THE BALLYGULLION BUS

Lynn Doyle has collected in this "omnibus" for the benefit of his many thousands of admirers the humorous Ballygullion stories which he himself likes best out of the many which have appeared since he first started writing them in 1908. The curious circumstances in which, as a modest bank clerk, he first "put pen to paper" he reveals in a characteristic preface.

The collection is published in good time for Ballygullion's fiftieth birthday. This kindly, tolerant, laughter-loving village is by now firmly engraved on the map of Ireland—though just where, and which side of the "border", the author might be hard put to it to say: and its characters—the infinitely resourceful Patrick Murphy, Sandy Morrison the auctioneer, and wee Mr. Anthony the solicitor—people the happiest memories of Irishmen all over the world, and will long continue to do so.

By LYNN DOYLE

BALLYGULLION
LOBSTER SALAD
DEAR DUCKS
ME AND MR. MURPHY
ROSABELLE
THE SHAKE OF THE BAG
A BOWL OF BROTH
GREEN ORANGES
BACK TO BALLYGULLION

—

AN ULSTER CHILDHOOD
FIDDLING FARMER
NOT TOO SERIOUS (*Essays*)

PATRICK MURPHY

The Ballygullion Bus

by

LYNN DOYLE

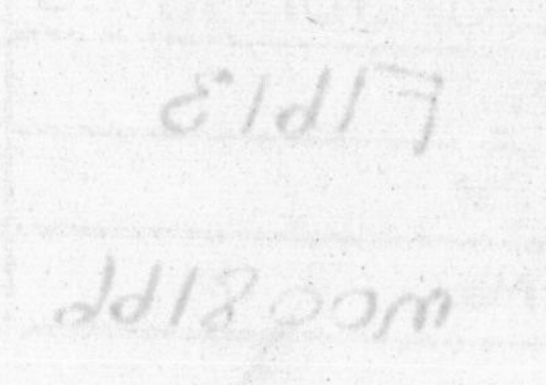

GERALD DUCKWORTH & CO LTD
3 Henrietta Street, London, W.C.2

This collection first published 1957

Printed in Great Britain by Richard Clay and Company, Ltd.,
Bungay, Suffolk

Contents

Preface

Away in 1906 I was a young married man, a bank clerk in a provincial branch. I was country bred, an only boy, with a taste for country life and country folk which has never left me. In particular, I had a country friend, a small depositor at my branch: an inveterate poacher, who was beginning to adopt me as an associate in his misdemeanours.

One evening he tempted me to go rabbit-trapping with him in the demesne of a local Big House of those patriarchal days. At first I refused. A dog was almost a necessity. The fruitful district in rabbits lay near the Big House itself. If the animal made a noise, and we were caught, I, at any rate, would be ruined.

My tempter got round me. He owned a shooting-dog, he said, that never, even in the most provocative circumstances had been known to bark. The three of us crept along in the dusk, far too near the Big House, *I* thought; and I was right. What forms of emerging game overcame the dog's reticence I never learned; but as we drew near a ditch-side, the brute suddenly gave way to a torrent, to a roaring crescendo of barking.

Need I go on? My least imaginative reader can picture the immediate sequel: the clatter of feet, the shouting, the slamming of gates, the dawn and dancing of lantern lights, the call and answer of voices. I could see and hear it all as I ran, saying farewell to my wife and children, and my comfortable home.

I may as well tell you here, that I was *not* dismissed from my job, after all; but the current of my life had been deflected, though I did not know it at the time. Henceforward I became—to myself, that is—a writer, an artist; a liar who breaks up the realities of life, and moulds them into something he deems more enjoyable to mankind. All life became the material for my new part. I let my tea grow cold on the breakfast-table while my hero's horse galloped up the "straight" to victory and the heroine's thrilling lips. After I had taken in a new five-pound note over the counter from a hastening customer, I would pause to jot down on the back of it—so as to fix the matter *really* in my mind—that the hero's horse fell at the wall, not at the water-jump.

I had been stirred by the incident of the poacher's barking dog. A few days after that happening, I bought a large school exercise-book; and, sitting down on a ditch-side I wrote—I thought happily—the title: "The Silent Dog", for the first story in my first little book, *Ballygullion*. That was in 1906, and I wish it wasn't! Yet I have compensation for the vanished years. Modestly but gratefully I record that, though the "Silent Dog" first barked in print in 1908, he is barking yet, and does so again in this new collection of my Ulster yarns selected from my nine volumes of "Ballygullion" stories, which purport, with a few exceptions, to be related by one Patrick Murphy of Ballygullion (a small town and district of Ulster) a generation ago.

L.D.

Malahide
June, 1957

Prologue

WHEN I looked up from my desk, and saw my old friend Patrick Murphy of Ballygullion once more, after his long absence, my spirits rose above the dull job I was working at. Then they fell a little when I saw the size of the bundle of printed and hand-written papers he was carrying in his arms; for it was nearly four times as big as the largest he had ever, up till then, unloaded on me. But I plucked up heart in spite of the bulk. The public and myself had, so far, more than cheerfully listened to what Mr. Murphy called his "ould crack"; and I had hopes that they could put up with some additions to it, if he had made them.

"More work for the undertaker, Pat?" said I.

"More laughs, I hope," said he, "for the folks that have laughed with me so kindly already. At least I think so; for it's the same ould fellow that is uttering it all: one Patrick Murphy of Ballygullion. Some of what I've got here is new, an' some of it is old; but had got clean wore-away with thumbin'; an' has come out of it so well that it is being printed here for the ninth or tenth time.

"It's sandwiches, this parcel of mine," said Mr. Murphy, "if I might put the thing that way. Here an' there is a slice of bran-new stuff. But the rest is just the ould brown bread of Ballygullion, with a few fresh currants in it.

"I have impident hopes that the 'Bus' is going to run here an' there over the whole English-speaking world; for folks, that far apart, have been asking for it. An' I'm trying to please them with this big gather-up of the ould stuff that has run out of print, forbye a brave wee bit of new."

"Will they understand it over *all* the world, Pat?" I asked him.

"Over a deal of it," returned Mr. Murphy: "Ireland an' England, Scotland an' Wales—in wee pockets of folk here an' there. An', forbye that, a big handful of 'Mericay men an' weemin have written an' said they liked it; an' wanted more."

"But do all these folk understand your kind of *fun*, Pat?" said I. "Will they laugh at your jokes?"

"They will, I do believe," said Mr. Murphy; "an' I'll tell you why. We don't try to make jokes in Ulster. We say serious things in a way that makes them appear funny when you see how serious they are."

"Sit down and give me some examples, Pat," said I.

There was a short interval while Mr. Murphy lighted his pipe and took a few thoughtful puffs.

"Listen to me, now," he said; "for I think I'll be worth listening to. But the things I'm going to tell you are not jokes made-up by myself. They're just a wee harvest of fun that I've gathered because, like yourself (if I may say it) I'm fonder of fun than of paying attention to my regular work. In the stories in these bundles of mine that I hope are going to be printed again, an' in the new ones that have been put in as well, you're looking at a few of the things that, during his lifetime, have passed before the eyes an' been listened-to by the ears of one, Patrick Murphy of Ballygullion; an' maybe, I'm willing to admit, been given a wee bit of a twist in the telling.

" 'Can you ate that?' says the cook in a Big House kitchen after there had been a five- or six-course blow-out of a dinner for the Quality upstairs.

"She was speaking to a working-man who had been doing a rough job of work in the yard outside. An' she had laid before him a big dish of leavings of every kind: fish, flesh, and fowl; pudden, pies, an' cakes; all in one mix-up, an' just short of fighting with each other.

" 'Can I ate that?' says the handyman, laying hold of a tablespoon—'What I can't eat, throw about me!' But he was merely saying, in Northern Irish: "Yes, thank you;" as if he meant it."

"I'll give you another example of what I mean," said Mr. Murphy. "Ould Robert Dumphy, up the road from me, was well-liked by his farm hands, an' took particular notice of them. His ploughman was going-out, one Saturday evening, to bring his girl to a wee tay-party in a country cottage. He was a good-looking, well-set up young fellow, with a brave notion of himself; an' he was all dressed-up, except about the chin, where there keeked-out a very tattered shirt-neck. Robert, guessin' where the lad was heading-for, took pity on him.

" 'Hold on!' he says, goes up the room, an' fetches down a stiff white-linen collar that he always wore himself on the anniversary of his wedding, to let on to his wife that she hadn't been a disappointment to him.

" 'Put that on you,' he says to the lad. 'Her father has twenty acres of good ground; an' she's a fine girl, an' you might get her.'

"So the young fellow set to work; an' with the help of safety-pins an' Robert's strong fingers the collar was got on his neck. But the laddie was shocking uncomfortable, with his chin in the air; an' Robert seen that.

" 'Are you all right, William?' he asked.

" 'I'm all right about the neck, sir,' says the ploughman; 'but plaze God nothin' goes wrong about my feet!' "

"Mind you," said Mr. Murphy, "this Ulster fashion of tellin' the truth round a corner isn't always calculated to turn away wrath.

"One of the Bank men in Ballygullion town got promoted to another branch. He wasn't a manager yet; an' had been living in a private house instead of in a bank one. Just before the news of his change came he had papered the drawing-room of the house he was goin' to leave, an' very flash, too; an' he thought he should get compensation from the in-comer, an' told him that.

"The other looked at the wall of the room, an' ran his hand over it very thoughtful. 'A lovely bit of wall-paper,' says he. 'A lovely piece, indeed.—You'd better take it with you,' says he. 'You'd better take it with you.' "

"There you are now, Mr. Doyle," says my visitor, pushing the big parcel over to me with his foot. "Do your best with it! For that is Patrick Murphy an' the folks he has seen an' listened-to down the years; maybe laughin' too loud an' too often; maybe a wee bit out of date, like himself; but still Ballygullion!"

DEDICATED

TO MY WIFE

The Silent Dog

THE minit I clapped eyes on the baste I knowed there was an unlucky look about him. But if there was bad luck wi' him sure the most av it fell his own road. It was this way I come across him. Wan afthernoon I was workin' about the yard, whin who should come intil it but wee Mr. Anthony, the solicitor, an' Mr. Barrington av the Bank.

"Good evenin' to yez both," sez I; "what has sthrayed ye out av Ballygullion the day, gintlemen?"

"Pat," sez Mr. Anthony, "are ye on for a night's sport?"

"That'll depend," sez I.

I wasn't goin' to let on what I'd do till I knowed what they were afther. For if it's shootin', sez I to meself, I'm otherwise engaged.

Mr. Anthony's as dacint a wee man as iver stepped,—divil recave the betther; but a bigger ould dundherhead niver wint out wi' a gun in his fist. Between his short sight, an' his ramstam way av runnin' at things, it was the danger av your life to go within a mile av him. Didn't he blow in the end windy av the Presbyterian meetin'-house wan prayer-meetin' night in the month av May, thryin' to shoot a crow off ould Major Dennison's tombstone in the buryin' ground outside; an' wanst he thrailed me two miles to Ballybreen bog afther a flock av wild geese he said he seen, an' before I could stop him he killed ould Mrs. Murphy's gandher that lives in Drumcrow, an' had to pay her a cowld pound, forbye a new gandher he bought her.

So whin he sez "Are ye on for a night?" thinks I, I'll know what yez are afther first.

"Well, Pat," sez he, "Mr. Barrington an' me has planned to have a night's rabbit-nettin' up at Mr. Hastings's at The Warren——"

"Is it mad yez are?" sez I. "Sure ye'll be right fornent the house, an' the ould gintleman'll hear the first bark; an' doesn't the whole counthryside know he's a fair lunatic about poachin'."

"Aye, but," sez Mr. Anthony, "we've got a silent dog."

"A what?" sez I.

"A silent dog," sez he. "A dog, Pat," sez he, "that'll hunt rabbits, or rats—aye or cats," sez he, "an' niver even give a whine. I have him chained to the gate here."

Wi' that he goes round the corner an' fetches back a dog on a chain.

"There he is, Pat," sez he; "an' you wouldn't get a bark out av him if you thried him for a month."

"Faith," sez I, "it's well he's some good points about him, for be me sowl he's no beauty."

An' nayther he was;—a low-set, crooked-legged baste, wi' a dirty brown coat, an' a wee bunty tail. Wan av his ears was half tore off, an' he'd lost two teeth in the front.

"An' what do you think about it, Mr. Barrington?" sez I.

Between ourselves, Mr. Barrington was supposed to be coortin' the youngest wan av the Miss Hastings's, an' I thought it a quare thing if he'd run the risk av a row wi' the ould fellow for the sake av a night's sport.

"There'll be Ould Nick himself to pay if we're catched, an' that'll be no good till any av us," sez I, lookin' hard at him.

"Oh! I know rightly what ye mane, Pat," sez he, "but it doesn't matther. The ould fellow an' me has fell out," sez he, savage-like, "an' I don't mind the chance av a row if I can spite him a bit."

"I'm wi' you there," sez I; "for he's no friend av mine. But what about the dog? Can yez depend on him not to bark?" sez I.

"I tell ye, man," sez Mr. Anthony, "he'll not bark. Hit him a kick," sez he, "an' see if he even whines."

"Hit him a welt yourself, Mr. Anthony," sez I; "he knows you betther nor me." For there was a quare glitter in the baste's eye I didn't like.

So Mr. Anthony fetched him a lick wi' the toe av his boot; an' wi' that the dog turns on him, an' without even a girn, catches him be the ball av the leg, an' houlds on like grim death, worryin' at him. Mr. Anthony he lets a screech an' begins to pull away from the dog.

"Haul him off, Pat!" sez he, "I'm bit till the bone! Kick the brute. Why don't ye pull him off, Archie?" sez he, dancin' round on wan leg an' cursin' like a haythen.

As luck would have it, he'd on a pair of them putty leggin's, an' the dog only had his teeth in wan av them; an' afther the first fright, whin we seen he wasn't likely to be hurt, Mr. Barrington an' myself couldn't do nothin' for the laughin', till Mr. Anthony was fair wild.

"What the divil," sez he, "are yez grinnin' at, ye pair av monkeys? Pull him off quick, or he'll be through to me leg."

So I lifts a bit of a stick, an' hits the dog two or three lundhers wid it; but divil a bit would he let go.

"He's a terrible hoult, anyway, Mr. Anthony," sez I. "What'll I do wi' him at all, at all?"

"Bate him over the head wi' a stone," sez he.

"I'll hurt the baste," sez I, "if I do."

"I don't give a damn," sez he, "if ye kill him. Get him off anyhow," sez he.

So I ups wi' a stone an' runs over till the pair av thim; an' whin the dog seen me comin' wi' the stone, he lets go Mr. Anthony's leg all av a suddint an' turns sharp on me. Mr. Anthony, he was pullin' the other way, an' whin the dog let go he went on his hands an' knees intil the sheugh, an' I took a run-race an' got up on the ditch, thinkin' I felt the baste's teeth in me leg ivery minit.

Whin I looked over my shoulder I seen Mr. Barrington had him be the chain.

"More power to ye, Mr. Barrington," sez I; "it's well ye were there, for I've no leggins on, an' if he'd got me he'd 'a massacred me."

"He's safe enough, now, Pat," sez he, "come on down."

So I come down an' give Mr. Anthony a pull out of the sheugh.

I thought Mr. Barrington would have died laughin' at him; an' in troth it was small wondher, for he was a shockin' sight wi' gutthers an' clay. But for all that he wasn't a bit daunted.

"Ye may laugh, Archie," sez he; "but the dog didn't give a squeak anyhow. Ye're satisfied av that."

"Oh, I'm quite satisfied," sez Mr. Barrington. "I think we can depend on him. Anyway, I'll not bother thryin' him," sez he.

So we trysted to meet the nixt night at Mr. Anthony's gate, as bein' the handiest place for all parties; for it's about half-roads between me an' Ballygullion, an' just across the river on the other side av the county road an' you're in the Warren grounds. I was to bring me nets.

It was a gran' moonlight night when I left home, an' when I come to Mr. Anthony's gate the two av them was there wi' the dog.

Mr. Anthony was in great heart.

"We couldn't have picked a betther night," sez he. "We'll be able to see what we're doin'."

"Aye, an' the rabbits'll be able to see what we're doin' too," sez I. "There's no good startin' till it clouds over a bit." It was risin' a bit cloudy behind the wind, an' I knowed the moon would be soon covered.

"Maybe you're right," sez Mr. Anthony. "I'll tell you what I'll do while we're waitin'. I'll run back an' get the air-gun," sez he. "It'll make no noise, an' I might get a shot at a rabbit. Hould the dog, Archie, till I come back."

"If ye take my advice," sez I, "ye'll let the gun alone."

But he never listened to me, an' made off up the avenue at a trot, lavin' Mr. Barrington an' me standin' there.

Mr. Barrington was very heavy an' down, an' said nothin', but kept suckin' away at the pipe; not like himself at all; for he's mostly full av jokes an' fun, an' ready to laugh at nothin'.

"What's up between yourself an' Mr. Hastings above, Mr. Barrington," sez I, "if it's not bould av me to ask?"

"Nothin' much, Pat," sez he. "Only I spoke till him about what ye know, an' he's forbid me the house.

"The ould upstart," sez he between his teeth till himself, "because av his dirty money turnin' up his nose at a man whose gran'-father was a gintleman when his was carryin' a hod."

Ye must know the Hastings made their money in the buildin' line, an' none av them was very much before the present man.

"What need ye care," sez I, "about the ould fellow at all, at all, if the young lady an' you has made it up?"

"Oh, it's willin' enough she'd be (the darlin'!" sez he under his breath); "but I'd be a nice hound to ask her to marry me on two hundred an' fifty a year."

"Divil moan her," sez I, "if she niver gets a man wi' more. Sure I've brought up a wife an' family on the fift' av it."

Mr. Barrington he laughs a bit at that, an' just then Mr. Anthony comes up an' stops the crack.

"The moon's well hid, now," sez he; "we'll make a start."

So we crossed the river an' took to the fields, an' afther half a mile av a walk we come to the plantin' below the big house. There's about fifteen acres av it in a sort of half-moon, then a big stretch of grass land they call the lawn, right up to the hall-door, wi' an odd big tree in it here an' there. The upper end av the plantin's fair alive wi' rabbit-holes, an' av a fine night the rabbits does be feedin' on the lawn in hundhreds. Our schame was to run the nets along in front of the holes, an' thin get around an' let the dog loose to scare the rabbits intil them.

As soon as we got the nets set we slipped round to the horn av the plantin', close up to the house. Mr. Anthony puts the end av the chain he had the dog on in my hand.

"Now, Pat," sez he, "you hould the dog in till we get to the middle av the lawn, an' I'll maybe get a shot," sez he, puttin' a pellet in the air-gun.

"Ye ould fool," thinks I, "wi' your pop-gun; it's well if ye don't lame somebody." For his hands was in such a thrimmle wi' narvousness that he could hardly snap the breech.

Howiver, out we moves, an' just thin, as ill-luck would have it, out comes the moon.

"Bad cess to ye," sez I, "ye ould divil ye, weren't ye all right behind there, but ye must come out an' spoil sport."

But Mr. Anthony was well plazed.

"Wheesht, Pat," sez he, "I see wan."

Wi' that he puts his foot in a rabbit-hole, an' down he slaps on his face, an' the gun snaps an' pins the dog in the side somewhere.

Maybe it was more than mortial baste could stan', for thim wee pellets is cruel, but anyway the dog sets up the horridest howlin' ye iver heard, an' I was that taken in at him I dhropped the chain an' let him go.

An' thin the fun began,—Mr. Anthony rippin' an' cursin' an' spittin' out bits av grass, an' the silent dog runnin' round an' round in rings an' yowlin' murther, wi' the chain rattlin' behind him like a tinker's cart.

Mr. Barrington,—divil miss him, but he'd see fun in it,—he begins to laugh.

"For a silent dog, Anthony," sez he, "he's makin' a brave noise."

"Shut up, ye fool," sez Mr. Anthony, as mad as you like, "an' catch the brute. Be the mortial," sez he, "if I catch him, I'll make a silent dog av him."

But the divil a catch him could we do; an' the more we went near him the louder he yelled.

"We'd better run," sez I; "the house'll be up."

But I didn't spake in time. All av a suddint the big front door opens wi' a clatther.

"Come on, men," I hears in ould Mr. Hastings's voice. "Scatther across the lawn, an' ye can't miss the blackguards."

Ye niver seen three men run faster than we did for that plantin'.

Divil a much laughin' there was in Mr. Barrington then.

"If we're caught, Pat," sez he, as he run, "I'm done entirely. I'll be disgraced for iver," sez he.

"We'll not be caught," sez I, as well as I could wi' thryin' to keep up wi' him. "Sure we've over three hundhred yards av a start. Look out for the nets!" sez I.

But wee Mr. Anthony was runnin' like a red-shank ten yards in front av us, an' niver heard me. The net just took him on the shin-bone, an' he riz about two feet in the air, an' lit on his belly on the plantin' ditch wi' a sough. Whin we got up till him he could hardly spake.

"Up wi' you, quick, Anthony," sez Mr. Barrington.

"I can't," sez he wi' a groan or two; "me heart's bursted," sez he.

"Not a bit av it," sez Mr. Barrington, feelin' him; "it's only your braces."

"Come on, Mr. Anthony," sez I, "you're not bate yet." But he couldn't move.

"Run yourselves, boys," sez he, in a kind av a whisper.

"Come on, sir," sez I to Mr. Barrington, "they'll be on us in a minit."

The words wasn't right out av me mouth till he catches me be the throat.

"This way, men," sez he, at the top av his voice; "I've got wan o' the villains."

"It's not goin' to sell me, ye are, Mr. Barrington," sez I.

"Hit me a good knock wi' your fist in the face, Pat," sez he. "Quick, man!"

"Be me sowl will I," sez I, "if ye don't let go."

"I won't let go till ye do," sez he.

"Here goes, thin," sez I to meself. "It's a quare business anyway, but if ye've sould me ye desarve it, an' if ye haven't, sure ye asked for it yourself;" an' wi' that I fetches him wan on the right cheek-bone would ha' felled a bullock, an' off I goes like the divil, lavin' him where he fell.

I was away safe an' well, for the moon was hid again, an' it was gey an' dark; but I hadn't run above a hundhred yards till I come on that unfortunate divil av a dog whimperin' in the bushes. He took till his heels whin he heard me comin' an' kep' in front av me about ten or fifteen yards; an' if he'd been silent all his days before, be me sowl he made up for it that night, for the gowls av him was lamentable.

"The divil choke ye, anyway," sez I, when I'd run near a quarther av a mile an' him niver stopped; "for if I'm not catched it's no fault of yours." I stopped a minit to get me wind, an' at first I thought there was nobody follyin'; but thin I hears ould Billy the game-keeper's voice.

"This way, boys," sez he. "They're not away from us yet; I hear their dog."

"An' divil thank ye," sez I to meself; "sure ould Pether of the Bog could hear him, that's been stone deaf this fifteen years."

So away I goes again, wi' the dog in front av me, him yowlin' an' guldherin' harder than iver, thinkin' I was comin' to kill him fair out this time. But whin he comes to the river bank, he takes down the sthrame nixt Ballygullion.

"Good-bye, me darlin'," sez I, and' I off up the sthrame as hard as I could belt. Before I'd gone very far, I hears a sound av men runnin', an' thin a shout or two down the sthrame, an' a couple av shots, an' then nothin'. But I niver stopped till I was at home an' in me bed.

All night long I lay wondherin' what could have come on Mr. Barrington. The more I thought about it the more it looked like some thrick, but divil a bit av me could see through it.

"Howaniver," thinks I, "I'll lie low," an' I keeps to the house for a week, lettin' on I'd a cowld; till on market day the wife comes home from Ballygullion in a terrible flutther.

"Did ye hear about the poachin' at Mr. Hastings's, Pat?" sez she.

"Holy Pether," sez I to meself, "I'm done."

"What poachin', Molly?" sez I.

"Sure," says she, "poachers broke intil Mr. Hastings's on last Tuesda' night,—above ten av thim—to thrap his rabbits, an' Mr. Barrington, of the Bank, an' Mr. Anthony, the solicitor, follyed thim to catch thim an' got nearly killed. Wee Mr. Anthony's been in bed iver since, an' Mr. Barrington has a face like a prize-fighter.

"Ould Mr. Hastings's tarrible plazed about thim both. They say he's promised Mr. Anthony the agency av the estate whin ould Jenkins dies, an' there's a sough in the town that Mr. Barrington's goin' to marry Miss Anne."

Thin I seen the whole thing in a wink.

"Well done yourself, Mr. Barrington," thinks I, "sure you're the able one. Thrust you to get out av a hole, if ye were up till the neck in it."

"I'll just slip down to the town, Molly," sez I, "an' hear all about it."

Whin I got intil Ballygullion I sends a message till the Bank to Mr. Barrington, askin' him if he could step down the length of the bridge to see a couple of ferrets I had,—just for a blind.

Prisintly down he comes, an' in troth I hardly knowed him.

There was a big lump av stickin'-plasther above his right eye, an' the whole cheek was all puffed up, an' as yellow as a duck's foot.

"Aye, ye ould reprobate," sez he, catchin' me look; "ye see the hand ye've made av me."

"Sure," sez I, "ye brought it on yourself. Didn't ye ask me to hit ye."

"I didn't tell ye to hit me such a skelp," sez he. "You've loosened every tooth in me head, an' I've been livin' on slops an' mashes for a week past. But niver mind, Pat," sez he, "I've had good luck out of it. There's no wan would think I got an eye like this from a friend."

"Be me sowl, Mr. Barrington," sez I, "ye're a cliver wan. Ye've bamboozled the ould gintleman finely,—wi' your ten poachers. An' is it true what they're sayin' about the young lady an' you?"

"True enough, Pat," sez he. "We're to be married within three months. The ould fellow has behaved uncommon handsome, an' I feel a mane baste for deceivin' him. But anyhow, I tould Anne—Miss Hastings," sez he, gettin' very red where his face wasn't yellow.

"An' what did she say, Mr. Barrington?" sez I.

"Whin she'd done laughin'," sez he, "she tould me to tell ye ye'd niver want a day's shootin' in The Warren as long as she could put in a word for ye; an' she's goin' to get the best kennel in Ireland for the dog. Have ye any notion what's become av him?"

"Divil a bit av me knows," sez I.

Wi' that I sees somethin' comin' floatin' down the river.

"Be the mortial, Mr. Barrington," sez I, whin I'd looked at it a minit. "It's him!"

"What?" sez Mr. Barrington. "What is it, Pat?" sez he.

"The dog," sez I, pointin'.

"Not a bit av it," sez he, "that's twice the size."

"Maybe he's a bit swelled," sez I; an' whin it floated down the length av the bridge, sure enough it was himself.

Mr. Barrington stands lookin' at him till I was near turned, for in troth he was smellin' higher nor a daisy.

"Come on, Pat," sez he, at the last, turnin' away. "I'm sorry the poor baste's killed, for he done me a good turn, an' I can't return him another wan now. But I'll send down somebody to fish him out an' give him a dacint burial."

"It's all ye can do for him, Mr. Barrington," sez I. "Rest his sowl, if he has wan, though I did lose two good rabbit-nets be him, he's a silent dog now, anyway."

It's a brave while ago since it all happened, an' Mr. Barrington an' the wife, Miss Hastings that was, is in Dublin now, in the big Bank there; but to this day there's a wee headstone in the Bank garden at Ballygullion, wi' words on it that has bothered the whole countryside but me an' Mr. Anthony:

"IN LOVING MEMORY
OF
THE SILENT DOG."

The Ballygullion Creamery Society, Limited

'TWAS the man from the Department of Agriculture comin' down to give a lecture on poultry an' dairy-farmin' that set the ball a rowlin'.

The whole farmers av the country gathered in to hear him, an' for days afther it was over, there was no talk at all barrin' about hens an' crame, an' iverybody had a schame av their own to propose.

Ould Miss Armitage up at the Hall was on for encouragin' poultry-farmin'; an' give a prize for the best layin' hen in Ballygullion, that riz more scunners in the country than the twelfth av July itself. There was powerful stir about it, an' near iverybody enthered.

Deaf Pether of the Bog's wife was an aisy winner if her hen hadn't died, an' nothin' would satisfy her but it was poisoned; though divil a' all killed it but the gorges of Indian male the ould woman kept puttin' intil it.

Ivery time the hen laid she gave it an extra dose av male, "to encourage the crather," as she said; an' wan day it laid a double-yolked wan, she put a charge intil it that stretched it out stiff in half an hour.

After that there was no doubt but Larry Thomas's wife would win the prize; for before the end av the month Miss Armitage had allowed for the test, her hen was above a dozen ahead of iverybody else's.

Howiver, whin it came to the countin' there was a duck-egg or two here an' there among the lot that nayther Mrs. Thomas nor the hen could well account for, so the both av thim was disqualified.

An' whin it come to the test, and Mrs. Archy Doran won the prize, she counted up an' made out that between corn an' male she had paid away double the value av it, so she wasn't very well plazed; an' thim that had spint near as much on feedin'-stuff, an' had got no prize, was worse plazed still.

The only wan that come out av it well was Miss Armitage herself; for she kept all the eggs, an' made above twice the prize-money out av thim. But there was nobody else as well plazed about that as she was.

So all round the hen business was a failure; an' it looked as if there was nothin' goin' to come av the lecture at all.

However, iverybody thought it would be a terrible pity if Ballygullion should be behind other places; an' at last there was a move made to start a cramery, an' a committee was got up to set things goin'.

At first the most av us thought they got the crame in the ould-fashioned way, just be skimmin'; but presently it begin to be talked that it was all done be machinery. Some av us was very dubious about that; for sorrow a bit could we see how it was to be done. Thomas McGorrian maintained it would be done wi' blades like the knives av a turnip-cutter, that would just shave the top off the milk, an' sweep it intil a pan; but then he couldn't well explain how they'd avoid shavin' the top off the milk-dish too.

Big Billy Lenahan swore it was done with a worm like a still; but although we all knowed Billy was well up in pot-heen, there was few had iver seen him havin' much to do wi' milk; so nobody listened to him.

At last the committee detarmined they'd have a dimon-sthration; an' they trysted the Department man to bring down his machine an' show how it was done; for all av thim was agin spendin' money on a machine till they were satis-fied it would do its work.

The dimonsthration was to be held in Long Tammas McGorrian's barn; an' on the night set above forty av us was there. We all sat round in a half-ring, on chairs an' stools an' any other conthrivance we could get, for all the world like the Christy Minstrels that comes to the Market House av a Christmas.

The dimonsthrator had rigged up a belt to Tammas's threshin'-machine, an' run it from that to the separator, as he called it.

The separator itself was a terrible disappointin' con-thrivance at the first look, an' no size av a thing at all for the money they said it cost. But whin the dimonsthrator begin to tell us what it would do, an' how by just pourin' the milk intil a metal ball an' bizzin' it round, ye could make the crame come out av one hole, an' the milk out av another, we begin to think more av it.

Nobody liked to spake out wi' the man there, but there was a power av whisperin'.

"It's a mighty quare conthrivance," sez wan.

"Did ye iver see the like av it?" sez another.

"Boys-a-boys," sez James Dougherty, "the works av man is wonderful. If my ould grandmother could see this, it would break her heart. 'Twas herself was the handy dairy-woman, too; but what'd she be till a machine?"

But most av thim wouldn't say wan thing or another till they seen it workin'; an' 'deed we were all wishin' he'd begin. We had to thole, though; for the dimonsthrator was a bumptious wee man, an' very fond av the sound av his own voice, an' kept talkin' away wi' big long words that nobody knowed the manin' av but himself, till we were near deaved.

So we were powerful glad whin he sez to Mrs. McGorrian: "Now, madam, if you'll be good enough to bring in the milk, I will proceed to give an actual demonstration."

But Mrs. McGorrian is a quiet wee woman, an' wi' all the crowd there, an' him callin' her madam, she was too backward to get up out av the corner she was in; an' she nudges Tammas to go, tellin' him where to get the milk.

So Tammas goes out, an' presently he staggers in wi' a big crock in his arms an' sets it down.

"Now," sez the dimonsthrator, "if you'll just get the horses goin', an' pour the milk into that receptacle, I'll start the separator working."

Tammas in wi' the milk, an' the wee son whips up the horses outside, an' away goes the separator bizzin' like a hive av bees.

"In a few seconds, gentlemen an' ladies," sez the dimonsthrator, "you will see the milk come out here, an' the cream here. Kindly pay attention, please."

But he needn't have spoke; for iverybody was lanin' forrard, holdin' their breath, an' there wasn't a sound to be heard but the hummin' of the separator.

Presently there comes a sort av a thick trickle out of the milk-hole, but divil a dhrap av crame.

The dimonsthrator gathered up his brow a bit at that, and spakes out of the barn windy to Tammas's wee boy to dhrive faster. The separator hums harder than iver, but still no crame. Wan begin to look at the other, an' some av the wimmen at the back starts gigglin'.

The dimonsthrator begin to get very red an' flusthered-lookin'. "Are ye sure this milk is fresh an' hasn't been skimmed?" he sez to Tammas, very sharp.

"What do you say, Mary?" sez Tammas, lookin' over at the wife. "Sartin, sir," sez Mrs. Tammas. "It's fresh from the cows this very evenin'."

"Most extraordinary," sez the dimonsthrator, rubbin' his hair till it was all on end. "I've niver had such an experience before."

"It's the way Tammas feeds his cows," sez Big Billy Lenaham from the back; "sure iverybody knows he gives them nothin' but shavin's."

There was a snigger av a laugh at this; for Tammas was well known to be no great feeder av cattle.

But Tammas wasn't to be tuk down so aisy.

"Niver mind, Billy," sez he; "av you were put on shavin's for a week or two, ye'd maybe see your boots again before you died."

There was another laugh at this, an' that started a bit av jokin' all round—a good dale av it at the dimonsthrator; till he was near beside himself. For divil a dhrop av crame had put in an appearance yet.

All at wanst he stoops down close to the milk.

"Bring me a candle here," sez he, very sharp.

Tammas reaches over a sconce off the wall. The dimonsthrator bends over the can, then dips the point av his finger in it, an' puts it in his mouth.

"What's this?" sez he, lookin' very mad at Tammas. "This isn't milk at all."

"Not milk," sez Tammas. "It must be milk. I got it where you tould me, Mary."

The wife gets up an' pushes forward. First she takes a look at the can av the separator, an' thin wan at the crock.

"Ye ould fool," she sez to Tammas; "ye've brought the whitewash I mixed for the dairy walls!"

I'll say this for the dimonsthrator, he was a game wee fellow; for the divil a wan laughed louder than he did, an' that's saying something. But sorrow a smile Tammas cracked, but stood gapin' at the wife wi' his mouth open; an' from the look she give him back, there was some av us thought she was maybe more of a tarthar than she looked.

Though troth 'twas no wondher she was angry, for the joke wint round the whole country, an' Tammas gets nothin' but "Whitewash McGorrian" iver since.

Howaniver, they got the machine washed out, an' the rale milk intil it, an' there was no doubt it worked well. The wee dimonsthrator was as plazed as Punch, an' iverybody wint away well satisfied, an' set on havin' a cramery as soon as it could be got started.

First av all they wint round an' got the names av all thim that was goin' to join in; an' the explainin' av the schame took a dale av time. The co-operatin' bothered thim intirely.

The widow Doherty wasn't goin' to join an' put in four cows' milk, she said, whin she'd only get as much out av it as Mrs. Donnelly across the field that had only two. Thin, whin they explained to the widow that she'd get twice as much, ould mother Donnelly was clane mad; for she'd thought she was goin' to get the betther av the widow.

Thin there was tarrible bother over barrin' out wee Mrs. Morley, because she had only a goat. Some was for lettin' her in; but the gineral opinion was that it would be makin' too little av the Society.

Howiver, all was goin' brave an' paceable till ould Michael Murray, the ould dundherhead, puts in his oar.

Michael was a divil av a man for pace-makin', an' riz more rows than all in the county for all that; for whin two dacent men had a word or two av a fair-day, maybe whin the drink was in them, an' had forgot all about it, the next day ould Michael would come round to make it up, an' wi' him mindin' them av what had passed, the row would begin worse than iver.

So, whin all was well set agoin', and the committee met to call a gineral meetin' av the Society, ould Michael he gets up an' says what a pity it would be if the Society would be broke up wi' politics or religion; an' he proposed that they should show there was no ill-feelin' on either side by holdin' this gineral meetin' in the Orange Hall, an' the nixt in the United Irish League rooms. He named the Orange Hall first, he said, because he was a Nationalist himself, an' a Home Ruler, an' always would be.

There was one or two Orangemen beginnin' to look mighty fiery at the tail-end av Michael's speech, an' there's no tellin' what would a' happened if the chairman hadn't whipped in an' said that Michael's was a very good idea, an' he thought they couldn't do betther than folly it up.

So, right enough, the first gineral meetin' was held in the Ballygullion Orange Hall.

Iverything was very quiet an' agreeable, except that some of the red-hot Nationalists kept takin' quare skellys at a flag in the corner wi' King William on it, stickin' a man in a green coat wi' his sword.

But as fortune would have it, little Billy av the Bog, the sthrongest wee Orangeman in Ulsther, comes in at half-time as dhrunk as a fiddler, sits down on a form an' falls fast asleep. An' there he snored for the most av half an hour, till near the end av the meetin', whin the chairman was makin' a speech, there was a bit av applause, an' up starts Billy all dazed. First he looked up an' seen King William on the flag. Thin hearin' the chairman's voice, he gives a stamp wi' his fut on the flure, an' a "hear, hear," with a mortial bad hiccup between the "hears." The wee man thought he was at a lodge-meetin'.

All av a sudden he sees ould Michael Murray, an', beside him, Tammas McGorrian.

Wi' that he lepps to his feet like a shot, dhrunk as he was, an' hits the table a terrible lick wi' his fist.

"Stap, brethren," sez he, glarin' round the room. "Stap! There's Papishes present."

Ye niver seen a meetin' quicker broke up than that wan. Half the men was on their feet in a minit, an' the other half pullin' thim down be the coat-tails. Iverybody was talkin' at the wan time, some av them swearin' they'd been insulted, an' others thryin' to make pace.

Thin the wimmin begin to scrame an' hould back men

from fightin' that had no notion av it at the start, an' only begin to think av it whin they were sure they wouldn't be let.

Altogether there was the makin's of as fine a fight as iver ye seen in your life.

However, there was a lot av dacent elderly men on both sides, an' wi' arguin' an perswadin', an' houldin' back one, an' pushin' out the other, the hall was redd without blows, an' bit by bit they all went home quiet enough.

But the Cramery Society was clane split. It wasn't wee Billy so much; for whin people begin to think about it the next mornin', there was more laughed at him than was angry; but the party feelin' was up as bitther as could be.

The Nationalists was mad at themselves for givin' in to go to a meetin' in the Orange Hall, for fear it might be taken that they were weakenin' about Home Rule; an' the Orange party were just as afeard at the papers makin' out that they were weakenin' about the Union. Besides, the ould King William in the corner of the Hall had done no good.

I'm no party man, myself; but whin I see William Robinson, that has been me neighbour this twinty years, goin' down the road on the Twelfth av July wi' a couple av Orange sashes on, me heart doesn't warm to him as it does av another day. The plain truth is, we were bate at the Boyne right enough; but some av us has more than a notion we didn't get fair play at the fightin'; an' between that and hearin' about the batin' iver since, the look of ould Billy on his white horse isn't very soothin'.

Anyway the two parties couldn't be got to join again. The red-hot wans av both av thim had meetin's, wee Billy leadin' wan side, and Tammas McGorrian the other, an' the nixt thing was that there was to be two Crameries.

The moderate men seen that both parties was makin' fools av themselves, for the place wasn't big enough for two; but moderate men are scarce in our parts, an' they could do nothin' to soothe matthers down. Whin the party work is on, it's little either side thinks av the good av thimselves or the counthry either.

It's "niver mind a dig yourself if ye get a slap at the other fellow."

So notices was sent out for a meetin' to wind up the Society, an' there was a powerful musther av both sides, for fear either of them might get an advantage over the other wan.

To keep clear av trouble it was to be held in the Market-house.

The night av the meetin' come; an' when I got into the room who should I see on the platform but Major Donaldson and Father Connolly. An' thin I begin to wondher what was on.

For the Major was too aisy goin' and kindly to mix himself up wi' party-work, an' Father Connolly was well known to be terrible down on it, too.

So a sort av a mutther begin to run through the meetin' that there was goin' to be an attempt to patch up the split.

Some were glad and not afraid to say it; but the most looked dour an' said nothin'; an' wee Billy and Tammas McGorrian kept movin' in and out among their friends an' swearin' them to stand firm.

When the room was well filled, an' iverybody settled down, the Major gets on his feet.

"Ladies an' gentlemen," sez he—the Major was always polite if it was only a thravellin' tinker he was spakin' to—"Ladies an' gentlemen, you know why we've met here to-night—to wind up the Ballygullion Cramery Society. I wish windin' up meant that it would go on all the better; but, unfortunately, windin' up a society isn't like windin' up a clock.

"Now I'm not goin' to detain you; but before we proceed, I'd like you to listen to Father Connolly here for a minute or two. I may tell you he's goin' to express my opinion as well as his own. I needn't ask you to give him an' attentive hearin'; ye all know as well as I do that what he says is worth listenin' to." An' down the Major sits.

Thin Father Connolly comes forward an' looks roun' a minit or so before speakin'. Most av his own people that catched his eye looked down mighty quick, for they all had an idea he wouldn't think much av what had been goin' on.

But wee Billy braces himself up an' looks very fierce, as much as to say "there'll no priest ordher me about," and Tammas looks down at his feet wi' his teeth set, much as he meant the same.

"Men an' wimmin av Ballygullion," sez Father Connolly —he was aye a plain-spoken wee man—"we're met here to end up the United Cramery Society, and after that we're going to start two societies, I hear.

"The sinsible men av Ballygullion sees that it would be altogether absurd an' ridiculous for Catholics an' Protestants, Home Rulers an' Unionists, to work together in anything at all. As they say, the two parties is altogether opposed in everything that's important.

"The wan keeps Patrick's Day for a holiday, and the other the Twelfth av July; the colours of the one is green, an' the colours of the other orange; the wan wants to send their Mimbers av Parliament to College Green, and the other to Westminster; an' there are a lot more differences just as important as these.

"It's thrue," goes on the Father, "that some ignorant persons says that, after all, the two parties live in the same counthry, undher the same sky, wi' the same sun shinin' on them an' the same rain wettin' thim; and that what's good for that counthry is good for both parties, an' what's bad for it is bad for both; that they live side by side as neighbours, an' buy and sell among wan another, an' that nobody has iver seen that there was twinty-one shillin's in a Catholic pound, an' nineteen in a Protestant pound, or the other way about; an' that, although they go about it in different ways, they worship the same God, the God that made both av thim; but I needn't tell ye that these are only a few silly bodies, an' don't riprisint the opinion av the counthry."

A good many people in the hall was lookin' foolish enough by this time, an' iverybody was waitin' to hear the Father tell them to make it up, an' most av them willin' enough to do it. The Major was leanin' back, looking well satisfied.

"Now," sez Father Connolly, "after what I've said, I needn't tell ye that I'm av the opinion av the sinsible men, and I think that by all manes we should have a Catholic cramery, and a Protestant wan."

The Major sits up wi' a start, an' wan looks at the other all over the room.

"The only thing that bothers me," sez the Father, goin' on an' takin' no notice, "is the difficulty av doin' it. It's aisy enough to sort out the Catholic farmers from the Protestant; but what about the cattle?" sez he.

"If a man rears up a calf till it becomes a cow, there's no doubt that cow must be Nationalist or Orange. She couldn't help it, livin' in this country. Now what are you going to do when a Nationalist buys an Orange cow? Tammas McGorrian bought a cow from wee Billy there last month that Billy bred an' reared himself. Do ye mane to tell me that's a Nationalist cow? I tell ye what it is, boys," sez the Father, wi' his eyes twinklin', "wan can av that cow's milk in a Nationalist cramery would turn the butther as yellow as the shutters av the Orange Hall."

By this time there was a smudge av a laugh on iverybody's face, an' even Tammas an' wee Billy couldn't help crackin' a smile.

"Now," sez Father Connolly, "afther all its aisy enough in the case of Tammas's cow. There's no denyin' she's an Orange cow, an' either Tammas may go to the Orange cramery or give the cow back to Billy."

Tammas sits up a bit at that.

"But, thin, there's a lot of mighty curious cases. There's my own wee Kerry. Iverybody knows I bred her myself; but, thin, there's no denyin' that her father—if that's the right way to spake av a bull—belonged to Major Donaldson here, an' was called 'Prince of Orange.' Now be the law a child follows its father in these matters, an' I'm bound be it to send the wee Kerry's milk to the Orange cramery, although I'll maintain she's as good a Nationalist as ever stepped—didn't she thramp down ivery orange lily in Billy Black's garden only last Monday?

"So, boys, whin ye think the matther out, ye'll see it's no aisy matther this separatin' av Orange an' Green in the cramery. For if ye do it right—an' I'm for no half-measures —ye'll have to get the pedigree av ivery bull, cow, and calf in the counthry, an' then ye'll be little further on, for there's a lot av bastes come in every year from Americay that's little betther than haythin.

"But, if ye take my advice, those av ye that isn't sure av your cows'll just go on quietly together in the manetime, an' let thim that has got a rale thrue-blue baste av either persuasion just to keep her milk to themselves, and skim it in the ould-fashioned way wi' a spoon."

There was a good dale av sniggerin' whin the Father was spakin'; but ye should have heard the roar av a laugh there was whin he sat down. An' just as it was dyin' away, the Major rises up, wipin' his eyes:

"Boys," sez he, "if it's the will av the prisint company that the Ballygullion Cramery Society go on, will ye rise an' give three cheers for Father Pether Connolly?"

Ivery man, woman, an' child—Protestant and Catholic—was on their feet in a minit; an' if the Ballygullion Market-house roof didn't rise that night, it's safe till etarnity.

From that night on there was niver another word av windin' up or splittin' either. An' if iver ye come across a print av butther wi' a wreath of shamrocks an' orange-lilies on it, ye'll know it come from the Ballygullion Cramery Society, Limited.

The Green Cheese

It all begun wi' me meetin' Pether Boylan comin' from Ballygullion one Sathurday night.

"Good evenin', Pat," sez he, stoppin' the cart; "wud ye take a parcel up till ould Davis's for me? Major Donaldson sent it, tell him."

"What'll it be?" sez I.

"I don't know," sez he. "But it has a mortail quare smell. It's nothin' livin'," sez he.

"Show me it," sez I. "It's green cheese," sez I, "I'll bate a pound. An' maybe it's livin' too, for all ye say. The quality does ate it whin ye could hardly keep it on the plate wi' a pitchfork. I'll take it up till him if ye're in a hurry."

"It's as good as a shillin' to ye," sez he, laughin', as he drives on.

"If it is," sez I, callin' afther him, "it'll be the first he's give away this ten years."

For though ould Mr. Davis was a gentleman born, an' a brave decent ould fellow at that, he was heart mane. Whin the wife was livin' he was a great sportin' man, an' open-handed an' hearty enough; but afther she died he begin to get terrible wee an' greedy.

He sacked all the servants wan by wan till there was nobody left but an ould housekeeper; an' him an' her lived at the big house up the road from me, all be their lone.

Whin I got up till the house, just at the hall door I came on the ould gintleman himself, dhressed in a shabby ould suit an' a hat would have affronted a scarecrow.

"What have you there, Pat?" sez he.

"It's a present from the Major," sez I; "cheese," sez I, "be the smell."

"So it is, Pat," sez he, twinklin' all over his wrinkled ould face. "Thank ye, thank ye kindly. I'd give ye a drink, but I'm clane out of whiskey just at the minit. Howiver, we'll have wan another time. Anything fresh in the counthry?" sez he.

"Not much," sez I. "They do be sayin' that Mr. Hastings has entered 'Black Billy' for the Grand National."

"He may lave it alone," sez he; "for the baste is no manner of use at a ditch."

"He may," sez I; "for they say the favourite'll win. I'd back him meself, but sure there's no money in it at six to four. If it was a twelve to wan chance like 'Junius,' now."

"Twelve to wan again' 'Junius,'" sez he; "it's big odds,

an' he's no bad horse. Twelve to wan," sez he, to himself like. "No," sez he, startin' up. "Keep your money in your pocket, Pat. Bettin's the way to lose it; an' it's hard to get—hard, hard to get," sez he, goin' into the house.

I thought that was all goin' to be about it; but next mornin' I wasn't right out av the door till I meets Mr. Davis himself.

"Good mornin', sir," sez I. "How are ye this mornin'?"

"Not well, Pat," sez he, "not well. I had my supper of them cheese," sez he, "an' I slept powerful bad. Pat," sez he, sudden like, "do you believe in dhrames?"

"Some av thim," sez I. "What were you dhramin', sir?"

"Pat," sez he in a whisper, "I dhramed that 'Junius' won the National. Three times I dhramed it," sez he. "I wondher—I wondher would it come thrue?"

The ould fellow was all in a thrimble wi' excitement, an' in troth I was a bit excited meself; for they do say if you dhrame a thing three times runnin' it's sartain to come thrue.

"I'll put a pound on him," sez I, "anyway. It would be a terrible pity to miss the chance. They say ould Harrison beyont made his fortune by dhramin' av a gold mine whin he was in Australia."

"He did," sez he; "he did right enough. Give me your pound, Pat," sez he, "I'm goin' to put a thrifle on meself with a Dublin man I used to do a bit with, an' I'll send your pound too. Ye'll get better odds that way."

So away the ould chap goes wi' my pound in his pocket; an' whin I come to meself a bit, thinks I, "it's the right ould fool ye are, puttin' a pound on another man's dhrame.

"But, how-an'-iver, it's away now," sez I to meself, "an' anyway it's in good company; for the ould fellow doesn't part aisy. Who knows what luck we'll have?"

For all that I was like a hen on a hot griddle from then till the National.

The big day come, an' about half-past four, in comes ould Davis intil the yard, an' ye niver seen a man in such heart in your life.

"Pat," sez he, "it's come off—Junius has won! Twelve to wan, as I'm a livin' sinner. It's a hundred an' twenty pound in my pocket," sez he.

"An' it's twelve in mine," sez I. "More power to the Major's cheese!"

"D'ye think it was the cheese that done it?" sez he.

"Divil a doubt av it," sez I. "Ye should take another feed av it—before the Two Thousand, say."

"In troth will I," sez he. "I've hardly touched it since, for it agrees mortial badly wi' me; but I like it a dale betther now, Pat.

"Send me up any sportin' paper ye got between this an' that. We needn't both be buyin' them," sez he. "I'll just keep me eye on what's happenin' an' maybe I'll dhrame somethin' before then."

So I sent him up *Sport* for a week or two, an' wi' readin' at it he begin to get that keen he couldn't wait for the 'Two Thousand,' but begins to the cheese again.

For a while divil a thing it did for him, but give him heartburn; but afther about ten days he dhramed the winner of a Sellin' Plate, an' a week afther that, two more.

Between the three av thim he made near five hundhred pound, an' me near fifty.

Thin he stopped; for the 'Two Thousand' was comin' on, an' he didn't want to spoil himself for that.

About ten days before it he came in to me lookin' very miserable an' down.

"Pat," sez he, "I've done me best, but I can't dhrame av the race at all, an' I've near disthroyed meself wi' that cheese. It's a mortial pity nothin' else is any good, for this cheese atin' is terrible bad for the inside."

"Did ye niver thry nothin' else?" sez I.

"I did, Pat," sez he; "but it was no use. I took a shockin' male av salt herrin's the other night," sez he; "but divil all I dhramed but nonsense. I niver closed an eye at all till twelve, an' thin I fell asleep an' dhramed I was ridin' Widow Murphy's goat in the Derby, an' just on the winnin' post the baste threw me an' butted me in the stomach. Terrible real it was, too, for a dhrame; for whin I awoke I could feel the pain in my inside still. No," sez he; "I'll have to stick to the cheese if it kills me."

Whin it came on till a week before the race, an' him niver dhramin' anything was any good, he was near demented; for the more he made, the greedier he was gettin'. An' to tell the truth I was a bit cut meself; for there was no doubt he was dhramin' powerful at the first.

To make matthers worse, the mice got in at the Major's cheese, an' ate it ivery crumb, although the smell might ha' daunted a man let alone a mouse.

Down comes the ould gintleman the next mornin' in a terrible way.

"Have ye any cheese in the house," sez he, "Pat?"

"Divil a crumb," sez I; "it's a thing I niver lip. What's wrong wi' what ye have?"

An' thin he begins cursin' the mice something lamentable, an' bemoanin' his luck, till I could hardly get out av him what had happened.

"Ye'll have to buy more," sez I. "There's time enough yet to dhrame a dozen winners."

"It's terrible dear," sez he, groanin'.

"What about it?" sez I. "Sure ye're makin' a fortune out av it. Give me a shillin' an' I'll run down to Ballygullion, an' get ye a pound av good stuff."

I'd ha' paid for it meself, but, thinks I, "Ye ould miser; it's a heart's blessin' to make ye spend somethin'."

"No," sez he; "I'll go meself."

Away he goes, an' afther a while he come back wi' a pound av quare yellow-lookin' cheese, that looked more like soap. He was lookin' terrible well plazed, to.

"Man, Pat," sez he, "I'm in luck. I got a pound av Meriky cheese for sevenpence."

"Ye'll not dhrame many winners on that," sez I. "It's poor lookin' stuff."

"Ye niver know," sez he. "Anyway, we'll give it a chance."

An' wi' that off he goes like a shot; for he was afeared I might banther him intil buyin' betther.

The next mornin' down he comes leppin' like a yearlin' calf.

"Pat," sez he, "I've dhramed again. I seen 'Buttercup' win the 'Two Thousand' as plain as I see you. An outsider, too," sez he, "we'll not get less than twenty to wan."

"Did ye dhrame it more than wanst?" sez I; for "Buttercup" wasn't thought much av, I may tell ye.

"No," sez he, "but I'll give it another thrial the night."

That night he dhramed it again, an' the nixt night afther that as well.

He's niver dhramed av a race three different nights before, an' that put any doubt av "Butercup" out av our heads.

So I made up me mind to make a death this time, an' I give him the whole fifty pound I'd made.

I niver knowed what he put on himself; but it must ha' been somethin' purty big. For there's no man as venturesome as your miser whin the greed gets the betther av him.

Anyway, ye may guess the state of thrimmles he was in whin he sent an extra sixpence to get the result telegraphed. 'Twas the best thing he could ha' done, too; for he was that busy frettin' about the sixpence he was spendin' that he hadn't time to worry about the race.

The day av the race came, an' whiniver I seen the boy passin' on the red bicycle I down wi' my spade an' away to the big house. The minit I clapped eyes on the ould gintleman I knowed we were done.

He was sittin' on the hall-door steps lookin' fair dazed, wi' the telegram crumpled up in his hand.

"Is it bad news, Mr. Davis?" sez I.

"Bad news," sez he in a sort av a scrame, startin' up; "ay, bad news indeed. I'm broke," sez he—"broke an' ruined. The baste niver got a place even. Och, och," sez he, wringin' his hands an' rockin' backwards an' forwards on the stone steps, "my money's gone, my good money's gone, that I gathered hard an' sore. Curse the baste," sez he. "Curse him! Curse him!"

He bate his head wi' his hands, an' lamented till ye'd been sorry lookin' at him.

"Well, well, now," sez I, "don't fret yourself like that. Sure *I'm* near broke too."

But that was small comfort till him; for divil a hair he cared I was broke all out.

"Anyway," sez I, "we'll get it back. Sure you've dhramed four winners an' only missed wanst. It's that cheap Meriky cheese has done us. If you'd had the pluck to buy a bit av dacent cheese, this wouldn't ha' happened. But your heart wouldn't let you," sez I. For by this time I was beginnin' to get vexed at the thought av me own good fifty pound.

"You're right, Pat," sez he, comin' round a bit. "I give in, you're right. I was mad not to find out from the Major what sort the first was. But I'll do it this day," sez he, gettin' on his feet.

"Ye won't," sez I, "worse luck; for the Major died this mornin' at half-past ten."

Wi' that I thought he was off in his tantrums again; for whin he minded to send to the Major he thought he seen his money back an' more.

At long last I got him quietened down to go into Ballygullion an' get as near as he could to the first.

The next night he dhramed a horse sure enough; but the divil a betther it done than third. I lost five pound, an' himself a bit more, I'm thinkin'.

Away he goes like a madman to Ballygullion again, an' buys a pound av another kind, dearer nor the first. But sure he might as well not; for his luck was clane gone, an' he dhramed an' ould mare that niver left the post at all—divil keep her there still.

Afther that I stopped; for I seen he was clane done at the dhramin'. But the poor ould gintleman niver went mad at it till thin.

He ransacked every shop in Ballygullion an' through the countryside for green cheese, an' whin that was no good he sent to Belfast, an' Dublin even. But he niver had a bit av luck at all, at all. Half-time he niver dhramed av a horse, an' if he did dhrame of wan, it wasn't in the first five.

Afther a while I stopped goin' up at all, for whin I wasn't

bettin' he took no manner av intherest in me; an' besides wi' the eatin' av so much cheese he got as carnaptious as a clockin' hen, an' him an' me always fell out whin I advised him to give it up.

But I still heard odd rumours from the neighbours about him; for people's tongues soon begin to go about all the cheese he was buyin'; an' iverybody thought he was mad, not knowin' anything about the bettin'.

Then I heard he wasn't well, an' wan afthernoon the ould housekeeper come down to tell me the masther wanted to see me.

As the two av us was walkin' up the road we fell intil crack.

"How's he doin' lately, Molly?" sez I.

"Doin'," sez she. "The ould divil's clane crazy. Ye've heard the notion he's tuk about atin' cheese—divil choke him on it. Sure the house is full av it, an' there's a fresh dose comes ivery post. The money he's spendin' on it is lamentable, him that would ha' wrestled a ghost for a ha'penny. But divil the bite or sup else has come intil the house for a month barrin' potatoes an' oatmale. If it wasn't that the ould fool is near his end I'd ha' left long ago, for I'm near dead wi' the heartburn, an' me guts does be rumblin' all the time like an empty churn."

"Near his end, Molly," sez I. "Is he bad, thin?"

"Bad," sez she. "The docthor's been with him ivery day for a week past. He's with him now. Sure 'twas him sent me for you." An' right enough the docthor met me in the hall.

"Tell me, Pat," sez he; "do you know anything of this notion Mr. Davis has got about the dhramin'?"

"Well, docthor," sez I, lookin' a bit foolish, "he dhramed a winner a while ago, afther a supper av cheese, an' him an' me made a bit av money on it; an' iver since he's been thryin' to do the same again. I've tould him over an' over to give it up, but divil a bit will he."

"Well, go in an' thry again," sez he. "He'll maybe take more notice of what ye say now; for I've tould him he'll not live above a fortnight if he doesn't quit the cheese."

So away goes I up to the bedroom, an' troth 'twas a cruel sight to see him lyin' there. Terrible failed he was; all gathered up lookin', an' not more than half the size he was when I seen him last.

"Och, Mr. Davis dear," sez I, "what have ye been doin' to yerself at all, at all."

"I've been ruinin' meself," sez he, "that's all. I'm near a pauper," sez he, in a sort av heartbroken way, wi' the tears rollin' down his cheeks—"me that was a well-off man if I had a' had sense."

"Come," sez I, "you're not as bad as that yet; you've still a fine place behind ye."

"Have I?" sez he. "Do you see that letther? Well, there's six notes av fifty pound in it, an' that's all that's left av what I raised on the same place," sez he.

"Och, och," sez I, "this is terrible altogether. I niver thought it was as bad as this wi' ye."

"Wheesht, Pat," sez he, risin' on his elbow an' spakin' in a whisper. "I'll get it back yet. I've found the right kind av cheese at last. It come just before I tuk to me bed," sez he, "an' I kept a bit in the dhressin'-table unbeknownst to the docthor. I've dhramed 'Clematis' for the 'St. Leger' for sivin nights now, an' she's a twinty to wan chance. You post this letther to Dublin to-day for me," sez he, "an' I'll come out right yet. The wire'll come to you, an' the doctor'll niver know."

"Is it mad ye think I am," sez I, "to post your last shillin' away. Divil a fear o' me."

"Listen to me, Pat," sez he, "if 'Clematis' wins I'm set up again for me day; an' I'll niver back a horse again av I was to dhrame a whole circus av thim. An' if she loses, sure I've neither chick nor child to be the worse."

"But what about yourself, Mr. Davis?" sez I.

"Pat," sez he, "if she loses I'll not be long here. It'll break me heart if I don't get me money back. I can't stop thinkin' av it day nor night—day nor night.

"But she'll not lose," sez he. "Somethin' tells me she'll not lose. I've got the right kind av cheese again. I know I have. Ye don't believe it, I see that, an' I'll not tell ye what it is or where I got it—now. But when I've won, an' ye're convinced, I will. Sure there's a fortune in it—aye, a fortune," sez he.

He was sittin' up in the bed be this time, wi' his eyes all bright an' glitterin', an' it come over me whin I looked at him that, sure enough, he wasn't all there.

However, thinks I, what he sez is thrue—he'll not be long for this world if he doesn't get his money back, an' I'll give him his chance. Sure we'll know wan way or another in a fortnight. So away I goes an' posts the letther.

Two days afterwards whin I got me *Sport*, I seen that "Clematis" was riz in the bettin' from twinty, till twelve to wan. "That looks well," sez I. An' up I goes to the big house to tell the ould gintleman. He was weaker a good deal, but the news heartened him up a bit.

"Here, Pat," sez he, gropin' under the pillow, "here's a shillin'. Get a paper ivery day, an' let me know how the bettin' goes."

I had mighty little hope av him afther that, for I don't believe he'd spent a penny on a paper since the misthress died, let alone a shillin'.

But the nixt day the mare was up till eight to wan; an' afther that she riz in the bettin' steady, an' the ould gintleman kept mendin' ivery day.

Three days before the race she was at four to wan, an' I was cursin' meself that I hadn't the heart to back her whin there was a dacent price to be got.

Thin the nixt mornin' comes out a report in the paper that "Clematis" had broken down in thrainin' an' was scratched.

"It's all up wi' him now," sez I.

Up I goes, intendin' to say nothin' about it, an' make out the mare was doin' well; but whin I wint intil the room, sure I seen death in his face.

"I'm done, Pat," sez he. "The docthor was here an' towld me about the mare. I didn't want him to know I was bettin'; but I couldn't thole till you came."

"Divil stretch his long tongue another fut!" sez I. "He

might a' had more gumption. But keep up your heart, there'll be better news in the mornin'."

An' so there was. Next mornin' the paper says the report about "Clematis" was only partly thrue, an' she'd start alright. For all that, she was back to the twinties in the bettin', an' all I could do I couldn't cheer the ould gintleman up.

The docthor met me comin' down the stairs, an' afther givin' me the divil's own dhressin' down for deceivin' him, forbids me to go up again.

"He's too wake to stand any excitement," sez he. "If I'd caught ye in time ye'd not have been in wi' him the day."

"But docthor," sez I, "sure the race is on to-morrow, an' if the mare wins you'll let me tell him."

"If the sky falls!" sez he. "Ye might as well expect my pony to win." An' in troth, I couldn't conthradict him.

All the nixt afthernoon from dinner-time I was goin' about like a ghost round a graveyard, lookin' for the telegram. At last, about half-past three, I sees the boy comin' up the road. I run down to meet him an' tuk the invilope out av his han', but me own was thrimmlin' that I could hardly open it.

There was just three words:—"Clematis won easily;" an' whin I read them the sight near left my eyes.

Thin I to my heels an' up the road for the big house wi' me heart in a twitter. I niver looked to right or left, but up to the ould gintleman's room.

The docthor heard me comin', an' steps out on the landin'.

"Wheesht, Pat," sez he, "an' go quietly down if ye have any dacency at all. The man's dyin'," sez he.

"He'll not die," sez I, "if ye'll only let me in. The mare's won I tell ye."

"It's too late," sez he; "he's at his last gasp."

"Let me in," sez I, pushin' past him; "it's not too late yet," an' before he could stop me I was in the room.

The ould gintleman was lyin' very still an' quiet, wi' his eyes half shut; an' whin I seen him me heart near failed me.

But I fell on me knees be the bedside.

"Mr. Davis," sez I, as softly as I could.

He opened his eyes a bit, an' I seen that he knowed me; for they brightened, an' a wee bit av colour come in his face.

"Pat," sez he, in a whisper, "Pat!"

"The mare's won, sir," sez I. "The mare's won! Ye're all right yet. Sure ye'll niver give in now."

The poor ould fellow stretched out his hand, an' laid it on mine that was lyin' on the bed. A sort av a smile come on his face, an' his lips moved a thrifle. When I seen that, I learned over him.

"Pat," sez he, very slow an' faint, "Mooney's—Sackville Street—thirteenpence a pound." Thin he stopped.

I looked at his face, an' run out av the room cryin' like a child.

The Wooden Leg

It was a black day for Michael Carlin whin he first took the notion av soldierin'. In troth, though, ye could hardly blame him; for it was all over the two things that bothers the whole men kind av us—dhrink an' the wimmen.

Michael an' Susy Bryan was coortin' sthrong for a long time, an' iverybody thought it would ha' been a match. An' a right good match it was for both av thim. Michael lived wi' his uncle, an' was sartin to get the bit av land whin the ould man died; an' Susy lived wi' an aunt on twinty-five acres av the best land in the county, that they said was her own, barrin' a life intherest the aunt had in it. The aunt got money left her at the same time, an' even if Michael an' Susy didn't come intil that in their own time—for the aunt was a tight, fresh body, not above thirty-eight or so—sure the childher were bound to fall in some day.

There niver should ha' been a match aisier to make, an' that's just what bate it. It was too simple and complate altogether; an' the wimmen bein' the divil for pure crookedness, Susy must be carryin' on wi' wan or another, just to let

Michael see he wasn't goin' to get things all his own way, till he was clane wild wi' jealousy.

Wan day as Michael was goin' in to Ballygullion fair, he happened to come on James Doran and Susy walkin' along the road.

They were brave an' close together for a start, an' whin Susy sees Michael comin', she slithers still closer to James. James, bein' a man av spunk, didn't make much av a move away, as ye may guess; so altogether they were a very lovin' lookin' couple whin Michael come near them.

Michael he never let on, though, but just said, "Good-mornin'," and walked by. He niver turned his head either, or Susy niver catched him doin' it anyway, an' she turned hers brave an' often to see.

But for all that Michael took it quiet, he was badly cut; an' all that day he kept thinkin' about it, an' drinkin' half-wans av whiskey to dhrive the thoughts out av his head.

The more he took the angrier he got with Susy, till, bein' clane beside himself wi' whiskey an' jealousy, an' happenin' to meet the Ulsther Fusiliers route-marchin' on his way home, what does he do but list. The sodgers were campin' outside av Ballygullion for two days, an' at the end av that time Michael was to join thim.

But when Michael got home, thin there was the fun. The ould uncle nearly wint mad. It was bad enough losin' Michael about the place, but that was nothin' to the disgrace av him goin' for a sodger.

There was a muttherin' av war wi' the Boers at the time, and terrible bad feelin' again England among the red-hot Nationalists; an' to list for a sodger in the British army was like turnin' your back on your politics altogether.

So ould Pether he ramped up an' down, an' cursed somethin' dhreadful, an' poor Michael sat on the dhresser very miserable lookin'; for the dhrink was dead in him by this time, an' he begin to see he'd made a fool av himself.

But if Michael's uncle was mad, it was nothin' to the rage Susy was in whin she heard av it. Susy was by way av bein' a terrible pathriot, an' used to dress herself up av a holiday wi' a wee green hood an' a cloak wi' shamrocks embroidhered on it, for all the world like what you'd see on a Christmas card. An' mortial well she looked too, wi' a handful of brown curls stickin' out on each side av as red a pair av cheeks, and two as bright eyes as was in Ireland.

'Twas well the green suited her, though; for, in troth if she'd ha' looked as well in it, there's no tellin' but she'd ha' wore orange.

Anyhow, she was clane wild wi' Michael, an' wouldn't even see him, though he hung about the house the whole two days. If she hadn't been a bit in the wrong herself, she'd maybe have come round; but that was what finished his chance entirely.

The end av it was Michael marched away wan mornin' wi' divil a wan to say "good-bye" till him, an' wasn't heard av for more than a year.

Thin word come that he was goin' out to South Africa wi' a lot more recruits to bring up the regiment to full strength; for they'd lost heavy again the Boers. For near a year again there was no word more. An' thin a letther come for the uncle sayin' Michael had been badly wounded an' was comin' home.

For all the uncle was so mad about the soldierin' he was a kindly man at bottom, an' he made Michael welcome; though he was no manner av use till him, for wan of his legs was as stiff as a poker wi' the wound he'd got.

Wan evenin' after Michael had been home about a couple av days, I thought I'd go down an' see him. Whin I wint in he was sittin' before the fire wi' the game leg up on a chair before him, an' the uncle sittin' beside him talkin' very hard.

"How are ye, Michael?" sez I. "But I needn't ask. Sure you're lookin' rightly." An' he he was too, barrin' the leg. The soldierin' had made a man av him. He was square an well set up lookin' about the shouldhers, an' as brown as a berry.

"Troth, Pat," sez he, "I've not much to boast about. I'm little betther than a cripple. An' if the uncle here hadn't taken me in, it's the beggin' I might be at."

"Wheesht now," sez the uncle, shufflin' on his chair—he was a terrible fidgety wee man, always on the go—"sure you're welcome; an' if you take my advice," sez he, "you'll be undher a compliment to nobody very long. Not that I want to be redd av ye; but it's for your own good.

"I'll tell ye what it is, Pat," goes on the uncle, turnin' to me; "I'm just advisin' him to make up to the widow beyont."

It was on me tongue to ask Michael what about Susy, when the ould chap winks at me.

"Now that Susy's left her, an' not likely to be back, she'll jump at the chance av settlin' again," sez he.

"An' is Susy not comin' back from her uncle Joe's?" sez I.

"No," sez he, "she's goin' to marry her cousin, and they're both to keep house wi' the ould man. He's terribly lonely since the wife died."

I stole a look at Michael, an' he was lookin' very white.

"Look here, uncle," sez he, breakin' out suddenly, "I'm a burden here, an' if the widow would have me I'd ask her, for I'm not carin' much who I marry; but there's no wan would have a poor cripple like me, an' well ye know it. Help me up to bed," sez he, "an' let Pat know the whole story. He'll not tell anybody about me that he's known from a child. If he gives in to me makin' up till any woman, when he's heard, damme, I'll marry who you like."

So the ould fellow arms him up to bed, an' comes back to the fire. "Look here, Pat," sez he, "the whole trouble's this. The lad has lost his leg above the knee, an' has got a wooden wan. Ye wouldn't notice it when he's sittin', but he can't walk barrin' on sticks yet, an' very stiff at that. That's why I tould him the crack about Susy an' the cousin. There's no chance of a young girl lookin' at him now.

"But it's different wi' the widow. Whin a widow woman gets to her time av life, an' no word av a second market, there's very little in breeches she'll not face. It's not for a lame leg she'd refuse a likely young chap like Michael."

"Would ye not tell her 'twas a wooden wan, this?" sez I.

"Divil a bit," sez he, "if I have me will. She'll niver find out till it's too late, an' thin she'll have to thole. There's enough av Michael left to make as good a man as she's likely to get now, an' if he wanst gets her he's a made man. The ould hussy has bings av money, I'm tould. An' if Susy should marry the cousin, an' there is some talk av it, right enough, the aunt'll be able to buy out the place very chape. She has a life intherest in it as it is.

"The only bother wi' Michael is the leg. If him an' the widow was wanst married she'd niver tell, or if it come out she could let on she knew all the time. But if she finds out about it durin' the coortin' she'll not hould her tongue then, an' the divil a woman he'll get at all."

"Pether," sez I, "it's well ye tould me about the leg; for I know the very article for you."

"What, Pat," sez he; "what do ye mane?"

"It's just this mornin'," sez I, "I was readin' in a piece av a doctor's paper the vet brought round a linimint for the mare, about some man in Dublin that makes legs betther than the rale thing,—that's if you're to believe what he sez in the advertisement."

"But could ye walk in wan?" sez Pether.

"Walk," sez I. "If the man's not as big a liar as the ould fellow himself, ye could dance a hornpipe in wan. It'll carry him up the church wi' the widow anyway," sez I, "an' that's all ye want."

"Pat," sez he, "bring down the paper, an' if they're all you say, we'll have wan for the boy should it break me. It'll not throuble him to pay me back if he gets the widow."

The end av it was ould Pether brings Michael round to let him send for a patent leg. An' though the price daunted him a bit, he was that sure av Michael gettin' the widow he screwed himself up to partin' wi' it.

It was no easy job gettin' Michael to agree, for he was no way keen on the widow, an' the game leg was a fine excuse. But whin he seen how the uncle was set on the match, what could he do but give in, him bein' only a sort av pensioner in the house.

"Pat," sez he to me, whin the uncle wasn't by, "I've lost Susy now, an' I can't sponge here all me days. There's nothin' for it but the widow, an' I might do worse. She's a kindly wee woman, an' an ould friend av mine. But I don't live decavin' her about the leg."

"Hould on till ye get the new wan," sez I. "If it's like the thing at all, ye needn't say a word. Niver mind about the decavin'. Sure all marryin' is decavin'. If she'd knowed the temper the first wan had, she'd niver ha' taken him. An' a bad temper's worse than a bad leg any day."

"Ay, but I'm not sure it's worse than a wooden wan," sez Michael, wi' the first smile I'd seen on his face since he come home.

Before the new leg come, Pether had the widow over for tay, an' I think he must have give her a hint that Michael was on the look out, for she was over near ivery day after that inquirin' for his health; an' all the time she kept askin' about the bad leg, an' how soon he'd be walkin'. Michael niver would say much about it, but left ould Pether to do the talkin'. I was over wan night she was there, an' it was as good as a play to see Pether squirmin' on his chair, an' lyin' like the divil.

An' in troth I think the joke av it egged Michael on a bit; for he was mighty friendly wi' the widow before the night was over.

A couple av days afther this Pether sends up for me, an' whin I got there he runs across the kitchen an' shakes me be the hand.

"Pat," sez he, "you've made the boy's future. Look at him," sez he, caperin' round. "Get up an' walk, Michael."

Up gets Michael, an' walks across the kitchen, an' faith 'twas wonderful. Barrin' a bit av a halt, you'd niver ha' known but he had two legs as sound as me own. He was greatly up wi' it himself too.

"Would any wan know, Pat?" sez he.

"Not a mother's son," sez I. "I can hardly believe it meself. It's wondherful altogether. Does it work aisy?"

"There's a bit av a catch in it I was just goin' to fix whin you come in," sez Pether. "Sit down, Michael, an' I'll do it now."

"Maybe you'd as well lave it alone," sez Michael; for he knowed his uncle.

He was by way of bein' a handy man, an' always would be meddlin' at things he didn't undherstand. There was hardly at clock in the counthryside he didn't spoil before the people found him out.

But Pether wasn't to be put off.

"Not at all," sez he; "I'll make it all right in a jiffey."

So he gets Michael down on a chair at the fire, pulls up his breeches, an' begins pokin' about the knee av the patent leg with a screwdriver. There was a desperate lot av springs an' joints about the thing, an' I misdoubted but Pether would do it little good. An' sure enough, afther pokin' a bit, whin he tries to work the joint,—"be the holy poker," sez he, "she's stuck."

An' stuck the leg was. It was bent well at the knee, but divil a bit would it go straight for all he could do, an' he tugged at it till he near pulled Michael off the chair.

"What's to be done?" sez he, afther he'd progged it for five minits. "I'm clane bate."

"Thry a taste av oil," sez I.

"The very thing, Pat," sez he; an' he reaches down a bottle av paraffin.

He put a dhrop or two in. "Now," sez he, "for a good pull. That'll shift it."

So it did. The leg straightened out wi' a snap, lit ould Pether on his back, an' the toe av it just took the wee tay-drawer that was simmerin' on the hob.

The cat an' dog was sleepin' in front av the fire; an' naythe of thim had any cause to complain av the other; for they just got the tay over thim in about equal shares. The dog run away up the house yelpin' murdher, an' the cat tears round the kitchen a couple av times, spittin' an' swearin', knocks two plates off the dhresser, an' thin out through a pane av glass.

"Holy Biddy," sez Pether, risin' to his feet; "there's eighteenpence gone. But niver mind, the leg's workin' again. Is it aisy, Michael?"

"It's all right, uncle," sez Michael, walkin' up an' down the kitchen.

"I'll just put a dhrop more oil in," sez Pether.

"No, uncle," sez Michael very firm. "Thank you, all the same, we'll just let it rest at this."

"Maybe you're right," sez Pether. "It might take another thraw. Man!" sez he, "it's doin' well. I'll dhrop over to the widow's in the mornin' an' tell her you're mendin' fast."

Whin the widow seen Michael walkin' about wi' only a bit av a limp, she begin to set her cap at him in rale earnest. Up till then she'd been afeared he was goin' to be a lamitor all his days, an' she wasn't right sure whether to face him or not. Besides, there was a pig-dealer in the neighbourhood, wan Tammas M'Gimpsey, was reported to be lookin' after her when the word av Susy's goin' to be married come out. But afther Michael got on his feet she had no eyes for anybody but him.

About three weeks after the patent leg come home, Pether calls up to see me.

"Pat," sez he, "the hob's as good as done. Michael's a made man. He's goin' to ask the widow after Mass next Sunday."

"It's well if Susy doesn't come home before it's settled," sez I.

"Tut," sez Pether, "she'd niver look at him now."

"Ay, but she might put him off the notion av the widow," sez I.

"Not a bit," sez Pether. "Sure the widow an' him's as good as trysted already. Michael has a terrible notion av her now."

I said nothin' to that, but I had an idea all the same that Michael's notion av her was little sthronger than at the first. He wasn't lookin' in big heart for a man that was goin' to be married, if it was only to a widow.

Sunday come, an' whin I sat down beside Michael an' the uncle, there was the widow right across the aisle, dhressed up to the nines.

A minit or so before the bell stopped, ould Pether give a jump an' sits well forrard in his sate. I seen him skellyin' across, an' whin I looked, who should I see but Susy sittin' down beside her aunt. From the look the widow gave her I'm thinkin' she was naythe r expected nor welcome.

"Pether, me man," sez I to meself, "your work's cut out for you now."

An' Pether knowed that as well as me; for he aye kept edgin' furdher forrard to keep Michael from seein' Susy. Very little throuble he had; for Michael niver turned his head at all, but sat there very glum, lookin' straight in front av him.

All wint well till Father Connolly was just beginnin' his sermon. Michael shifted round a bit to hear him, an' his eyes lights on Susy. He half riz from his sate, an' turned as white as a sheet. Sittin' down again his wooden leg slips off the wee stool he had it restin' on, an' hits the flure a brave knock. Wi' that it gives a whirr an' a bizz the same as in the kitchen at home, an' fetches the sate before us a thump ye'd have heard all over the chapel.

Ould Mrs. Malone in front lepped above three inches in the air, an' dhropped her glasses, an' Father Connolly took a mortial hard look our way.

But sure lookin' at Michael was little use, for the leg was clane away wi' it, kickin' fourteen to the dozen, an' threatenin' ivery minit to break down the partition in front.

Ivery man, woman an' child in the church was standin' up, or cranin' over to see what was wrong, an' as for Father Connolly, he was near chokin' wi' rage. The cowld sweat was runnin' down Michael's face, an' poor ould Pether was near as bad.

"Stop the cursed thing, Michael, for Hivin's sake," sez he, in as near a whisper as he could get to bate the noise av the leg.

"I can't," sez Michael in desperation. "Thry an' catch it, uncle."

So Pether stoops to get hould av it; but he missed his grip, an' the leg comes again the partition wi' a dunt that split the board for two feet.

Be this time the people was near mad wi' curiosity, an'

Father Connolly had stopped in his sermon, an' was comin' down from the pulpit.

"Let me out," says Michael, sthrugglin' to his feet; an' out he comes, wi' the leg goin' like a flail.

The first skite it kicked ould Pether's Sunday tall hat into the organ-loft. Be good luck the nixt missed Pether himself by an inch; but if it did, the third one took me on the knee-cap, an' near desthroyed me.

However, out in the aisle he gets at last, an' just that minit Father Connolly comes marchin' down it, wi' a face like a turkey-cock.

Whin Michael seen him comin' he jams the toe av the leg undher the heatin' stove, an' steadies himself as well as he could.

"An' is it you, Michael Carlin, that has been disurbin' the house av God wi' your dhrunken frolics?" sez Father Connolly. "I might have known it. I might have known it could be none av the dacint boys av Ballygullion; but a blackguard av a soldier, that fears nayther God nor man. Lave the sacred precincts av the church, before I forget my duty as a priest," sez he, turnin' away.

But sure enough the Ould Fellow himself was again Michael that day, for just as he dhrew the toe out to go, the leg lashes forrard an' catches Father Connolly where he didn't expect it.

Before ye could dhraw your breath the half av the congregation was on top av Michael, Tammas M'Gimpsey at the head av thim.

"Out wi' him," sez he, "out wi' the dirty sodger, an' tache him whether he'll kick our priest in his own church!"

"Out wi' him," sez iverybody.

An' out they goes in a sthrugglin' crowd, Michael in the middle av thim, an' the wimmen hangin' round, pullin' the skirts av men's coats, an' cryin' melia murdher.

Poor Michael would ha' had a poor chance wi' them be himself, but they didn't reckon on the leg. If it did get Michael intil the throuble, manly and well it stood to him in it.

Between the middle av the church an' the door it shifted more teeth than Docthor Cargill pulled in a year before; an' thim that only got a peeled shin or a black eye was well plazed the next day.

Be the time they got him intil the churchyard the bulk av thim was at Michael's head, an' only Tammas M'Gimpsey would face the right leg—the wooden wan, I mane;—though sorrow a wan av thim knew it was wood, thin.

"Throw him in the road!" sez the men at his head.

"Put him in the river," sez thim at his feet. They were the angriest at him, small wondher.

"Ye'll dhrown him," sez the first party, pullin' nixt the road.

"Divil a odds, if we do," sez Tammas M'Gimpsey, pullin' nixt the river.

At that minit the sthraps av the leg give way.

Down goes the men at Michael's head over Father Dorrian's tombstone, an' down goes Tammas M'Gimpsey wi' the leg in his hand. Whin he riz, he takes a look at Michael an' the boys lyin' on the ground in a heap, an' wan at the boot an' leg in his hand. An' thin wi' a screech like a stuck pig he over the churchyard wall, an' across the fields like a madman. He had his passage booked for Amerikay the nixt day, before he heard the leg was wood.

For the first minit or two the rest av the boys was near as much scared as Tammas; but they soon seen how the thing was; an' thin there was such a laugh riz as Ballygullion niver heard. Even thim that had broken heads an' bloody noses joined in—afther a while.

The wimmen that was hurryin' out to save Michael's life, they chimed in too, an' the only sober face I seen was the widow's. She had come out hot-foot to rescue Michael, an' near thripped over Tammas M'Gimpsey an' the leg as they both wint down.

Wan look at the leg an' another at Michael was enough for her. She stood a minit or two dumb-foundhered, an' thin down the path for the gate.

An' if the crowd laughed before, they laughed twice as

much thin; for there was few didn't know about the coortin' match.

But och, och, ye would ha' been sorry for poor Michael, sittin' there in the middle av the ring av thim, the laughin'-stock av the parish. An' maybe the thought that Susy was among thim wasn't the laste av his sorrow.

In the thick av the laughin' an' jeerin' out comes Father Connolly; for somebody had tould him what had happened.

"Michael," sez he, puttin' his hand on his head, "Michael, me poor fellow, I miscalled ye inside. I said things to ye I shouldn't ha' said, an' things I didn't mane. But ye'll forgive me, me son, for I was angrier than a Christian man should be, let alone a priest, an' I didn't know your thrial. But keep up your heart," sez he; "it's not the coward that gets the knocks, an' a brave man, Michael, has no cause to be ashamed av anything. God comfort ye, Michael," sez the ould man, turnin' away.

"An' now, boys an' girls," sez he to the rest av thim standin' round, "go in there," pointin' to the church, "an' I'll see if I can't tache ye more Christian charity than to laugh at a fellow-creature's affliction. It's little betther than haythens ye are."

It wasn't long till they were all in again, I can tell ye; all but me an' Pether.

"Uncle," sez Michael, "lift me up on the stone there, an' do you an' Pat lave me for a bit. Maybe you'd borrow Joe Crawley's cart from down the road an' take me home. I'm only lumber, an' the world knows it now. I've thried to decave people, an' I'm punished for it this day."

"We'll go, Michael," sez ould Pether. "Pat," sez he to me in a whisper, "stay here an' keep an eye on the lad."

So I tip-toes round behind Michael's back, an' plants meself on a stone a bit away, lavin' Michael sittin' there wi' his head between his hands.

Prisintly, who should comin' slippin' out av the porch but Susy. She comes right over to Michael, an' puts her hand on his shouldher.

"Michael," sez she. Quick enough he looked up thin.

"Susy," sez he; "Susy, me dear, is it you?" Maybe 'twas the words, maybe 'twas the way he said thim, but Susy's face that was glum enough before broke out in a smile like sunshine on a runnin' sthrame.

"Och, Susy," sez poor Michael, "don't you laugh at me, too. I know I'm a mock an' a laughin'-stock,—well, well, I know it; but if ye iver had a kindly thought for me, an' wanst I believe ye had, lave me to me shame, if ye can't pity me. If I did go soldierin' have I not paid the price? Och, och," sez he, dhroppin' his head on his hands again, "if I'd only lost me life be it. But I've lost dearer than me life, an' it's this day I know it."

"In troth, Michael," sez Susy, "ye've lost me aunt right enough, if that's what ye mane. She'll niver take ye now."

"Ye little divil ye," sez I to meself, "if I didn't see your face I'd think ye'd no heart, to say thim words."

But Michael didn't see her face, an' his head dhropped lower than iver.

"I desarve it, Susy," sez he; "it's a hard word you're sayin', but God knows I desarve it. But me dear," sez he, "some day if ye should happen to think av a broken man, a man that was a burden to his friends, an' thim friends eggin' him on, ye'll maybe see some excuse for him. For all that, till I heard ye were to be married to your cousin, I niver give in. Not that I had hopes for meself. But sure till you were another man's wife, I could think av ye without sin."

"Well, Michael," sez Susy—the smile was still on her face, but I thought there was a glint av tears in her eye—"I'm not goin' to marry me cousin that I know av, an' if me aunt won't have ye,—and I don't think there's much chance av it,—I'll just have to take ye meself—if you'll ask me, that is," sez she, gettin' very red.

"Susy," sez Michael, sittin' up, "are ye mockin' me?" "No," sez he, lookin' at her a minit; "God bless your soft heart, I believe you'd do it for pity; but, child, ye don't know what you're sayin'. Is it to marry me, a cripple, an' a pauper forbye? Niver," sez he. "I've behaved like a scoundhrel, but plaze God I'll be an honest man now. I'll love ye, Susy, till they carry out this maimed carcase av mine, but I'll niver let ye join yourself to three-quarthers av a man. God bless ye again, dear," sez he, wringin' her hand, "an' send ye the man ye desarve."

"Well, Michael," sez Susy, "I don't know what about gettin' the man I desarve, but it seems I'm not goin' to get the man I want; an' all because he's too fond av me, that's the annoyin' part av it. I didn't say what I said out av pity, though me heart's sore for your throuble, but just because I couldn't help it. I lost ye by me folly an' empty head before, an' if I'm only gettin' three-quarthers av ye back I've nobody to blame but meself. An' I'd rather have that three-quarthers av a man, Michael dear, than the best whole man in Ireland."

An' thin in a minit Susy was lyin' on his breast an' croonin' over her poor boy, an' Michael strokin' her hair and sayin' niver a word. Maybe his heart was too full to spake.

It was no place for me, anyway, so I stepped quietly out be the gate.

Comin' up the road I meets ould Pether wi' the horse an' cart.

"Pat," sez he, "maybe this is all for the best. Ould Crawley was executor under the uncle's will, an' he tells me the farm's Susy's altogether. The aunt only got two hundhred pound an' no life intherest. So maybe Michael's well out av her, afther all."

"What?" sez I, "the farm's Susy's? Come here, Pether," an' I dhraws him over to the churchyard gate. "Look at thim," sez I. "Wheesht now, ye ould fool. Lave thim there for a while, an' thin put thim in the cart an' let thim go home together. You an' I'll walk it. But if it wasn't that Susy's not far off bein' an angel, I'd say Michael had the divil's own luck."

I don't well know how it come about, but whin Tammas M'Gimpsey got the notion av Amerikay in his head, he stuck till it, an' whin he wint, he tuk the widow an' the two hundhred wi' him.

A fortnight afther that Susy and Michael was married;

an' now there's a lump of a gossoon runnin' about the place that thinks his daddy's the cliverest man in the country because he can stick a fork in his right leg.

The wee fellow thinks all the more av it since he thried it on himself.

The Alarm Clock

'TWAS just in the middle av Ballygullion sthreet I met Billy av the Hills, the last man in life I thought to meet there on a market-day. In his spare time Billy does be makin' an odd dhrop av potheen; an' the market-day bein' a throng day for the polis in Ballygullion, 'twas ginerally Billy's throng day outside av it, deliverin' a wee keg here an' there.

"You're a sight for sore eyes, Billy," sez I. "What has fetched ye intil the town the day?"

"Ye know ould Dick Taafe, me uncle be marriage," sez Billy. "His brother's dead, away in Donegal, an' he's goin' off to the funeral in the mornin'. I'm sleepin' in the house a night or two to keep the aunt company, an' I come in the day to rise me uncle in good time for the thrain; for he's desperate heavy-headed, and the aunt's little betther, though she wouldn't give in till it. Come on down an' have a crack before ye go home."

So away we goes down to the house, an' whin we got that length, who should be there wi' Mrs. Taafe but wee Jinks, the pedlar,—Peddlin' Tam as they call him,—wi' a whole packful av stuff spread out on the table.

"Good evenin', gintlemen," sez he. "Ye might come an' give me a hand. I'm just thryin' to sell the misthress here the very thing she wants."

"What's that?" sez Billy. "It'll be somethin' in the way av clothes, I'm thinkin'."

"Not a bit av it," sez the pedlar, "it's just an alarm clock. Sure her heart's broke wi' wakin' the man in the mornin's; an' this is the boy'll do it for her."

"I don't believe in thim conthrivances," sez she; "ye could niver depend on thim."

"Hould on till I show ye how she works," sez Tam, "an' then ye'll change your mind. She's set for five," sez he; "now listen till her ringin', for it's herself can do it."

"Ay, there ye are now," sez the aunt. "Sure it's seven o'clock now, an' she'd be ringin' two hours slow. That'd be a dale av use in the mornin'."

"But ye can set her for any time ye like," sez Tam. "Wait a minit an' I'll set her to seven."

"An' mightn't ye as well get up to raise the house as get up to set the clock to do it," sez she. "It bates me to see the use av it at all."

I wish ye'd seen the pedlar's face. 'Twas little compliment to the ould woman's brains was in the back av his head, I'm thinkin'.

But he wasn't to be bate, an' at long an' at last he got the workin' av the clock insensed intil her.

"Now," sez he, "listen till her;" an' he set the clock down on the table.

The divil a such a whirroo ye iver heard in your life. The first birr-r she made she near lifted herself off the table; an' then she hopped an' jigged round it, fair burstin' herself wi' noise, for all the world like a hen after layin'.

"What d'ye think av that?" sez the pedlar, whin she stopped. "An' if ye set her on a tin pan she'll make double the noise."

"Ye don't need it," sez Billy; "she's a terror. Be the hokey, if ye set her on a tomb-stone in Ballybreen church-yard there'd be a general resurrection."

"An' what do you think av her, mem?" sez the pedlar, turnin' to Billy's aunt.

"How much do ye want for her?" sez she, feelin' for her purse.

"Half-a-crown," sez he, seein' how keen she was lookin'.

But the ould woman wasn't that soft, for all ye could see she was dyin' for the clock.

"I'll give ye two shillin's," sez she, "take it or lave it."

"Well, well," sez the pedlar, "seein' it's you, Mrs. Taafe, ye can have her."

"Don't let on what I paid for her, Billy," sez she when the pedlar was gone. "The good man'd have me life if he knowed."

She wasn't far wrong there, for the ould fellow was heart miserable about money.

"Wait till he hears her," sez Billy, "an' he'd not grudge half-a-crown. I'll tell ye what," sez he; "just slip her into the room the night, an' niver say a word, an' then he'll know the good av her before he hears the price."

"It's a right good idea," sez she, "an' I'll just thry it."

"You're a terrible blackguard, Billy," sez I, when the ould woman was left the room. "It'll frighten the ould fellow out av his seven senses."

"Divil a bit," sez Billy. "I niver seen him frightened but wanst, an' that was whin he dhropped a shillin' in the pig-market, an' thought he wasn't goin' to find it. But, Lord," sez he, "but I'll make him lepp. He'll think it's the Fenians. I'll fill him full av stories about dinnamite an' infernal machines before he goes to bed."

"Here he's comin' up the sthreet wi' Davis the polisman," sez I.

"Is it Davis?" sez Billy. "Begad I'll spoil his dhrames for him too. 'Twould be a charity, for he's as timid as a chicken. Look at him wi' the fat white face av him. He's big enough to be a man, if he'd only the heart av wan."

"Good evenin', uncle. Good evenin', constable," sez Billy, as they come up.

"Good evenin', Billy," sez the uncle, hearty enough. But the constable was very dhry an' cool. None av the polis was very fond av Billy. He was too many for them; an' nobody likes to be got the betther av, laste av all a polisman. It's more av a come-down for him than for another body.

"It's a wondher you're not out at Ballybreen, constable," sez Billy.

"What'd I be out there for?" sez the constable very short.

"Did ye not hear about it?" sez Billy. "Man, there's the

divil himself to pay. Nayther Bates nor Keown'll sell their estates, an' the whole counthry's in a blaze about it; for ivery other landlord in the country has sould, an' brave an' chape too. They're goin' to start a Land League, an' clear the counthry av landlords altogether, they say. There hasn't been as bitther feelin' in the counthry since I was a lump av a boy runnin' about. I wouldn't be surprised if ye were to see the ould Fenian work over again, wi' shootin' av landlords, an' dinnamittin' av houses,—an' polis-barracks, too," sez Billy, takin' a skelly at him wi' the tail av his eye.

"What'd they touch the polis-barracks for, Billy?" sez I, just to give him a lift. "They'll niver come near Ballygullion, anyway."

"Will they not?" sez Billy. "Doesn't half the town belong to ould Keown? Sure the house me uncle's livin' in is his. An' the people is terrible wicked agin the polis, I hear. Ould Bates has wired to Dublin for fifty av thim, and the counthry's set for givin' thim a warm welcome. 'Twould be odd if they didn't give the polis in Ballygullion a touch too."

"Ye seem to know a good dale about this affair," sez the constable, very suspicious. "Maybe you're a sympathizer?"

"'Deed no," sez Billy, "except that I'd like to see the polis get a lick. Not, av coorse," sez he, very hasty by the way, "that I'd like to see anythin' happen to our own polis here, Misther Davis, for, faith, they're harmless enough. An' troth, it's a pity av them all. It's terrible hard life, too, whin ye come to think av it; wi' iverybody wi' a grudge agin ye, an' niver knowin' whin ye'll be blown intil etarnity."

"I'll tell what it is, me fine fellow," sez the constable, "ye'd betther mind yourself. If ye get mixed up in any Fenian work ye'll see whether the polis here is harmless or not. I've a good mind to lift ye on suspicion as it is, an' I'd do it too, if I thought there was any truth in what you've been sayin'. But ye're twinty years behind the time wi' your dinnamite. Dinnamite!" sez the constable, wi' a sneer, movin' off, "dinnamite nowadays!"

For all that he footed it off to the barracks a very soberlookin' polisman; an' whin ould Pether Linchey's donkey let a hee-haw just as he passed the stable, he give a lepp in the air that near bounced the helmet off his head.

"What nonsense is that ye've been fillin' the man's head wi'," sez ould Taafe. "Some more av your jokes, I suppose, Billy. But ye needn't be thryin' thim on here. It'll maybe do for a yarn for the constable, but it's no manner av use for me. I know ye too well now. Good night, Pat," sez he, goin' past us intil the house.

"The ould chap's too cute," sez Billy, lookin' a bit gunked; "but, anyway, he'll get a bit av a start in the mornin'."

"Is it all lies about the throuble out at Ballybreen?" sez I.

"Not *all*," sez Billy, wi' a grin. "There's a bit av bad blood right enough, an' the head-constable an' two av the polis is away out just to show themselves; 'twas that put it in me head. But, 'deed, the most av it is nather more nor less than just lies."

"Well, good night, Billy," sez I. "Ye'll be hanged for some av your jokes, but it'll not be for this wan. It's mortial like a miss."

"Is it?" sez he. "You lave the clock an' me till it, an' there'll maybe a laugh out av it yit."

An' troth so there was, an' if ye don't laugh too, it's because I can't tell the story as well as Billy.—But here goes for it, anyway:

About nine o'clock or so ould Taafe gathers himself together to go upstairs to bed.

"Ye'll give me a bit av a call about six, Billy," sez he, "if I should sleep in. Not that I'll likely need it."

"No, ye'll hardly," sez Billy. "Me aunt tells me you're a grand riser. Ye'll need no call from me the morrow mornin', I'm sure," wi' a wink at the aunt.

Away the ould fellow goes, an' Billy an' the aunt sits crackin' at the fire till they thought he'd be sure to be asleep.

"I'm thinkin'," sez Billy, as she riz to go, "ye'd betther let me slip up wi' the clock afther ye're in."

" 'Twould be betther," sez the aunt. "Give me two or three minits to get me clothes off."

Whin Billy thought she'd be settled, he slips off his boots, an' up the stairs, an' just sets the clock inside the door.

Thin he pushes the door till, an' listens for a minit. 'Twas like a watchmaker's shop, as he said afterwards.

The ould wag-at-the-wall was goin' "tack-tack-tack-tack," very slow an' steady, an' the wee alarm was rattlin' away "tick-tick-tick-tick;"—for all the world like long Tammas M'Gorrian an' the wee wife goin' down the road together av a frosty night.

"It'll wake him, sure," sez Billy to himself. An' whether it was the tickin', or the creakin' Billy made on the stairs, I don't know, but anyway ould Taafe sits up sudden in the bed.

"What's that?" sez he, very sharp.

No answer at all but the tickin' av the two clocks.

"Jenny," sez he, nudgin' the wife, "Jenny; wake up, there's somethin' in the room. Do ye hear it?"

"No," sez the wife, very sleepy be the way, "I hear nothin'. Go to sleep, ye ould fool; ye've been dreamin'. 'Twas thim salt herrins ye had for your supper. Ye've got the nightmare."

"I've got the divil!" sez he very mad. "I tell ye there's somethin' in the room. This is some av Billy's conthrivances. He'll set fire to the bed, or some mad action av the kind. Billy!" he shouts at the top av his voice.

"Wheesht, wheesht, man," sez the wife. "If ye must know, it's a 'larmer clock I got to rise ye in the mornin'."

"A 'larmer clock," sez he, "who give it to ye?"

"Niver mind," sez she, "who give it to me."

"Where did ye get the clock?" sez he. "Ye'd betther tell me. Ye'll not sleep the night till ye do."

"I got it from Peddlin' Tam," sez she, "if ye want to know. An' if ye'd like to know more,"—for she was gettin' a bit vexed by this time—"I paid two shillin's for it. Now are ye satisfied?"

"Two shillin's," sez he, "for a 'larmer clock; two cowld shillin's to that wee thief. Oh! Holy Biddy, but I married the right gomeril. Is it the workhouse ye'd bring us to? Two shillin's—— An' what the divil did ye want wi' a 'larmer clock anyway? Did I iver sleep in yit whin I wanted to get up, tell me that, ye——"

"Don't miscall me, Dick Taafe," breaks in the wife. "An' don't sin your sowl wi' lies either. Did ye iver sleep in? Didn't ye sleep in last fair day an' miss the sale av the heifer? Didn't ye sleep in the mornin' the pig was to be killed, an' wasn't able to get him killed till ten days afther-wards, whin he'd ate five shillin's worth more of potaties an' male, an' pork was down eighteenpence? Didn't ye sleep in—ay, didn't ye sleep in the mornin' we were married, and had to be fetched to the chapel wi' your boots not tied?"

"Ay, an' 'twas an ill turn the man did that wakened me that day," sez he; "to get me tied to an empty-headed cab-bage av a woman that's ruinin' me wi' her capers an' non-sense. Get out av the bed an' put that clock outside the door; an' the morrow you'll go an' get them two shillin's back from that wee peddlin' vagabond, or, be the mortial, I'll be hung for him. Out wi' ye," sez he wi' a roar.

An' out the poor woman had to get, an' put the clock on the stairhead, all the time Billy lyin' low half-way down the stairs.

Another man would ha' been satisfied an' gone till his bed; but it wouldn't ha' been Billy if he'd let well alone.

There he sits on the stairs till all was quiet wanst more, an' thin puts the clock in again; an' shovin' her well in be-hind the table he makes a bit av a noise.

The uncle stirs in his sleep, an' thin sits up again in bed.

"Ye ould faggot, ye," sez he; "ye've brought her back again. Do ye want me to murdher ye? Get up this minit, an' put that clock down in the room below."

"She *is* out," sez the wife. "I put her on the stairs."

"She's not out," sez he; "I hear her in the room. Will ye get up an' put her out whin I tell ye?"

"No!" sez she, as mad as a hatter; "I'll not put her out whin she's not in. If ye want to make a fool av yourself get up an' look whether she's in the room or not."

"Wait till I get me hands on her," sez he, "an' be hivins I'll alarm her," an' out he bounces. "Where's the matches?"

"Look for thim," sez she, "whin you're so smart."

Billy could hear the uncle pattherin' about on the floor, an' gropin' round for the matches. Thin there was a clatther, an' a blissin' from the ould man.

"Blast your big feet, couldn't ye put your boots undher the bed," sez he, leppin' round. "I've sprained me big toe. Where's thim matches, this minit?"

"Ye may sprain your neck for me," sez she from the bed, "before I'll tell ye, ye obstinate ould mule."

Wi' that there was another clatther, an' a roar from the ould man. "Oh, 'tarnal wars, me shinbone's broke."

"I wondher would ye come to your bed," sez the wife. "Ye'll kill yourself."

"I will whin I get this blasted clock," sez he, "an' ye'll be sorry whin I do. I have her too!" sez he; for he heard her tickin' at his feet.

But he hadn't reckoned on the table; an' as he stooped down he near brained himself on the corner av it.

An' thin he wint clane wild. First he made a glam at the table, an' pulled off the cloth, wi' two or three bottles, and a pair of chaney dogs. Thin down wint the lookin' glass, an' the next charge over goes the table itself. An' ivery clatther there was a guldher av an oath from him, an' a screech from her in the bed.

"Billy, Billy," shouts the aunt, "for gracious' sake come up; your uncle's wreckin' the house," an' she gives a screech fit to raise the roof.

Wi' that there comes a knockin' on the front door, an' Constable Davis's voice very thrimblin': "What's wrong, Mrs. Taafe? Is he murdherin' ye? Hould on till I run for help."

"Here's the polis, uncle," shouts Billy from the foot av the stairs. "For marcy sake quiet yourself till I put thim off" —an' Billy makes for the door.

But that minit the uncle lays his hand on the clock, an' in the blind rage he ups with her an' fires her at the windy.

There was a tinklin' av broken glass an' a rattle in the in the sthreet, an' thin whir-r-r-r! away goes the alarm full bindher.

Thin they hears a shout from the constable outside, an' a clatther av feet up the sthreet, an' in a minit the house was as quiet as a graveyard, barrin' the sobs av Billy's aunt upstairs in the bed.

"It was," sez Billy. " 'Twas Davis," sez he, chokin' down a laugh, "an' he's away for help. Hould on till I get a light, an' we'll get the place straited up before they come back. What in the name of wondher were ye doin'? I thought the house had fell, whin I waked."

"Niver mind, now, Billy," sez the uncle,—he was beginnin' to calm down, an' to see what a fool he'd been makin' av himself,—"fetch a light."

So Billy lights a candle an' goes upstairs. I believe the room was like a battle-field. The table was lyin' in wan corner wi' a leg broke, the lookin' glass in another wi' the face all starred; an' the whole place in a litther wi' broken ornaments an' bottles. The aunt was sittin' up in bed cryin'; an' the husband houldin' on to the bottom av it on wan foot, wi' the other up in the air dhroppin' blood where he had thramped on a piece av wan av the chaney dogs.

"Here, aunt," sez Billy, "I'll light your candle; an' do you fix up me uncle, an' the two av yet get intil bed. I'll run down and get rid av the polis all right. I hear them comin'. Ye can tell me all about it in the mornin'."

Down goes Billy to the front door, an' that minit there came a powerful battherin' on it, an' a shout: "Open the door, Mrs. Taafe, if you're not killed. Open to the polis."

Billy opens the door, an' there was the head-constable an' two or three more polis, wi' a neighbour or two that had heard the noise.

"There's the murdherin' villain," sez Davis. "He's killed iverybody in the house, an' thin thried to blow it up, an' me wi' it. Seize him!" sez he, edgin' well back.

"Who's killed, ye gomeril?" sez Billy. "Here, head-constable," sez he, "shout up an' ask me uncle if he's killed."

For though the mess he'd made av the uncle had daunted him a bit, the divil was beginnin' to rise in him again.

"Are ye there, Misther Taafe," shouts the head-constable up the stairs.

"It's all right, Head," sez he down till him. "There's nothin' wrong. Spake up, Jenny," sez he; an' the wife answers too.

But there was a sound av cryin' in her voice, an' the Head wasn't right satisfied.

"What did ye say, Constable Davis, about the infernal machine bein' thrown? Where did it fall?" sez he.

"Just behind here, sir," sez Davis. He was as white as a ghost, in the candle-light, an' thrimblin' like a leaf. "There it is," sez he, wi' a shout, an' right enough there was a glitther av the candle on the platin' av the clock.

The wee crowd starts away back like a dhrove av sheep, all but the Head.

"Come out here, you," sez he, layin' hold av Billy. "Fetch that bucket av wather, Johnson," sez he, "an' give me the shovel. Here, hould this man."

Thin the Head takes the shovel in his hand, gathers himself together, makes a race at the clock, an' has it in the bucket in a twinklin'.

Iverybody dhrew a long breath, an' there was a mutther av a cheer, an' "well done, Head-constable."

"Here," sez Billy, "there's been enough av this tomfoolery. I'm gettin' me death av cowld. There's no infernal machine, nor nothin' av the sort. I'll show ye what it is," makin' a move for the bucket.

But the Head had him by the arm in a minit. "Keep back, sir," sez he, very fierce. His blood was up, an' afther liftin' the infernal machine he was on for anythin'.

"Now listen, Head," sez Billy. "I'll go an' lift out the—what's in the bucket," sez he; for he wasn't goin' to spoil the joke yet. "I'll show it to ye, if ye'll come forward too. Ye're not afraid, I know. An' I'm not goin' to blow *meself* up, ye may swear. 'Twould make too big a mess in the sthreet."

"I'll do it," sez the Head, settin' his teeth. "Go on."

"Far marcy sake, sir," sez Davis, "don't let that dispirate fellow touch it. He'll blow us all to etarnity."

"Maybe you'll lift it yourself, Constable Davis," sez the Head, very sharp. "Ah, I thought not," whin he seen him lepp back a couple av feet at the very idea. "Go on, Billy; I'll hould the candle."

So Billy steps forward, the Head close behind him; an' ivery man held his breath. Av coorse, Billy had to keep up the joke, stoppin' ivery foot or two, an' hesitatin' by the way; an' ivery time he checked his step the ring round the bucket widened out bigger. At last he gets to the bucket, an' stoops down an' lifts the clock.

"What is it?" sez the Head, shrinkin' back a thrifle.

"It's a quarther past eleven," sez Billy, lookin' at the clock face.

"What d'ye say?" sez the Head, very cross.

"Just a quarter past eleven, to the minit. Look for yourself," sez Billy, houldin' out the clock.

The Head lifts the candle an' looks at it; thin he steps nearer an' takes it in his hand. For a minit he sez nothin', an' then: "May the divil fly away wi' me," sez he, an' the Head was a man that didn't often swear, "but it's a common alarm clock."

"Just that," sez Billy, "an' nothin' more. The uncle took a scunner at the tick av it, an' threw it out of the windy. That's the whole murdherin' an' blowin' up there was the night. I doubt, head-constable," sez Billy, "this man av yours is no hero. This night'll not be much av a credit to the force. But niver mind, ye've give a dale av innocent pleasure to your neighbours," sez he, lookin' round at the grinnin' wee crowd. "An' they'll not tell anybody—barrin' wan or two."

The head-constable took it like a man.

"Billy," sez he, "the joke is on us, there's no denyin' it; an' they can tell it to who they like. 'Twill maybe shame this crather Davis out av the force.

"Go back to barracks," sez he to the constable, very wicked, "an' if ye're wise," sez he, "ye'll seek a more suitable employment. It's mindin' chickens ye should be at, or flowerin' handkerchiefs like the ould woman ye are. Good-night, Billy," sez he. "Tell your uncle an' aunt I'm sorry for puttin' thim about. An' you, good people, away home wi' ye. The performance is over."

In a couple of minits the sthreet was cleared, an' Billy steps intil the house wi' the clock. But he might as well ha' left her outside; for between the fall an' the dhrowndin' in the bucket, divil a chime she iver rung since.

A Wild-Goose Chase

HAVIN' a taste for a thing and bein' able to do it isn't altogether the same, though there's some people thinks it is.

An' wee Mr. Anthony the solicitor was one of them. He had the terriblest notion of all kinds of sport of any man I ever knowed, an' in particular of shootin'; an' he was a bigger dundherhead at shootin' than he was at anythin' else, an' that, mind ye, is saying a good deal.

If it hadn't been that he was always at the safe end of the gun there'd ha' been a crowner's jury sittin' on himself before he even seen twenty-five; an' if there hasn't been one sittin' on some of his friends up till now, it's only puttin' it off.

Everything else, fish, flesh, and fowl, he'd shot some time or another, down to the tin weathercock on Tammas Dorrian's barn, that he took for a wood-pigeon, an' never knowed to the differs till he heard the jingle of it on the slates.

In the first place, he was a wee, nervous, twittery kind of a man, with his hands always ready to shoot a couple of seconds or so before his head was; an' in the next, he was as shortsighted as a ten-days-old pup.

Not that that would ha' mattered if he'd put on glasses like another body—my ould grandfather wore specs an' could ha' shot snipe till he was seventy,—but Mr. Anthony was a natty, dressy wee body, an' would wear divil a thing but an eyeglass; an' half his time he was either unwindin' the string of it from round the barrels of the gun, or pickin' bits of the glass out of the breech.

Eye-glasses must ha' come heavy on him. He always carried a stock of them with him. I remember him using up three in one while of an afthernoon, an' divil a' all he shot in the end but a setter pup that the mercy of Providence sent between my legs an' him when the gun went off.

So though he was mortial fine pay, an' the best of good company, he was no great shootin' companion for a man with a young family; an' when he come into my yard with the gun in his hand a couple of days afther he shot the pup, I'd very near as soon ha' seen the Ould Fellow himself.

But there wasn't a bit of use of me tryin' to put him off.

"Now, Pat," sez he, "ye'll have to come, that's all about it. Wee Sonny Burke came into Ballygullion this afthernoon, one errand, to tell me there's a flock of wild geese in Miss Armitage's bog; an' I might never have a chance like it in my life again. I never shot a wild goose yet," sez he, all fidgetin'.

"No," sez I, "an' ye never shot a tenant-farmer yet, but you're goin' to do it now if ye don't stop footherin' with that gun. For mercy sake put it down on the ditch there till I talk to ye. Don't ye know there hasn't been a shot fired in Miss Armitage's demesne these two years an' more."

An' that was true enough.

Ould Miss Armitage was one of them ould ladies that never havin' got a man or a child of her own to turn their kindliness an' good-heartedness on, was always squandherin' them on somethin' else that hadn't the same need of them.

Many's the thing she took up wi' from the time she lost all hope; dogs an' cats, an' pigs, an' the heathen—at home an' at Ballygullion; but at the time I spake of she was all for kindness to animals in general.

Not a finger dare ye lay on a livin' thing about the place.

The pheasants an' partridges was as thick as sparrows, an' the country for a mile round the demesne fair polluted wi' rabbits; but the divil a trigger would she let be drawn where she had any say.

And about the Big House itself it was worse than all. Every hen an' duck in the yard had its name on a wee brass ring round its leg, an' knowed its name too, an' would come when it was called by it; but if the whole household was starvin' ye daren't put a knife on one of their throats. The best cook ever she had she sacked at a minit's notice for killin' an' servin' up a young pullet called Emily Ann one day the District Inspector turned up unexpected for lunch; forbye that she held a burial service over the bird, an' put up a headstone to it in the back garden.

The yardman had an extra five shillin's for everybody he caught killin' flesh or fowl about the house an' grounds, an' each of the gamekeepers the same for every poacher he caught; so that between one thing an' another, to walk across an acre of Miss Armitage's land was as good as layin' down forty shillin's an' costs; keepin' off the disgrace of bein' up before the Bench.

I put all this before Mr. Anthony, an' more to the back of it; but I might as well ha' saved my breath; for he was as obstinate as a he-ass when he had his mind made up about a thing. He was out to shoot a wild goose, an' a wild goose he would shoot, an' all the good I did by talkin' was to make him that nervous of bein' caught that he fetched me over four barbed-wire fences an' a march-drain instead of goin' into the demesne by the road. An' if it did lift my heart a bit to see him leave the seat of his new shootin' breeches on the first wire-fence, I fell into the drain myself an' got a cold that nearly brought me to my grave.

We were pushin' along the edge of the wee wood that lay between us an' the marsh, Mr. Anthony leadin' the way, wi' both barrels cocked, though the watter was a quarther of a mile off yet, when all at once he jukes down behind the stump of a tree.

"Wheesht, Pat," sez he. "I see a rabbit on the path in

front of us—not eighty yards away. I'll have a shot at it. It'll get my eye in."

"Will ye be wise?" sez I. "Isn't it bad enough runnin' the risk of a shot in the marsh without firin' one here, where we're as near again to the Big House."

"Hang the Big House," sez he, all in a flurry; "we're not within half a mile of it. An' I never seen a rabbit sittin' betther for a shot. I couldn't miss it if I tried. It's away," sez he, all disappointed, peepin' over the stump. "Wait, it's not, I see it. But it's farther off than I thought; stay you here, an' I'll double in among the trees."

An' away he goes, stalkin' in an' out, an' crouchin' an' crawlin', till he'd taken the price of half a dozen rabbits out of the remains of the shooting suit. The divil of a rabbit could I see; an' presently Mr. Anthony straightens himself an' steps out into the path again. When I got up to him he was rubbin' the eye-glass on a piece of shammy leather, an' swearing most lamentable.

"What was it, Mr. Anthony?" sez I. "Is it gone?"

"A most extraordinary thing, Pat," sez he, lookin' a bit foolish, an' rubbin' away like fury wi' the shammy. "I'll be blest," sez he, "if it wasn't a bit of hayseed on my eye-glass all the time. I'd have taken my oath it was a rabbit. I saw the scut an' the two ears as plain as I see you. If ye laugh, ye ould scoundrel," sez he, "I'll put the two barrels in ye."

"Is it laugh at ye, Mr. Anthony?" sez I. "I wouldn't think of such a thing." An' the next minit I was holdin' on to a tree an' laughin' till I lost my breath.

I'd ha' been laughin' yet, I believe, between the fun of the thing an' the look of Mr. Anthony, but just as I was in the middle of a kink there comes a whistle from up the path in front of us.

"By the Lord Harry, it's a gamekeeper," sez Mr. Anthony. "Quick, Pat" He grabbed the gun by the muzzle, an' stuck her well into a bunch of briers, an' the two of us down behind the briers on our hands an' knees.

Sure enough, it was Long James, the head gamekeeper. He passed us that close he could ha' touched us. I suppose, to a man like a solicitor, brought up in the middle of them, an oath or two isn't the same as to another body; but there's no doubt that when Mr. Anthony was in a tight place he swore like a bailiff's officer.

"In the name of goodness, Mr. Anthony," sez I, "will ye stop swearin'? Sure, the man's clean gone, an' no harm done."

"Bad luck to him again for a long string of misery," sez Mr. Anthony, still muttherin' as he riz from his knees: "what brought him round this way? He has me all in a twitter. Come here, you," sez he, very vicious—takin' a pluck at the gun by the muzzle.

An' wi' that bang goes the right barrel. When the smoke riz, an' I looked for the bits of Mr. Anthony; he was standin' there thrimmlin', as white as a ghost, an' lookin' a kind of a stupid way at the tails of his coat, that was all chattered wi' the shot.

"Did ye see that, Pat?" was all he could get out. "Did ye see that? I ruined my breeches on that infernal wire fence, an' now there's the coat gone too."

"Never mind your coat, Mr. Anthony," sez I, snappin' up the gun. "Long James'll be back on the top of us." We could hear the shouts of him comin'.

"Make for the crown of the wood," sez I, as we ran. "We can hide in the bracken."

I never seen Mr. Anthony run like it. If the eye-glass hadn't lapped round an ash saplin' an' fetched him up with a jerk that near sthrangled him, I'd ha' never caught up with him till he was in the middle of the marsh.

"Are we safe, Pat?" sez he, gaspin', on his face in the bracken. "Are we clean away from the rascal? I wouldn't for ten pound he'd get a catch at me. I beat him in a poachin' case at the last sessions, an' he's had it in for me ever since.

"This is all Brown the gunsmith's fault," sez he, gettin' savager as he found his breath, "the clumsy, brainless ould fool. First he had the gun pullin' off that stiff that I shot Joe Nevin's ferret, an' me aimin' at a rabbit ten yards to the left of it; an' now he has her that light that she'd go off if ye blew your breath on her. If I'd been pullin' her wi' the muzzle towards me just now I'd have had an action again him."

"If ye'd been pullin' wi' the muzzle towards you, Mr. Anthony," sez I, "ye'd never have throubled the law courts again, barrin' the takin' out of probate on your will. It's on your knees ye should be, givin' thanks that you're alive, instead of lyin' there cursin' an innocent man that had no more to do with it than I have. Long James must ha' missed us," sez I. "Gather up that gun an' come on home out of this."

"Gimme her," sez he, sittin' up an' screwin' in the eye-glass very determined. "Ye can please yourself, Pat; but out of this demesne I don't go till I get a shot at them wild geese."

"Ye'll be here then till the last trumpet frightens them away," sez I, "for ye wouldn't hit a wild goose till the Day of Judgment wi' the state of nerves you're in now."

But no, he wouldn't give in. His blood was up all the more wi' the vexation, an' the fright he'd got. I kept him arguin' there till I thought the gamekeeper would be gone home, an' then for peace sake I settled with him that he'd have one shot an' no more. After that we were to go home, goose or no goose. For, thinks I, he's sure to let the gun off at the first tuft of rushes he sees, an' then we'll be away out of this as hard as we can.

But luck wouldn't have it that way. We weren't right at the edge of the marsh till, sure enough, half a dozen geese dashes out of the rushes. Bang goes Mr. Anthony; there was a terrible splashin' in the wather, an' when the smoke riz there was a goose scutterin' here and there on the surface of the bog-hole with a broken wing.

Mr. Anthony gives one wild yell of delight, an' into the marsh. It never come into his head to fire the other barrel an' shoot the goose outright; but he grabs the gun near the muzzle wi' both hands, an' runs round the edge of the bog-hole thryin' to brain the bird with the butt.

Och, ye should ha' seen the spangs of him round that bog-hole, trippin' over tussocks of rushes, an' stumblin' in an' out of wee side drains, cursin' an' thrashin' away at the goose, an' all the time callin' on me to help him. If I hadn't run up as quick as I could wi' the laughin' and whished the goose over towards him, the second barrel would ha' been out through his backbone, sure. He aimed a most lamentable blow at the goose as it come within range, an' more by good luck than good guidin' put it out of it's pain with a dunt on the head would ha' felled an ox. The next minit he had it by the neck, an' was dancing on the edge like a madman, shoutin' an' wavin' it round his head.

"For the love of goodness, Mr. Anthony," sez I, "keep quiet and make for the wood, or every gamekeeper in the demesne'll be down on us. There's Long James!" sez I. "Run!"

I was only makin' that up, but it sobered him; an' he made for the wood like a lamplighter, the gun in one hand an' the goose in the other.

When I caught up with him he was lyin' in the bracken admiring the dead goose.

"Did ye ever see a finer goose in your life, Pat?" sez he, all excited. "Isn't it a beauty? an' as fat as mud. Feel the breast of it."

I took the bird in my hand. "It looks very big for a wild goose," sez I.

"What do you mean?" sez Mr. Anthony.

He took a hard look at the goose. His jaw fell. I could see the red risin' in his face. "Ye don't mean to say——" sez he, stammerin'. He looked at the bird again.

"Pat," sez he, in a kind of whisper. "Pat. There's somethin' on it's leg."

I looked. Round the right leg of the goose was a wee brass ring.

"There's writin' on it, Mr. Anthony," sez I. "What does it say?"

"It looks like a name," sez he, puttin' the glass in his eye. "Blast me, but it looks like a name. It *is* a name," sez he—" 'Algernon Charles.' "

"Oh, Mr. Anthony dear," sez I, "ye'll be the death of me.

Ye've shot Miss Armitage's prize gander that she named afther her uncle, the ould Major."

Mr. Anthony never said a word, but riz up an' walked away behind a wee clump of bushes. I could hear him holdin' a very bitther argument with himself an' gettin' a deal the worst of it.

Presently he come back, a bit quietened down, but still very vicious-lookin'.

"Curse the bird," sez he, lookin' at it. "It serves it right. Sure it flew. You saw it, Pat. What the divil made a tame gander fly, anyway?"

"The same thing as brought us here, Mr. Anthony," sez I, "want of sense. Hide it in the bracken, an' come on home. Nobody'll be a bit the wiser."

"I'll hide none of it in the bracken," sez he, settin' his teeth. "I killed it," sez he, "an' I'll eat it, if it was only for spite."

"Have a bit of wisdom, Mr. Anthony," sez I. "Sure ye can't walk home in broad daylight carryin' one of Miss Armitage's tame geese. If it came out on ye, she'd have ye struck off the rolls."

"Tie the legs round my neck," sez he, "an' let it hang down undher my coat. Nobody'll notice it from a distance, an' if I was the length of your house, I'll wait there till dark."

"Ye couldn't do it," sez I. "Sure the neck would be hanging below your knees."

"Well, you take it, Pat," sez he. "You're taller than I am."

"Divil a fear of me," sez I. "If I'm taller I have more wit. An' if anybody's goin' to jail over this job, it'll be the man that fired the shot. But if ye're wise, ye'll leave it here. Ye'll have no luck over it. Wait till ye see."

An' it turned out the way I said. Just as we were well into the back road out of the demesne, round the corner comes Ruddell, the huntsman, an' the whole pack of staghounds.

The two of us were over the ditch in a crack.

"Lie down, Mr. Anthony," sez I, crouchin' behind a bush. "Lie down or he'll see you."

"Divil a bit of me'll lie down," sez Mr. Anthony. "We're out of the demesne land. I'll keep my face to him, an' he'll see nothin' but the gun."

"He'll see the feet of the gander undher your chin," sez I.

"It makes no odds," sez Mr. Anthony. "He'll think it's a breastpin. I near blew the intestines out of myself for a gamekeeper today already, an' I'll not risk my life for a huntsman."

"A fine day, huntsman," he shouts, as the pack went past.

The huntsman touched his hat an' rode on, never noticin' anythin'.

"Now, ye ould fool," sez Mr. Anthony, as we walked along the road, "didn't I tell ye it would be all right? An' that's an alibi established. The huntsman seen me at four o'clock, an' I had no goose in my possession. For an ould sportsman, Pat, ye have little gumption. Now we're well out of it all, whatever happens. What's that behind us, Pat?" sez he suddenly. "Oh, it's only a stragglin' hound. Go home, ye brute," sez he; "ye frightened me."

But the dog had no notion of going home. We weren't ten yards further till he was sniffin' at Mr. Anthony's heels again.

"What the deuce does the animal want?" sez Mr. Anthony. "Go home, sir."

"He must smell the gander," sez I. An' with that the dog bones the bird by the neck.

"Ah, ye brute!" sez Mr. Anthony; "let go, let go this minit."

But the dog didn't let go. Instead of that he took a fresh hold, an' near lit Mr. Anthony on his back.

"Confound the dog," sez Mr. Anthony, in a rage. "I'll murdher him. Chew, sir, chew!" An' he lashes behind him wi' the gun.

"Easy with the gun, Mr. Anthony," sez I. "Ye know what happened the day already." But I was too late. There was a flash an' a bang; an' the next minit the dog was kickin' in his death-thraw in the middle of the road.

For a minit the two of us stood lookin' at him, dumbfoundhered.

"May the divil fly away with ould Brown, the gunsmith," sez Mr. Anthony at last, in a kind of lament. "He's goin' to be the ruin of my whole career. This is dreadful—dreadful. If I'm not struck off the rolls, I'll be laughed out of the profession anyway. What'll I do now, at all, at all?"

"If ye could get the divil to fly away wi' the gander an' the dog, Mr. Anthony," sez I, "it would be more to the purpose. Ruddell'll be back any minit, lookin' for his hound, an' he'll see the two of them, an' then you an' I may lave the counthry. What are we goin' to do with them?"

"To the divil with both of them," sez Mr. Anthony, in a dancin' rage all at once. "I'll show ye what I'll do. Here," sez he—he cut the gander free of his neck, an' took the bird by the legs—"away you to blazes," an' he pitched it as far as he could over the hedge. "Fly now, blast ye," sez he; "ye could fly when ye weren't wanted to. An' go you afther it," sez he, staggerin' over to the ditch with the body of the dog. "Worry the goose now, if ye can," sez he, "an' the divil choke ye on it. An' to pot wi' you as well," sez he, "it was you got me into all the bother, you an' the ould fool of a gunsmith that begot ye." An' before I could say a word the gun went spinnin' over the ditch too, an' away goes Mr. Anthony down the road, fair foamin'.

"Mr. Anthony," sez I, runnin' afther him, "Mr. Anthony, show some kind of sense. Ye might as well give yourself up at once. Sure, your name's on the breech of the gun."

He stopped dead, an' looked at me with his mouth open.

"Away for the gun, Pat," sez he, at the last, "an' blow out my brains with it. No," sez he, "no; I have no brains. I'm not fit to be trusted out by myself. Take me home, an' put me to bed."

"We'll have to hide the dog, Mr. Anthony," sez I. "Sure, Ruddell seen ye with the gun, an' he'll put two an' two together. Wait, an' I'll hide him in the sally-bushes over yonder, an' then we'll go to the length of my house for a spade an' bury him. We'll ha' time enough. Ruddell'll never miss him till he gets to the kennel. Will I bring ye the gander?"

"No," sez Mr. Anthony, breakin' out again, "bring me no gander. Bury it," sez he, "an' bury the gun—an' bury me too, if ye like, for there's neither luck nor grace about me. Come on, Pat. I'm away for the spade. There's no time to be lost."

It was wearin' on to dusk when we got back.

"Now, Mr. Anthony," sez I, "you keep watch on the road here, an' I'll go an' bury the dog on this side of the sally-bushes. The gander is well enough hid in the rushes where he is."

"Is it me keep watch?" sez he. "The whole hunt might be on top of us before I'd seen them. Gimme the spade," sez he, "an' you look out. I can handle a spade as well as a gun, I'd have ye know," sez he, seein' me lookin' at him.

"An' troth," sez I to meself, "if ye can handle it no betther the huntsman'll catch us yet." But it was true what he said about the watchin', so I let him go.

All the same, it was in my mind about the huntsman; an' afther a bit I slipped along by the sallies to see how Mr. Anthony was gettin' on.

I could hear the spade goin' as if it was half a dozen men digging: an' troth, afther a minit, I couldn't persuade myself that there wasn't more than one at it.

"Lord," sez I, afther listenin' again, "am I bewitched? For, sure enough, there was another spade goin' on the far side of the sallies from Mr. Anthony.

I keeked through the bushes, an' who was diggin' away for dear life but Ruddell the huntsman himself!

I looked at him, an' looked at him, an' then I rubbed my eyes an' looked at him again; and it was still Ruddell. The first thought in my mind was to warn Mr. Anthony, an' I into the wee thicket an' makes for him. But I was too dumb-foundhered to mind my feet, an', before I was well started, I tripped over a rush-bush an' down like a bullock.

"I've done it," sez I, an' I had.

The huntsman quit diggin' at once, looked round him, and slipped quietly over to the bushes, spade in hand, an' the same minit I hears Mr. Anthony stop dead.

"Begad," sez I to myself, "it's all up wi' Mr. Anthony now." An' the next minit he riz up face to face with the huntsman across a sally-bush.

Ye never seen two men so much taken aback in your life. They just stood there with their mouths openin' and shuttin' like goldfish in a bowl.

But Mr. Anthony was the worst stuck of the two; for the spade fell from his hand, an' it was the huntsman spoke first.

"Mr. Anthony, sir," sez he, touchin' his hat, "ye'll not say anythin'."

It wasn't just what I was expectin', I may tell ye, or Mr. Anthony either. But he hadn't served his time in the law courts for nothin'.

"Certainly not, huntsman," sez he. "I'll not breathe a word of it." Ye'd ha' thought by the tone of him he was doin' the man a favour, an' all the time his knees knockin' together, as I knowed right well.

"The fact is, Mr. Anthony, sir," sez the huntsman, "one of my hounds strayed to-day, an' I doubt," sez he, lowerin' his voice till I could hardly hear him, "I doubt he has been huntin' game an' one of Miss Armitage's keepers has come on him, for I found him here in the bushes with a charge in him. I'm just goin' to bury him quietly here, an' say nothin' about it. You'll say nothin' either, sir, if ye please."

"Well," sez I to myself, "if Mr. Anthony ever tells me he's unlucky after this!"

But it wouldn't be him if he'd let his luck alone.

"You can depend on me, huntsman," sez he—an' ye could hear the delight of him in his voice—"ye can depend on me. We'll shake hands on it, huntsman," sez he, "we'll shake hands on it!"

The huntsman looked at him in a wondherin' kind of a way.

"Certainly, Mr. Anthony, sir," sez he. An' he reached out his hand.

An' as he leaned across the bush his eye fell first on the grave an' then on the spade at Mr. Anthony's feet.

The whole thing flashed on him in a twinklin'.

"I might ha' knowed who it was shot my dog, Mr. Anthony," sez he, very low an' bitther. "When I seen you with a gun in your hand this afthernoon I might ha' knowed that the pack wasn't safe in the same county with ye, let alone the same town-land. Ye're a danger to every man that walks the road, an' to every man's baste. But this'll be an end to your shootin'—an' to your huntin' too. I've put up with a good deal from ye, Mr. Anthony, an' said nothin'. Ye thramped two good pups lame on me the first time ye were on a horse this season; the off fore-leg of my best mount'll never grow hair again where that ould grey screw of yours kicked him last November; an' the same dirty brute beat in two panels of the stag-cart on St. Stephen's Day, an' all the time I never raised my voice.

"But this is too much. To go an' shoot the best hound in the pack, an' then bury him an' never say ye did it or were sorry for it. It's more than any man could thole. Forbye that ye stood there an' listened to me makin' a fool of meself an' blamin' the poor innocent brute wi' chasin' game. I take that worst of all. A gentleman wouldn't do it, an' I'll have the opinion of the Hunt on that. I will. I'll——"

An' on he went like a mill-race. I didn't think the huntsman had it in him.

All the time Mr. Anthony just stood there.

"Why the divil," sez I to meself, "does he not offer the man a five pound note to keep it dark! Sure it's worth ten times that to him to save the exposin' he'll get." I could hardly sit quiet for wantin' to get at his ear.

An' wi' that Mr. Anthony turns round to the road an' lets a shout: "Pat,—Pat Murphy!"

Ye could ha' knocked me down with a feather.

"Oh, the weary take ye for a blundherin' wee dundherhead," sez I to myself, "are ye not content wi' makin' a byword of yourself but ye must bring me into it. An' me a tenant of Miss Armitage's too. I'm ruined, ruined an' desthroyed. She may put you off the shootin', but she'll drive me out of the counthry."

For a minit I swithered would I show myself. But, thinks I, he has sold me now, an' I may as well face the music.

So I doubles back along the sallies, an' then comes runnin' up, by the way I was just straight from the road. An' all the prayers Mr. Anthony had prayed on himself that day, an' that wasn't a few, was nothin' to what I called down on his head in the time it took me to cover twenty-five yards of ground.

"Have ye done now, huntsman?" sez Mr. Anthony as I come up.

"No, nor half done," sez the huntsman, still ragin' away. An' troth, by the sound of him, he could have kept on for a fortnight, an' never repeated himself.

"Well, give me my turn," sez Mr. Anthony. "Pick up that spade, Pat." An' away he walks to where the gander was lyin', an' picks it up.

"Well, by all the saints," sez I to meself, "are ye not even goin' to make a fight for it?"

"Do ye see that, huntsman?" sez Mr. Anthony, comin' back. "Wait a minit, now," sez he, holdin' up his hand, "an' then ye can talk for a week. Do ye know what that is? It's one of Miss Armitage's prize geese. There's the ring about its leg. When I looked back as I was walkin' along the road wi' Pat Murphy, an hour ago, I saw your dog wi' that goose by the neck an' the goose was dead. Isn't that so, Pat?"

"It's the gospel truth, huntsman," sez I.

Ye could see the huntsman's jaw droppin'.

"Now, Ruddell," sez Mr. Anthony, "ye were a man I had some respect for till ten minutes ago. An' once or twice when my horse has been a bit restive"—I turned away my head—"ye have been civiller than many another man in your position would have been. An' I know what happens to a pack of hounds that would kill anybody's geese, let alone Miss Armitage's; an' I shot your dog an' was goin' to bury him here, an' the goose too, an' say nothin' about it. I'll say nothin' about it yet," sez Mr. Anthony, "an neither will Pat, here. But if your pack of mangy mongrels was to eat every bird an' beast in Miss Armitage's demesne, an' finish up wi' the two stuffed peacocks in the entrance hall, they may do it for me from this day on. Bury your confounded dog," sez Mr. Anthony, by the way of bein' in a rage—an' troth, by this time I think he was beginnin' to believe in himself—"an' go into mournin' for him if ye like; it's nothin' to me——"

"Mr. Anthony, sir," sez the huntsman, breakin' in—an' ye never seen a man as much come down in your life—"I haven't a word to say."

"It's a change," sez Mr. Anthony.

"Well, I was vexed, sir," sez the huntsman. "But I should have knowed betther. Will ye look over what I said? I'm a bit hasty, I know, an' ye'll admit the thing looked queer. But it was kindly done of ye, Mr. Anthony, an' it's not every man would ha' had the wit to think of it.

"Ye've saved the credit of the pack, an' me, too; an' I'll not forget it to ye. An' if ye'll excuse me for the impidence I give ye, an'll come out again to the hunt, ye may thramp every hound in the pack, and kick the stag-box into pipe-lights, before I'll say black is the colour of your eye.

"Ye offered to shake hands wi' me, a minit ago. Will ye shake hands now, sir, an' let bygones be bygones?"

"Not a word now, huntsman," sez Mr. Anthony grippin' him by the hand. "An' there's somethin' to make up the loss of the dog. Now say no more. There, Pat, bury that gander. An' do you cover up the dog, huntsman. The sooner we're out of this the better. Good-bye, huntsman. You can depend on me—an' Pat, too."

"Good-bye, sir," sez the huntsman. "Ye're a gentleman, Mr. Anthony, every inch of ye."

When I caught up wi' Mr. Anthony he was in great feather.

"I bamboozled him, Pat, eh?" sez he, chucklin' to himself. "I bamboozled him, what? The great thing in a case of this sort is to take the right line of defence; an' I saw it in a minit. Damme," sez Mr. Anthony, "but I'm thrown away as a solicitor, I should have been at the bar."

"Ye should be in the dock," sez I; "an' will be yet if ye don't throw that gun behind the fire."

"Get away, ye ould croaker," sez Mr. Anthony. "Could ye have bowled over that gander any better than I did? I'll be blest," sez he, "if I don't get ould Brown to fix the lock, an' come back an' have a slap at the wild geese the first clear night. There would nobody see us, Pat."

"There'll nobody see me," sez I; "for I won't be there."

"Now, ye'll come with me, Pat," sez Mr. Anthony, stoppin' at the foot of the loanin'. "We can't get into a worse hole than we did to-day; an' ye saw the way I got out of it."

"Well, get the lock fixed first of all, Mr. Anthony," sez I, "an' then we can talk it over. There's be a full moon in a week or so."

"You're right, Pat," sez he, "you're right. I'll go up to ould Brown in the mornin'. The full moon, then, Pat. It's a bargain. Good night. I'll be up with Brown before my breakfast to-morrow."

An' away he goes, hot-foot, as if he thought the moon might come to the full before he got home.

"Don't forget.—The full moon," he calls out as he turned the corner.

"All right, Mr. Anthony," I shouted back.—"The full moon."

But the next time Mr. Anthony an' me goes out shootin' wild geese together there'll be two moons in the sky—an' one in the garden.

The Saucepan

THE childher about Ballygullion is just like the childher everywhere else, they're terrible fond of imitatin' their eldhers. An' whenever the Orangemen marches out of the town on the twelfth of July, an' you're beginnin' to think ye'll get a bit of peace for your ears till they're comin' home again, out comes every wee fellow that can get hould of an ould tin can, an' batthers about till folks is near deaved.

I need hardly tell you, too, that them that stays behind in Ballygullion on the twelfth is not of the persuasion that's likely to thole it the best.

However, it's like Christmas, an' only comes once a year; an' as the one day does it, they put up wi' it the best way they can.

But about four or five years ago a lot of wee boys took the notion that it was a pity not to have more of a good thing; an' a party of Orangemen settin' out on the thirteenth for the sham fight at Scarva, nothin' would do the childher but they'd have a sham fight of their own at home.

It might ha' done all right, an' lasted to this day, if they'd kept it among their own sort; but wee Billy Black's son, that started the idea, thought it would give a kind of reality to the whole affair if they had some of the other side to do King James's men. An' so it did, an' a thrifle more than some of them expected.

There wasn't much throuble gettin' up the sides.

Wee Black's army was easy gathered, for most of them had got a holiday, an' wi' the other fellows keen to keep up the honour of the Irish, an' maybe seein' a chance of gettin' their own back afther all they'd tholed the day before, enough of them mitched from school to make up brave an' near as many to fight for King James.

The two armies took up their positions on each side of the wee river at the bottom of Ballygullion, both of them rigged out in great style, wi' belts an' wooden swords an' paper helmets on them. Billy Black's wee fellow, as bein' the one that got up the fun, couldn't be kept out of bein' King William, especially as he'd borrowed ould John Linchey's donkey to do the white horse; an' Murray, the pawnbroker's son, got doin' Schomberg on account of an ould horse-pistol an' a handful of caps he had stole out of the father's shop.

There was a deal of wranglin' an' disputin' about who was to be who on the other side. The biggest rush was for Pathrick Sarsfield, but when big Jacky McGra, the blacksmith's son, buttoned up his coat an' swore if anybody else wanted to be Pathrick Sarsfield he'd blacken his eye for him, they all turned their attention to who'd be King James. The wrestlin' an' wranglin' riz near as big as if it had been the rale thing, an' for a while it looked as if they were goin' to have a battle without waitin' for the enemy at all; till wee Sonny Morrison comin' up with a shield made out of a three-gallon pot lid, an' his mother's best saucepan on his head for a helmet, he was made King on the spot. An' troth, as it turned out, like ould King James himself, he had no great luck of the crown.

The leadin' men bein' once picked, the battle begun with a deal of spunk on both sides. For a good while it was fought at long range wi' balls of clay out of the river-banks. Wee Brown, the rector's son, that was doin' Walker of Derry, got a clay ball in the pit of his stomach that give him the colic from that till Christmas; an' Pathrick Sarsfield got one in the face that made a sore differs to his side, for the battle was all over before he got the gutthers scooped out of his eye. But barrin' this, an' a terrible spoilin' of good clothes, there was no great harm done.

Then there riz a bit of a difference in the Orange Army. Schomberg kept blazin' away caps on the horse-pistol so like the rale thing that every boy on his side was fair green wi' envy, an' King William, seein' he was bein' made as good as nobody by it, rides up till him an' insists that it was time he died accordin' to the arrangement before they started.

Schomberg was no way willin' to do this, but his caps bein' at an end he makes a blarge wi' the last of them that near blew one of the ears off the ass, an' lies down dead in the clay at the edge of the river. His mother warmed him for that later on.

When the ass comes-to afther the dazin' of the shot he gives his ears one shake, lets a couple of skreighs out of him between a squeal an' a hee-haw, an' intil the river, teeth an' heels goin'; an' King William afther near goin' out over the tail makes the best of it, shouts to his men to come on, an' puts the ass at the opposite bank.

For a minit or two it looked as if it was to be the ould story over again. King James an' his men stood up manful again the rest of the army, but they couldn't hould out again the ass. The squealin' an' bitin' an' kickin' of him was somethin' lamentable, an' if King William could ha' sat him at all the battle was as good as won.

But a bad shot from his own side takin' the ass very threacherous in the rear, he clean forsook his colours altogether, rid himself of poor William wi' an exthra lift of his hind-end, an' away as if the divil was afther him, an' never stopped, barrin' for thrippin' every now an' then on the bridle, till he reached home.

This was great heartenin' for King James's men.

Down the bank they come with a rush, throwin' clay balls an' blowin' peas an' leatherin' round them wi' sticks, King James himself at the head of them doin' desperate execution with a four-foot length of garden hose he had stole out of Major Donaldson's garden, an' would ha' won the battle with his own hand only for the time he lost unwindin' it from his neck every time he missed his blow.

As it was, him an' his men were well through the river an' the battle the same as ended, when, makin' a mighty sprang up the bank, he puts his foot on Schomberg's face as he lay there dead.

'Twas an unlucky step for James.

Divil a word says Schomberg good or bad, but lepps to his feet an' fetches the butt end of the horse-pistol down on King James's helmet wi' both hands; an' the next minit the saucepan was sittin' on poor King James's shouldhers, an' him yellin' melia murdher from the inside; for the rim had had a difference wi' his nose on its way down, an' the nose had come badly out of it.

The battle was over in the clappin' of your hands.

Schomberg takes one look at what he'd done, dhrops the horse-pistol, an' off home for his life; an' both armies gathers round King James thryin' to quiet him, for the gowls of him inside the saucepan was like nothin' earthly, an' they were afeared of some of their mothers comin' down on them.

None of them thought very much of it at the first, for they deemed it wouldn't be much harder to get the saucepan off than it had been to get it on. But when they had worked at it for a quarther of an hour, an' near wrung King James's neck, an' still nothin' comin' of it, they begun to slip away quietly by ones an' twos, till at the last there was only about half a dozen or so left.

By this time King James begin to see that he was of some importance, an' stopped cryin' an' commenced to put on airs, an' was content enough to let the saucepan stay where it was. But the others was too uneasy in their minds to hear of that, an' when Pathrick Sarsfield come up from the rear they were as glad to see him as ever the Irishmen was at the Boyne.

"Here's bit Jacky McGra," sez one. "Aye, here's Jacky," sez another, "he'll have it off in no time." An' Jacky, bein' a big lusty fellow wi' a fair conceit of himself an' some experience of handlin' tools, was much of the same opinion himself.

"Stan' back an' gimme a chap at it," sez he. "If a horse-pistol put it on, sure it can take it off again."

So they stood back an' let him at it.

Maybe it was the dirt in his eye, or maybe he was a bit nervous, but the first lick he took he missed the rim of the saucepan by about an inch, an' near put the rings of his backbone out of joint wi' the twist he give himself; an' the next blow takin' King James about the shoulder-blade an' startin' him on a worse gowl than ever, the whole party took to their heels an' away, thinkin' they had finished him, an' left him to make his way home the best he could.

More by good luck than good guidin', poor wee Sonny gropes his way up ontil the road. The mother's house was only a step or two away then, an' he got the length of it without breakin' his neck.

But och! the Boyne itself was nothin' to the row that riz when he did.

At the first fright of seein' the saucepan walk in an' sit down cryin' by the fire the mother dhrops the pot she was liftin' an' makes for the room door without a word, she was that frightened.

But when she made out 'twas wee Sonny was inside the saucepan, an' afther tuggin' at it till she was tired an' couldn't get him out of it, between cryin' an' lamentin', an' scoldin' at them that had put the saucepan on him, an' shoutin' at himself because he didn't take it off, she riz the very divil's own row; an' happenin' to be passin' by on my way intil Ballygullion I steps in to see who was bein' killed.

For a minit or two I couldn't for the life of me make out what was wrong; but when I did come at it nothin' but the disthress the poor crather of a mother was in would ha' kept me from laughin'.

First she'd start to tell me a bit more of the story, an' then in the middle of it break out roarin' an' cryin' that her wee son was ruined an' desthroyed, an' then all at once she'd get mad at the wee fellow for bringin' himself intil the scrape, an' would make at him wi' her hand up till she'd mind that his ears was well protected by the saucepan; an' wi' that she'd burst intil another tanthrum wi' the vexation that she couldn't get at him—all the time the saucepan hoppin' about with its hands up to save itself every time she took a run-race at it, an' liftin' a cup or a plate off the dhresser every other minit wi' the handle. The divil a such a circus ye ever seen.

"Hould on, Mary, hould on," sez I, at the last. "Have ye thried all ye can to get it off him?"

"Thried is it, Misther Murphy," sez she, breakin' out in a fresh roar. "If I pulled an' ounce harder I'd a' had the ears off the child.

"An' 'deed small pity too if I did," sez she, gettin' mad again, an' takin' a race at him. "I've a big mind to pull it off him ears an' all, the——"

"Wait now, Mary, wait a minit," sez I, gettin' between her an' the wee chap. "Put on your shawl an' come up wi' me to the docthor's till we see what can be done. For if the child's head swells in it, you'll never get it off him till they trail him to the graveyard by the handle."

"You're right, Misther Murphy, you're right," sez she,

all in a splutther. "Sure I might ha' thought of that before if my head hadn't been near turned. Come on, ye wee heart-scald ye, an' if I don't warm your lugs when the saucepan comes off them, my name's not Morrison. Gimme you hand." An' she out wi' him with a tug that near pulled the arm off him, an' up the road.

When he got intil the surgery down comes ould Dr. Dickson chewin' the last bite of his dinner he'd put in his mouth, an' lookin' mighty cross at bein' disturbed.

"What's wrong now, Mrs. Morrison?" sez he, feelin' for his glasses. "What's this!" sez he, as he puts them on an' sees the saucepan. "How'd he get this on his head? How'd ye get your head in this, boy?" sez he very sharp, bendin' down his ear to the child.

"Spake up an' tell the docthor," sez the mother, bendin' down to the other ear—unlucky enough, as it happened, for the wee fellow turnin' round sharp to the mother's voice, fetches the docthor a welt on the bridge of the nose wi' the handle of the saucepan that knocked his eyeglasses intil the fendher an' starred one eye like a shop-windy with a stone through it.

"Away out of this, you an' your brat," roars the docthor, dancin' round in a rage wi' the glasses in his hand. "I'll charge ye wi' these, mind ye; I'll charge ye wi' these. I'll put them down in the bill—I'll——"

"Och, charge me what ye like, docthor dear," sez the poor woman, half-cryin', "only take the pot off his head for the love of God, or——"

"Take the pot off his head," sez the docthor, still in a rage. "How the divil would I take the pot off his head, barrin' I take the head off wi' the handsaw an' then prise it off wi' a cold chisel. This is a job for a blacksmith," sez he, feelin' round the boy's neck; "take him away out of this.

"Fetch him up to the blacksmith, Pat," sez he to me. "Ye aye like to have your finger in every pie."

"But, docthor," sez the mother, "could ye not do *somethin'*? Could ye not pour somethin' on the pot would melt it?"

"I could," sez he, "only ye could put all would be left of the pot an' his head in a naggin bottle when I'd done. Away out of this, ye ould fool ye," sez he, openin' the door an' pushin' the child out. "Take him up to the blacksmith's, an' he'll have the thing off his head in half an hour with a file. Here, come back," sez he—he was a kindly man for all his short temper—"wait till I make ye up a pot of ointment. The child'll be bruised.

"Never mind, Pat," sez he, as I went to call the boy back. "Let him dandher on down the road. I'll not be more than a minit, if ye'll wait till I get my dinner over."

So the mother an' I sits down for a bit, waitin' on the docthor, an' while we were there wee Sonny wandhers on down the road till he come to the wall between it an' the school-house; an' just as he come fornent the school-house itself, the masther happened to be lookin' out of the windy.

The masther, as everybody knowed, was no teetotaler, an' the twelfth of July comin' in at the end of the holidays, he had wound up wi' a terrible burst wi' one or two Orangemen he met comin' home from the field—just to show, as he said, that there was one broad-minded man in this benighted counthry.

I'll say this for the wee man, he was no way bigoted about who he took a dhrink wi'. There's a deal of the same kind of broad-mindedness about Ballygullion.

But anyway, whether the masther's mind had been broader than usual, or whether Michael Casshidy's twelfth of July whiskey didn't lie kindly on a Catholic stomach, the wee man was in a mortial bad way this day, an' wi' the thrimmle in his hand had put as many ins an' outs in the map of Ireland he'd been dhrawin' on the blackboard as would ha' bothered the best pilot on the coast. So thinkin' to steady his nerves a bit he went to the schoolroom windy for a mouthful of fresh air.

The first thing his eyes fell on was the saucepan—'twas all he could see, for the wall.

"Who's been puttin' rubbish on the school wall," sez he

very cross. "Here, Mickey McQuillan, run out an' take that thing away."

"What thing, sir?" sez Mickey, comin' forward.

Just at that minit the saucepan begins to move. The masther takes a hard look at it, an' turns very pale.

"Mickey," sez the masther, very quiet, "do ye see a saucepan out there?"

"Where, sir?" sez Mickey, all in a flusther wi' the eyes of the whole school on him.

"Out there, on the wall," sez the masther, very short. "Don't ye see it, ye gomeril!"

"Yes, sir; oh yes, sir," sez Mickey in a hurry, though divil a thing he saw, good, bad or betther. An' small blame to him; for the sash of the windy was a good two inches higher than his head, though the masther was too flusthered to notice that.

The saucepan stopped an' turned round, wi' Sonny Morrison turnin' his head to listen for the mother, an' then it begin to move on again, very slow.

"Do ye see it movin', Mickey?" sez the masther in a kind of an off-hand way, as if it was nothin' much to him. "Don't say it's movin'," sez he, breakin' out very fierce.

"No, sir," sez Mickey, edgin' away from the cane in the wee man's hand, "it's not movin' at all, sir."

The masther looks hard at the saucepan again, an' there, sure enough, it was walkin' along the wall.

"Mickey," sez he, takin' a sthrong grip of himself, an' spakin' very slow an' quiet, "are ye *sure* it's not movin'—positive?"

"Yes, sir," sez Mickey, very anxious to please him—"positive, sir." An' wi' that the saucepan passes out of sight, with a desperate waggle of the handle through wee Sonny thrippin' on a stone.

"Holy Biddy," sez the masther to himself, turnin' very white, an' thrimmlin' all over, "this is terrible, this is terrible altogether. 'Twas that last glass in Michael's, or maybe the half-pint I took home.

"I deserve it," sez he, very bitther, "I deserve it. This is what comes of dhrinkin' holiday whiskey—me that knows what good liquor is, too.

"But what's to be done at all," sez he, dhroppin' down on a seat wi' his head in his hands. "There's nothin' for it but the docthor," sez he, startin' up again.

"Boys," sez he, turnin' round to them all starin' at him, "the school is dismissed. I'm not feelin' just at myself.

"Never mind me," sez he, as one or two of them made to go over till him, "I'll just sit down a minit or two an' then go home. Gather up your books an' slates quietly—*quietly!*" he roars as young Rafferty dhrops a slate wi' a clatther that made the wee man jump six inches sthraight up from the chair. "An' if there's any—any rubbish on the school wall as you're goin' past, dhrive it—I mean, take it away."

So the childher gathers up their bits of things, an' slips out very quiet, leavin' him sittin' there lookin' hard at the blackboard, an' ready to jump out of the windy if it as much as budged.

In the meantime Mrs. Morrison an' me had been sittin' at the docthor's, she still lookin' down the road an' gettin' fidgetier every minit as she watched the wee chap stumblin' along; till at last when he thripped over the stone at the school-house she could thole no longer, but down the road afther him, tellin' me to wait for the ointment.

The docthor kept me a brave while waitin', what wi' laughin' at the idea of the wee chap in the saucepan, an' then pickin' up his glasses an' gettin' angry when he looked at the wreck of them; an' at last when I did get out, who should I meet but the wee masther comin' up the road, desperate white an' shook-lookin'.

"What's wrong wi' ye, masther?" sez I; for, troth, 'twas sthrange to see the same wee man without a bit of a twinkle in his eyes. "Has anythin' happened, that you're lookin' so glum?"

"Pat," sez he, lookin' at me very hard, "ye take a dhrop of dhrink like meself—maybe less, maybe less," as he seen me goin' to say somethin', "but still a brave dhrop. Tell me, did ye ever see anythin'—anythin' movin' about?" sez he, moistenin' his lips.

"Not that I mind," sez I. "I niver thried just that hard. But I've heard of people that did, customers of Michael's mostly, about a holiday or a fair-day."

"Did ye ever see a saucepan walkin' along a wall?" sez he, bendin' forward an' spakin' undher his breath.

I spotted the whole thing in a flash, but still kept my face straight. "Never," sez I; "I never even heard of such a thing."

"Well, I saw one walk along the school-house wall a wee while ago," sez the masther, lookin' back at the wall, an' then turnin' his head away very quick. "Right along the wall it walked, from one end of it to the other, an' when it come to the far end it stopped an' wagged its tail at me, Pat," sez he. "I've got them, I've got them bad."

"Tut," sez I, "ye'll be all right in a day or two. It might ha' been far more serious. A saucepan's not as bad as a snake," sez I, to cheer him up; for I seen he was badly shook, an' I didn't want the thing to go too far.

"It's worse," sez he, "far worse. I could work wi' a snake. Sure St. Pathrick banished them long ago," sez he, wi' the wee'st bit of a twinkle in his eye, "an' if I seen one I'd know 'twas only imagination. But when the kitchen utensils comes out an' prances up an' down the open sthreet in broad daylight it's time somethin' was done. An' all, mind ye, on less whiskey, spread over a whole day an' a deal of the night, than I've had many a time between my dinner an' my tea.

"I'm a done man, Pat," sez he, lookin' at me very melancholy. "I'm goin' down the hill fast. The last of the MacDermotts is goin' to end his days little betther than a teetotaler."

"Ye should go up an' see the docthor," sez I.

"It's just where I'm goin' this very minit," sez he. "Tell me, though, Pat," sez he, cockin' his eye at me very anxious, "he wouldn't want me to take the pledge, d'ye think? For troth, if he did, I'd rather thole. The remedy would be worse than the disease."

"He'd never think of it," sez I. "Sure he's been livin' in Ballygullion too long."

"Come on back wi' me then, Pat," sez he, "an' we'll hear what he says."

But when the docthor heard the case, wi' all the winkin' I did, an' I near give meself paralysis of the right side of my face, he could hardly contain himself. He'd never ha' kept in if he hadn't seen the chance of a lifetime to straighten the masther up.

"There's no use disguisin' it, Misther MacDermott," sez he, lookin' very solemn, "this is a very serious business."

"Divil a doubt of it," sez the masther. "The cold thrimmles is runnin' down my backbone this minit. Ye should tell that servant of yours to shut the kitchen door when she comes to open for anybody at the front. There was a wicked-lookin' ould saucepan sittin' on a shelf that near turned me back again, an' me in the very hall."

I could see by this the masther was comin' round a bit.

"Don't make a joke of it, Misther MacDermott," sez the docthor. "You're on the verge of a nervous breakdown, an' maybe of insanity," sez he, very slow an' weighty. "There's only one thing can save ye."

"What's that, docthor?" sez the masther. But I could see by his face he knowed right well.

"You'll have to abstain from all intoxicatin' liquors for some time," sez the docthor. "Nothin' else is of any good."

"How much do I owe ye, docthor?" sez the wee man, gettin' up. "I'd rather face the saucepans. Maybe I'll get used to them in time."

"Ye owe me nothin'," sez the docthor. "I'll take no money from a dyin' man. It's my duty to tell ye that it's very unlikely, if ye persist in your present way of livin', that ye'll be alive this day month. Good-bye, Misther MacDermott," sez he, houldin' out his hand.

The cold sweat broke on the wee man. First he looked at me an' then at the docthor, but we were both as solemn as judges, though I'd ha' given half-a-crown for a good laugh.

"How long would do, docthor?" sez he, in desperation. "I'll face it for a while. 'Twould be a pity for me to go off before the school examinations, an' lose my result fees."

"Three months," sez the docthor, "at the very least."

"Ye might as well say years, docthor," sez the wee man. "It couldn't be done at all. Sure I might as well die of the horrors as the drouth. When are the Ballygullion races, Pat?" sez he to me.

"This day four weeks, masther," sez I.

"Very well, docthor," sez he. "I'll take the pledge for four weeks short of a day, an' divil an hour longer, should the kitchen range come out an' dance a polka in front of me."

"It's no manner of use," sez the docthor. "Ye wouldn't ha' lost the taste for dhrink by that time."

"An' who tould ye I wanted to lose the taste for it?" sez the masther very sharp, "a man wi' the gift of dhrinkin' whiskey that I have. What would become of Michael Casshidy if I lost the taste for dhrink? He'd be in the poor-house in a twelve-month. Sure he white-washed the whole premises an' re-painted the signboard out of my last quarther's salary. Ye have no considheration for the public institutions of the town at all, docthor. Four weeks, short of a day, as I said—or nothin'."

There was no use aimin' too high an' missin' altogether, so afther arguin' a bit more the docthor give in an' bound the masther over for the time he said, wi' me for a witness; an' the wee man an' I goes back down the road.

There wasn't a word spoke. The masther walked wi' his head down, an' the tall hat on the back of his head, as miserable-lookin' as if the whole of his friends was dead an' buried; an' as for me I aye kept wondherin' what he'd do or say when he found out how he'd been thricked. I hadn't long to wait.

Just as we come to the school-house, who should we meet but Long Tammas McGorrian, in a great hurry.

"Masther," sez he, all out of breath, "I wish ye'd step up to the blacksmith's an' see what ye could do wi' wee Sonny

Morrison"—("Now for it!" sez I)—"he's got his head fixed in a saucepan," goes on Tammas.

"What's that ye say, Tammas?" sez the masther, all thrimmlin'. "What's that about a saucepan?"

"The wee fellow's got his head fixed in a saucepan, God knows how," sez Tammas, "an' has been walkin' about all mornin' an' can't get it off. The blacksmith has it by the handle in a vise, an' has creeshed the child's head well an' wants him to pull hard enough to get out; but he won't, for all we can do. Maybe you could persuade him. He'd be afeared of you."

But the masther said nothin' for a minit or two, but leaned up again the wall.

"Four weeks," sez he till himself, very low an' bitther, "four weeks, wantin' a day. Oh, Holy Biddy, an' me passin' Michael Casshidy's twice every day at the very least. Wait a minit, Tammas," sez he, leppin' up, "wait till I get my cane, an' if I don't have him out of it, should he leave the whole side of his head behind him, he'll not sit down aisy from this to the Ballygullion races anyway." An' he intil the school-room like a ragin' lunatic.

But he fumbled a while at the gate, wi' the splutther he was in, an' I just had time to explain matters to Tammas.

"Run, Tammas, run now," sez I. "You're longer in the legs than I am. If the wee fellow isn't out before the masther comes, the blacksmith himself won't be able to save him. Run, man!"

Away goes Tammas like a hare, an' me afther him all I was fit, to see the fun. But before I reached the forge the masther was near on top of me.

I could hear the shouts of Tammas, an' the rest of them inside. "Pull, Sonny, pull; he's comin'!"

"Pull, ye boy ye," shouts Tammas; "here he's at the door. By the mortial, he's got ye!"

But that minit wee Sonny gives a last wrestle an' a yell, an' out of the saucepan an' through the back-door just as the masther in at the front one wi' the cane swishin' round him like a flail. One or two of us got in front of the masther, but we needn't ha' bothered ourselves. If the real King James only run as hard from the Boyne as Sonny Morrison did from the blacksmith's shop, it's small wondher he was the first of his men to get to Dublin.

The Bridge

No, said Mr. Murphy, this bridge isn't long built. It was put up by the ratepayers ten years or so ago, afther Simon Harvey bought Grierson's farm over there, an' put this wee loanin' on the county. An undherhand job it was, too, for the divil a one either the loaning' or the bridge serves but himself; an' I never could see why I should be payin' an extra tuppence in the pound of rates, just to save Simon Harvey's carts a journey of two miles round by the big county bridge.

Oh, aye; there was a bridge here before that, a foot-bridge about two planks wide, restin' on two piers of mason-stone in the middle of the river. A bad, dangerous bridge it was, an' a bad history connected with it. By the time I mind it first it had fell into a very poor condition. The three spans of it was all sagged in the middle, an' pulled away from the hand-rail in places, an' the planks was all green an' slimy with the water pourin' over them when there was a spate. Ye mustn't take the river by what it is now, in the summer's day. It's a very angry, greedy river in the month of December, an' would turn your head to look down on it tumblin' an' swirlin' by. Aye, a greedy river, a greedy treacherous river, an' has devoured men's lives an' weemin's happiness in its time. Grierson's river it was called about here; an' this was Grierson's bridge, an' yon, as I told ye, was Grierson's farm. Now the very name of a Grierson is gone out of the countryside; an' it was that river you're lookin' at, with the sun shinin' on it this minit, swept the same name away. Sit down on the parapet here, an' I'll tell ye the whole story:

They say it all begun through a Grierson puttin' a poor

widow woman out of them two fields there on the wrong side of the river from the farm. He put up the foot-bridge I told ye of, to get to the fields handy, an' then run this loanin' up to the county road. An' they say the first time he crossed the bridge afther it was finished the widow was standin' waitin' for him, an' knelt down on her knees an' put a sore curse on him, an' said that for every span there was in the bridge there would be a life paid. But the old fellow was a reckless, careless divil, like all the rest of them, an' he only laughed at her. Nothing happened to him anyway. He died in his bed, twenty years afther. The widow was gone years before, an' the memory of the curse had near died out.

The eldest boy, Alexander, succeeded to the place, an' got married—she was a Miss Halfpenny of Toberrann, I heard my mother say—an' the night his son Ezekiel was born he slipped off the far span of the bridge, comin' back from warnin' the midwife, an' was found half a mile down the river lyin' in the bulrushes. That was the first life.

The poor wife died of the news, but the child lived, an' was brought up by his Aunt Eliza on her husband's farm at Ballybruff, an' lived at Ballybruff till he was twenty-one. Then he came back to the home-farm here, an' started to labour it himself. The whole sough in the country was that the first thing he meant to do was to pull down the old bridge an' build a new one. However, the land was a good deal run down an' the houses in bad repair, an' he thought he would put the place in ordher first, an' then build the new bridge. But when you start tinkerin' at houses an' fences an' drains you're never done. There was always somethin' wanted doin', an' even what should ha' been done let lie many a time, for Ezekiel was a devil-may-care feckless creature like the father before him; an' the buildin' of a bridge got less pressin' every year, till in the end there was no word of it at all barrin' among a lot of cronies of old weemin that used to wag their heads together of a winter's night an' spey ill-luck.

But keepin' off the curse altogether you'd wondher that Ezekiel never done anythin' to the bridge, if it was only for the safety of people comin' an' goin' from the farm; for it kept gettin' rickettier every year, till a body could ha' got drowned off it without havin' a curse connected with him at all. Nothin' was done anyway. There might be some talk of repairs, afther a bad flood, an' a nail or two dhriv in here an' there, but that was all. Afther the first spasm of work when he came into the place Ezekiel got very slovenly an' lazy, an' he married a wife near as bad as himself. They had just the one child, a son Robbie; an' when Robbie grew up to be goin' to school I used to listen to him at the father about buildin' a new bridge, for he'd heard about the curse from his mates. But Robbie was a bit easy-goin' too, an' though he used to talk about tacklin' the job himself when he got old enough, he never seemed to get old enough to do it.

However, the near span of the bridge, where the water runs hardest, got into a very bad state, an' somethin' be't to be done. Robbie promised to fix it, but kept puttin' it off, an' puttin' it off, till the father got angry at the last, an' one very rough October day, when there was nothin' to be done about the fields, he laid hold of an old piece of plank that was lyin' kickin' about the yard an' started to the bridge himself. He didn't make a bad job of it either—for Ezekiel wasn't unhandy—an' just as he had finished he seen Robbie comin' down the loanin' from the county road an' calls to him to come an' see the work, beckonin' with his hand at the same time in case Robbie shouldn't hear him, with the wind. The hammer slipped from his hand; he made a glam at it as it fell, missed his foot, an' pitched head-foremost into the river, an' was never seen again alive. That was number two gone.

I need hardly tell ye that all the talk there ever had been before about the widow's curse was nothin' to what riz then. A most lamentable lot of people gathered for the funeral, an' they all went down an' viewed the bridge, an' everybody beseeched Robbie to pull it out of that, even if he should never build a new one. But there was no need of sayin' anythin' to Robbie. He had been desperately cut up about the father's death, an' blamed himself with bein' the cause of it; an' the mother blamed him, too, an' wasn't slow to tell him either. An', troth, there was some thought of himself as well; for he was daunted about the curse, an' didn't know when it might be his own turn, with one life to go still. Him an' I walked home together from the funeral, an' he swore to me that before another week went over his head the old bridge would be down, let whoever liked build the next one.

When he got home and told the mother what was in his mind she wouldn't hear of it at all. Near the bridge she would not let him go. If the bridge was goin' to be pulled down, let Taylor, the carpenter, be got. Her man had been dhrowned workin' at it, an' her son would be dhrowned, too, if he went near it; an' she screamed an' cried an' went on till Robbie gave in to wait for Taylor.

But Taylor wasn't to be had. He was roofin' a house for John Torney, an' wouldn't be done for six weeks. So the pullin' down of the bridge was put off till Taylor would be free. Robbie didn't engage him definite, but was to let him know. At the end of the six weeks Robbie was thrashin' corn, an' put off sendin' for Taylor till Taylor was fixed up for another long job, so the bridge was let lie again.

But Robbie's mind was made up that the bridge was comin' out of that, sooner or later. For a long time afther the father's death he hated the very sight of it, an' used to curse it an' threaten it as if it was a livin' thing an' had killed his father an' grandfather on purpose. It wasn't till months aftherwards that he put a foot on the bridge at all. I was there that day myself.

Robbie had been courtin' Minnie Watson off an' on for about a year in Ezekiel's time; but he had to do most of his courtin' on the sly, for Robbie had no means of marryin' for many a long day, an' her people didn't want him to be spoilin' their girl's market. Minnie was a likely lookin' wee girl, very bright an' merry, but wise with it, an' she was apt to make a good match if she got a fair chance. But she never had a chance of anybody else once she got in tow with Robbie, an' didn't want one. So the pair of them used to humbug the old people an' meet at all sorts of odd times an'

places just as they could manage. But when Ezekiel was dhrowned Robbie was as good a match as even her own folk could wish for, an' he used to go straight up to the house an' court in the ordinary way. It was a great drawback him havin' to go round by the big county bridge, an' by the end of the winter he was very tired of it.

We were talkin' about that in his own yard one February day, an' as I walked down to the foot-bridge—for I wasn't a bit afraid of it—Robbie walked down beside me. It was a bright mild day—the sort you'll sometimes get in the month of February. The river was low, an' with the sunshine on it, an' the reflection of the blue sky, it looked a very harmless bit of a stream.

The same thought must ha' come into Robbie's head. "Now, amn't I the great fool," sez he, "listenin' to a lot of old weemin's clash, an' walkin' round a mile an' a half when I might be in Watson's in ten minutes. Ye old divil," sez he to the bridge, "ye'd think ye were temptin' me."

But all the same he kind of hesitated, an' we stood a while at the bridge-end, talkin'; for I wouldn't ask him to cross. An' as we stood we saw a girl walkin' along a hedge-side on the opposite hill.

"Yon's Minnie," sez Robbie, wavin' his cap; an' the girl waved back. "It is," sez he. "Ach, come on." An' across the bridge he goes.

From that on he began to use the bridge just the same as ever, an' was across it every time Minnie showed herself on the opposite side. It was that handy for him that when Taylor turned up to do away with it Robbie wouldn't let him, but put him off till the end of summer.

"By that time I'll be married, John," sez he; "an' then ye can take it out of this an' we'll put up a new one."

"Ye'd betther let me start the job while I'm here," sez John. "Puttin' off the fixin' of this bridge has cost two men's lives; an' it'll maybe cost three."

But the scare of the father's death was beginnin' to die in Robbie, an' he only laughed at him; so John went off, shakin' his head.

He went round the whole country, too, tellin' what had happened, an' speyin' ill-fortune, sayin' that what was to be would be, an' that the bridge wouldn't be pulled down by him or anybody till Robbie Grierson was dhrowned, too, an' the widow's curse filled up.

Of course somebody made it their business to tell all this to Minnie, an' it frightened the very life an' soul out of her.

She made one errand over to Robbie's that afthernoon an' fell into his arms cryin', an' would have him start pullin' down the bridge that very day; an' troth, if she could ha' used a hammer I think she'd ha' got at it herself. Of course the country clash wasn't so much news to Robbie as it was to her, an' he was inclined to laugh at her a bit; but when he seen the state she was in he changed his tune an' ended by swearin' he'd have the work started within a week, an' then left her home round by the road an' the county bridge; for the very look of the foot-bridge near put her into hysterics.

He had to go home the same way as he came to please the girl, an' got well wet in a shower of rain, an' I'm inclined to think that cooled him a bit about pullin' down the bridge till he'd have her on the same side of the water with him. Maybe, troth, it was just his natural laziness; but anyway a week went past an' a fortnight afther that, an' still nothin' was done. At last his sweetheart came over to me—she knowed Robbie an' me was very thick—an' nearly went on her knees to me to get Robbie to carry out his promise. She was all pale an' worried lookin', an' black rings undher her eyes, an' I was sorry for the girl. So when she left me I walked straight across to Robbie's an' told him that he was behavin' very badly to Minnie, an' should be ashamed of himself, for she was just clean worryin' herself to death an' him not carin' a straw about her——

"That's enough, Pat," sez he, when I'd finished. "I'll not let the wee girl be vexed. The job'll be done."

He set his teeth as if he meant it this time, so I left things at that.

But the divil a thing was done to the bridge for the next three weeks. I don't know how Robbie managed about his sweetheart, but he kept out of my way altogether; an' the one time I did meet him he fairly took over the ditch an' across the fields sooner than face me.

A week afther, he met me in Ballygullion sthreet on the market-day, an' stopped me. He was all flushed in the face, an' his hat a bit cocked on one side. I seen in a minit he'd been takin' a dhrop, an' troth I was surprised, for it was a thing seldom happened to Robbie.

"In the name of goodness, Robbie," sez I, "what has put you on the spree. Have ye come into money?"

"No," he sez, laughin' very hearty, "a far more exthra-ordinary thing. I'm on the road to do a job that has baffled three generations of the Griersons. Do you see that?—John Taylor's comin' to start pullin' down the old bridge to-morrow, an' there's a receipt for the timber for the new one. No more delays. The wee girl was too uneasy about me. A good bridge it's to be; three foot wide, with a hand-rail on each side. A dhrunk man could walk across it. Whoever else the river dhrowns, it'll not be a Grierson. Come in and have a bottle of stout with me over it."

An' right or wrong I had to go in with him into Cass-hidy's pub an' dhrink a bottle of stout to the health of the new bridge. I came out then an' brought Robbie with me, for I seen he'd had enough. When we got to the corner of the sthreet he stopped. "Good-bye, Pat," sez he, shakin' me by the hand. "I'm away home to get a couple of carts an' fetch that timber. Now that I am started I want to push on. Let me see, this is the fourth of October; six weeks to my weddin'-day, Pat. We'll have the new bridge up long before that, an' then the ould widow an' her curse may go to the divil for all I'll care."

"Hush, hush, Robbie," sez I; for it was an unchancy thing to say. "Away home now, an' get the carts. Ye've been here long enough. An' the sooner ye set about it the betther. There'll be rough weather before night."

"Good-bye, Pat," sez Robbie. "I can look ye in the face now, ye old sinner." An' he hits me a great slap on the back an' goes off roarin' an' laughin'. I thought even at the time there was somethin' byordinary about the spirits he was in.

However, I had my oats to sell, an' afther that a whole lot of things to buy for the house, an' I met this one an' that one, till Robbie an' his affairs went clean out of my mind. I suppose it was a couple or three hours afther I parted from him that I run into Minnie at Hogan's corner. She was all worried an' excited-lookin', an' that out of breath she could hardly speak at the first.

"Pat," sez she, gaspin', "have ye seen Robbie lately?"

"Not this three hours, Minnie," sez I. "He's away home long ago to get carts an' dhraw the timber for the bridge."

"He's not, Pat," sez she. "He never left the town. He started dhrinkin' with one an' another. My aunt seen him about twelve, an' come home an' told me, an' I put on me hat an' come into the town hot foot; for he's not used to dhrink, an' might get more than is good for him. But he must be away home by now, for I can't find him.—Oh, my God," sez she, "would he have gone home by the wee bridge?"

We stood lookin' at each other for a minit, an', troth, I think my face was as white as hers.

"Pat," sez she, "I'll get my bicycle—it's at Larney's round the corner—an' I'll ride to Robbie's as fast as I can. There's bad news."

"We'll hope not, Minnie," sez I. "But you'd betther do what ye say. I'll follow ye on foot, an' take the short-cut by the bridge."

"No, no!" she cries, checkin' her step. "No, Pat. Don't go near that unlucky spot. Follow me round by the county road."

"Now don't bother about me," sez I. "I'm due sober. I'll save time by it, an' be there near as soon as you."

"I suppose you would," sez she, hesitatin'. "It is shorter. But be careful, Pat; now do." An' away she goes.

I hurried on out of the town, stoppin' for nobody, till about half a mile up the road I met Tom Scott, the blacksmith. "Ye didn't meet Robbie Grierson?" sez I.

"I did not," sez he. "But they told me at Dornan's

cottages he went by an hour ago an' him singin' dhrunk an' staggerin'. I met his sweetheart a quarther of a mile back an' passed the news on to her; an' I wish now I hadn't, for she was frightened enough as it was. But he surely would never think of goin' by the bridge?"

"I don't know, Tom," sez I. "Oh, man, I don't know."

I took off up the road at a half run, an' all the time it kept beatin' in my head: "He's dhrowned, he's dhrowned." As I hurried down the loanin' to the bridge my hat blew off. I jumped into the ditch to get it—an' there, a bit along, was Robbie Grierson, lyin' sleepin' among the nettles.

I pulled him out of the ditch, an' shook him till he opened his eyes an' looked at me; an' then I took to the laughin' an' the cursin' and the prayin' till even Robbie, that was still all dazed, begun to wondher at me.

"What's wrong with ye, Pat?" sez he. "What has happened?"

"Nothin' has happened, Robbie," sez I, "nothin' has happened. But oh, lad, do you see where you are an' what might have happened this evenin'?"

He looked round him stupidly, an' then he saw where he was standin'. "The road to the bridge," sez he, in a kind of whisper. "The road to the bridge, an' me dhrunk—Pat," sez he, layin' his hand on my arm an' lookin' at me very solemn, "it's true. I've put it off this time, but it's only puttin' it off. I wanted to desthroy that bridge for years, an' my father before me, an' my grandfather before that, but we couldn't. It has to be. The third life must be paid. I'll be dhrowned down below there, yet; an' poor Minnie'll be another heart-broken Grierson woman."

"Come on home out of this," sez I. "Here's the two of us standin' bletherin' here, an' her away round by the road on her bicycle near out of her mind about you."

"Aye," sez he. "Come home. We mustn't vex wee Minnie. If dhrownin' myself in the river below would save Minnie one sore heart, now or ever, I'd do it——

"Wheesht!" sez he, catchin' my arm; "listen!"

We stood there a minit, quiet. Across the river, risin' an'

fallin' on the wind, we could hear a long wail like a woman lamentin'.

"Pat," sez Robbie, grippin' me tighter, "what's that? That's my mother's voice," sez he. He let go my arm, an' ran down the loanin' towards the river. An' as he ran it came into my mind what had happened.

"Robbie," I shouts, "Robbie! Come back! I know what it is. Minnie's at your house by now, an' your mother thinks you're dhrowned."

But he was out of sight.

"Oh, merciful heavens," sez I, startin' to run. "He'll cross, he'll cross, an' it's all come true."

But when I turned the corner Robbie was kneelin' at the broken bridge, beatin' his head an' callin' on his God, an' beside him on the bank was lyin' Minnie's bicycle.

A Tale of a Tinker

As every intelligent Irishman knows, there's a close connection between porther an' hard work. A man that's workin' with his hands, an' sweatin', as he's bound to do if he works at all, 'll need moisture of some kind or another, an' if there's a pleasanter way of administherin' it than through the neck of a porther-bottle the secret hasn't leaked out, in Ireland, anyway.

But whiskey is no dhrink for the labourin' man. Whiskey catches ye about the head mostly. It takes a man of brains an' education to dhrink whiskey an' keep out of the hands of the police. Solicithors, an' docthors, an' bank-clerks, an' them class of people can dhrink a deal of whiskey, an' still keep brave an' respectable-lookin', barrin' about the nose; an' whenever they want to make their wives miserable they can do it in an educated sort of way; but the more ignoranter people, when they get a glass or two, can think of nothin' better nor their two fists for the job, an' very soon finds themselves at the Petty Sessions.

That was how it was with Lanty Rogan the tinker. There's no doubt Lanty was a regular professor at the tinkerin'—any brains the Almighty had bestowed on him was in his two hands—an' for a tinker he worked very industhrious. As long as Lanty stuck to the porther he was as merry as a cricket, an' as pleasant as the flowers in May to everybody except the ass, maybe; but all the bad boiled out on him when he took to whiskey. He always took a terrible scunner at the ass when he had porther in him, but was very fond of the wife; but when he got a feed of whiskey he hated the very look of the wife, an' loved the ass like a brother. As soon as he begun on the whiskey he started to sing. The more whiskey he had in him, the louder he sang; an' when the wife could hear the singin' of Lanty above the rattle of the ass's cart as he came down the road, she always reached for her shawl an' took off across the fields to her mother's.

But she wasn't always out of the house in time; an' whenever that'd happen, an' Lanty'd get his hands on her, he'd give her a sore lambastin', just to learn her that she might 'a had more sense than to marry a man with no head for whiskey.

This sort of thing went on for a long while. The wife was a quiet loyal wee body, took the rough with the smooth, an' never complained; an' none of the neighbours liked to intherfere; the weemin sayin' she deserved all she got for puttin' up with it so peaceable, an' the men thinkin' at the back of their heads that they might want to give their own wives a lick some time or another. But as time went on the thing begun to get serious, an' people begun to see that if somethin' wasn't done it would end in manslaughter; an' at last, one night, afther Lanty had give the wife a cruel doin'-over, Mrs. Jarvis made her man go an' inform to the polis. Lanty was fined ten shillin's; an' then that evenin' he went down an' broke all the front windows in Jarvis's cottage, an' was fined a pound an' had to pay thirty shillin's for the glass. There's a deal of kettle-mendin' in two pound ten, an' for about two months there was great peace an' concord in the

Rogan family; but at the end of that time Lanty got a skinful of whiskey at William Dempsey's wake an' come home an' broke all records on the poor wee woman. The polis was on the watch for him this time, an' he went down thirty shillin's an' costs. The next bout was forty shillin's or a month, an' the next afther that a month without the option.

It was all no good. He wasn't out of gaol six weeks till he chased the wife two mile up the road with a soldherin'-iron, an' would surely ha' been the death of her if she hadn't been runnin' straight an' him zigzag. People seen that gaol wasn't goin' to meet the case at all. It wore off just as quick as a fine, an' besides, when he was in there was no money bein' made, an' the wife was half-starved. Everybody was at their wits' end what to do, from the P.P. to the Resident Magistrate, an' the only end they could see to the business was for Lanty to kill the wife clean out, an' then be hanged an' done with.

But just about the time people had come to that opinion, the ass fetched Lanty home one evenin' by-ordinary full. He couldn't sing, itself, an' even forgot about the wife; an' when the cart dhrew up at his own door he just lay there with his head in a tin can an' kicked kettles into the road. Afther a while he gathered himself together a bit an' slid down off the cart an' kissed the ass an' staggered into the house; an' afther fallin' down the stairs twice he climbed up them an' fell asleep on the bed in his clothes.

A few of the neighbours had been lookin' at his antics from a respectful distance, an' followed him in just to see what he would do. The wife, I may tell ye, was a mile an' a half away by this time. As luck would have it, the Rector's son was home in Ballygullion on his vacation. A very antic lad he was, too, a medical student, an' never likely to be anythin' else. He seen the wee crowd goin' in to Lanty's, an' followed them upstairs, an' as he stood there lookin' at him a notion come intil his head.

"Pat," sez he to me—I was about his own age, an' he knowed me well—"fetch one or two of the boys downstairs an' we'll arrange a wee surprise for Mr. Rogan when he wakes."

So downstairs three or four of us went, an' young Mr. Donaldson took command.

First of all we unyoked the ass, an' then we took out the linch-pins an' pulled the two wheels off the axle.

"Now," sez he, "carry the body of the cart upstairs—you can do it if you turn it sideways—an' then fetch up the wheels an' put them on again." So we done that. I don't suppose anybody had ever seen a donkey-cart in an upstairs room before; an' it looked very queer.

"That'll surprise him sure enough," sez I. "I'd like to see his face when he wakes."

"Take your time," sez Masther Bob. "We have to bring the ass up yet."

We looked at him to see was he serious—an' he was. So we tied the ass's legs together, an' carried him up, with no harm done barrin' two front teeth that Joe Walsh lost through forgettin' that he was at the kickin' end; but it's not a job I'd like to undhertake again. Then with a deal of coaxin' an' squeezin' we got the ass between the shafts, an' harnessed him, with his head towards the bed; an' then we stood in the doorway an' laughed till we cried.

Ye've maybe seen one of them conthrivances of a full-rigged ship inside of a glass bottle. When I was a child it used to be a sore puzzle to me how the ship got in; but a grown man would ha' been puzzled to guess how that ass an' cart got into Lanty Rogan's upstairs bedroom. Even ourselves, that done the business, could hardly think how it was done, it was that impossible-lookin'. But the ass wasn't a bit put about, an' started to eat the straw out of the bed-tick as composed as if it was used to bein' put to bed every night an' sung to sleep.

"Come on downstairs, boys," sez Masther Bob. "He'll do no harm.—I suppose we'd better wait about till Lanty comes to?"

"Wait!" sez Billy Lenahan. "I wouldn't miss it if I should sit up all night."

So we lit our pipes an' sat down by the kitchen-fire.

In about an hour's time we heard a bit of a stir upstairs an' a groan or two.

"He's comin' round," sez Masther Bob, an' tiptoes up the stairs, wi' the rest of us afther him. When we keeked in, the ass had ate all of the stuffin' of the tick he could get at, an' part of the quilt, an' was nosin' at Lanty's face, an' Lanty gruntin' an' thryin' to brush him off as if he was a fly. Presently the ass begins lippin' at Lanty's hair, an' at last he puts his teeth to it an' takes a good tug; an' with that Lanty throws out his closed fist an' pins the ass on the nose. Back goes the ass with a jerk, an' shoves one of the trams of the cart out through the window with a powerful crash; an' at that Lanty starts up in the bed an' looks round him. He took a stupid stare at the ass, an' then reached for the reins an' give a great tug at them.

"Come out of the ditch, ye brute ye!" sez he. "How the divil did ye get down there?" An' then he raised himself on his elbow an' looked round him. For a minit or two he lay there blinkin', with his eyes slowly thravellin' from one thing in the room to another, an' from that to the ass an' cart; an' then all at once the whole thing came home to him. He let one screech out of him an' rolled off the bed on the far side of it from the ass, an' in undher it like a rabbit, an' lay there on his mouth an' nose, roarin' like a fog-horn in a sea-mist.

With that we all begun to push into the room, an' Masther Bob climbed over the cart an' thrailed Lanty out from undher the bed.

"What's wrong, Lanty?" sez he. "In the name of goodness what's wrong?"

"Oh, Masther Bob," sez he, clingin' tight to him, "it's the divil, it's the divil. He has followed me home an' fetched up the ass an' cart for me. Run for the priest," sez he. "Run for Father Connolly, or one of the curates—or even your father would do at a pinch, if you can't get them. Oh, Lord deliver us!" An' he fell to the prayin' an' cryin' time about.

"Away for Father Connolly, somebody," sez I—for I

didn't want to miss the fun.—"There never was a better chance of gettin' the pledge on him."

So off goes young Tommy McGorrian; an' the rest of us stood there listenin' to Lanty. He was soberin' every minit, an' the soberer he got the frighteneder he got, till at the last one of us had to go an' help Masther Bob to hold him in the room.

Presently we heard a noise below.

"Here's Father Connolly," sez I. But it wasn't. It was the sergeant of police. We could hear the big boomin' voice of him.

"An' he thinks the ass an' cart is up in the bedroom with him, an' it an upstairs room. Did ye ever hear such blethers? It's the horrors of dhrink is on the man."

"I wouldn't be surprised," we could hear Billy answerin' —the rascal. "Ye'd betther go up an' reason with him, sergeant."

"I will, then," sez the sergeant, very determined; an' up the stairs he marches, with every step of him shakin' the house.

But when he walked into the room an' seen the ass an' cart there sure enough, there wasn't much to choose between him an' Lanty as far as bein' scared went. For though he was a big man, an' plucky enough with a thramp or a dhrunk-an'-disorderly, he was very superstitious an' cowardly at night-time, an' wouldn't ha' gone out afther dark without a couple of constables with him, not if he was to get his pension doubled.

However, seein' the eyes of everybody on him, he pulled himself together an' looked over very wicked at Lanty.

"How did this yoke get here, Rogan?" sez he.

"It was the divil done it, sergeant dear," sez Lanty, with his teeth chatterin'. "The last thing I mind was myself an' the ass comin' down the hill below Pat Devlin's, an' all at once there come a terrible clatther like all the tin cans in the world fallin' about us, an' in the clappin' of your hands I was lyin' on my bed here an' the ass eatin' the hair of my head as if it was turnip-tops. Send for Father Connolly," sez he, "for it's touch an' go with my sowl this minit."

"It mightn't be any harm," sez the sergeant crossin' himself on the quiet, "if one of yez did go for him. An' in the meantime I'll hold a bit of an investigation.—Had ye dhrink taken at the time this happened, Rogan?" sez he, fetchin' out his notebook.

"Well, I might have had a couple of spoonfuls of whiskey, sergeant," sez Lanty; "but sure the ass was as sober as you are, an' he's here too."

"He is, he is," sez the sergeant, "an' the question is how the divil—Lord pardon me," sez he, "I mean how did he get here? Lend me your two-foot rule, Joe Davison. For we must thry all natural means of inquiry before the case passes out of the hands of the civil authorities."

So he run the two-foot rule over the door an' over the cart, all of us lookin' on very solemn.

" 'The dimensions of the cart,' " sez he to himself, writin' all the time in his notebook, " 'rendhered it impossible for it to pass through the doorway. I then proceeded to measure the window.' "

"You need hardly bother doin' that, sergeant," sez Masther Bob. "We can see for ourselves that the donkey wouldn't go through it, let alone the cart."

"As an officer of the Force," sez the sergeant, "I must pursue the investigation in a legal an' proper way, Mr. Donaldson. 'I then proceeded to measure the window, one pane of which appeared to have been recently broken——' Can you explain this breakage, Rogan?"

"I cannot, sergeant," sez Lanty. "It was as whole as the bottom of a new kettle when I left home this mornin'. But sure you couldn't get the ass's tail through the hole, not to speak of his body. It was never through the window he came."

"The breakin' of the window I would regard as immaterial," sez the sergeant; "for three times the size of the window wouldn't admit the cart. Is there any other orifice in the room?"

"Only the chimney," sez Masther Bob. For none of the rest of us was quite sure what the sergeant was dhrivin' at.

"Examine it carefully, sergeant," sez he. "I've heard of the divil ridin' down a chimney on a broomstick before now."

"He might do that in the present case," sez the sergeant, peerin' up the chimney; "but nobody less than himself could ha' dhriven an ass an' cart down here. 'The size of the chimney,' " sez the sergeant, at the notebook again, " 'which did not appear to have been swept for a considerable time——' "

"An' that's the God's truth, anyway," sez Peter the sweep. "I haven't taken eighteenpence out of the house since the year before Lanty's father died. As far as I'm concerned the divil may get Lanty anytime."

"Oh, Lord forgive ye for them words, Pether," sez Lanty, half-cryin'. "Isn't my sowl in a bad enough way as it is? Will some of yez go an' hurry up Father Connolly?"

"Here he is," sez somebody. "That's his step on the stairs." But when we looked it was ould McSwiney, the schoolmasther from Tullydrum.

"There'll be fun now," sez I to myself. An' I could see by Masther Bob's face that he was very much of the same opinion as myself.

Ould McSwiney had come down from the mountains when he was a lump of a fellow, an' was a native Irish speaker, an' a great man for ould times an' ould stories. If ye once got him started—an' was in no great hurry home—he'd ha' deaved ye with yarns about fairies an' will-o'-the-wisps, an' leprechauns, an' them sort of bein's. He didn't believe in the English divil at all, but had rooted out a deal of information about another ould Gaelic chap that he thought was twice as good; though, troth, if it come to spendin' the balance of eternity with either of the two there wasn't much to choose between them.

When the story of Lanty an' the ass was explained to him he was in great heart.

"Fairies," sez he, clappin' his hands; "by the Hokey, fairies. I never heard of a clearer case. There's a story in *The Annals* as like this as two peas."

"Fairies!" sez the sergeant curlin' his upper lip till it near pushed the helmet off his head.

"Ay, fairies," sez McSwiney. "Where did you hear the noise, Lanty?—There you are, now! There's a fairy ring not half a mile from that."

"Did you ever see a fairy?" sez the sergeant.

"I did not," sez McSwiney, "not that I was sure of. But my father was the seventh son of a seventh son, an' he seen plenty of them.—Ye don't believe that," sez he to the sergeant.

"No, nor I wouldn't believe it if he was the seventh son of Lord Ross's telescope at Birr," sez the sergeant. "Was your father a teetotaller?" sez he.

"I wouldn't say he was," sez McSwiney. "What are ye thryin' to make out?"

"Oh, nothin'," sez the sergeant. "But we had a dhrunk man in the lock-up not a fortnight ago that seen two sea-serpents an' a talkin' frog. Will ye tell me what would the fairies—if there *is* fairies—would be botherin' themselves about this unfortunate being for?"

"That's just it," sez McSwiney. "That's what proves my case up to the hilt. For it's well known—to any knowledgeable an' educated man—that it's just such an extraordinary bit of rascality as this that they would put their hands to. They're full of tricks an' divilment, the fairies. There's no reason with them at all."

"I'm with you there," sez the sergeant very dhry—"nor with them that believes in them."

"Well, if it wasn't the fairies," sez McSwiney in a rage, "who was it then?"

"Afther a careful investigation of all reasonable explanations of the occurrence," sez the sergeant, "I have come to the conclusion that the divil is mixed up in it."

"You're a poor superstitious creature, for all your three stripes, sergeant," sez McSwiney. "Why should the divil bother with Lanty Rogan, when he's sure to get him anyway?"

"He mightn't be willin' to wait for him," sez the

sergeant. "I mind my grandmother—rest her soul—tellin' me——"

Poor Lanty had been listenin' to the whole conversation, an' had been greatly cheered up in his mind to hear that it was maybe only the fairies he had to deal with, but at this he give way altogether, an' fell forrard on the bed cryin' an' roarin' for the parish priest.—An' with that we heard Father Connolly's voice on the stairs, an' more along with him. The next minit he pushed his way into the room, an' in afther him comes Lanty's wife an' his mother-in-law. It seems the news of Lanty's mishap had reached beyond their length already.

When the wife seen the ass an' cart she started the roarin' an' cryin' too, an' made to go over to Lanty. But the mother-in-law let a skreigh out of her an' fell on her knees.

"It's a miracle!" sez she, "it's a blessed miracle has fell from Heaven to warn that dirty scallywag from his murdherin's ways an' give him one more chance before the divil gets him.—Get down on your knees, ye miserable wee scut, an' thank God an' the saints for what they've done for you this day, warnin' ye from your dhrink an' your wickedness; an' then get up an' take the pledge with Father John here, an' save your useless sowl while ye have a chance.—It's a miracle has been performed in Ballygullion this day; your Reverence will tell him that."

Father Connolly looked across the room at Masther Bob, an' there was just what ye would know of a twinkle in his eye.

"Well, Mary," sez he, "in the matther of miracles the Church is inclined to be very cautious, an' I wouldn't recommend anyone to jump to a rash conclusion; but if ye'll all leave me here alone with Lanty I think I'll be able to convince him about the advisability of takin' the pledge. Just go down, the whole of you, to the kitchen."

So as I went out of the room I took a keek over at Lanty, an' even with the scare was on him it come into my head that Father John would have his work cut out. For by the look of the same Lanty it was no spring-water drouth was on him that minit.

We sat in the kitchen for a quarther of an hour or more, an' at the end of that time Father John came down lookin' very plazed with himself.

"Mary," sez he, "do you an' your daughter go upstairs an' fetch Lanty away home with you. This house will be closed to-night; an' I think you'll find when you come back in the mornin' that the ass an' cart will be removed to their natural habitation."

He took a squint over at Masther Bob as he said it, and Masther Bob just returned him a wee nod, with a wink thrown in.

"But, Father, dear," sez the mother-in-law, "did he sign the pledge? For if ye let the ass an' cart off the premises till he does it we're done for ever."

"He has taken the pledge again whiskey for the rest of his life," sez Father Connolly; "an' he's a man of his word.—About porter I've allowed him a little latitude."

"Oh, Father John, Father John," sez she, half-cryin', "why didn't ye pledge him again porter, too, when ye had this blessed chance?"

"Mary," sez Father Connolly, lookin' at her with a very wise wee smile on his mouth, "as I told you, I wouldn't commit myself about whether there was a miracle performed here this evenin' or not; but there's one thing I will tell you: I've been livin' in the parish of Ballygullion these twenty-two years past, an' I know far too much about the place to expect two miracles in it in the one day."

Dear Ducks

WEE Mr. Anthony, the solicitor, was one of them men that hasn't room in their heads for more than one idea at a time. Him bein' a solicitor, ye might think it was law his head was full of; but not a bit of it. Outside of his own office or the Petty Sessions Court, law never troubled him; he just passed his final examination an' then placed the whole business in the hands of the divil. Sport was his weakness. In the summer he played tennis as if he made his livin' by it; an' it was well for him he didn't, for with him bein' so short-sighted he stopped a deal more balls with the pit of his stomach then ever he did with his bat. But with the end of the good weather he dhropped the tennis like a hot potato an' took to the shootin'. An' then the Coroner sharpened his pencil; for when Mr. Anthony turned out a charge shot on the world only an all-seein' Providence could tell where some of the pickles would come to a full stop.

I was standin' whettin' my scythe one October evenin' when Mr. Anthony comes into the yard. "Pat," sez he, "is there any wild-duck about that a body could shoot handy?"

"Lashins of them," sez I. "Do you want a brace or two?"

"I do," sez he. "The fact is, Pat," he goes on, "Miss Livingston an' I is a bit friendly lately——"

"Oh, well," sez I, "what odds? If it comes to a breach of promise ye can conduct your own defence."

"I haven't got the length of a promise yet," sez he, "let alone a breach of it."

"What's holdin' ye?" sez I, "that can talk round a whole bench of magistrates, let alone an' innocent slip of a girl that might be your daughter."

"You're a liar," sez Mr. Anthony; "I'm not even ten years older than her.—It's the shootin' is holdin' me back," sez he. "She's clean death on my takin' up a gun; an' I'd as soon live single all my life as give it up now that I have masthered it."

"Masthered it, God forgive ye!" sez I to myself—an' then out loud: "There's no doubt you've come on extra-ordinary well at it this last winter or two."

"Haven't I, Pat?" sez he, all pleased, "haven't I now? D'ye mind that grouse I shot, last June was a year?"

"Wheesht! Mr. Anthony," sez I.

"I don't care a fig," sez he. "Close season, or no close season, didn't the bird rise up fornent me an' just ask for it? I never made a prettier shot in my life. Blast it, why wasn't it in the month of August, when I could have told people?

But that's neither here nor there," sez he. "It's in my mind to shoot a couple of nice ducks an' send them round to Miss Livingston. If she had a wing an' a bit of the breast of one of them sittin' before her on a plate, she might think betther of my shootin'."

"Does she not think well of it, as it is?" sez I.

"Well," sez Mr. Anthony, lookin' a wee bit foolish, "there was an accident happened to me one day lately when I was walkin' across the fields with her. A rabbit got up in front of us, an' I fired a bit hasty an' missed it."

"Is that all?" sez I. "She surely wouldn't expect even you to hit everything you fire at."

"It wasn't that," sez Mr. Anthony, rubbin' his chin. "The fact is, Pat," sez he, "I hit her dog. It was that blasted wee Pomeranian, that goes along with its tail arched over its back as if it was as proud of its hind-end as it is of its face; an' of course in the tail it got it. Curse the misbegotten little brute, if it carried its tail decently out behind it like an ordinary dog the divil a pickle it would ha' got, an' I might even have killed the rabbit. However, that's past prayin' for now. Where do you think I could get a pair or ducks?"

"Try the marshy ground where the Ballygullion river flows into the lake," sez I. "It's clean alive with ducks, an' most of them flappers, an' flyin' very slow."

"Flyin' slow," sez Mr. Anthony, a bit vexed. "Flyin' slow, is it? What do I care whether they're flyin' slow or fast. You'd think I was a novice to hear you talkin'." An' off he goes in a huff.

But about three days afther, back he comes again, an' not near as cocky this time.

"Did she like the ducks?" sez I.

"I always thought this tennis playin' was bad for a man's shootin'," sez Mr. Anthony. "Would you believe it, Pat, but I've been down at the marshes these three evenin's, an' fired away as many cartridges as would fill a counsellor's wig, an' the divil a feather I've brought down."

"Did ye not as much as wound somethin'?" sez I, chaffin' him.

"Well," sez he, "there *was* one, a drake, I think, that flew away very slow an' heavy afther I fired at him."

"I wouldn't think much of that," sez I. "He might have a touch of rheumatism, sleepin' in the damp. You'll have to take another evenin' or two at them."

"It's no good," sez he, "till I get this infernal tennis out of my system. Besides, I haven't time. There's a dinner-party at Mr. Livingston's on Friday, an' I wanted the ducks for that."

"Ye needn't bother your head," sez I. "My wife has a pair of young ones fattened for them."

"Has she?" sez he, lookin' disappointed; "that's a pity. Pat," sez he, all excited, "would she sell them to me? Hold your tongue, now. Let her send word to the Livingstons that the rats ate them; an' then I'll come along with a pair just in the nick of time. Don't talk to me," sez he, hoppin' round as the notion took hold of him, "there's not a bein' about the place would know a duck from a wather-hen barrin' Mr. Livingston himself, an' sure they'll be plucked naked before they get his length."

"Ye've no sense, Mr. Anthony," sez I. "Wouldn't the very scullery-maid know when a bird had its throat cut instead of bein' shot?"

"So she would," sez Mr. Anthony. "That's awkward.—Wait now," sez he; "I'm not beat yet. Dhrive them through the gap in the hedge there, one at a time, an' I'll shoot them as they come through. What about that, eh? It's hard to get the betther of me, mind ye, when I lay my brains to a thing. Go on, now, an' get them. What are ye waitin' for?"

"It's clean murdher, Mr. Anthony," sez I, "forbye that ye might miss them."

"Miss them!" sez he. "Miss them, ye imperent ould vagabond. An' them walkin'! Didn't ye see me bringin' down a woodcock in the Drumnaquirk wood only last February?"

"I did," sez I; "but you were aimin' at a wood-pigeon at the time.—However, I suppose I'll have to be as big a fool as yourself. Away an' post yourself, an' I'll drive in the ducks. What size of shot are ye usin'?"

"Number three," sez he.

"It's too big," sez I. "Ye'll damage them."

"It's all I have," sez he. "I've killed ducks with it before."

"Ye have," sez I; "an' ye killed a terrier dog of mine with it, too. If Mr. Livington breaks one of them gold teeth of his on a pickle of number three shot, I wouldn't give much for your chance of marryin' his daughter. But have your own way. Ye'll have it anyway, I know."

So off I goes an' brings the two ducks, an' them quackin' away as if they'd ten years to live. Ye'd ha' thought somebody had told them what sort of a shot Mr. Anthony was. When I came back he was on the far side of the gap with the gun in his hand.

"Are ye ready, now?" sez I. "Here's the first of them."

"Hold on a minit," sez he—an' I could tell by his voice he was flusthered—"I want a good steady shot. I'm going to lie down on my belly."

"If one of them two-year-old bullocks of mine steps on ye, ye'll get up again," sez I.—"Bless my soul," sez I to myself as a thought struck me; an' I ran over to the gap an' peeped through. It was well I looked at Mr. Anthony first. If I hadn't ha' shouted, I was a dead man.

"Good Heavens, Pat!" sez he, lowerin' the gun, "I thought it was one of the ducks."

"Ye didn't think a duck had a pair of nailed boots on it, did ye?" sez I. "Ye'll do ten years for manslaughter, yet.—I wanted to make sure the bullocks was out of your line of fire."

"Will ye dhrive out them d——d ducks an' have done with it?" sez Mr. Anthony in a rage ."Ye have my nerve near ruined as it is."

"Come on, then," sez I. "Blaze away!"

I whished the first of them through the gap, keepin' well to the rear myself, I may tell ye. There came a terrible roar of a report. When I run through the gap there was as much smoke dhriftin' down the field as if the kitchen chimney was on fire, an' Mr. Anthony rowlin' over an' over in the middle of it, an' cursin' most lamentable.

"In the name of goodness, Mr. Anthony," sez I, "what's wrong? Did ye shoot out of the wrong end of the gun?" For, troth, he was capable of it.

"It was you, ye ould fool ye," sez he, risin' to his feet an' rubbin' himself. "Ye had me scared into thinkin' I might miss the beast, an' I pulled the two triggers at the one time. My backbone is out of joint," sez he, reachin' round between his shoulder-blades. "But I'll go bail I killed the duck, anyway."

"Where is it, then, if ye did?" sez I, lookin' all round. For there was no duck to be seen.

"It's the most extraordinary thing," sez Mr. Anthony, stickin' the eyeglass in his eye an' looking all round him. "I'll swear, an' kiss the book, that I hit it."

"I'll tell ye what ye've done," sez I, "ye've blew it to pieces." An' that's what he *had* done. We searched up an' down, but divil a all we ever discovered of the same duck but the neb an' one of the feet.

"Aw, well," sez I, at the last, "it had a lovely death, even if there isn't much eatin' about the carcass. Will I dhrive out the other one for ye, now?"

"Dhrive it to hell if ye like," sez Mr. Anthony, fair boilin' over. "Have ye any whiskey about the place?—Then, come an' rub my shoulder with some of it.—An' ye may throw that blasted gun in the well," sez he, an' stalks off into the house.

But by the time his shoulder was well rubbed with the whiskey, an' him had a good jorum of it in his inside, he begun to come round.

"Say what ye like, Pat," sez he, "it was a great shot. Plumb in the middle I must ha' got that duck."

"Ye must have," sez I, sootherin' him. "It was only outlyin' bits like the neb that was found. There's no doubt ye have a very straight eye."

"Haven't I, Pat?" sez he, swellin' himself out. "Haven't I now?—Curse that tennis," sez he; "if I had let it alone an' practised with the gun all summer, I could shoot midges by now.—Look here," sez he, "I'll send Miss Livingston that brace of wild-duck yet. They'll be late for the dinner-party, but what matter?"

"They needn't be," sez I. "Couldn't ye come out to-morrow evenin' to the marshes?"

"I can't," sez he. "The Quarter Sessions is on. It's a pity too, an' me shootin' the way I am. But I'm prosecutin' in some poachin' cases, an' I must turn up.—But wait, Pat," sez he; "the ducks'll be plentier in a week or two, won't they?"

"With the first touch of frost," sez I, "there'll be dhroves of them."

"Very well," sez he, "the next likely evenin' that ye see any plenty of ducks in the marshes, send for me an' I'll come should it be rainin' conveyances an' snowin' wills. I've got the true knack of shootin', this time. Give me the neb of the duck, till I show it to my articled clerk.—Ye'll not forget, now, to send me word."

So I promised I would not; an' clean forgot all about it till a fortnight aftherwards when I was out myself lookin' for ducks with the old muzzle-loader, an' Big Billy Lenahan of the Hills with me. It was a fine frosty evenin', with just enough ice about to fetch the ducks to the open water, an' I knowed there'd be strings of them coming down the river presently.

"Billy," sez I, "this is just the very night for Mr. Anthony. I must send him word."

An' then I remembered I was makin' a mistake.

"Let him stay at home, the wee gas-bag," sez Billy, with a growl. "Five pounds his long tongue cost me at the Quarter Sessions, bad luck to him."

"If ye let yourself be caught poachin', Billy," sez I, "ye needn't blame Mr. Anthony. He's prosecutin' solicitor, an' he has his duty to do."

"I know he has," sez Billy, "but he needn't have done it that wicked. He promised me he wouldn't press the case; an' then he goes an' gets himself all blew up with his own talk, an' I'm fined five pounds through him, the vain wee cockatoo.—But take your time," sez Billy, "I'll be even with him yet."

"Ach, don't bear malice, Billy," sez I. "There's no harm in Mr. Anthony."

"There's a deal too much of the blether about him in a law-court," sez Billy, still very sour. "He's all gab and guts, like a young crow. But let him come. We'll have some fun out of him, anyway."

So we sent one of the young Robinsons for Mr. Anthony, an' Billy an' I went on afther the ducks. In about half an hour's time he come up behind us, an' him an almighty swell with a fur-lined coat an' his evenin'-dhress below it.

"You're never goin' to shoot ducks in that rig, Mr. Anthony?" sez I.

"I am not," sez he, "worse luck. I'm going out to dine at Miss Armytage's of the Hall. Have ye shot many?"

"Half a dozen, up till now," sez I; "but they'll be comin' along thicker presently."

"Well, bad cess to it," sez Mr. Anthony, very savage. "An' just the evenin' I can't get at them. You'd think they knew they were safe."

"Away home an' change your clothes," sez I, "an' send Miss Armytage word you're not well."

"I can't," sez he, bitin' at his nails; "no, hang it, I can't. Miss Livingston is to be there. Between you an' me, Pat," sez he, "I've given her a hint that I'm going to ask her a question to-night.—But do you an' Billy go on, an' I'll walk with you. I've been readin' up about duck-shootin' since I saw you, an' I might be able to give ye a wrinkle or two."

"Come on, then," sez I. For I seen some very offensive expressions thremblin' on Billy Lenahan's tongue.

A couple of minutes later along comes a pair of ducks just barely within range, an' I fetched the near one down.

"If ye'd waited till the two of them was in line," sez Mr. Anthony, "the one shot would have killed both."

"If you could fly afther them, you could catch them with your hands," sez Billy, very sour. "It's a pity it's not you is carryin' the gun."

"I wish I was," sez Mr. Anthony. "Bad cess to it, I wish I was. I could shoot to-night, I know I could. An' look at the strings of ducks comin' along there, far out. Where's that old pair of wadin' boots I gave you, Pat? If you were only out in the middle there you could shoot rings round you.—Pat," sez he, dancin' round with excitement, "away home for them, quick. Damme, I'll put them on an' have a shot myself. Run; an' don't waste a minit. I must turn up at the dinner. My whole future life might depend on it. But I'd like to have a couple of shots before I commit myself to matrimony. There's no telling what effect marriage might have on my shootin'. Away with you now, quick."

"Ye'd betther wait till you're coming back from the dinner, Mr. Anthony," sez I. "The moon'll be up by then."

"There'll be two moons up by then," sez Mr. Anthony. "Did you ever taste Miss Armytage's port wine?—Go on an' get the boots. Gimme your gun an' the powder an' shot. I'll be loadin' the empty barrel while you're away."

"Betther let Billy load it," sez I. "You have no great experience with a muzzler-loader."

"Blethers," sez Mr. Anthony, layin' hold of the gun, "you'd think I was a beginner to hear you talkin'. I blew the nail off my thumb with a muzzle-loader before Billy was born."

"Keep an eye on him while he's chargin' her," sez I to Billy in an undhertone, "only if you're wise it'll be from behind a tree. I'll be back before he has time to shoot much more than the dog." An' off I went, hot-foot; for I knowed there would be fun before the evenin' was over.

When I got back he was sittin' on a stone in his stocking-feet, waitin'.

"In the name of goodness what kept ye all this time," sez he. "The toes is near froze off me. An' there's not less than five hundhred ducks gone past us.—Here, pull the boots on me, the pair of you, an' I'll lean on the gun."

"If ye fill the muzzle of that gun wi' dirt, Mr. Anthony," sez I, "all ye'll kill this evenin' 'll be a solicitor; for the charge'll come through the near end of her."

"Blast it," sez he, in a splutther, "am I doin' that?—Wait a minit, an' I'll lean on the butt."

"Well, if you think I'm going to pull on your boots with the muzzle of a loaded gun proddin' me in the small of the back, you're mistaken," sez Billy. "I'll hold him, Pat, an' do you pull.—There you are. Away ye go, now; straight in front of you."

"Where are ye sendin' the man, Billy?" sez I. "Come back, Mr. Anthony. You're headin' right for the main dhrain; an' if ye go in there it's a submarine ye'll need instead of wadin' boots.—Keep to your left.—Easy now; don't fire! That's only a coot scutterin' along the top of the wather. Wade as far out as the boots'll let ye. The ducks is frightened of us on the bank here."

"Bad manners to you anyway, with your main dhrain," sez he. "You've shaken my nerve. How will I know the main dhrain if I come on it?"

"You'll know by goin' in over your ears," sez I. "But you're not headin' that way now."

So off he moves through the wather an' mud, going very cautious.

"Why didn't ye let him go on the way he was goin'," sez Billy. "There'll be no sport with him now."

"I never seen him go out with a gun yet that there wasn't sport," sez I. "He'll shoot somethin' he oughtn't to before he goes home; take care it isn't yourself, ye black-hearted ruffian.—Wait; here he's comin' back. What has he done now? Listen to the language of him.—What's wrong, Mr. Anthony?"

"It's them cursed coots," sez he. "The wather was just lippin' up to the top of the boots when a couple of them came splattherin' by, makin' a wake like a steamer; an' there's about two gallon of mud gone down the legs of my evenin' breeches. An' the moths has ate the seat out of the only spare pair I have. Confound it, anyway," sez he, "I may stay at home now."

"Such nonsense," sez I. "Won't your feet be undher the table. If it was your shirt-front was round your legs you might be talkin'.—Hurry up an' try a shot. The light's goin'."

"I might as well let it alone," sez he; "I'm goin' to have

no luck to-night. But I'll have a try, seein' I'm here." An' off he wades again.

"It's the first time I ever went out with him," sez I to Billy, "that he wasn't cock-sure he'd fill his game-bag with one shot. It's a good sign. He'll hit somethin' to-night, see if he doesn't.—Do ye think he loaded that second barrel all right?"

"He did," sez Billy. "I kept a careful eye on him. Just a fair charge he put in, an' no more."

"Watch him, then, Billy," sez I, 'till we see how he does—— Juke down! There's a sthring of ducks comin' between us an' him.—He doesn't see them, the wee donkey. Shout to him, Billy."

"No, don't shout," sez Billy. "There's some beyond him as well.—Is he never goin' to shoot?" sez he, fidgin'. I could see Billy was near as excited as myself. "He sees them," chuckles he. "Look out for fun now."

Up goes Mr. Anthony's gun to his shoulder. He followed the ducks with the muzzle till I was near bursted with holdin' my breath. I could see him bracin' himself up as he pulled the trigger.

"Now for a shower of ducks, Billy," sez I.

There came nothing but the crack of a cap.

"Bad luck to it," sez I, "a missfire. I knowed he wouldn't load her right.—Behind you, Mr. Anthony!" I shouts, leppin' up. "Behind ye!"

He wheeled half-round at the sound of my voice, seen the second lot of ducks, up with the gun again, an' fired. There was a report like the blastin' of a quarry. Mr. Anthony staggered back, recovered himself a bit, clawin' in the air, an' then souse down he went on the broad of his back, an' disappeared.

"Quick, Billy," shouts I; "follow me. He'll be dhrowned! He's in the main dhrain."

"Easy," sez Billy, quite cool, layin' hold of my arm. "He's fifty yards from the main dhrain. There he is on his feet again. Oh, great Christopher," sez he, beginnin' to laugh, "will ye look at him!"

An', troth, though I was heart-sorry for the wee man, I could hardly keep my own face straight. It was just like one of them sea lions bobbin' up out of a tank at the circus, only instead of havin' a sealskin coat on him he was one solid mass of mud an' glar. He turned round a couple of times, gropin' in front of him with his hands, an' then he started off straight for the main dhrain.

"This way, Mr. Anthony," I calls out, when I could find my voice. "Come this way."

He started to come towards the voice, all the time gropin' with his hands, an' wandherin' here an' there as if he was playin' blind-man's buff, an' at last he made the land. The only feature ye could make out in his face was his mouth, an' only that because he kept spittin' out mud an' bits of bulrushes.

"What happened to you at all, at all, Mr. Anthony?" sez I, when we got him a sort of a way cleaned. "Did you trip on anything?"

"Take me home," he splutthers, "take me home out of this. An' send word to Miss Armytage that I'm dying of typhoid. I will be, too, before breakfast-time to-morrow," sez he, spitting out another mouthful of mud. "There's as much sewage gone down my throat as would give typhoid to a carrion-crow.—It was all that d——d old blundherbus of yours. I can handle an ordinary fowlin'-piece with anybody," sez he, "an' well you know it; but I won't undhertake to stand up against the kick of a field-gun. By Heavens, it has a recoil like a howitzer! Take me home, I tell ye; an' if ye ever dig that old infernal machine out of the marsh where it's lyin' this minit, by this an' by that I'll be hanged for ye."

An' not another word could we get out of him till we helped him into his own hall, afther persuadin' the housekeeper that it *was* him.

I walked down the road with Billy, thinkin' very hard, an' every now an' then takin' a look at his face. But he was as solemn as a judge.

"Look here, Billy," sez I, "tell me the truth. Did Mr.

Anthony put only a fair charge into the empty barrel of that gun?"

"He put a fair charge in," sez Billy. "The only thing I wasn't quite sure of at the time," sez he, backin' away from me a step or two, "was whether he was puttin' it into the empty barrel."

I suppose I shouldn't ha' done it; but afther a minit or so I sat down beside Billy, an' laughed till I minded that it was my gun that was lyin' at the bottom of the marsh.

The Footwarmer

I WAS comin' back from Donegal one winter night after buryin' my sister's youngest son,—the only time I ever was in the same cowld county. The train was terrible crowded through there bein' a fair in the neighbourhood, but I happened on a porter that was a Co. Down man, an' he put me intil a first-class carriage all by myself.

I lay back on the cushions, feelin' like the Lord-Leftenant, an' here at the next station wasn't another passenger shoved in as well, an' him third-class, too, by the look of him.

I wasn't a bit pleased, I may tell ye, an' the porter that put him in was less pleased nor me.

"There's a first-class carriage for ye," sez he, very snappy, as if there had been words already between the pair of them. "Maybe that'll content ye. Don't be wipin' your feet on the cushions, now."

But the wee chap he had pushed in—a dapper horsey-lookin' wee fellow—didn't turn a hair.

"If I haven't wiped my feet on your ugly puss," sez he, "it's because I don't want to dirty my boots. Run along to the van, my good fellow," sez he, putting on a great lah-di-dah accent all at once, "an' see if my golf clubs an' the three leather trunks is all right. Here's tuppence for ye."

He picked up the two coppers that the porter threw back at him, an' settled himself down on the seat. I could see him all the time takin' me in with the corner of his eye, an' presently he tries to get me into talk. But I'd been takin' the boy in with the corner of *my* eye; an' when I seen three cards peepin' out of the pocket of his waistcoat I knowed the nature of his business straight away, an' made up my mind to keep myself to myself.

All he could do, he couldn't get me to answer more nor "Yes" and "No"; and in the end he give up in disgust.

"The cushions of a first-class carriage is a d——d sight betther nor the conversation, I'm thinkin'," sez he, half to himself an' all to me. "Give me a decent third for business an' pleasure. Heaven for climate, as the sayin' goes, but hell for company."

With that the door opened an' an ould counthry-lookin' fellow was shoved in—a farmer by the look of him, an' a wee farmer at that.

"Get in there, now," sez the porter, "an' don't be wastin' time. They'll not ate you."

"Quite right, porter," sez the Three-card Man in his fine accent again.—"Make yourself at home, my good fellow," sez he to the ould counthryman. "My friend and I don't mind in the least."

He winked over at me as he said it, an', troth, I had to smile back at him; for he done the thing well. All that the like of them chaps wants is a bit of encouragement; an' he was as pleased as Punch. He took a very hard searchin' look at the ould counthryman.

The ould fellow was sittin' very cautious on the edge of the seat, afther he'd got a bad fright when he sunk down among the springs; an' he wasn't very up-to-date lookin'. The Three-card Man jerks his thumb towards him as much as to say, "Watch me an' you'll see sport," an' moves over opposite to him.

It was a great performance, I'll say that. Before ten minits he had the ould fellow chirpin' like a cricket, an' disgorgin' all the information he had gathered in the whole course of his life; his name, an' where he lived, an' how much land he had, an' what stock he had on it, an' how many childhren an' grandchildhren there was, an' what rent he paid, an' what his wife was called before she was married. An' the whole of it, I declare to you, without him seemin' to ask a question at all. I was glad I hadn't spoke to him myself, for God knows what he'd ha' got out of me.

Then he started to talk himself, an' the lies he told was fit to put the train off the lines. North, South, East an' West he had thravelled,—by his own account; an' everywhere he went there was some bigger wondher happened to him. He had climbed mountains, an' dug gold-mines, an' caught fish, an' killed wild animals, ay, by Heavens, as many as would ha' filled two menageries an' left what over would ha' done a circus. Before he was half through, the ould counthryman's eyes was as big as the headlights of the engine, an' he was clean beyond speech altogether.

In the end the Three-card Man did stop; not because he was done, for he was as full of lies as if the divil had stuffed him like a cushion; but I think he wanted to see what new roguery he could be up to. So he lay back in his seat an' took fresh stock of the old man. Then he saw the ould fellow lookin' very puzzled at the copper footwarmer on the floor, and he sat up again.

"You've never seen one of them before, my friend?" sez he. "Eh?"

"I have not, then, your Honour," said the old man. "A wondherful great traveller like yourself would hardly believe it, but it's the third time in my life I've ever been in a railway-thrain at all. If I dare make bowld to ask your Honour, what might it be for?"

"Thry puttin' your feet on it," sez the Three-card Man, pushin' it over with his toe. "Don't be afraid. It's meant for that. Do you feel any heat?"

"I do, then," sez the old man, afther a minit. "It's the great invention surely."

"That one has been all over the habitable earth with me," sez the Three-card Man, "from Japan to the Cove of Cork. It's been in my father's family for five generations. It's not much to look at, but the price of it would buy a cow."

"Do you tell me that?" sez the old man. "It's not made of gold is it?"

"It is not," sez the Three-card Man. "It's made of fourteen different kinds of metals mixed into one; but the secret of mixin' them has been lost, an' that's why there's such a price on it. There's only seven of them contrivances in the world."

"Do you mind that?" sez the old man, starin' at it. "Only seven of them."

"Only seven of them," sez the Three-card Man. "It's the truth I'm tellin' you. King George has one, an' the President of the United States has one, an' the Emperor of China has one, an' the Czar of Rooshia had one—if the Bolshies hasn't melted it down——"

"They might have," put in the old man; "bedad, they might have."

"An' the Pope has two——"

"It's only right," sez the old man, liftin' his hat.

"He's always had one," said the Three-card Man, "and when the Big War broke out the King of Austria sent him his one, in case he should be beat an' the French get it. That's six of them; an' your two feet is on the seventh."

"It beats all," sez the old man, takin' his feet off it.

"The real beauty of them is this," sez the Three-card Man: "when you once pour the hot water intil them it's a year an' a day before it gets any cooler than when you put it in."

"I've heard of them, now," sez the old man, brightenin' up. "There was a gentleman shootin' over my farm last year had a bottle like that."

"The like of them bottles," sez the Three-card Man, "is only an imitation, an' not the same thing at all. The best of them'll only keep warm for a fortnight, an' even at that you'll have to leave them near the fire. But with these the water won't get cold for the time I tell you. Feel that fellow, now. An' it was filled last July."

"The Saints preserve us!" sez the old man, "it's scaldin' yet."

"It would be a great comfort to ye up among them cowld hills of yours," sez the Three-card Man.

"Ah, them things is not for the likes of me, your Honour," sez the old man, risin' to his feet as the thrain slowed down; "but I'm proud to have seen one of them, anyway. An' I'm thankful to your Honour for lettin' me see it, an' for tellin' me about it."

"Not at all, my good fellow," sez the Three-card Man, mindin' about his fine accent again. "Good night. Don't get out till the train stops. Look here," he sez; the notion catchin' him all at once, "I've taken a fancy to you. I'm going home to be married, an' I'll be thravellin' no more. Damme, I'll give it to you!"

"It's makin' fun of me you are," sez the old man, shakin' his head.

"Not a bit of me," sez the Three-card Man, all excited. "When I take a likin' to a man I'd do anythin' for him. Get out, an' I'll hand it to you."

"The Heavens preserve your Honour," sez the old man, climbing down, "but do you mean it, really?"

"Of course I do," sez the Three-card Man. "Quick, or the thrain'll be started on us. Hold hard, now; it's heavy. Good-bye," he calls out as the thrain begun to move. "Watch nobody takes it off you.—He's away with it," sez he, his head out of the window an' him prancin' his feet with delight. "If he once gets through the station door, he's safe. Wait! The station-master has him—an' the porther. Hold on to it, ye boy ye! Bedambut, the porther's down? Stick to it, ye divil, stick to it!—They're hid round the corner," sez he, dhrawin' in his head. He rowled back on his seat an' crowed wi' delight. "I'd give a pound-note," sez he, "to know will he get clean away."

An' troth, I wouldn't ha' grudged half a sovereign myself.

Link Law

UP till the time the Golf Club was started in Ballygullion there was nothin' for the better class of people to do but drink whiskey an' play tuppeny nap. Very severe the same two occupations was on them, too. We used to use up a dispensary doctor in about ten years; a bank manager seldom lasted above five, an' a cashier about eighteen months; an' as for district inspectors of the polis, they melted like snow off a ditch. The thing begun to be a bit of a scandal in the end, an' at last a few of the leadin' men put their heads together an' determined that some other way of killin' spare time ought to be provided. After a lot of cogitation they hit on the notion of a Golf Club; the divil, I suppose, thinkin' he'd more than make up on his turnover of bad language what he was likely to lose over drink, furthered the scheme all he could; an' a committee was formed, includin' wee Mr. Anthony, the solicitor.

First of all they took a likely piece of ground in Mr. Hastings's demesne. The next thing to be done was to get some knowledgeable man that would show them how to lay it out. The general opinion of the committee was that they should get down one of them fellows that plays golf for their livin'; an' hearin' there was a great swell of a professional player, a Scotchman, comin' over to Belfast about another club, they wrote an' trysted him to come to Ballygullion as well.

So the Scotchman come along, a wee wiry-lookin' hard-faced fellow, an' could lower a power of whiskey without makin' any fuss about it after it was down. He put them all in great heart about the new course, an' told them they'd the makin' of the finest eighteen-hole course in the Three Kingdoms; but I misdoubt somebody must have fetched over a splinter of the Blarney Stone to Scotland a while before he left home; for the night he quitted Ballygullion him an' me had a couple of drinks together, an' he told me it would never be a course till the Day of Judgment.

I went into Ballygullion the next day to tell Mr. Anthony; but when I got to his office, about four o'clock, who should I meet comin' out but himself, an' the wee office-boy behind him with not less nor half a hundred-weight of clubs in a bag on his back.

"The very man I want," sez Mr. Anthony. "There," sez he to the wee boy, "away back an' copy them letters. Do you take the clubs off him, Pat, an' come on to the links with me. Fitzsimons down the street has started the golf. They have a kind of a makeshift hole fixed up, from the bottom of the Whinny Hill to the top, an' Fitzsimons says he did it in fifteen. He's a liar, Pat," sez Mr. Anthony; "an' even if he isn't, I can do it in less. Fifteen!" sez he, "an' it not longer than eighty wards. I shot a rabbit on the top of the same hill last year, an' me standing further back than where they play from. If I can't get into the same hole in five shots I'll give in that Fitzsimons can draft a conveyance better than I can; an' I needn't say more than that.—Away you up to the top of the hill, now. You'll see a jam-pot sunk in the ground beyond the whins; that's the hole. I'll shout before I let fly, an' do you keep a keen eye out for the ball."

"Watch ye don't hit me, Mr. Anthony," sez I.

"What odds if I do?" sez he; "sure the ball is Indian-rubber. It'll bounce off you.—Hold on a minit," pullin' a wee book out of his pocket. "I can't find it," sez he, puttin' the book back in his pocket again; "but I believe I'd lose strokes if I hit you. Better stand well away from the hole."

So I went to the top of the hill an' stood with a foot on each side of the hole, thinkin' that would be the safest place; an' presently Mr. Anthony gives a shout. I seen him square himself an' wave the stick about in the air awhile, an' then he took a terrible wind at the ball.

"I don't know where it's gone, Mr. Anthony," I calls down to him. "I neither heard nor seen it."

"I wasn't tryin' to hit it that time," he shouts. "I was just loosenin' myself a bit. Look out now!"

"I didn't see hint or hare of it, Mr. Anthony," I calls. "Did it come this far?"

"I missed it that time, too," he shouts back, very wicked. "Do you think it's a football I'm aimin' at?"

By this time I could see it was goin' to be a longer job than I'd expected, so I lay down in the bushes an' lit my pipe. The next six wipes Mr. Anthony took at the ball he hit nothin' but wind, an' with every welt he made the eyeglass fell out of his eye. Then he laid the stick down on the ground an' walked about a bit, talkin' to himself. He up with the stick again, an' this time he hit somethin', anyway, for a sod of turf riz up in the air as big as a saddle-cloth; an' with that he turned round towards the wee wood behind him an' threw the stick as far as he could in among the trees. I thought by this he was done for the day, an' riz up to go back to him, when I seen him pluckin' another club out of the bag an' takin' a run-race at the ball. The next minit it come singin' over my head, an' pitched on the ground not twenty yards from the hole. When I looked back Mr. Anthony was gatherin' up his bag. I seen my chance in a flash, run out of the bushes bent double, an' picked up the ball an' popped it into the jam-pot.

"Mr. Anthony," I calls down the hill, "Mr. Anthony, you've put it into the hole."

He stopped dead, an' fixed the eyeglass in tighter.

"What's that?" he shouts. "Did you say *into* the hole?"

"Right in," sez I. "Come an' see for yourself."

He dropped the bag like a hot potato, give a yell an' a couple of steps of a Highland fling, an' then up the face of the hill as hard as he could tear.

"Show me," sez he.

"There it is," sez I. "Look."

I was waitin' to hear him let another yell; but you never knew Mr. Anthony.

"Not a bad shot, Pat," sez he, quite cool, "eh? An' me only a beginner, too. Wait till I'm at it a while. I knew I could do it," sez he, "I knew I could teach that big-headed fellow Fitzsimons a thing or two. It's the theory, Pat. That's where I have the pull over the rest of them; I've read the books.—But they say you have to buy a bottle of whiskey when you get a hole in one. Come on back to Ballygullion till I get a bottle an' fetch it down an' give Fitzsimons a glass. He'll choke on it, he'll be that gunked.—A hole in one shot, Pat," sez he, gettin' excited again. "It'll be a record on this course till all eternity."

"What about the times you missed the ball altogether, Mr. Anthony?" sez I.

"Eh?" sez he, very sharp. He stopped his jigs all at once, an' stood lookin' at me.—"That's all right, Pat," sez he, after a minit. "The game doesn't start till you hit the ball.—Come on down till I get my clubs, an' then we'll be off an' catch Fitzsimons before he leaves his office."

He pushed through the whins lookin' as if he was thinkin' very hard. "Pat," sez he, presently, "I wouldn't say anything to Fitzsimons about the times I missed the ball. He's an ignorant fellow, an' might try to make little of me. I'll go down to his office by myself. I wouldn't like to crow over him before anybody. But I tell you what I'll do. The Golf Club'll be open in a month's time. I'll go into trainin' from now till then, an' I'll challenge Fitzsimons to play me for ten pounds. If I do, will you come an' carry my bag?"

"Come!" sez I. "I'll come if I have to leave the praties rottin' in the drill."

"Very well," sez he, "I'll send you word."

Right enough I got a letter from him in about five weeks' time sayin' the match was on for the followin' day.

As I was goin' up the street next day to keep my appointment I met the wee office-boy, an' he told me I was to turn back an' wait for Mr. Anthony at the end of the town. Presently he comes along, an' a most lamentable swell he was, in a shootin'-jacket an' knickbockers, an' a pair of fancy stockin's with tops on them as bright as the head-lights of a motor-car.

"I had to meet you here, Pat," sez he. "Old Mrs. McIlheron, of Pennyquirk, sent word she was comin' to the office to make her will, an' I wouldn't ha' got clear of her before dark. Confound her, anyway," sez he. "I wish she'd go mad all out instead of stoppin' half-way, an' then we could put her in the asylum an' have done with her."

Ye must know that this Mrs. McIlheron was an old widow-woman wi' no children, that had left Belfast an' bought a place near Ballygullion when her husband died. She had got very odd, livin' by herself, an' spent near her whole time knittin' stockin's for the heathen an' makin' whatever kind of wills she thought would give most annoyance when she was dead. One time she'd go to Fitzsimons, an' the next time she'd go to Mr. Anthony, an', troth, the pair of them must ha' made near as much out of her as kept them in pocket-money.

"I wonder you'd run the risk of missin' her, Mr. Anthony," sez I. "She might ha' left you a legacy. Maybe she's away to Fitzsimons now."

"Let her go," sez Mr. Anthony, "the thrawn old divil. When I make her will she leaves a legacy to Fitzsimons, an' when he makes her will she leaves a legacy to me. She says it's for fear the will would be disputed. To pot with her. I'll make more out of Fitzsimons this evenin' than I would out of her."

"You think you'll beat him, then?" sez I.

"Beat him!" sez Mr. Anthony. "I could beat Vardon. An' mind you, Pat, I wouldn't ha' said that this time yesterday. It's a most cursed game. You'll be drivin' like a professional on Tuesday, an' if you part your hair differently on Wednesday d——n the ball you can hit. But I've bottomed it at last. I don't suppose there's another man in Ireland has mastered it but myself. There was just the one wee thing wrong, an' I found it out yesterday evenin'. Show me one of them clubs," sez he, bringin' an' old ball out of his pocket.

"Wait till we get off the county road," sez I. "You'll only break the stick here."

"Not a bit of me," sez he. "I could play a ball off a soap-bubble.—But never mind. We're late as it is. You'll see it all when I'm playin' Fitzsimons. Do you hear me, Pat? I wouldn't take nine pound nineteen an' ninepence for my chance of that ten-pound note. Hurry up, till I get started to him."

When we got to the course we could see Fitzsimons standin' waitin' for us with one of his clerks holdin' his bag of clubs.

"Blast him," sez Mr. Anthony, "he's a long-headed fellow too. Now he has two legal opinions to one, an' that blackguard of his would swear a hole in a door. Do you take this"—he handed me a wee book—"an' if there's a difference between Fitzsimons an' me look into that as wise as you can, an' whatever I say you swear to.—Here we are, Fitzsimons. Blaze away."

Fitzsimons is a long dry cautious fellow, an' I could see he wasn't goin' to be rushed.

"After you, Anthony," sez he. "You're the senior solicitor in the town."

"So I am," sez Mr. Anthony, all pleased. "So I am. I'd better drive, then.—Wait a minit, till I get out my notebook. I want to mark down my score."

He turned his back on Fitzsimons, took a hasty skelly at the notebook, an' put it back in his pocket. Then he pulls a club out of his bag, an' perches his ball up on a wee hill of sand. Whatever he read in the book, I could see his lips goin' as he muttered it over to himself. He laid the head of his club down behind the ball, kept it there till he must have counted five-an'-twenty at the very least, then drew back like lightnin' an' fetched a most wicked dunch at the ball. He just all but missed it. It flew off at right angles an' took Jones, the articled clerk, in the waistcoat. Jones doubled in two with a gulp, the clubs flew out of his hand, an' he sat down sudden on the grass an' started rubbin' himself.

Fitzsimons run over to see was his man killed; but divil a hare Mr. Anthony cared whether the ball had went out through him.

"That's my hole, Fitzsimons," sez he. "That's my hole.—I aimed for him, Pat," sez he, in a half-whisper. "He was standin' too far in front, an' I saw my chance. Fetch out the wee blue book an' look up rule eighteen. One up to me," sez he as Fitzsimons pulled the clerk to his legs; "I get that hole."

"You should get fourteen days for assault an' battery," sez Fitzsimons, very savage. "How do you make it your hole?"

"Your caddy interfered with my ball," sez Mr. Anthony. "Read him rule eighteen, Pat.—Wait, I'll read it: 'If a player's ball when in motion be interfered with in any way by an opponent or his caddie'—I think you'll admit that my ball was in motion——"

I took a look at Jones, an' by the colour of his face he didn't look like disputin' it, anyway.

"An' Jones is your caddie," goes on Mr. Anthony.

"He is not," snaps Fitzsimons. "He's my clerk. A caddie is a boy employed by the Club——"

"Blethers," sez Mr. Anthony, breakin' in. "Of course he's your caddie. Isn't he carryin' your clubs?"

"It doesn't matter," sez Fitzsimons, settin' his lips very obstinate. "The Club doesn't pay him.—Now you can't get over that, Anthony."

"I can get over it, an' I will get over it," sez Mr. Anthony. "Are you content to state a case to the Golfin' Union?"

"I am," sez Fitzsimons, "an' I'll draw up a memorandum when I get back to the office. Are you better, Jones? All right; reach me my driver."

So Fitzsimons made another wee hill of sand an' perched up his ball an' took a shot at it. As I said, he was a cautious old boy, Fitzsimons; an' he didn't go back near as far as Mr. Anthony, an' not half as fast. But for all that he missed the ball teetotally altogether.

"One!" sez Mr. Anthony.

"What's one?" snaps Fitzsimons at him. "The game doesn't start till you hit the ball. Didn't you tell me that in my own office the day you said you got the practice hole in one, an' repeated it over an' over again till I was scunnered listenin' to you?"

"That's right, Mr. Anthony," sez I. "I mind you tellin' me——"

But Mr. Anthony give me a look that near burned a hole in me.

"I may have thought that at the time, Fitzsimons," sez he, "but on reading the rules I found out my mistake."

"Ay, but read this one," sez Fitzsimons, luggin' out a wee book of his own. "Rule two: 'A match begins by each side playing a ball from the first teeing-ground.' I haven't played my ball off the teeing-ground. There it's sittin'. This match isn't started yet."

"Show me," sez Mr. Anthony. He read the rule over very carefully, pluckin' at his lower lip.

"Well, what do you make of it?" sez Fitzsimons, crowin'.

"For the love of goodness, Mr. Anthony, give in to him," sez I. "We're here a quarter of an hour as it is, an' if we go on at this rate we'll not be finished till about Tuesday week."

"You can go on, without prejudice," sez Mr. Anthony. "I'll look up the authorities afterwards. But seein' that the match isn't started, I'll have another shot, too."

So Fitzsimons takes a gingerly sort of whack at his ball, an' knocked it about fifty yards along the course. You could see Mr. Anthony's lip curlin' at all the length it travelled.

"I can betther that, Fitz," sez he. He screwed the eye-glass tight into his eye, set his teeth an' knocked the ball a good hundred an' fifty yards as straight as an arrow.

"Didn't I tell you I had mastered this game, Pat," sez he. "It's hardly decent to take the money off him. I should ha' laid him two to one."

"Take your time, Mr. Anthony," sez I. "You have a lot of lepps to clear yet."

An' sure enough the next wallop he took he sunk the ball out of sight in a grassy bank in front of him. The ground was purty soft, an' I don't believe any man livin' could ha' found it, short of puttin' in a ferret. So Mr. Anthony lost the hole; an' he was that mad about the simple way it had happened that he took five skites at the next teein'-ground, as they call it, before he hit the ball at all, an' lost that hole too. I thought he was clean beat altogether, for Fitzsimons kept askin' him every five or six yards if that was two up, till Mr. Anthony was near purple in the face wi' rage. However, the anger stood well to him, for he hit the ball such a punch that it took Fitzsimons three goes to get up to him, an' Mr. Anthony won that hole four shots to the good.

The next three holes was among the whinny ground, an' they both lost their balls at the whole three, an' had to call quits. Then they come to the hole that Mr. Anthony had done at one, an' tryin' to do it over again he knocked the ball into a whin-bush behind him, an' took twenty-four. That left him two holes to the bad; but he wasn't a bit daunted, an' won the next hole in a canter, through Fitzsimons losin' count.

Fitzsimons was only one up now; an' he didn't hold his lead very long.

At the next hole he was switherin' what club he should take, an' turned an' asked Jones. Jones, by the look on his face, didn't care what club he took, but advised again a wooden one.

"That'll do," sez Mr. Anthony, pullin' out his wee blue book. "My hole. Rule four: 'A player accepting advice from any one but his caddie loses the hole.' "

"Jones is my caddie," snaps Fitzsimons.

"He wasn't at the first hole," sez Mr. Anthony. "You can't have it both ways."

"We stated a case at the first hole," sez Fitzsimons. "It's not decided yet."

"I'll make you a present of the case," sez Mr. Anthony. "If you win it, you lose this one."

"All I have to say, gentlemen," sez I, "is if you're goin' to make this a lawsuit instead of a golfin' match ye'd betther put it off till the Assizes an' engage a Special Jury."

"Murphy's right," growls Fitzsimons. "You can have the hole to save time."

"I settled him there, Pat," sez Mr. Anthony to me. "What? He's beat now. I've established my legal superiority. I'm better than he is even with my hands, but it's the head that counts. This is a game you play with your head. I've been forgettin' that. I'll out-general him now—damme, I'll out-general him. How many holes are there to go?"

"Seven," sez I, reckonin' up.

"Very well," sez Mr. Anthony. "I'll beat him seven up.—Wait; we'll allow one for accidents; say six up. Gimme that driver."

However, whether Mr. Anthony's brains wasn't workin' at their best, or whether it was his hands was at fault, or whether the two weren't comin' in at the same time, when they got to the last hole but one nobody was anythin' to the good.

Mr. Anthony should ha' won the hole hands down.

Fitzsimons had been doin' great work in the bad ground with a weapon he called a niblick, a short-handled club with a face on it the size of a full moon; but working along the edge of the county road he hit a "Trespassers Prosecuted" notice crossways with it, an' the head of the club took near five minutes to come down. All Mr. Anthony had to do then was to keep cool; but takin' a lamentable wallop just to make sure of the hole, the club flew out of his hands into the Scroggy Wood an' was never seen again, an' that made him as mad as Fitzsimons was. Jones an' I told them they were quits when they both got into the hole, but, troth, it would ha' took an accountant to come to the rights of the matter.

"Never mind," sez Mr. Anthony to me, full of heart; "you can't help your hands gettin' slippy. If I'd bought tuppence-worth of cobbler's wax in Ballygullion, I'd 'a had him beat half an hour ago. Watch me now, Pat, when I'm up again it."

Fitzsimons was shakin' like a leaf when he stood up to play, but the ball must ha' got in the way of a bad trimmle of his hands, for it went off well down the course. As Mr. Anthony reached for his club, who should come out from among the trees but old Mrs. McIlheron, an' makes towards the teein'-ground.

"Gimme that club quick, Pat," sez he. "If she gets a hold of me before I drive, the hole is lost."

"Stop, Mr. Anthony, stop!" sez I. "You'll kill the woman."

"I don't give a d——n," sez he. "Sure her will's made."

I suppose the hurry put the nervousness out of him; anyway he hit that ball near two hundred yards, an' well over her head.

"Come on," sez he. "The old divil can wait till I've the hole won."

An' as we went along hot-foot, out strolls one of Mr. Hastings's bullocks from the bushes, picks up Mr. Anthony's ball in its mouth and starts to chew it as unconcerned as if it was a carrot.

With that Mr. Anthony let one yell and up the course like a madman, whirlin' the club round his head an' cursin' like a tinker. The old lady seen him comin', an' just give a squawk an' sat down in one solid lump. Mr. Anthony went past her like an express train at a country station, makin' at the bullock. But the bullock was as cool as a china egg, an' stood there chewin' away, with the strings of guttapercha hangin' out of his mouth. When Mr. Anthony got within ten yards of him he begun to see there was no great friendship intended to him, an' he slipped by Mr. Anthony at a trot, headin', as luck would have it, right for Mrs. McIlheron. All the yells Mr. Anthony had let out of him was nothin' to the screechin' of the poor old lady then. The three of us started the runnin'; but Mr. Anthony came in first an' headed the bullock off just in time.

It took us fifteen minutes by the clock to persuade her she wasn't dead, an' another fifteen to get her to Mr. Hastings's gate lodge. I thought the golfin'-match was ended by all this; but I might ha' knowed Mr. Anthony better. Back he would go to finish it out; an' Fitzsimons, hopin' the bullock was chewin' his cud on the pulp of the ball by this time, was just as keen. So we tucked Mrs. McIlheron up at the fire, sent the lodge-keeper's wee son into Ballygullion for the doctor, an' back to the course again.

Mr. Anthony wouldn't give in that the bullock could ha' swallowed the ball at the rate he'd been runnin', an' sure enough we found it on the edge of the long grass—what was left of it. The whole cover was full of dinges an' cuts, an' the inside was hangin' round it in strings like the whiskers of a mountainy farmer.

"The match is mine," sez Fitzsimons, rubbin' his hands. "You can't play that thing."

"Can I not!" sez Mr. Anthony, scringein' his teeth. "I could play it if it was in jelly. Gimme that iron."

He hit at the ball most vicious, an' knocked it out on the cut grass, an' then started flailin' it along next the hole, the rest of us followin' without a word, for I believe he'd ha' killed any man that spoke above his breath. Every welt took the ball along about twenty yards; for, of course, it wouldn't carry in the air; an' wherever it lit it stopped. But there was an advantage in that, too, for Mr. Anthony kept the course for the first time that day—till he got within thirty yards of the hole, an' then, hittin' extra hard, he went out to the right. The ball struck a long trailer of a brier an' hung there by the whiskers, about three feet off the ground.

"That ends him," sez I to myself; an', troth, I was sorry, for he was showin' a great heart.

But not a bit of it. He aimed a bitter blow at the brier. Up went the ball in the air, an' lit on the green not six inches from the hole.

"Did you see that, Pat?" sez Mr. Anthony. "Did you see the generalship of them last two shots, one to get the ball up off the ground an' the next one beside the hole? I could never have rolled it up as accurate as that. You must pitch the ball up to the hole—Vardon says that. I'll be down in one more, an' I'm only twenty-two so far. Where are you, Fitzsimons?"

One of us looked at the other.

"God bless my soul," sez Fitzsimons, "I forgot all about my ball!"

An' so he had, an' so had all of us, watchin' the antics of Mr. Anthony.

"Come on back an' we'll watch you playin' up," sez Mr.

Anthony. "Walk alongside of him, Pat," he whispers, "an' just smile every time he misses a shot. His nerve'll be gone with the recovery I've made when he thought he had me beat. It'll be like fallin' out of a balloon to him. He has only twenty-one to win, an' it'll take him fifty.—Begad," he sez, "shootin's nothin' to this game; an' look at the money you make!"

There's no doubt Mr. Anthony had a head on him, though some of his capers would make you think he hadn't. The divil a ball could Fitzsimons hit. He hit them into the ground, an' he dug holes behind them you could plant a bush in, an' he welted them up trees an' into rushes; but anywhere except along the course. Mr. Anthony opened his mouth two or three times to encourage him, an' I'll do him the justice to say that he closed it again; but the smile on his face was deservin' of sudden death. At last Fitzsimons hit a lucky one an' landed on the green.

"How many is that?" sez Mr. Anthony.

"Twenty-nine," sez Fitzsimons; an' he wasn't more than ten short of the count.

"You needn't hole out," sez Mr. Anthony. "I'm down in twenty-three."

"I *will* hole out," sez Fitzsimons, very short.

So he steadied himself an' was down in five more shots.

"That's thirty-four," sez Mr. Anthony. "An' this is twenty-three, as I said," sez he, knockin' his ball into the hole. "Hand over ten pounds, Fitzsimons. You never had a chance. I'll give you five up the next time."

"Wait a minit," sez Fitzsimons. "Your ball's not in the hole yet."

We all gaped at him.

"Are you blind?" sez Mr. Anthony. "Don't you see it's in the hole."

"It's not all in the hole," sez Fitzsimons. "The half of the stuffin' isn't in yet."

"Bless my soul, Mr. Anthony," sez I, dumbfoundered, "he's correct there." For wee worms of rubber were stickin' out all round the hole.

"That's all right," sez Mr. Anthony, not a bit put about. "I have ten strokes to spare." An' he starts to scrape in the bits of rubber.

"My hole," sez Fitzsimons, with as near a chuckle as I ever heard him give, "an' my match.—Rule five: 'The ball must not be pushed, scraped, nor spooned.' "

"I wasn't scrapin' the ball," sez Mr. Anthony. "The ball's in the hole."

But I could hear by the sound of his voice his heart wasn't in the words.

"You were scrapin' part of the ball," sez Fitzsimons, "an' you know it, too. I'll trouble you for ten pounds."

"Wait till I read that rule again," sez Mr. Anthony. He took out his own wee book an' looked at it a long time, fluttherin' the leaves an' readin' here an' there. Then the eyeglass fell from his eye an' he reached for his pocket. Ye'd ha' felt sorry to look at him.

But Fitzsimons wasn't a bit sorry, nor Jones either; Fitzsimons smiled over at Jones, an' Jones give his waistcoat a rub an' smiled back at him, as much as to say, "He's paid out now."

It was too much for Mr. Anthony. He pulled his hand out of his pocket again.

"I won't pay a penny," sez he, "till I get a decision on this, not if that long ruler of a fellow of yours should rub the buttons of his waistcoat into the rings of his spine. I'll state a case, Fitzsimons, I'll state a case to the Golfin' Union; an' when it's decided you'll pay me, you'll see that. Come on, Pat." An' away he tears towards the county road.

"I doubt them fellows'll give it again you, Mr. Anthony," sez I, as we went along.

"Let them," sez he, between his teeth. "I'll take it to the House of Lords.—Could you identify that bullock?" sez he. "If you think you can I'll come back some evenin' an' assassinate the dirty brute. Go on home now, Pat. I'm in a bad temper. Don't say a word till ye hear from me."

Nothin' happened for the next four or five weeks barrin' that old Mrs. McIlheron went back to Belfast an' died there.

But one day I got a note from Mr. Anthony to meet him at Fitzsimon's office.

When I went in, there was Fitzsimons an' Jones sittin' as solemn as undertakers, an' Mr. Anthony smilin' like a basket of chips.

"By the hokey," sez I, "he's won after all."

"Now, gentlemen," sez Mr. Anthony, "you know why we're met—to hear the decision of the Golfin' Union. Well, here it is——" We all craned forward.—" 'Mr. Fitzsimons wins the last hole, an' the match.'—There's your ten pounds, Fitzsimons," sez he. "You'd better bring a performin' goat next time, that'll swallow the ball altogether. But there's another communication I want to read you. It's a letter from Samuels an' Samuels, the solicitors in Belfast, to say that the late Mrs. McIlheron has left me a legacy of three hundred pounds in recognition of my gallant conduct in rescuin' her from the attack of a mad bull on the Ballygullion Golf Course.—That leaves me two hundred an' ninety pounds up, Fitzsimons. Good-day to you. Come on, Pat."

"Did you think, Pat Murphy," sez he, as we went down the road, "that I was such an ass as to let the game of golf interfere with my business? What did I care if that greedy crow of a bullock give himself appendicitis eatin' golf-balls when I saw such a chance of clenchin' my position with a client, an' one with a weak heart, too. I may tell you I'm disappointed. I expected five hundred at the least."

I looked at him to see did he mean it; but he was payin' no attention to me at all.

"Yes," sez he. "Five hundred at the very least.—But never mind, Pat," sez he, brightenin' up. "If I play Fitzsimons once a fortnight for ten pounds, I'll have it up to five hundred by Christmas."

The Homecoming

I MIND young Dick Leonard as well as if it was yesterday —a wee white-haired laddie goin' down the loanin' to school, as lively as a cricket an' as mischievous as a monkey. Ye'd ha' heard the laughs an' kee-hoes of him a couple of fields away.

God alone knows how it was he grew up the way he did; for he had the good care an' the kindly rearin'. But, troth, there's times I think there were mistakes made.

The mother was a wee, nervous, timid bein'; an' with Dick the only child, she lived in a continual dread that somethin' would happen to him, an' jinneyed after him an' danced attendance on him till he used to play outrageous pranks just to show his comrades he was no mollycoddle.

Then the father went to clean the other extreme. He was just as much wrapped up in the boy as the mother was—maybe more; for he was a quiet distant man, an' said little. But seein' the mother too soft, an' dreadin' the lad bein' spoiled, he was that hard on him that, 'deed, he helped to make a kind of a hypocrite of him.

For when the boy got into some divilment or other, as boys will, an' it came out, the fear of the father's stick made him lie like a Trojan. An' with the mother at his elbow to back him up—for she dreaded the lickin' worse even than the boy did—he got that clever at the last that he could ha' looked ye straight in the face an' told a lie that would have imposed on a counsellor.

An' so when Dick, like many another high-spirited young fellow goin' out among company, begun to take a glass or two, he was always able to throw dust in the father's eyes. He was a merry, takin' chap, an' well liked on all sides; an' though everybody soon begun to see he was fonder of dhroppin' into Michael Casshidy's public-house than was anyway good for him, nobody would split; an' the poor foolish mother would see nothin'; till the dhrink had got a fair hold of Dick before the father had even an inklin' that he took a dhrop at all.

But when it all came out, as sooner or later it was bound to do, there was fair murdher—bargein', an' swearin', an' threatenin'; an' one night a wicked thrashin' that only hardened the young fellow.

Of course the poor mother still stood Dick's friend.

If it could be done at all, she smuggled him out of the father's way till he was fit to be seen. An' if that couldn't be done, she stood between the father an' him, an' saved him an' excused him all she was able.

"There now, there now, Hughey, be aisy on the boy, be aisy on him," she'd still cry. "He didn't mean to take too much, oh, no, he didn't mean it. Sure it's the last half-glass that does it all."

But, troth, poor Dick begun to take the last half-glass too often, till he was little betther than a common tippler; an' when the mother could hide it from herself no longer she just quietly took to her bed an' died.

The death of the mother sobered Dick a bit; an' for a couple of days he never touched the whiskey. But the father's upbraidin' dhriv him back to it in a kind of despair; an' at the funeral the old man walked behind the coffin alone; for Dick was lyin' at home speechless drunk.

Everybody said it was only a matther of time with him, now that the mother was gone; but they were wrong, as it turned out.

All at once there came a change in Dick. He stopped goin' into Ballygullion near altogether; an' the odd times he did venture in he could never be got to go near Michael's for all his old cronies could do in the way of jeerin' an' persuadin'. He begun to work about the farm again, too, as hard an' regular as if he was earnin' his day's pay; an' the father an' him, that hadn't 'changed friendly words for six months before the mother's death, got as thick as thieves again. Before long the ould man's pride in him grew up stronger than ever; an' he begun to spake of "my son Dick" with the ould tone in his voice.

I need hardly tell ye there was a girl in the question; for sure they're at the bottom of all the good an' bad is in the world.

The sudden turn in Dick bothered all the ould weemin in the parish to explain, at first; but it wasn't long till it come out that Dick an' big Margit Stevenson was trysted to be married, an' that she'd made him swear off the drink for the rest of his days before she'd promise him.

It seemed desperate sudden to happen so soon afther the mother's death, an' no word of it before; but I think maybe it was the mother's death was the cause of it.

For Dick had been used to havin' a woman makin' much of him from he was born, an' when the mother went the world was a very cold place to him. So he just turned to the first one he could get sympathy from; an' Margit was the nearest-hand. She an' the aunt lived only a couple of fields away; an' it had always been a comfortin' kind of place to drop into when the father made it clean unbearable for Dick at home.

If he had got the right woman, it might ha' been a thorough job wi' Dick. A wife can do more with a man than his mother can; partly, in troth, because she won't put up with as much from him. But Margit wasn't the right woman.

A dashin', tear-away girl, that could ha' kept him a bit in hand, an' laughed at him when he made a fool of himself, might ha' held him all his days. Margit was too miserable an' melancholy, an' took things too serious altogether.

When the first freshness begun to wear off Dick's good behaviour, an' he begun to take an odd drop again, instead of lightin' on him with a skreigh, or laughin' at him an' coaxin' him a bit, Margit always took to the cryin'.

Now Margit was one of them tall, stoopin' delicate weemin, wi' not too much blood in them, that a cold wind blows all the good looks out of; an' whenever she cried the sorrow went to the point of her nose, and clean ruined her appearance; so I need hardly tell ye her cryin' did more harm than good.

It was a pity, too; a pity for Margit worse than for Dick.

For she was a lovin', big-hearted, anxious crather, the kind of woman that everybody tramples on, an' everybody turns to; an' if God had been good to her she might ha' been the great mother to some man's childher. But as for Dick, I doubt the bad was in him.

For a long while he behaved wondherful, considherin'; but all at once he made a break; an' the latter end of him was worse than the beginnin'; drinkin' an' card-playin', an' bettin'—ay, an' worse, if all people said was true.

It fell on the poor ould man like a thunderclap.

I think he'd thought more of Dick when he took himself up than ever he did before he fell away at all; an' the pride of him to watch Dick an' Margit walkin' arm-in-arm about the place was somethin' wondherful to see.

He'd taken the terrible fancy to Margit, partly on her own account, but more for the hand he thought she had made of Dick; an' he could hardly bear to let her out of his sight. An' when Dick turned to his ould way of goin' again, he took near as much throuble to hide it from Margit as the mother used to take to hide it from himself.

When the son would come home of a night, dhrunk to the world, the ould man would trail him up to bed, and then make off across the fields to explain to Margit that the boy wasn't well an' had just laid down for a while. An' then the next mornin' he'd have her over by the skreek of day an' leave the two of them together, hopin' she'd get a fresh hold of Dick.

It was pitiful to see him hangin' about, eyein' them every time he thought they weren't lookin', an' muttherin' to himself—troth, I think it was prayers.

'Twas about this time I begun to notice a great change in Hughey. All the ould distant, stand-off manner was goin' off him, an' he begun to blether an' wander to me about Dick in a way I'd never knowed him do before—all anxious and disthressed, instead of angry an' savage the way he used to be.

An' still he would pretend that Margit had done wondhers wi' the son.

"Ay, Pat," he'd say to me, when he'd meet me of a mornin' afther Dick had been on a bad spree, "I was just watchin' Margit an' the boy there takin' a walk to themselves. She's a fine girl Margit, a great girl, an' a great hand she's made of Dick. He used to take a wee dhrop, Pat; but Margit has worked the quare change on him. He's another lad now, Pat, another lad. He maybe takes an odd wee dhrop still; but he'll never be the same ould wild Dick while Margit's there. It's a comfort to know that, Pat, it's a comfort, isn't it?" An' all the time he'd keep lookin' up in your face to see if he could gather a bit of hope to himself.

But when things begun to go from bad to worse a kind of anger begun to grow in him again Margit.

He had seen the change she wrought in Dick before, an' he still trusted an' persuaded himself that she could do the same again; but when he couldn't deceive himself any longer he began to turn again her day by day.

At first it was a kind of a blind anger at her disappointin' his hope; but it wasn't long till he begun to blame Dick's dhrop-back on her, an' make her an excuse for him.

An' Dick was sharp enough to see what was in the ould man's mind, an' wicked enough to play up to it.

When he went off on one of his bursts it was a fine excuse to say that 'twas Margit was dhrivin' him to it. She was hard on him, he said, an' cold with him. She didn't want him any longer. It was breakin' his heart, an' sendin' him to the divil.

"The boy's ill-used, Pat; the poor fellow's ill-used," the ould man would say to me. "Sure he worships the very ground she walks on; and she doesn't care a traneen for him. Oh, ay, ye may talk. But it's true, it's true;—ye don't know all I know. An' it's ruinin' him, that's what it's doin'! Look how he took up afther the mother's death. Would he be goin' the way he is now if somethin' wasn't dhrivin' him?" An' ye might as well save your breath as try to reason with him.

Of course it all turned out as ye might expect.

There was a terrible scene in the kitchen one night, with the ould man takin' Dick's part; an' the end of it was Margit slipped the ring off her finger an' ran home to cry herself sick, an' Dick took away upstairs to bed with a bottle of whiskey an' dhrank himself near into the horrors.

The ould man stuck to it all ways that the whole thing was Margit's fault; an' when Dick still went as fast to the bad as ever, he railed at her on every side as the ruination of his boy.

But Margit just moved about pale an' red-eyed, an' broken-hearted lookin'; an' when some of the ould man's talk come back to her, as ye may be sure it did, she turned quietly away an' said nothin'.

An' presently his tongue quit Margit.

For all sparks of decency seemed to leave Dick as time went on; an' one mornin' the whole countryside was ringin' wi' the news that he'd put another man's name to a bill an' had 'listed an' left the counthry.

The father paid the money, an' never gave a sign; but the disgrace near killed him.

For a wheen of weeks nobody seen him at all; an' when he had to go the length of Ballygullion at the last, he just slunk in an' out like a ghost, speakin' to nobody, an' crossin' over the road if he seen a neighbour comin'. He even sacked the servant-girl at home, and begun to cook an' do for himself.

Every now an' then a letther come for him in Dick's handwritin'; an' the next day he'd go into the town an' buy a postal ordher, an' send it off to some barracks in London.

I doubt there was no good news in any of the letthers. Every one he got seemed to add a year to his age; an' Pether the Post tould me he'd as soon deliver the whole rest of the mailbag as one letther to Hughey, it was that miserable to see him thrimmlin' when he took it in his hand.

He got desperate suspicious about his letthers, too—for he knowed the curiosity there must be about Dick—an' used to turn them all round in his hand to see if they'd been interfered with; an' at last one day he got a letther of Dick's a bit tore he flew into a fearful rage, an' swore there'd no more letthers of his come through the pack of busybodies was in Ballygullion post office; but he would get them sent to Belfast an' travel for them; an' so he did, from that on.

But odd rumours about Dick went round from time to time, nobody knowed from where.

One had it that he'd taken himself up, an' was doin' well; an' another that he was behavin' badly, an' had been threw out of the army. An' at last somebody brought out a yarn that he was dead.

Margit came round cryin' to me the night she heard that report, to ask if it was true; but I was just as wise as herself. Indeed, God forgive me, I tould her it was very likely; for there was a heavy farmer in the neighbourhood, one Robinson by name, comin' a deal to her aunt's house at the time. The sough was that he was afther Margit; an' I thought a pity that she should be losin' her chances for the sake of a blackguard like Dick. The truth is, nobody knew anything about Dick but the ould man, an' he would say nothin'.

But after a while everybody began to notice a difference in him. The anxious, frightened look left him, an' he began to pass the time of day with a neighbour again, an' go out among people a bit, brighter an' happier-lookin' than he'd been since Dick left home.

Nobody had the face to mention the son to him for a long time, till at last big Mrs. Renaghan—"Ould Curiosity," as they called her—stopped him one day in Ballygullion sthreet an' asked him plump an' plain had there been any news of Dick lately.

The ould man turned as white as a sheet, an' went all of a thrimmle, but never spoke.

"Ye won't think it imperent of me askin' ye, Misther Leonard," sez she; "but Dick was a great favourite with us all, an' we'd be glad to hear of him doin' well. He had his wee failin's like the rest of us, but for my part I always said ye'd live to be proud of him yet."

Still the ould man never spoke; but the tears come rushin' to his eyes, an' he wrung her hand as he turned away. But everybody in Ballygullion that day noticed that he was houldin' his head higher all afthernoon, and no one knowed what to make of it when the story went round.

The next market-day he met "Ould Curiosity" face to face on the footpath. She looked four ways at once, not knowin' what to say or do; but this time the ould man stopped her himself, an' wrung her hand again.

"It was kind of ye to ask about the boy, Mary," sez he, "kind an' friendly." Then he stopped dead for a minit an' looked all round.—"There's good news of him, Mary," he burst out at the last, "good news. I'm havin' letthers regular from him, an' he's doin' well."

The word went through Ballygullion market like wildfire, an' 'deed, I thought better of people to see the way they crowded round the ould man, an' shook hands with him, an' wished him joy, an' cracked up Dick for what he never was.

For a week or two Hughey was kind of frightened an' nervous when one an' another stopped him an' spoke about Dick, an' could say little or nothin' but that the lad was doin' well, doin' well; but after a while he begun to talk a bit more an' give the inquisitive ones news.

It seemed that the regiment had been ordered to India, an' that Dick had been very ill after he'd got there, with the climate, an' when he thought he was dyin' he wrote to the father that if God spared him he'd be a changed man. He did get better, an' kept his promise; an' from that on he never looked back, but was as steady as a rock, an' was a corporal now, an' soon lookin' to be a sergeant.

It was great news, sure enough, an' did the ould man good to tell it. The whole nervousness an' oddness left him. He couldn't talk enough about Dick now; an' when he'd been speakin' to one or two, an' minded somethin' more, he'd run back after them to tell it.

Bein' a neighbour, I wasn't the last to look in on him, as ye may guess; an' him an' me had some powerful collogues.

"Pat," sez he to me one night, lookin' at me very hard as I was risin' to go, "can ye keep a thing to yourself, can ye now?"

"Of course I can," sez I, all agog; "what is it, Hughey?" —For he was still lookin' hard at me, hesitatin'-like.

"D'ye mind Peter O'Rourke's son," he goes on suddenly, "that joined the army, an' they took him intil the Paymasther's office because he was a smart fellow; an' he got on, an' got a good job, an' his father had to go security for him? D'ye mind that, Pat?"

"To be sure I do," sez I.

"Well," sez he, "the same has happened to Dick. He was aye smart at the figurin', ye know, an' they've took him intil the office out there.—I didn't know whether to tell it to ye or not," sez he, looking away from me, an' all stumblin' over his words. "The boy was in trouble before he left, an' people might say he'd get into trouble again if he was in among money. Ye'd maybe better not mention it. I'd be afraid of what folks might think."

"An' is that all?" sez I. "Such nonsense. Nobody would think anythin' of the kind. They'd all be delighted, an' Peter O'Rourke the most of the lot. Tell everybody. There'll not be a man or woman in the parish won't envy ye."

"Do ye think so, Pat? Do ye think so?" sez he. "They'd be envyin' me, eh? They'd be thinkin' Dick has turned out the fine fellow after all?"

"Everybody'll be grudgin' him to ye," sez I. "But they'll be as pleased as Punch, all the same."

An' indeed so they were. Peter O'Rourke come over one errand to compare notes with Hughey, an' the two of them talked half the night. But old Leonard fair out-bummed Peter; an' Tom O'Rourke was soon no pride to the countryside at all, wi' the way Dick was gettin' on.

In troth the ould man became a bit of a nuisance after a while. He got intil a kind of a ramblin', bletherin' way, an' at fairs an' markets he clean scunnered people with "his son Dick in the dhragoons." An' if anybody went near the house he was sure to go up the room an' bring down a letther of Dick's an' read them a bit here an' there about how well he was doin', till one letther would be fallin' to pieces before another one come.

All this time Margit an' Hughey had never spoke.

When he'd meet her on the road he'd look hard at her as if he wanted badly to say somethin'; but he could never musther up the courage; an' Margit was the last in the world to make a push herself.

But from ever the first good news came of Dick she fair haunted me for word about him. I could hardly go out at night but she'd be waitin' for me at the corner of the road; an' if I hadn't been over at Hughey's for a while she'd be beggin' me to go that length an' see if there was anythin' fresh.

I used to put her off at the first; for I couldn't see what benefit Dick's well-doin' was likely to do her now, an' Robinson was still shapin' hard for her. But I could soon see that Robinson was goin' to do no good. She still kept at me for news of Dick; an' I begun to cast round for a chance of reconcilin' her an' the ould man.

It come at the last, an' just when I'd made up my mind that I needn't take the trouble. The aunt died very sudden, an' poor Margit was left alone. Robinson was very kind an' attentive at the wake an' the funeral; an' on all hands it was bein' said that Margit would have a new home in no time.

But two days afther the funeral she come round to me cryin' bitther.

"Pat," sez she, "ye know what they're sayin' about me; I see ye do. But it's not true; it's not true; an' if the word of it goes out to India it'll break my heart. Ye'll go over an' tell his father it's all lies, won't ye now, for ould times' sake? He might be writin' to India this very night. Oh, go over an' tell him it's all lies."

An' what could I do but what I did?

I just took her by the hand, an' over an' intil the ould man's kitchen where he was sittin' by the fire.

"Misther Leonard," sez I, "here's a girl that you were bad to, and your son Dick was bad to. But she's just breakin' her heart about him; an' if ye don't make her some amends, God forgive ye."

The ould man never spoke, but sat lookin' at her as if he'd seen a ghost. An' then he give a terrible cry:

"Oh, Margit, Margit!" sez he; an' the next minit she was kneelin' on the floor, her head on his knees, an' him bendin' over her wi' the tears runnin' down his face.

From that minit all bittherness again Margit seemed to die in the ould man, an' he went clean to the other extreme. He'd be runnin' over to see her ten times a day, an' bringin' her back with him, an' walkin' round the fields with her; an' all the time the talk of them nothin' but Dick.

An', troth, though I let on to be glad at what I'd brought about, I was far from sure in my own mind; for, thinks I, if nothin' comes out of all this I've only made a bad job worse, as far as Margit is concerned.

But at last there came great news. 'Twas Margit herself brought it to me.

"Pat," sez she, burstin' into the kitchen one night, between laughin' an' cryin', "Dick has answered his father. An' he's forgiven me everythin'—all the cold an' the hard things I said to him, an' the way I turned my back on him when I should ha' stood by him most. That's all he has said about me so far; but there has been nobody else, Pat; an' when he comes home I think he'll be comin' home to me too." An' she fell to the laughin' an' the cryin' till I could hardly believe it was the same big quiet Margit I'd seen growin' up before my eyes.

From that on the ould fellow didn't need anybody else to talk to about Dick. He had always somebody just across the fields that was glad enough to listen if he babbled about him from mornin' to night. I begun to see that I wasn't as welcome myself in the house as I used to be, an' fell into the way of meetin' Margit somewhere about the road an' gettin' the news from her.

An' still the news was good.

Dick was risin' fast in the depot, an' writin' to the father regular, an' sendin' him money home. Margit used to slip over, as proud as a peacock, to show me the notes that the ould man had brought from Belfast when he got Dick's letter.

Dick was savin' money, too, forbye; an' when he had three hundhred gathered he was comin' home to live like a gentleman, an' make a lady of Margit. Less wouldn't content him, it seemed.

But less would ha' done Margit.

For as time went on, I could see her wearyin' an' wearyin' for him; an' every now an' then it would break out of her in spite of herself.

"Now isn't it good of him," she'd say, "to be slavin' an toilin' in that dreadful climate, an' all that I may have ease an' plenty some day. But oh, Pat," she'd burst out at the last, "I wish he would come home!"

An' I begun to wish it myself more an' more every month.

For, with all Dick sendin' him money, the ould man was doing badly. He was failin' fast, an' fallin' into a kind of a dotin' way. The farm might mind itself for all he cared. Bit by bit the stock begun to be sold, an' the decent look to go off the place. He had started borrowin' money too, Margit let out to me; first from herself, till he'd ate up near all the wee bit she got from the aunt, an' then from other people. I begun to see that when Dick did come 'twould take all he had saved to clear the farm of debt.

Many a time I wanted Margit to write an' tell him the way things was goin'; but no, she wouldn't expose the ould man or vex Dick by lettin' him know the money he was sendin' home was doin' no good.

"No, Pat," she'd say, "he'll come back in his own good time. We can hold on till then. It would be selfish to coax him home, an' him doin' well. He's trustin' me; an' I'll trust him, an' wait for him in silence."

But there was worse than the money matthers in it.

For Margit's good looks had never been of the kind that wears; an' the waitin' an' the pinin' begun to tell on her sore. Every day she failed an' failed. The comeliness left her face, an' the weariness settled down on it, till I begun to dread that when Dick did come home it would be to a faded, dry old maid.

An' then, thinks I, what'll happen?

For if Dick didn't stick to her when she was a bloomin' young girl, how would she hould him when all the freshness is gone?

Other people took to thinkin' the same thing, too; an' some of the girls begun to look more for Dick's comin' back than they'd done at the first. Wee Susy Moore was only speakin' what was at the back of other people's heads when she tould me sthraight out one day that maybe when Dick did come home he'd be lookin' for somethin' fresher than that ould thing.

I could see who was in Susy's mind by the way she tossed her head; an' 'deed, when I looked at the red cheeks an' the bright dancin' blue eyes of her, I misdoubted what would happen more than ever.

Worst of all, it begun to come into Margit's own mind.

"I'm beginnin' to be an ould woman, Pat," she'd say to me sometimes in a kind of a sorrowful joke. "I doubt my looks is goin'? Dick'll get a sore set-back when he sees me, I'm afeared." Then she'd try to laugh.

An' I'd still hearten her up.

"Tut," I'd say, "it's fresher every day you're lookin'. An' sure Dick's not gettin' any younger himself; forbye that it's four good years since he's seen anythin' but black weemin."

But I doubt there was no great heart behind the words, an' maybe Margit seen it; for she'd turn away heavy and down.

"Och, och," I'd say to myself. "Is it goin' to end in misery afther all?" An' when at long last the word of Dick's home-comin' arrived I didn't know whether to be sorry or glad.

He was comin' too late for one of them, anyway.

For a long time Hughey had been goin' quietly, just a kind of fadin' away. Then he got a bad wettin' goin' up to Belfast one terrible day in November—it was the day he brought the news about Dick comin' home—an' the next thing I heard he had taken to his bed an' Margit was gone to nurse him.

I went over a couple of nights after, an' I was sorry I went.

There he was lyin', all wild-eyed an' babblin'; and for one word of sense he'd talk it was ten of blethers. Sometimes it was about Margit, sometimes it was about the wife that was gone; but always in the end it came round to his son Dick.

His son Dick was comin'—comin' home to him, he'd say, pullin' out a letter from under his pillow.—"It's a far-off country, India, Pat, an' a long journey an' sore; but wouldn't it be a queer thing if a man's son wasn't here to close his eyes at the last?"

"An' he won't be, Pat," poor Margit said to me, cryin', as we stood at the kitchen door. "I doubt he won't be; that's the worst of all. I can't find in my heart to worry the old man with questions in the state he's in—he's been just as you see him for two days—an' he would never let anybody touch Dick's letters but himself. But I've asked at the post office here. The first boat Dick can be on isn't due in London for near a week, an' the father'll never last that long.—Oh, Pat, Pat," an' the poor girl clean broke down, "I knowed he wouldn't be spared to us; but I thought Dick an' me might ha' stood by his bedside an' comforted his last hour."

I wasn't right home till there was a message for me to go back, that the ould man had taken a turn. When I went into the room the hand of death was on him. He didn't know me when I bent over him. His eyes was all glassy an' the breath was sobbin' in his throat.

"Hughey," sez I. "Hughey, man. Do you know me?"

An' as I spoke his eyes cleared an' he looked up at me.

"Pat," sez he, very quiet an' sensible, "I'm goin' to see my son Dick."

He sunk back on the pillow with a wee sigh. His lower lip trimmbled a little, an' he was gone.

When I leaned over to close his eyes I seen the letther crushed up in his right hand. I turned to Margit. There was nobody in the room but our two selves.

"Wheesht, now, Margit," sez I, "wheesht. It can do him no good now. The dead is gone, an' it's time to think of the livin'. Take this letter from the poor ould man's hand an' see when Dick'll be home."

For a wee bit Margit sat there chokin' down the sobs.

Then she got up, wondherful calm an' composed, an' walked over to the bed. "Ye'll forgive me, father," sez she, kissin' him on the forehead, an' took the letther quietly from his dead hand.

She stood lookin' at it for a minit; then she turned as white as a sheet, an' begun to shake.

"What's this, Pat?" sez she, "what's this?" Her voice was all changed an' frightened.

The letther fluttered from her hand, an' she stood there with a wild stare in her eyes.

I ran over an' picked it up. An' when I looked at it there was nothin' but an empty sheet of paper.

The Divil and Johnny Magee

It was my ould grandfather that told me this yarn, so you may guess that it goes a good while back, to a time when people wasn't as well up as they are now, an' believed in a whole lot of things that they wouldn't swallow these days.

My grandfather knew the change that had come over people's minds; an' before he would start the story he would always say that unless you believed in the divil there was no use tellin' it. For it was my grandfather's opinion that in his young days, anyway, the divil was still livin' an' very active, an' that it behoved people to take no liberties with him, because he was sure to best them in the end. "An' to prove my case," he would wind up, "I'll tell you the story of the Divil an' Johnny Magee."

He told it to me that often, that in the end I was able to tell it as well as himself; so it's in my own words I'll give it to you.

It seems that when my grandfather was a young man there was one Johnny Magee kept a public-house at the Ballymawhaw cross-roads; an' the same Johnny was a real bad pill. He drank, an' he gambled, an' he cursed, an' he went cockfightin' on Sundays. A place of worship never seen him from one year's end to the other, an' he would have cheated St. Peter out of the gate-money to Paradise. An' above all, an' what brought him the worst name of the whole lot, he kept very bad drink. But the extraordinary thing was that for many a long year he prospered.

It was a terrible puzzle to everybody, but most of all to the religious people, particularly the clergy. The clergy of all denominations wasn't as mealy-mouthed then as they are now, an' thought very little of denouncin' a man by name if he wasn't just what they thought he should be. Johnny was the text of many a sermon; an' his downfall, in this world an' the next, was speyed for him about every other Sunday in the year.

But seein' that Johnny persisted in thrivin' in this world, they were driv to lay all the more stress on the next. There was only the one way of accountin' for Johnny's success. It was hinted at from one pulpit an' another for a long time; till at last Mr. Gordon, the Presbyterian clergyman of Drumnaquirk, hearin' that two members of his congregation had gone off cockfightin' with Johnny the Sunday before, gave out plump an' plain that beyond all manner of doubt Johnny had sold himself, body and soul, to the divil. The notion was taken up very kindly in the countryside, an' from that time on Johnny was known far an' wide as the Divil's Bargain.

But there was a few level-headed people that didn't see any necessity for bringin' the divil into the matter at all. In the first place, Johnny's pub was just alongside the Drumnaquirk flour mill. That threw him custom every day of the week, while other publicans had to depend mostly on market an' fair days; an' a man with a mill-dam lappin' up again the back wall of his house could never run short of cheap drink. Besides all that, there was two or three irreligious rascals to hint that the Reverend Mr. Gordon's sermons were long an' drouthy, an' that Johnny's pub being only about a couple of hundred yards away, his Sunday afternoon trade by the side-door was as good as two week-days to him.

Anyhow, Johnny never minded what people said. He had long lost the fear of his Maker, an' wasn't likely to pay much attention to mankind, or to the divil either, for that matter. In troth he rather traded on his reputation; for it greatly blew up his name in the district for cuteness an' cunnin'.

But at long last the tide began to turn again him. Constant droppin' wears away a stone, they say, an' in time Mr. Gordon's sermons had an effect even on the light-minded class of people; an' his own rascality done the rest. Folk began to fight shy of Johnny an' his public-house, an' his trade fell off. To balance matters he took to goin' too often to the mill-dam; an' his whiskey got a worse name than ever. One or two desperate pushes at the cards an' the horses made things worse instead of better, an' at last Johnny made up his mind that the only thing for him was a moonlight flittin'. But he had no notion of goin' off empty-handed; an' what bothered him was how to get his fingers on enough cash to give him a fresh start somewhere he wasn't known. The cards had failed him, an' the horses had failed him, an' the last cock-fight had been near ruination altogether. With the state of trade in the pub there was no chance of gatherin' any money worth talkin' of that way. He was just at his wits' end.

An' then a great notion struck him. I suppose it would be Mr. Gordon's preachin' put it in his head. All at once he stopped cards, an' cock-fightin', an' horse-bettin', an' took to sittin' quietly in his own pub. He wouldn't drink, or he wouldn't sing or tell a story among his greatest cronies. There he would sit in the bar-parlour looking very melancholy into the fire, an' every now an' then he'd fetch a long sigh an' wag his head without sayin' a word. One an' another of his friends would try to hearten him up an' find out what was wrong, but there was no satisfaction to be had out of Johnny.

At last it began to be talked about outside. One would have it that something serious had gone wrong with his health, another would maintain it was the goin'-down of his business was what was botherin' him. An' some even made out that he was repentin' of his sins, and was goin' to turn religious to see if there was any money to be made out of that.

But it was all guesswork, for nobody liked to put a question to him plump an' plain. But one night Peter Short an' him was settin' by themselves in the bar-parlour. Peter had come home out of Ballygullion fair well primed an' on for a bit of a jollification, an' kept doin' his best to stir Johnny up a bit. He might as well have saved his breath. If Johnny had been down in the mouth before, he was ten times more down in the mouth that night. There he sat by the fire sighin' an' mutterin' to himself, till at last Peter could stand it no longer, but put it to Johnny straight out, what was the matter with him.

Johnny said nothin' for a wee while, then he took a kind of a frightened skelly behind him.

"I daren't tell ye, Peter," sez he.

Of course that set Peter all agog, an' he kept at Johnny all ways to tell him whether it was good or bad, an' swore—an', I suppose, meaned it—that he wouldn't let on a word to mortal.

Then Johnny got up an' barred the door an' the windows, an' after makin' Peter promise again two or three times that he would repeat it to nobody, he told him that for a long while he'd been in a bad way for money. He knew well, he said, the report that people, especially the Reverend Mr. Gordon, had spread about him in the country, an' thinkin' he might as well have the gains as the name, he *had* sold himself to the divil. He had been taken in, too, he said; for though he'd been allowed to dig up a crock of gold big enough to make him an independent gentleman, it had slipped through his fingers with the cards an' the bettin' as fast as he got it, an' now his time was up an' he had received notice that at twelve o'clock on a certain night a few weeks away the devil was comin' to claim his bargain an' carry him off.

When Peter heard this tale he was very sorry he had asked any questions, an' got himself off the premises as quick as he could, an' away home, very badly scared. But, of course, when he got home he told the wife all about it, in a dead secret, an' the next day she told somebody else's wife, still in a secret, an' before a week the whole countryside was ringin' with the news. Within sight of the pub, or easy walk of it, Johnny's own story held pretty good, but the further it travelled the wilder it got, till anythin' above five miles away it was taken for gospel that the premises had been burned down with fire an' brimstone the Saturday night before, an' that the divil had carried off Johnny Magee before him, squealin', on a broomstick.

By degrees it all simmered down to Johnny's own account of the business, an' a most lamentable sough of talk riz all over the country.

The wily ones laughed an' smelt a trick of some kind or another; but very few of them was goin' to spoil sport, an' most of them spread the story all they could to keep the joke goin'. The religious people be't to believe such a thing could be, an' there was nothin' in Johnny's past life to contradict it. The followin' Sunday every place of worship for miles round was crowded to the doors; half a dozen old weemin was carried out in hysterics out of Mr. Gordon's meetin'-house alone; an' two new religions was started in Belfast.

But curiosity will beat fear any day. Johnny's wee trick soon began to serve his purpose. A constant stream of people visited the pub every day, just to look at Johnny, an' see how he was takin' it; an' the hardier lads made up parties so as to have company goin' home, an' filled the bar every night.

Johnny was cunnin', an' never said a word about the report, good or bad. But he dressed himself in a black suit, as if he'd been goin' to a funeral, an' stood behind the bar with a set face, servin' out drink as hard as he could go, but hardly sayin' a word. That was in the daytime, when the more respectable kind of people was there. In the evenin' he'd change his tune, an' get wild an' reckless, an' drink with everybody would ask him, an' sing an' carry on as if he was distracted, every now an' then comin' off that it was a short life an' a merry one for him, throwin' in a string of oaths, an' cryin' that he was afraid of neither man nor divil.

After a while, however, the novelty of the thing begun to

show signs of wearin' off, an' trade fell away again; so Johnny played his trump card an' give out to a bar-full of his cronies that the followin' Thursday was his last day in this world, an' that if they'd all turn up at the pub, between him and them there'd be a night of it.

"At twelve o'clock, boys," sez he, "I'm goin' to an upstairs room to lock myself in an' see what'll happen me. I'm layin' in an extra supply of drink, an' if there's any left when I'm gone an' ye still have the pluck left to drink it, ye can have it for nothin'. It'll be no more good to me."

From that till the Thursday ye might say Johnny's pub was never empty, an' most terrible scenes of drink went on. Johnny couldn't cope with the trade at all, an' in the end had to send for a young nephew of his that lived four or five mile away. The father and mother was no way keen to let the young fellow go; but Johnny promised him the pub after he quit it, an' they all made up their minds it was worth the risk.

By the time the big Thursday come the whole countryside was near gone astray altogether. Some laughed at the whole business still, an' some still swallowed the story wholesale, an' some hung in the wind an' didn't know what to think; but one thing the bulk of them made up their minds about, an' that was that, far-off or near hand, they would be about when Johnny went, if he did go.

Long before dusk people had gathered in crowds on all the roads leadin' to the pub, most folk thinkin' it would be just as well to arrive in time for a daylight drink for fear that, later on, Old Nick might miss his man in the dark an' pick somebody else up so as not to have his journey for nothin'.

By nine o'clock every road up to the pub was choked with people young and old, an' even some weemin among them. As for the pub itself, it was fairly besieged, men fightin' their way up to the bar, an' Johnny's nephew servin' out drink from the side window as well. Between nine an' ten Johnny seen that supplies would hardly hold out till the divil was due, so he doubled the price of drink; an' I may as well tell you that from that minit the number of people that were sorry the divil was goin' to get him went down about three-quarters.

Still the sale of drink went on near as brisk as ever, but about half-past ten it got a check; for just on the stroke Mr. Gordon an' his choir marched into the field beside the pub and set up a very dismal skreigh of a psalm. The sound of it brought things home to a good many of the thirsty boys, an' some of them began to slip away; but Johnny went out an' threw two empty porter bottles at the choir an' hit the precentor in the ribs with the second one. The choir moved a couple of fields off then, an' hadn't near the same effect, so the pub filled up again as crowded as ever.

But from eleven on there began to be a change. A kind of nervousness began to come on people, even them that had a few drinks in them. The first sign of it was when a porter-bottle blew up in the bar-room about a quarter past eleven. The whole crowd in the bar took to their heels like one man, an' near tore the clothes off each other's backs fightin' their way down the passage. Old Joe Mackay tripped an' fell just outside the door an' had two ribs broke before they got him trailed from in under people's feet.

When they all found what had frightened them, everybody started to laugh, an' a lot went back into the bar, but more than half of them stayed where they were, includin' Johnny's nephew.

The crowd outside in the dark had been gettin' quieter an' quieter, an' gradually drew away from about the front of the pub. After the flurry over the porter-bottle had died down they stopped talkin' among themselves altogether an' stood there without a sound—just a kind of a thickenin' in the darkness. The choir had stopped singin' long before.

An' then all at once the church bell started tollin'. They say the first chap of it would ha' chilled the very marrow of your bones, comin' in the darkness an' the hush. A kind of a shiver ran through the crowd. Here an' there weemin cried out, and began to sob; and some of the men started to pray.

But when Mr. Gordon heard the bell he lepped up from where he'd been kneelin', callin' to the sexton to follow him, an' marched off to the church. He was an overbearin' big man, everything be't to be done by his orders, an' he had give no orders about ringin' the bell, an' flew into a towerin' rage when he heard the sound of it.

Half a dozen or so followed him an' the sexton, an' when they got to the belfry door it was closed an' locked. Mr. Gordon wasn't a bit daunted, but began to hammer on the door an' to call out for it to be opened, an' when the sexton came up asked him very sharply had he dared to give the key to anybody without his authority.

The sexton answered, "No, sir," an' drew the key out of his pocket. When he did that, five out of the six men that had followed them turned tail an' made back to the crowd. The sixth man, an' that was my grandfather, followed Mr. Gordon an' the sexton up the belfry stairs; an' when they got into the belfry an' Mr. Gordon struck a light an' lit a candle the bell was tollin' every now an' then above their heads, the rope goin' up an' down, and the end of it twistin' and tumblin' about the floor; but there was nobody in the room.

My grandfather, bein' a Catholic, stepped down one of the stone stairs, not wishin' to offend Mr. Gordon, an' blessed himself two or three times as well as he could manage with the knees of him knockin' together an' his teeth chatterin'.

Lookin' in out of the dark, he could see Mr. Gordon standin' with the candle in his hand steady as a rock, but his face very white an' stern an' his lips set tight. Then Mr. Gordon motioned to the sexton to go before him, an' the three made their way down the stairs. When they came to the bottom Mr. Gordon locked the door, an' threw the candle on the ground an' put his foot on it.

"Say nothing about this," sez he, very short an' stern. "These poor people mustn't be alarmed."

But the harm had been done already by the men that had run back. As the three went down the church path they could hear the shoutin' an' the clatter of feet, an' when they stepped out on the road the crowd was on top of them before they knew where they were, running like madmen, with hardly a sound. Mr. Gordon was a big burly man an' as obstinate as a mule, an' he stood his ground, however he did it; but my grandfather went with the stream, an' was carried a quarter of a mile down the road before he got clear. In this way he missed what went on at the pub; but if he wasn't obstinate he was inquisitive, an' he turned back, to hear what had happened at all costs.

It was about a quarter past twelve when he got to the pub. The door was wide open an' every window in the place lit up. He walked up to the door an' looked in; an' there was nobody to be seen. He listened, an' then he tiptoed to the foot of the stairs an' listened again; but there wasn't a sound. An' all at once a scare came over him worse even than at the church, an' he out of the house an' away towards home as fast as he could run. When he got to the top of the hill above the pub he pulled up an' looked back, an' there was the house with every window bright with lights, but not a soul to be seen or a sound of mortal. So he took to his heels again, an' never checked his foot till he was in his own kitchen.

Next mornin' he heard what had happened.

When the crowd had gone by, Mr. Gordon walked back to the pub an' marched in. It was then past twelve o'clock. There were four men sittin' in the bar, all of them drinkin' whiskey as fast as they could lower it, but still sober. They told Mr. Gordon that Johnny had sworn about ten of his pet cronies to stand by him; but that when the screeching started outside an' the crowd began to run everybody quit the pub but them four selves.

They sat lookin' at Johnny while he made up his cash an' took it away to lock it up in the safe as usual. He was very white an' nervous-lookin', they said, but quite cool. At ten minutes to twelve he come back an' beckoned them to follow him upstairs. If any one of them had had the pluck to run, they'd all have run, but nobody had. Johnny brought them to the big back upstairs room. It was empty, barrin' for one chair and a table, an' four candles on the table. Johnny went over to the window an' closed the shutters, an' hasped them. Then he handed the key of the room to Simon Mageean, one of the four men.

"Lock the door, Simon," sez he, "an' go downstairs. An' at ten minutes past twelve come back. There's one bottle of whiskey left, on the table in the bar. Take a drink before you come back. You'll maybe need it."

They made their way down the stairs without a word spoken, an' when they got to the bottom they looked the one at the other to see would they run this time. That minit they heard Johnny's voice upstairs. An' when they listened, here he was singin' an old song at the top of his voice, an' no very improvin' song either.

With that Simon Mageean slapped his thigh.

"Tut," sez he, "the whole thing's all blethers. Come on in to the bar an' have a drink." So they went in an' poured themselves out glasses apiece.

But nobody said very much, an' a minit or two before twelve they stopped talkin' an' turned to look at the clock. They could hear Johnny singin' away upstairs; an' with the first stroke of twelve his voice stopped dead. There wasn't a sound to be heard in the whole house but the strikin' of the clock, stroke by stroke, an' when it stopped there wasn't a sound at all.

The four men sat there listenin'. Still not a sound; but presently they noticed that the wind was risin'. A draught blew up the hall, an' slammed-to the bar door. It was then they seized on the whiskey-bottle an' started drinkin' hard.

When Mr. Gordon came in they told him all had happened. He looked at them for a minit, frownin'.

"Give me the key of the room," he said, holdin' out his hand. He went up the stairs, an' the four men riz an' followed him. An' when they opened the room door the table an' the chair were there, an' four candles burnin', an' the shutters closed an' hasped; but Johnny Magee was gone!

Mr. Gordon said never a word, but turned an' went down the stairs an' out of the house, an' the others after him. They left the door open an' the lights burnin', as my grandfather found them later on.

When Mr. Gordon an' the four men that was with him left the pub they walked up the road towards the manse, Mr. Gordon a little in front with his head down on his breast, still not sayin' a word. When they came to the manse gate he bid the men good-night an' told them to go quietly home an' say their prayers an' go to bed.

Next mornin' the pub was standin' as they had left it; an' all that day, an' for two or three days after, I suppose half the country passed up an' down by it, but nobody went in. Then Mr. Gordon an' the owner of the mill went an' closed it, an' had the windows nailed up. It stood there for years, empty—for Johnny's nephew never claimed it—an' gradually it fell to ruins. Even the trade of the mill began to fall off, an' in time it was closed too, an' fell into decay.

You might have thought there would have been powerful excitement an' talk in the country about the affair; but there was not. Everybody was too much scared to want to say anythin'; an' besides there was a kind of notion that it cast a slur on the district, an' that for everybody's credit it was better to hush the whole thing up.

Even Mr. Gordon kept himself very quiet; an' though for a long time afterwards he preached very wicked again horses an' cards an' cockfightin', an' give the divil a bitter hard name in connection with all three, he never mentioned Johnny's business at all or spoke of him from the pulpit by name.

It was just as well, too. For after five or six years had gone by the sexton of his own church took his last sickness an' sent for Mr. Gordon before he died, an' confessed that him an' Johnny had planned the whole trick. He himself had managed the tollin' of the bell with a cord to his wee son up a tree in the churchyard, an' had helped Johnny to rig a rope across the mill-dam from the upstairs room, an' took it down in the early hours of the mornin' after Johnny was safe away.

When my grandfather got to this point he always stopped and fumbled with his pipe, to give people a chance of sayin' somethin' or asking a question.

Somebody or other was near sure to say—in troth at times a bit disappointed: "An' so the divil didn't get Johnny at all?"

And then my grandfather would go on again as if nobody had spoken.

"Mark now," he would say, "how well Johnny had it all thought out. The tollin' of the bell frightened the people away when all the drink had been sold. The singin' of the song upstairs covered up the noise of the shutters openin' an' closin'. Johnny had scraped the slit between the two leaves of the shutters. When he was outside he just slipped in his knife an' hasped them again; an' off he went across the rope, laughin', ye may swear, at both the divil an' his neighbours, an' with forty-three pound eight an' tuppence in his pocket."

"An' how do you know he had just that amount in his pocket?" somebody would ask.

"I'll tell you that, too," my grandfather would say. "When the dam went dry, twenty years after all this, that was the exact money in the wee bag that was found lyin' in the bottom, among Johnny's bones."

"The divil *may* be dead," my grandfather would wind up; "an' I hope he is; for he was a very antic boy when he was livin'."

A Short Suit

It was just exactly at twenty minutes past seven, said Mr. Patrick Murphy, that my wife's aunt came into the kitchen of her house in Belfast—but I had better go back to the beginnin' of the whole business.

My wife's aunt, Mrs. McPeake, is married on a fitter in the Queen's Island in Belfast, an' they have a very snug wee house in Scullen Street.

About last October they invited the wife up to stay with

them. While she was on the visit here, doesn't a letter come to Mrs. McPeake from her brother, Sam, askin' if she could give him a bed for the night before Belfast fair. Sam has a nice wee farm in the Free State, about three mile over the Border; an' he had two or three good shorthorn bullocks that he thought he'd do better with if he fetched them up to Belfast.

It was a very tight fit for the McPeakes, I may tell you, puttin' up Sam; for their house isn't big; but by dint of lettin' the kitchen fire out early, an' makin' a bed for the twins on the top of the range, they managed to fix up a corner for him.

They were all sittin' in the parlour that evenin', talkin', as well as they could for the noise (for Sam had bought the children a pennyworth of sweets, an' that left one sweet short among them) when Joe McPeake lifts up the evenin' paper.

"Hold on," sez he, "till I read you a good one. Keep quiet, children! It's about some old fellow from the County Meath. He bought a pair of trousers in Belfast, an' didn't declare them as he was passin' through the Customs; an' what do you think they fined him? A hundred pounds; that's all! What's wrong, Sam?" sez he to his brother-in-law.

"Oh, my father," sez Sam, lettin' a most lamentable groan out of him, "an' didn't I buy a new suit of clothes here in Belfast this very evenin'?"

"How much did it cost you?" sez McPeake.

"Seven pounds I paid for it," sez Sam; "aye, seven good pounds. An' now I suppose I be to pay another pound duty."

"Twenty-one shillin's," sez McPeake. "There's fifteen per cent. duty, my boy. I'd risk smugglin' it through, if I was you."

"Is it risk a fine of a hundred pounds?" sez Sam. "No fear of me. D——n the Free State," sez he, very bitter. "I wish to heavens I had supported Carson."

"I'll tell you what you'll do, then," sez Mr. McPeake, winkin' at the wife (for the both of them knew Sam was no way rash); "wear the new suit an' leave that one you have on you behind. It'll make me a good boiler-suit."

"Boiler-suit, indeed," sez Sam. "You'll make no boiler-suit of it. It's a d——d sight better nor your Sunday clothes. But what the devil am I to do?"

"Pay the duty," sez McPeake. "That's the simple way out of it."

"What! Is it hand over one pound to them blood-suckers? Never!" sez Sam, "I'd pay the hundred pounds first—I don't mean that," sez he; "but I won't pay one shillin' of duty if I can help it. Have none of yez any brains, to give me a plan?"

Now my wee wife, Molly, has the name of bein' very lucky; but she had an unfortunate notion this time.

"Uncle Sam," sez she, "sure the railroad runs through your farm? What's to hinder you throwing the parcel into the field in front of the house as the train goes past to-morrow evenin'? It'll be near dusk."

"Tck, tck, tck," sez Sam, lookin' at her all vexed. "To think that the duty has been on clothes these two years, an' I never hit on that notion of yours before. I might have smuggled in as much both years as would ha' paid the rent. But it's never too late to mend. I'll make a start with the suit. Susan," sez he, "ye haven't by any chance a piece of strong brown paper you could wrap up the suit in? There's little better than tissue-paper on it now; and it might burst."

"Aye, have I," sez the sister; "an' a dirty crumpled oul' piece it is, the very thing for you. Ye don't want too swanky a parcel in the train, in case there'd be some fly boys about, spottin' for the Customs. Where's the suit?"

"It's in the hall," sez Sam.

"All right," sez the sister. "I'll go an' parcel it up now."

"Better let me do it," sez McPeake. "These children'll have the house down."

"I'll do it myself," sez she. "Maybe ye can use a hammer; but I never seen the man yet was much use with paper an' string."

But in the middle of the job the two children that had only one sweet between them, an' was suckin' it time about, fell out, an' in the tussle the youngest swallowed the sweet holusbolus. The mother had to run up the stairs hot-foot, first to save the one child from chokin', an' then to keep the other one from massacrin' it for boltin' the sweet; an' when she came down the second time, with the parcel in her hand, she allowed that she could ha' made it untidier if she hadn't been so flustered. But all the rest said she had made a great job of the parcel, an' that nobody would ever dream there was a new suit in it.

Molly told me after she came home that when Sam went off to the station the next afternoon you'd ha' thought it was a parcel of cotton waste he had under his arm; an' there's no doubt at all he'd ha' passed safe through the Customs if he'd let well alone.

But when he got into the carriage here was three or four cattle-dealin' men that he knew. As soon as the train was started one of them out with a pack of cards an' proposed a hand of Nap, an' Sam was asked would he join in? You might be surprised at him doin' it: but he was one of them men that never go three unless they have a Nap hand, an' live on other people's wreckage; so he wasn't afeared to play in any company.

The game wasn't right started till a stout little butt of a man with a blue serge suit on him, an' a very wise expression of countenance, riz out of the opposite corner an' sat himself down at Sam's elbow. As the game went on he gave Sam advice now an' then about calling, an' it was always good advice. Twice Sam, at his instigation, took the top card an' went Nap, though the cold sweat was runnin' down his back as he did it; an' twice he won; an' he began to see that the little man was just as wise as he looked.

Time run by, an' they all began to chat between deals, an' presently the talk came round to smugglin'; an' one an' another begun to boast how he'd got stuff through the Customs. Sam very soon seen that it was an easy business, after all, an' was inclined to be sorry he hadn't bought an overcoat as well. Then some of the boys started to tell about how cute the Customs people was gettin', an' how the Free State was payin' their army out of Customs fines alone; an'

Sam's heart went down intil his boots, an' he wished to heavens he had bought his new suit on his own side of the Border.

Up till now he had said nothin' about his smugglin' venture, bein' of a very cautious turn of mind. Besides that, he'd been a trifle shy of the wise-lookin' little man; for he thought his blue serge suit had a very great look of an old uniform about it; an' he misdoubted him. However, as the stories of people bein' caught went from bad to worse, he could thole no longer, but told his plan for throwin' the new suit out of the train. The other card-players allowed that it was a first-class notion; but the wise-lookin' little man shook his head very weighty.

"It was a good plan a month ago, that," sez he, "but it's no use now."

"How?" sez they all, lookin' at him open-mouthed.

"Well," sez he, "I don't know whether the Customs people has wind of it yet or not; but I do know that every servant-boy along the railway line within five miles of the Border is up to it. They lie in wait for the trains; an' now some of them is goin' about swankier nor their masters, with the hats, an' overcoats, an' boots, an' suits of clothes they're pickin' up near-hand every night."

"Do you tell me that?" sez one of the card-players.

"I do tell you that," sez the little man. "An' I know. I threw as nice a tweed overcoat out of the train three weeks ago as you'd wish to see; an' now my own first ploughman has been out to church these two Sundays wearin' it. God forgive me, I can't say my prayers for lookin' at him. An' I daren't say Boo! about it for fear it would cost me the price of a ten-acre field in a fine."

"Bless my soul," sez Sam, "this is terrible altogether. I had a right to make my old suit do another year, so I had. Should I pay the duty, do you think?" sez he, pickin' up his cards.

"Take the top card an' go Nap on the double, first," sez the little man, lookin' at his hand. "In the meantime I'll be thinkin' the matter out."

So Sam went Nap on the double, a thing he'd never done in his life before, an' got it, an' lifted eight shillin's in one scoop. After that he was prepared to back the little man again' King Solomon, an' ready to do anythin' he told him, short of throwin' himself out on the railway line with the suit on him.

"I have it!" sez the little man, as the cards were bein' dealt out again. "Change into the new suit in the lavatory, an' throw the old one out instead. They never charge you duty on a suit you're wearin'. An' if anybody does spot your old suit as it falls," sez he, in a very matter-of-fact tone, "they'll hardly bother to pick it up. Hurry though," sez he, payin' no attention to the look Sam gave him. "You've only one more station to go."

But Sam had seen the deal by now, an' here didn't he hold the ace, king, an' queen of hearts, an' a small one? He held up the cards to the little man, an' his hand was trembling.

"Have I time?" sez he. "It's a sure four."

"Blethers with your four," sez the wee man, near as excited. "Follow your luck. Take the top card, an' go Nap again."

So Sam lifted the top card, an' it was a heart. Four shillin's he took this time; an' he was that pleased about all the money he had won that he'd ha' died sooner than spend a penny of it on duty.

"Holy Moses!" cries the little man, lookin' at his watch, "you've left yourself bare time. Off with that old suit, an' bundle it into a parcel. I'll throw it out for you, an' you can put on the new suit at your leisure. The first house to the right past Ballindoyle Station, you said?"

"Yes, yes," splutters Sam, fumblin' on the rack for the new suit, "the field with the tarred wooden shed in it." An' off he dashes for the lavatory.

"Hurry!" sez the little man through the lavatory door. "We're not far from Ballindoyle now."

Sam tore the old suit off him, pulled the paper off the new suit, an' wrapped up the old one as well as he could, with the cold an' the splutter he was in.

"Hurry! Hurry!" sez the little man, outside.

Sam opened the door and pushed the parcel into his arms. The little man got to the nearest window just in time to throw it out.

That would be about twenty-one minutes past seven; for the Dublin train is due to pass Ballindoyle Station at twenty-past.

An' as I told you at the beginnin', it was just at twenty minutes past seven that my wife's aunt came into the kitchen of her house in Belfast.

"Would you believe it, Molly?" sez she to my wife, that was sittin' at the range fire, warmin' her shins. "Would you believe it, but I forgot to put in the trousers of Sam's new suit!"

The Rapparee

THE little body of soldiers moved in line over the vast desolation of the Bog of Allen, a slender ribbon of scarlet on the grey waste. As they passed along they beat each bush and tussock of grass, and scrutinized each pool and stream with a savage earnestness that seemed to spring more from personal hate than from mere devotion to duty.

The guerilla warfare that succeeded the Boyne and Limerick had fanned to cruelty the passions of the contending races; and the Bog of Allen had become the theatre of a long succession of sordid tragedies. Between the regular troops of both armies some show of military courtesy was still observed; but between the Rapparees and the Williamite forces the struggle had degenerated into mere savagery.

And so the soldier of this little company as he drove his bayonet home through bush or hummock had perhaps before his mind's eye the mutilated body of the comrade who had marched by his side but yesterday.

Presently on the extreme right of the line an outcry arose. The quartermaster hurried towards the sound. He found a knot of soldiers gathered by the side of a sluggish, sedge-covered stream.

"What is is, men?" he said.

"A Rapparee, sir," answered one of the soldiers. "I tell you it was," he said excitedly to his comrades. "I seen him. Here—he disappeared just here where we're standing." He peered eagerly into the stream, then suddenly threw himself on his face, and plunged his arm into the water.

"Here's his musket," he said, struggling upright. He handed the quartermaster a gun-barrel, plugged at the muzzle with an oiled cloth, and at the touch-hole with a quill.

"Yes, this is fresh," said the quartermaster, pulling out the plug. He uttered a hoarse shout to the halted line, which streamed in at the double.

"A Rapparee, boys," he cried. "Scatter—search the stream!" He ran up and down the bank, eager as a bloodhound. "Here, boys," he shouted suddenly, stooping over the water—"quick. By G—d, I have him!"

One or two of the men ran up and looked over the quartermaster's shoulder. The Rapparee lay in the shallow water close along the bank. From the pale face which alone appeared above the weedy stream his dark eyes looked up in sick fascination at the exulting faces of his captors.

The soldier on the quartermaster's right raised his musket. But the quartermaster beat the bayonet thrust aside with his sword.

"Easy, Jones," he said sternly; "we'll not dirty clean steel on the rogue. Have him out on the bank. There's a stout bush yonder will do his business."

The Rapparee was quickly dragged out of the stream, and stood shivering in the bitter wind, a meagre, famine-stricken object, his piteous shanks wrapped with straw ropes, his bare ribs gleaming through the rents in the tattered great-coat, his only garment. Beneath the matted hair that dripped over his face, the wild eyes darted here and there in agonized enquiry.

He was not long in doubt.

"The rope there, Dickson," said the quartermaster. "Corporal Knox, you will take a couple of men and settle with this fellow. Jones, enter up a Rapparee hanged at—never mind the place. Hurry, boys, there's snow coming."

The sight of the rope brought dreadful certainty to the prisoner. He threw himself at the quartermaster's feet, and clasped his legs. At frenzied torrent of entreaty poured from his lips.

"Away with the swine," said the quartermaster, pushing him off contemptuously with his foot. "How does he expect me to understand his cursed lingo."

Two of the soldiers seized the Rapparee; but he tore himself from their grip, leaving half his tattered garment behind, and again threw himself on the ground before the quartermaster.

"Money," he gasped painfully, "hide money—much money."

"What's that?" said the quartermaster sharply. The ring of soldiers narrowed.

"Money," cried the Rapparee, "much money." A light of hope dawned in his eyes. He sprang to his feet and began to drag the quartermaster towards a clump of bushes a little distance away.

"Money—give money—no hang," he said, and peered up piteously in the quartermaster's face.

"What does the rascal mean, Jones?" said the quartermaster.

"He's got treasure hidden, sir," answered the man, "and wants to buy off his life. I'd take the stuff, sir. You can hang the beggar afterwards. It's sure to be plunder."

The quartermaster hesitated. The faces of his men seemed to speak agreement with Jones. The Rapparee hung dumbly on his looks.

"We'll have a look at his money, anyway," said he; and signed to his prisoner to lead the way.

The creature uttered a yell of joy, sprang in the air, clapping his hands, and was about to dart off when two of the men seized him.

"That's right," said the quartermaster; "watch the treacherous dog. March ahead with him, Knox and Dickson. Spread, boys, and look to your priming. This may be an ambush."

The prisoner led the way to a patch of higher ground covered with thick grass and sheltered by a semicircle of low bushes. He crept under the branches of one of these, and began to ferret among the earth and stones.

The quartermaster bent over him eagerly. His men closed round with sparkling eyes, all thought of an ambush forgotten.

The Rapparee emerged from beneath the bush, a dirty cloth in his hand. His eyes shone with simple delight as he handed the rag to the quartermaster.

"Money," he said, smiling ingratiatingly in his face. "Much money. No hang."

The quartermaster untied the knots hastily. The soldiers crowded closer, and craned their necks to see. At last the cloth fell open in his fumbling hands and the treasure lay revealed. There were four half-crowns and three shillings in King James's brass money.

For a moment the soldiers looked at the little heap in silence. Then an outburst of laughter shook the whole group. They rocked back and forth, and laid hold of one another as they laughed.

The Rapparee looked at the circle of grinning faces in bewilderment, and smiled uncertainly. It seemed as if amid the laughter he detected a sinister note.

"Much money," he said to the quartermaster, with a rebirth of anxiety in his voice; "much money—no hang?"

The quartermaster had not laughed.

"Here, corporal," he said, "finish him off. I might have known it was only one of their tricks. Stop his cursed skirling, can't you! Fall in, men, and be ready to start."

"There might be more coin about, sir," said the man Jones.

"What's that?" said the quartermaster. "Gad, so there might. Fetch the rogue back."

"More money?" he demanded sternly of the shaking wretch. "More money——?" and he pointed to the bushes.

The Rapparee seemed to have abandoned hope. "No money," he said dully; "all give—all give," he repeated, looking in amazed distress from the little treasure to the quartermaster's face. "No hang," he burst out suddenly, trying to fall on his knees—"no hang!"

"I don't believe the dog, boys," cried the quartermaster sharply. "Do you see him looking at the bushes? Search all round, and I'll watch his face. That's right—along there. You're warm! You're warm! Look at the rogue's countenance. In there, boys. Hold the fellow back, Dickson!—Have you got anything?"

A shout came from the nearest group.

"Here's something, sir—something wrapped up in straw."

"Ha!" cried the quartermaster, hurrying forward, "we've found the fox's real den at last. Pull it out, whatever it it."

The men disinterred a considerable, straw-wrapped bundle, and carried it into the open.

"Good dogs," said the quartermaster, rubbing his hands; "good dogs. You've nosed out something worth our while. Hurry up till we see what it is."

They tore the bundle open. There fell out a confused mass of half-gnawed bones, potatoes, pieces of cheese-rind, and hunks of bread.

" 'Swounds," said the quartermaster, after the first pause of chagrin, "what was the fellow looking so plaguey anxious about? Pull all the stuff to pieces. There may be something hidden in it. And search the bushes further."

The soldiers tore at the fragments in greedy haste; ground the bread to crumbs, and burst the potatoes under their heels in a fury of disappointment.

The Rapparee threw himself beneath their feet with wild screams. He hung round their legs in a frenzy of supplication; he wept; he tore his matted hair; he grovelled before them; he threw himself upon the miserable relics of food, and tried to shield them with his body.

"No, no," he shrieked in an abandonment of anguish; "no, no!"

"Drag him off," said the quartermaster, motioning to two of his men. "There's something here." He fell on his knees, and groped eagerly among the straw. But his search was unrewarded. A few fragments of crust fell out, nothing more. He looked up in the faces of his men in bewilderment.

"D——n me if I can make the creature out," he said, rising to his feet. "Listen to the screeches of him. I'll be cursed if he isn't crying over his supper, and him going to be hanged in five minutes. We needn't waste more time over an idiot like that. Have another look round, and we'll be off.—Hullo! What's Tompkins got?"

A man came up with an armful of sticks and straw, and a flint and steel.

"No good, sir," he said; "only firing."

"Strike up a blaze," said the quartermaster. "It'll warm us up before we start. Just another look round, boys, while the fire's lighting."

But the preparations for making the fire roused the doomed wretch to a last paroxysm of distress. He struggled wildly in his captors' arms. He wrenched his mouth free, and uttered wail upon wail, high, quivering, despairing. His wild eyes darted from one to another in more than mortal agony.

"No, no," he screamed piercingly, and struggled vainly to reach the quartermaster—"no, no!"

"Now's he's howling for his fire," said the quartermaster. "He needn't. He'll have plenty of fire in a minute or two." He laughed brutally. "If I'd known he was only wasting our time he'd have been warming himself at it half an hour ago."

The straw roared out in a flapping standard of flame, and poured a torrent of flakes before the rising wind.

At the sight of the flame the Rapparee's screams died into silence. His struggles ceased. His guards released his arms a little; and he sank to the ground and crouched there, rocking to and fro. The moan of his keening rose and fell in a desolation of hopeless sorrow. Even his captors' hearts were wrung by the sound.

"Come, corporal," said the quartermaster, "off with you. Here are the men coming back. They've found nothing. Put the poor devil out of his misery."

The corporal and his men disappeared with their victim. The soldiers crouched round the dying flame, and strove to drive out the chill of the falling night. A little dusty snow fell, puffed here and there along the frozen ground, and hissed on the embers. Presently the fall thickened and quenched the last vestiges of fire.

The keen of the doomed Rapparee rose and fell, and mingled eerily with the soughing wind.

The shivering circle of men listened in gloomy silence.

Then the keening ceased. The quartermaster rose to his feet stiffly.

"Now, boys," he said, "fall in. Here's the corporal. We must step out. God send we don't miss our way this dreadful night.—Are you ready? Quick march, then."

The little band moved off, winding in and out among the frozen pools and quagmires.

One of the rear-rank men turned his head for a moment to look at the spot they had just quitted. But it was no longer visible. The tall columns of snow followed one another in endless procession across the darkening waste.

Suddenly the soldier gripped his neighbour's arm.

"Dick," he said, under his breath, "Dick—do you see anything! There—behind us—moving."

The man looked a moment, then turned to his comrade with whitening face.

"It's a woman and four little children," he said. "God forgive us all."

Bob Menzies Gives Alms

I

LITTLE Robert Menzies and his Uncle Hugh sat in the kitchen of Hugh Menzies's farmhouse, one on each side of the hearth. It was about nine o'clock on an October evening, and quite dark outside, but there was no other light in the kitchen than the glow of the red coals. Now and then a spurt of flame would cast a dancing gleam on the walls and light up the two faces. The boy's face was pale, with large, dreamy blue eyes; a sober face, lit up now and then with a slow but singularly pleasant smile. The psychologist would have deduced a dreamer and idealist, with a hint of humour, latent but undeveloped.

No trace of humour showed in the face of his uncle, a man of about fifty. The firelight disclosed a simple serious character, with a trace of wistfulness, imprinted by life. The tall stooping frame and long face and sparse pointed beard suggested something of Don Quixote.

Since the death of Bob's father, two years before, when Bob was almost ten, the pair had lived alone together, except for a housekeeper. It was their practice every winter night after the housekeeper had gone to bed to sit by the fire and talk. Hugh Menzies was a diffident man; and felt more at ease with Bob than with his grown-up neighbours.

The silence that had fallen between the two was broken by the uncle.

"Bob," he said, "here's a piece of advice for you: Be hard. That's the only way to get on in the world; and I've proved it."

The boy looked at his uncle, and laughed softly.

"I don't think you're very hard, uncle," he said.

Mr. Menzies compressed his lips slowly.

"Am I not?" he said. "Am I not? Don't get that notion into your head; for it's a foolish notion. Maybe I was a bit soft in my young days; but I don't want you to follow my example. I suffered for it, Bob; and so would you. There's a soft drop in you, too. Get rid of it, or you'll never do a day's good in this world. People will find it out. They found it out in me, and played on me. Many a pound it has cost me. But latterly I've changed my tune." He paused, and looked at the boy intently. "Bob," he said, "I'm going to put Mrs. Flanagan out of her cottage."

The boy stared at him. His mouth half-opened in his astonishment and dismay.

"Oh, uncle!" he breathed.

"Yes," said Mr. Menzies, violently, "she's going out this time. Why should I let that slippery old faggot humbug me any longer? The cottage costs me two or three pounds a year for thatch and repairs; I let her have it for sixpence a week, and she's ten shillings in arrear even of that. I need the cottage, too. I'm paying my ploughman two pounds a year extra because I have no cottage for him; and why should I let old Sally Flanagan sit in it rent free? Besides, it's a pure case of imposition. She has the money and could pay me to-morrow if she liked."

"Do you really think she could?" faltered the boy. "I'm afraid she's very poor, uncle."

"Now, Robert," said his uncle, shaking a finger at him, "this is just a case in point. This is where a young, inexperienced fellow like you gets taken in. The world is full of impostors and rogues; and the sooner we find that out the better for us. Anyway, to your bed now, and think over what I've been telling you. I've had a long experience of the world, Bob, remember that; and if I don't know what's what by this time it's a queer thing. Good night, son." He stroked the boy's hair affectionately. "God bless you."

Little Bob Menzies climbed slowly up to his attic, and began to undress. First he kicked off his boots. Then he stripped off his stockings, which lay where they fell. Next he took out of his jacket pockets three round pebbles and two pieces of flint. These he arranged in a row on his washstand, alternating the pebbles and the flints; and after contemplating the result with much satisfaction he knelt by the bedside and said his prayers. Then he finished his undressing hastily. His jacket and waistcoat he hung on the end of the bed; but his knickerbockers joined his stockings on the floor. Then he turned down the bedclothes, and, raising the candle, looked cautiously round the room. Gazing intently at one of the window-curtains, he perceived that its folds had assumed the form of a man's savage face. He straightened the curtain, and, blowing out the candle, leaped into bed and drew the bedclothes partly over his face, at the same time closing his eyes tightly.

But it was long before he went to sleep. The thought of poor Sally Flanagan and her approaching calamity haunted him more and more insistently. Her meagre bent figure, her sunken cheeks and nut-cracker nose and chin rose before him. He heard her plaintive voice, her complaining whine that "the world was a very hard place for the poor." He knew his uncle was not a hard man, was even by some persons regarded as a simpleton. In his childish acceptance of things as they were he was satisfied that Sally must either pay her rent or be evicted. The claim of William Wilson, the ploughman, to the cottage was unquestionable. As matters stood, William had to walk three-quarters of a mile to his work. Besides, he liked William, and would be glad to have him living so near the farmhouse. Plainly the eviction of Sally Flanagan was a just and even a desirable thing. Yet it was hard that she must go to the workhouse because she had not ten shillings. She had lived in the cottage thirty years, twenty with her husband and her son, and ten a lonely widow abandoned by her ungrateful child. Perhaps it was necessary to be hard. But the necessity was going to make life an unpleasant business for a certain small boy. Bother! Sally Flanagan's affairs were none of his business. He buried himself deeper in the bedclothes. He would go to sleep.

But Bob Menzies could not go to sleep on account of a very unpleasant fact that had all along been in the background of his consciousness, and now had come resolutely forward and driven out all other considerations bearing on the sad case of Mrs. Flanagan. There was a certain boy who had thirteen shillings in his money-box, and he, Bob Menzies, was that boy. Clearly it was his duty to arise in the morning and bestow ten shillings out of that hoard on Sally Flanagan. All the boys of whom he had read—the good boys, that was—would have done so. He himself had in his day-dreams given away pounds in even less deserving cases than Sally's, and had been rewarded a hundredfold. Ah, there was the rub. His ten shillings were real, solid silver shillings, more than a third of the price of that real shot-gun for which he yearned more than for anything else in the world; and his reward would be only day-dream gold. Even in the exceptional generosity of his uncle it would take him years to restore ten shillings. Perhaps he would be gone off to business, and a gun be useless to him. Better face the truth; he would never have a gun of his own if he gave the ten shillings to Sally Flanagan. That settled it. He had forgotten his uncle's advice. His uncle was quite right. It was necessary to be hard in this world.

But he had thirteen shillings; and with ten of those shillings he could save Sally Flanagan from the workhouse, preserve for her the poor little home, sole relic of her happiness. Oh, it was a shame, it was a *shame* that this trial should have been ordained for him.

Nevertheless, the struggle was over. His ten shillings were already dedicated to the service of Sally. His uncle might preach hardness, his boyish soul might yearn over his relinquished gun; but he knew it was impossible for him to let Sally be thrust out on the roadside while his money-box was full.

Presently compensation for his self-denial began to come to him. He thought with satisfaction of Sally's change from sorrow to relief and delight, of her protestations of gratitude, her fears and blessings. Then he remembered that this attitude of mind was sinful, and would diminish, if not cancel, his heavenly reward. There should be no self-seeking, no carnal pride about his gift, or the sacrifice would not be acceptable. He crept out of bed, and in simple fervour, but with a rotundity of phrase that was not his own, besought that the blessing of God would make fruitful his bounty to one of the poorest of His creatures, then crept reverently to bed, and in a few moments was fast asleep.

II

In the morning the fit of exaltation was still upon him. He felt strangely light-hearted as he moved about the room. He saw that only virtue made for happiness; and planned out a long life devoted to benevolence. Spiritual pride returned to him; but in the daylight he did not recognize it, and complacently saw himself set apart from the way of the sinful. That his life might be all of one piece he washed himself with unusual care, and descended to breakfast longing for the moment of immolation.

During the meal he observed that his uncle was ill at ease and ate in silence, contrary to his wont. Bob felt sorry for him. He knew Mr. Menzies must be suffering the pangs of conscience for the action he was meditating, and could not help contrasting their respective positions to his own advantage.

"Time you were off to school, Bob," said his uncle at last, gloomily. "Speak to Mrs. Ross as you go through the yard, and tell her I want her to take a letter to Sally Flanagan."

Mrs. Ross, a brisk, sturdy little woman of thirty-five or so, sniffed incredulously when she heard the message.

"Aye, another journey for nothin'," she said, carefully cleaning the last fragment of hens' food off the wooden spoon in her hand, and throwing the morsels on the backs of the unheeding crowd of gobblers. "About once a month I'm sent to give notice to that slippery old faggot; an' then the master goes down the next day an' countermands it. If he hadn't some sensible body behind his hand, God knows what would become of the soft old fool. Off with you now, Bob; I didn't mean all that. But he is, all the same," she said, testily, as she turned away, "an' ould soft-hearted fool."

For the first half-mile of his journey to school Bob was filled with dismay by these words of Mrs. Ross. He perceived that his struggle and his victory were likely to be in vain.

His crown of sacrifice was in danger of being withheld from him after all. Money became as dross to him compared with the spiritual triumph to which he had braced himself, and a gun vanity. Then, as he entered on the short-cut across the Quaggy Bogs, a pair of wild-duck clattered up out of a drain about thirty yards away, and he saw that a small boy possessed of a gun would enjoy many compensations. He had now, too, entered on the apache-haunted prairie; and a wary scout had no time to be thinking about Sally Flanagan and her troubles. But as he drew near home in the afternoon, tired and hungry, thoughts of her returned throngingly. He could not make up his mind whether to wish that his uncle had been firm or had relaxed. In either case it was better to end the uncertainty. He began to walk quickly. When he entered the kitchen his uncle was sitting there.

"Did you give Sally notice, uncle?" he asked, breathlessly.

"I did, Robert," replied his uncle, with firmness. "When I make up my mind to do a thing I do it."

Mr. Menzies's answer might have been decisive to Bob if he had not heard from the scullery the voice of Mrs. Ross pronouncing cautiously but heartily the response: "Aye, God knows!" Experience told him that the words were to be taken as ironical, and he wavered.

"And *do* you mean to put her out, uncle?" Bob asked, timidly.

"If she doesn't pay me ten shillings before dinner-time to-morrow, I'm off to Johnson, the solicitor," his uncle answered; and Bob knew from the raised tone that his uncle also had heard Mrs. Ross's voice, and had uttered a challenge, and was irrevocably committed to severity against Mrs. Flanagan. At once it became blindingly clear to him that his deed of sacrifice was not to be performed merely in imagination, that he must in actual fact part with his money beyond recall. He sat a little while in stunned silence, and through his brain ran a mingled thought of the desirability of a gun and the Sisyphus labour of saving a fresh ten shillings.

Yet he did not falter in his purpose. Some hidden force

impelled him. Whence it came he knew not, but the characteristic intuition of the Puritan warned him that it was a spirit of carnality, that the high essence of selfless benevolence was not for him. He perceived that he had been planning to wear a crown without bearing the cross, that he had never really believed he should have to give his money to Sally Flanagan, but had all along felt that his uncle would relent. In an impulse compounded partly of a desire for self-maceration, partly of a feeling that, after all, he might as well take a sporting long-shot for grace, he picked out the newest and brightest of his ten shillings; but in his heart he knew that his reward must come at the hands of Sally Flanagan only.

An errand sought from his uncle furnished him with an excuse for passing near the cottage. When he came in sight of the lighted window his heart failed him a little, and he slackened his step. Full realization of her calamity must by this time have come to old Sally. Before she could learn of his errand of mercy there would be a period during which she must look on him with hostility as the nephew of her oppressor, a spy sent to gloat over her anger or her grief. Bob shrank from the ordeal. Timidly he raised the latch, and, opening the door, stood on the threshold. The old woman looked up from the fire of sticks beside which she had been crouching, and peered sharply at him.

Her thin shoulders were stooped, the face was parchment yellow, and the matted hair was grey almost to whiteness. But the eyes were still bright and the glance keen. To Bob's tender conscience they spoke accusation and reproach. He did not dare to venture into the kitchen, but stood irresolute on the threshold.

The expression of Sally's face softened. When she spoke it was in the complaining whine punctuated by short breathless groans that Bob knew and dreaded.

"Auch—Master Bob—is it you, dear?—auch—these pains, these pains. Come in, dear; come in an' sit down. Take the good chair; that oul' stool is no seat for a young gentleman like you. Auch—I'm very bad to-night, Master

Bob; I think it's the change in the moon. An' I run myself off my feet after that woman's goat next door. She was in among my wee bits of winter cabbage. Ay, put there, my dear, put there on purpose. It isn't the first time—auch——"

"Did she do much harm, Sally?" asked the boy, staving off the evil hour.

"No, dear, no. I heard her in time," answered Sally, rising painfully to her feet with the help of a withered branch of firewood, and seating herself on a stool. "I heard her in time, Master Bob, an' run out an' caught her in the act—an' hit her a skelp or two with my stick that her hind-end won't forget till this time to-morrow."

Sally chuckled at the remembrance, then recollected herself, and fell back into her complaining tone.

"Auch—it's a sore thing—a sore thing to be old an' poor, an' put-upon. Auch—your uncle did a cruel turn to me this day, Master Bob," turning suddenly on him ('*Now* it's coming,' thought the boy, miserably)—"a cruel turn on a poor old woman with one foot in the grave. An' him with plenty of the best. He had little call, for the sake of two or three miserable shillings, to threaten the poor an' needy an' the afflicted. Oh, Master Bob, dear!" And Sally raised her voice in weeping.

"I'll do it now," said Bob to himself, and laid hold of his money. But Sally did not give him time to speak.

"Not that I blame him," she said, blowing her nose fiercely. "He may be a bit hasty at times, but he's kindly in the end. It was that woman Ross put him up to it. From the day she first put her foot in his house she was again me, an' Judased me, an' undermined me. She came down herself, Master Bob, this mornin', to give me the notice, an' tri*umph* over poor oul' Sally. 'Get out,' sez she; 'get out, ye ould bitch, ye.' As true as God's in heaven them was the very words she used. 'Ye've been here too long,' sez she. 'I've been here longer nor you,' sez I, back to her, like that, 'an' longer nor you'll ever be; an' I'll maybe be here after you're found out, an' threw out. Mr. Hugh Menzies is a dacent man,' sez I, 'an' a Christian man, an' he'll never send away an ould neighbour an' an ould friend at your instigation.'—An' he won't, Master Bob, he never will. He'll never have the heart to put me out of the wee home. Thirty long years I've been in it. My three childer was born here, the two wee girls that died, an' the boy that's run away an' left his ould mother to the mercy of the world. An' my good, kind man. He died sittin' at this hearth, in the very chair you're on this minit." Bob felt his back chill. "Aw, if he was here now, if he was only here now!"

The picture of the old woman's desolation oppressed the boy's soul to pain. All thought of self left him. It was in an impulse of pure compassion that he drew forth his ten shillings and pressed them into old Sally's hand.

"Uncle Hugh told me you owed him ten shillings, Sally," he stammered. "Don't cry, *please* don't cry. There's ten shillings. You won't have to go now."

Old Sally dried her eyes, and looked at the money in her palm. The boy quailed as he thought of the scene of wild gratitude and relief that would follow. To his bewilderment, she accepted the bounty quite composedly.

"Thank you, Master Bob," she said in a matter-of-fact voice. "God bless you, dear. You've a kind heart like your uncle. Of course you have plenty. But many a child of your age wouldn't have thought of this. Wait till I put it in my wee cupboard." She rose briskly, and went to a recess in the wall. When she had locked the cupboard door again, she stood a moment or two, thinking. "Master Bob," she said, "say nothin' about this to that woman—or to your uncle, or anybody. That's a bad woman, Master Bob; an' she would want to make out I coaxed the money from you; an' maybe your uncle would believe her. But, God bless you, dear, again. You've your poor father's kindly heart. He never passed the door but he gave me somethin'. Auch—auch——" Sally became suddenly feeble again, and hobbled toward the fireplace. "This has been a sore day on a poor old creature like me. Auch—I think I'll make a drop of tay. Would you have a drop, Master Bob?"

The boy took this speech as his dismissal, and made his way slowly along the road. He was conscious of an anti-climax. The great act of renunciation had been accomplished, and where was the glow of virtuous satisfaction? His heavenly reward he had thrown away by unwilling giving, he knew; but now even his earthly recompense seemed to be eluding him. He had expected voluble and tearful gratitude, and even shrunk from the thought of it; but from Sally he had had barely thanks. In his day-dreams he had imagined his beneficence accidentally coming to light, and had modestly glowed in the praise of his fellow-men; but now he wondered if the world might not share his awakening doubt of his own wisdom, and even hint ridicule. Yet he did not regret his kindness to Sally. If his ten shillings could be magically restored to him he knew he would give them back to her. Gradually light began to dawn in his puzzled mind. It was as Sally had said. There was no obligation of gratitude due from her to him. Compared with her indigence he had plenty. The uncomfortable burden of philanthropy settled on Bob's shoulders, thenceforward to insinuate misgiving into all his pleasures. He quickened his pace and strode manfully up the hill from Sally's house, fighting down the thought that when he arose that morning there had been thirteen shillings in his money-box, and now there were but three.

III

Next day being Saturday and a school holiday, Bob, as was customary, breakfasted late, and alone. When he went to the kitchen afterwards for his boots, he found his uncle sitting by the fire, waiting for him.

"Bring your chair over here, Bob," said Mr. Menzies in a mysterious whisper. "I want to say something to you before Mrs. Ross comes in. You remember my telling you that I meant to put Sally Flanagan out if she didn't pay me her arrears of rent. Maybe you thought me severe on the woman. It came into my head once or twice that you did. But I had a reason, Bob. I wanted to teach you a lesson, to show you what comes of softness, and what's the result of insisting on your rights.

"Now listen to this. Yesterday morning I sent word to Sally Flanagan to pay or go out. I had been soft with her for twenty weeks, and yesterday I turned hard. And what happened? What do you think happened?"

"I—I don't know, uncle?" said Bob, summoning up as good a pretence at wonder as he was able.

"She paid me," said his uncle, impressively. "She sent up this morning and paid me! It's not well, Robert, my boy, to be too hard; always remember that, so I sent her back a shilling by the messenger, wee Peter Maguire—I hope he doesn't stick to it, though I gave him sixpence to keep him out of temptation. Now, what lesson should you learn from what has happened? I'll tell you: 'Insist on your rights, or you'll be bamboozled!' You see now that your uncle knows what he's talking about."

Mr. Menzies leaned back in his chair and scanned the boy's face anxiously to observe whether the lesson had sunk in. As for Bob, he gazed steadily into the fire, lest he might betray himself. Here was a development of his action that he had never dreamed of. He was ashamed for his uncle, whom he had caused to become ridiculous before him; but, worse still, it was clear that though he had for the time relieved Sally's difficulties he had closed the gates of mercy on her for the future. With dismay he saw himself condemned by conscience to subsidize her with sixpence a week till her death. Life had suddenly become very difficult. He longed to go away and think. But his uncle was speaking again.

"Here's the money," said Mr. Menzies, triumphantly, groping in his waistcoat pocket. "Don't forget the lesson you have learned this morning, Bob. Being hard has been worth eight and sixpence to me—after all, what about eighteenpence?—and it'll be worth thousands of pounds to you before you die."

The boy looked at his uncle's oustretched hand, and saw two half-crowns, a florin, a shilling, and sixpence. He looked again, incredulously. There was no doubt possible. His eyes had not deceived him. But Sally had. Sally had. She had taken his ten precious new shillings, and all the time had possessed enough money to pay her rent. He felt hot all over at the thought. How *mean* of her, how mean! He had never imagined such deceit. Indignation flamed within him. He would march straight down the road to Sally's and tell her what he thought of her. Impatiently he listened to the rest of his uncle's homily, then sought his cap.

As he quitted the house doubt assailed him. Could there be any mistake? Had his uncle brought out of his pocket the actual coins from Sally, or just the same amount, as an object-lesson to drive home his sermon? Bob hesitated. Perhaps it was better to be certain. He saw Mrs. Ross coming from the farmyard, and decided to pump her.

"I suppose you know Sally Flanagan has paid uncle, Mrs. Ross?" he ventured.

The housekeeper sniffed.

"Oh, aye, Bob," she answered, dryly. "She has paid him."

Bob shuffled from foot to foot irresolutely. An impulse to confess his share in the transaction assailed him; but he remembered Mrs. Ross's hostility to Sally, and fell back on the indirect method.

"Do you think she had the money all the time, Mrs. Ross?"

The housekeeper banged down the buckets she was carrying.

"I don't know whether she had or not, Bob," she said with vehemence. "It's very likely. But it wasn't her own ten shillings she sent your uncle." (Bob's heart thumped.) Mrs. Ross paused and compressed her lips. "H'm, I don't know I should tell you—I will. It'll maybe keep you from following in the footsteps of that old idiot. Your uncle gave her the ten shillings. He sent Henry Larmour down with it to her yesterday after I'd come back from givin' her notice, an' gave him a shillin' not to tell anybody. But of course Henry came straight to me. Did you ever hear the like of such a man in your life as that uncle of yours?—the ould soft gawm.

Mind you, I know he had some fool notion of teachin' you a lesson—he let that out to me—but that makes it no better. To send thon greedy, two-faced ould baggage the money to pay her rent, an' then let on he was pressin' her; an' all the time her curlin' up her lip at him, an' talkin' about him behind his back. Aw, dear, dear. The country was laughin' at him before, but it'll be holdin' its sides now. I'm near ashamed to be looking people in the face myself."

Mrs. Ross picked up her buckets and went off. Bob scarcely remarked her going, but stood in the middle of the yard, half-stunned. Shame flooded his soul. An abyss of humiliation yawned before him. If his uncle was a laughing-stock, what would *he* be when old Sally told about him, as he knew she would? His soul sickened at the prospect. At home, at the forge, at school, he saw himself the helpless target of derision. Mrs. Ross would laugh at him. Even his uncle would laugh at him. He couldn't bear it. Life would be intolerable. He pictured himself ending his tortured existence in the gloomy waters of the big bog-hole.

What could he do? What *could* he do? Ah! He would appeal to Sally. He had been good to her. She had got his ten shillings. Surely that would satisfy her. If he besought her mercy surely she couldn't be so cruel as to betray the shameful secret of his gullibility. Breathless, half-sobbing, he stumbled along the road to her cottage.

He paused a moment or two before raising the latch, and strove to regain command of himself. He must dissimulate, he knew that; though his overwrought feelings impelled him to throw himself on his knees and beseech her with tears.

He opened the door; and at the sight of her hypocritical face little Bob Menzies first knew hatred.

"Sally," he said, "Sally." His voice trembled a little in spite of himself. "I—I gave you ten shillings last night; and I just came to tell you that I would rather no one knew about it."

The old woman looked at him shrewdly. A slow smile recreased her innumerable wrinkles.

"Is that what's botherin' you, dear?" she said. "Are you

afraid that people would laugh at you because you were kind to poor old Sally?"

The boy's self-command deserted him suddenly.

"Please don't tell, Sally," he entreated—"*Please.*"

The old woman did not answer. Her toothless gums showed in a silent laugh.

"Sally," he cried desperately, "I have three shillings in my money-box. I'll give you that, too."

The old woman hobbled forward and laid her hand on his hair.

"Well, well, well," she said; "is that all you think of poor oul' Sally? I'll not take your three shillings, child; an' I'll tell nobody nothing. You're a good, foolish child. You didn't say anything to your uncle about the ten shillings—or to Mrs. Ross?"

Bob shook his head. He was almost certain that if he spoke he would burst into weeping.

"Say nothing, then, dear, to either of them. Your uncle might be vexed, an' that woman would never forgive you for keepin' me off the roadside when she thought she was rid of me. An' you'll always be kind to me, Master Bob, if ever your uncle is hard—won't you, son?"

Bob nodded, and turning, hurried out of the cottage. Relief and shame contended in his bosom. He blushed for his panic. He must never be so foolish again. And he had wronged old Sally. She wasn't so bad as in his haste he had deemed her. She had refused his three shillings—but then she had continued to deceive him about his uncle's behaviour to her.

The sudden revelation of the complexities of life and character puzzled and dismayed the boy. Things would never be so simple to him again. Though he did not then know it, the Bob Menzies who walked soberly homeward from Sally Flanagan's cottage was a different boy from the one who had sat at the kitchen fireside with his uncle but two nights before.

Love Plucks a String

BOB MENZIES and his uncle sat by the kitchen fire, according to their usual custom in the winter evenings. This was their time for mutual unburdenings, and grave speculation. At least thirty-five years divided Hugh Menzies from his nephew and ward; but the world had made little mark on him; and they were both children together. At the back of them hard common sense—or so she said—in the shape of Mrs. Ross, the housekeeper ("a little thickened in the figure but still sonsy," as her master put it) hovered from kitchen to scullery, and dispersed whole clouds of romance now and then with a few bleak words.

This night Bob was anxious to avoid Mrs. Ross's comments, and spoke in a lower tone than usual.

A new field of emotion and disillusion had lately been opening to the boy. Gradually he was awakening to women as a separate sex. At the National School which he attended boys and girls were educated together, stood side by side in class, and romped together at play-time. Many of his boy fellow-scholars were much more advanced in sex-knowledge and feeling than he was; but to Bob, a shy child, holding rather aloof from his comrades, girls had hitherto been little more than a weaker species of boy, unsuited for sharing in the rougher games and the more adventurous deeds, more teasing and teasable, prone to weeping and to carrying tales.

It was the school-mistress who received his first tribute of homage to the power of womankind. Slowly she began to appear less awful to him, to awaken his admiration by her shining hair, her neat dress, her soft voice and shapely, well-cared-for hands. He became conscious of a feeling of mingled pleasure and discomfort when she bent over him during the drawing-lesson, and sometimes prolonged the disturbing sensation by pretending to be more stupid than he really was. But in a moment of exaltation he had been incautious enough to bring her an offering of flowers one morning. Both boys and girls united in a stream of ridicule. Worse still, the gratified teacher thenceforward singled him out for special attention, and with unthinking cruelty assumed something of the sweetheart; and Bob's first love impulse expired in misery and loathing. And when a little later on he began to experience a dawning tenderness for one Grace Henderson, a scholar in his own class, he was at pains to hide his sentiments even from the beloved one.

Concealment did not prey on him. The disease was not serious. Grace did not even leave a permanent image in his memory. In later years he could recall nothing but a vague impression of a tall girl with sunlit brown hair, who kept her hands very clean. But at this time she occupied his boyish mind many a month both by day and night. He wove timid day-dreams round her; and sometimes awoke in the night with a strange sweetness on his lips and thought that he had kissed her.

After a time the course of his affection began to be troubled by the intrusive image of laughing red-headed tomboy Molly O'Malley. No neat, clean-handed damsel, Molly; her chapped fingers were usually ink to the knuckle. But she was gay and bright-eyed and of an indomitable courage and an unquenchable effrontery. Bob's feeling for Molly was not altogether liking. She was a little older than he, and he was indeed rather scared of her; but her quizzical grey-green eyes and her mane of auburn hair and her transparent freckled skin and prematurely developed figure perturbed him nevertheless; and he sometimes wished he had the pluck to meet her half-way.

Such a height of temerity had hitherto proved beyond him. Even in the presence of the sweet shrinking Grace he was tongue-tied and awkward. He saw himself doomed to grow into old age a bachelor like his Uncle Hugh. This night he had determined to find out whether his uncle's bachelorhood was voluntary and cheerful, or whether it was due to some such infirmity as his own.

"Uncle Hugh," he asked cautiously, "do you think it's a good thing to get married?"

"Well now," returned Mr. Menzies in a considering impersonal manner, "I wouldn't just like to say. It's a chancy business, Bob, a chancy business. And if you don't have the good luck to get the woman that suits you I'd say it was a desperate affair altogether."

"Then you think a man is better to stay single?" asked Bob with a certain relief.

"I wouldn't say that either," said Mr. Menzies, after a moment or two. "You might be lucky, Bob. You might get a woman that suits one side of you anyway, and if God is good to you, you might even get a woman that suits all sides of you. It's maybe too much to expect, but if you should happen to get it you'll have the grandest gift that can be bestowed on a man. It's worth while marrying, Bob, even on the chance of getting it."

"But you never married yourself, uncle," said the boy, looking at him wide-eyed.

"I did not. I did not," answered his uncle, dwelling on each syllable, "and it was a mistake. Keep mind, Bob, marrying is a business with two parties to it. The one party asks—generally the man, though I've heard of women doing it—and the other answers—mostly 'yes,' but sometimes 'no.'"

The boy debated a question of delicacy with himself for a few minutes. Curiosity triumphed, though with difficulty.

"Did—did your girl say 'no,' uncle?" he queried shamefacedly.

His uncle remained silent for quite a long time. He, too, seemed to suffer an inward struggle.

"She did not, Robert," he answered finally. "She did not, and that's the truth. I—I never asked her. I wasn't oncoming enough with the girls when I was a young fellow; and I doubt I'm not a deal better yet, though there's times I think I'm mending. Bob," he said—he looked round the kitchen to see that Mrs. Ross was out of earshot, then leaned forward impressively—"remember one thing all your life: Be impident with weemin. A young woman is like a young horse. If you walk boldly up to her and take her by the headstall or the forelock she'll come along with you as quiet as a lamb; but if you go for her anyway timid or hesitating she'll prance and skip and squeal and show off, and maybe give you her heels in the end." He paused and remained in thought, then resumed, sighing. "That was how I lost my chance, anyway. I wasn't impident enough.—As far as I can see," he said disconsolately, as he rose and walked to the kitchen door, "I'll never be impident enough now."

"And that's the God's truth, anyway," said Mrs. Ross, looking after him. "A decent, kindly ould gawm.—What was he talking about, Bob?"

Bob yawned adroitly and brought fate on his head.

"But you're sleeping on your feet, child. Away off with you to your bed."

The boy obeyed willingly enough. His uncle's words seethed in his head, and filled him with daring thoughts. To-morrow was a half-holiday, too. As usual he and his school-mates would eat their "pieces," and play together in the afternoon before going home. A laughing vision of Molly O'Malley passed before his eyes. He jumped manfully be-tween the cold sheets, meditating impudence on the morrow.

On the morrow opportunity was thrust upon him. Molly was of the party, flushed with freedom, and even more hoydenish than usual. Her wildness infected the others. All was laughter, scampering, and horseplay; Bob, quick to take fire when some bolder spirit had kindled the flame, as frolic-some as any.

The most exquisite jest was to steal up softly, and violently jostle a comrade. Stimulated by the atmosphere of exhilara-tion Bob found courage and jostled Molly as heartily as the rest did, and in the end more frequently. Now Molly had for some time been well aware both of Bob's straying fancy and of his shyness; and the spirit of mischief soared in her. Suddenly, at the very top of Bob's glory the voice of doom sounded for him.

"I'm going to kiss Bob Menzies," called out Molly, and with the shrill cheer that arose, straightway swooped on him.

Disgraceful panic seized Bob. One thought alone emerged from the chaos of his outraged soul—escape. Pursued by shame, by fear of ridicule, and by Molly, he took to his heels, and blindly eluding the hands outstretched to detain him tore along the path to his home. He was a swift runner, but Molly's legs were longer. She gained on him; and but for her handicap of skirts and laughter Bob would have been kissed within the first hundred yards, in full sight of the jeering crowd. Terror gave him speed. He spurted desperately, and drew away a little. Then his better training began to tell. He held his own for a time. The chase settled down to steady flight and pursuit. Bob's brain cleared. In front of him was a small grove of trees and brushwood. If he could once gain that he might be kissed, but he would be kissed out of sight, and could deny the disgraceful fact. Presently a thought of wild daring entered his mind; what if safely out of view he should turn suddenly and kiss Molly? Better still, why not kiss her in full sight of the world? Ridicule would be killed; he would be the envy of his fellows for his boldness; and, with all his inexperience, he knew that he would gain in Molly's eyes.

Bob toyed with the thought as he ran, and it turned to sweetness. He wished to kiss Molly. How strange, how intoxicating it would be to press those warm red lips with his, to feel that slender body struggling in his arms. His speed had slackened as he yielded to his thought. She was gaining on him. Now was the time, before they were hidden by the trees. His heart failed him a little. He would not kiss her before the others. Perhaps Molly would be angry. She had once slapped a boy's face who had tried to kiss her. Girls were queer things. He would wait till they were among the trees. Now at last was the time! They were safely sheltered by the leafage. He slackened his pace again. Molly was drawing nearer, nearer. And then, as he strove to nerve himself for the great venture, he tripped over a fallen bough, and Molly was on him.

"Now, Bob Menzies, I have you," she cried.

Instant revulsion swept over Bob. At all costs he must escape this humiliation. He scrambled to his feet, avoiding Molly's clutch, and in a fury of scared modesty and outraged pride he seized on the bough that had been his downfall, and threatened the laughing girl.

"If you dare," he panted. "If you dare, I'll strike you."

Molly drew back a step, and stared at him. Something in his voice warned her that he was serious.

"I will," repeated Bob firmly. "I mean it."

The girl shrugged her shoulders and turned away indifferently. The thing had been a frolic; and the savour of the jest was departed.

"Who wants to kiss you, you little silly?" she said, and turned back on her steps, plucking idly at the leaves as she went, and humming stray snatches of song.

Bob threw down his piece of stick and followed her slowly. He was no longer afraid that she would kiss him. Her contempt stung him a little; but he did not think very much about her at all. The tumult of emotion had passed, and he was sunk in a slough of self-abasement. He had been a coward, a poor timid unmanly creature who might have kissed a girl, who had longed to kiss a girl, who had kissed more than one girl boldly, audaciously, in his day-dreams; and now when his visions might have found glorious realization he had turned his back on opportunity. Worse, perhaps, in his panic cowardice he had basely threatened a girl rather than be kissed. How he would be laughed at! What school-days lay before him now!

At first he thought of flying immediate torment; and turned his steps homeward. Then he saw that this would never do. Molly could tell her shameful story uncontradicted. He must be there to deny. He knew himself quick-witted, fertile in invention. Some turn could be given to the incident, whereby his humiliation might be lessened.

But when he regained his playmates he found Bill Jones and Joe Kinnear surrounded by an excited throng of partisans, threatening fisticuffs over a swap of marbles. The preliminary wrangle had been long and interesting; and he and Molly were forgotten. Hope rose again in Bob. If no one questioned her, perhaps Molly, too, would forget the episode. He hung around the ring of eager spectators watching Molly as she strove to elbow her way in. Then he saw little Susy Ryan—Inquisitive Susy—draw near Molly and pluck her by the skirts. He was lost! He crept closer, listening with all his ears.

"Molly?" he heard Susy persisting. "Molly, *did* you kiss him?"

But to Molly's volatile mind the present was the only moment.

"Go away, Susy," she cried, pushing her off. "No, I didn't kiss him. I was only humbugging. Let me alone. I want to see the fight."

The fight, as fights do, proceeded no further than the taking off of coats. The prospective combatants were only too easily dragged apart; and the spectators, divided into two wrangling groups, presently began to move on again. The groups slowly drew away from each other, bandying challenges as long as they were within earshot. Bob's adopted party split into twos and threes, talking of the recent squabble, of the exchange values of glass and stoney marbles, and other matters of boyish interest. The episode of the attempted kissing had passed from everyone's mind but Bob's. As he walked up the lane to his uncle's house he recognized that he had been fortunate beyond his deserving. But there was no elation in his thought, only depression and self-contempt. Regret for Molly did not trouble him. She was but a pawn in the game that he had so lamentably lost. Before his eyes rose up the swaggering image of the boy who would have strode home in pride and confidence if only he had kissed her. With a pang it came suddenly home to Bob that when most it would have availed him he had altogether forgotten his uncle's advice to be impident with weemin.

Bob's evening meal did a good deal to reduce the events of the afternoon to their true importance in a boy's life; but he still suffered from a sense of youthfulness and inexperience. His opinion of his uncle's wisdom had been greatly raised by the afternoon's happening; and that night he again brought round the conversation to the subject of love.

"Do you 'member, Uncle Hugh," he said, "telling me that you had a girl once. Were you very young then?"

"I was not, Bob," returned his uncle. "No, I wasn't exactly what you would call young. I suppose I would be about twenty-four or five. You'll be surprised to hear that. People thinks that because I have a very kindly feeling towards the weemin nowadays I was a tearin' rantin' courter when I was young. But, no; I put it off too long. I held away from the girls that long that in the end I came to think there was something terrible in making up to them; and the truth is it's just an ordinary transaction in life, and should come as easy to a man as suppin' porridge.

"I've been thinking about you, Bob, all day; and, do you know, I'm not sure that I came out strong enough in favour of marriage last night. I would not like that any remarks I made should discourage you. Of course, you're far too young to have anything to do with marriage—yet; but if you were thinking of having a little preliminary practice in courting I wouldn't say but it's nearly time you were making a start. Practice is what a young fellow wants, and plenty of it, too. Your whole system may be fair clogged with love, and what's the use if you can't deliver yourself of it in a handy, taking way?"

During this speech Mrs. Ross though appearing to bustle about the kitchen had contrived that her duties should lie within earshot of the speaker; and now she broke in without ceremony.

"What nonsense are you puttin' into the child's head about love?" she demanded. "Ay, nonsense," she repeated, intercepting Mr. Menzies's attempt to protest; "an' when you get to my time of life you know it. If Master Bob ever does come to think of marryin', an' he's time enough these ten years, let him look out for somebody with a bit of money, or a fine big farm, an' then if she dies on him he'll never be stuck to get another. A good secure comfortable position in the world is better nor love. It's a long time since I saw that."

"But didn't *you* marry for love, Mrs. Ross?" Bob ventured.

Mrs. Ross was silent for a moment or two, then passed her hand softly over the boy's hair.

"Bob," she said, "weemin is fools—one kind of weemin, anyway. That kind wants somebody or somethin' to be good to an' take care of an' dance attendance on. God made them that way. That's the sort I used to be myself. If I'd had the luck to have a nice boy like you I might be that way still. An' maybe when he grew up he'd turn his back on me, an' I'd be no better off in the end. No," she said, rubbing the table vigorously with the dish-cloth as she spoke; "it's better to mind number one. Money's what matters in this world. If I ever do it again it'll be for money."

Mr. Menzies stroked his chin thoughtfully, and looked into the fire.

"You uttered one very true thing there, Mrs. Ross," he said at last—"not about the money; for I wouldn't give a fig about that——"

"That's because you have plenty," interrupted Mrs. Ross, briskly.

"—it was what you said about care and attention," went on Mr. Menzies, not heeding her. "A man is a feckless bein' an' needs someone to look after him; an' only a woman can do it. After a deal of cogitatin' I have come to the conclusion that it doesn't matter who a man marries if he can only thole livin' with her till he gets used to her and she gets used to him.

"It's a great thing to get used to a woman. A man may differ with her about a whole lot of little matters. She may even annoy him a good deal at times. But then, she knows his ways. That oils life, Bob, that oils life. It's a great thing to feel that when you come in cold from the land there'll be a good hot tasty meal waitin' for you; an' when you want your boots to know that they'll be warmin' by the fire, instead of you paddin' round the house in your stockin' feet huntin' for them, an' maybe gettin' your death. If it's only the changin' of your socks you're heart-scalded unless there's a woman about the place. I know; for many a long day I endured. But how are you to get her?" demanded Mr.

Menzies, pursing his lips and looking first at Bob and then at the housekeeper. "You must make love to her first.—You would expect it yourself, Mrs. Ross?" he said with a certain note of timidity.

"I might like a bit of it, even yet," said Mrs. Ross, considering, "at the start, anyway. But I could do without it.—Ah, for goodness' sake stop talkin' blathers. I don't know what's come over us all."

She picked up her bucket, and clattered off to the scullery. Mr. Menzies looked after her a little wistfully.

"You'll find out that I'm right, Bob," he said. "A little courtin' has to be gone through, and early. If you don't learn the trick of it when you're young you won't have any skill of it if you should take a notion later on. Bob, my advice to you still is—start early, an' be impident.—You've heard me speakin' against drink, haven't you?"

"Yes, uncle," said Bob, drowsily.

"Well, the one time I think a man is justified in taking a little drink is when he goes courting. It puts heart an' courage into him, an' cheek; an' that's what the weemin like. I wouldn't just recommend whiskey, mind you. Weemin is nice in their ways. Something a little more genteel; say port, now. I've been thinkin' lately of keepin' a little sup in the house. You never could tell when it would come in useful. If I had thrown a couple of glasses of port wine into me on a certain occasion a good many years ago, the whole course of the world might have been changed."

When Mr. Menzies looked over at Bob for assent he saw that the boy had fallen fast asleep. For a while he sat on, staring into the dying fire and muttering to himself. Outside, in the scullery, Mrs. Ross was crooning a low song as she worked. After a little she ceased singing and listened, then stole to the kitchen door and peeped in. Mr. Menzies, too, had fallen asleep, his head drooping forward on his chest. Now and then he murmured a few words of expostulation that died into a groan. Mrs. Ross tiptoed across the kitchen and stood looking down on the pair, smiling and shaking her head. Once more she passed her fingers tenderly through

Bob's tousled hair, and, stooping, kissed him on the cheek. When she stood up again her eyes were wet. She shook the boy gently by the arm, and motioning in warning towards the other sleeper led him from the room. At the foot of the stairs she halted, and kissed him again, and pressed him hungrily to her bosom.

"Good night, son," she whispered. "Remember that no matter what happens Mary Ross won't see you harmed."

"Good night," Bob answered, and heavily began to climb the stairs. The chord that had prematurely vibrated in his heart was still again. He was a sleepy little animal; and sought his dreamless lair, untroubled by the knowledge that his feet had taken the first steps on a path of mingled pain and delight.

Mrs. Ross crept back to the kitchen door, and looked again steadily at her sleeping master. Mr. Menzies's head had fallen a little more forward, and his waistcoat lay open at the top. The housekeeper shook her head in playful despair.

"Would anybody look at the shirt he has on!" she said to herself, "an' this Thursday." She stepped cautiously into the kitchen, and lifting a saucepan-lid from its nail cast it on the floor with a clatter, then fled laughing. But when she reached her room she stood a while in thought, and sighed.

The Change in Liza

It has for many years been my practice to spend some of my annual holiday in the company of my friend, Mr. Murphy, for the purpose of refreshing my town-jaded soul with what he would call his "crack."

Of this commodity Mr. Murphy possesses an almost unlimited supply. To set the tap running is the difficulty. After long experience I have found out that the best vintage flows unsought. A chance word may do the business, or some trifling incident. The prudent will then confine himself to the part of listener.

I was returning one day after a somewhat unfruitful walk with Mr. Murphy, when, passing a farmhouse, I observed a very slatternly woman emptying a bucket of soapsuds down the steps from her kitchen into the yard. It is difficult to perform the duties of a working farmer's wife and remain trim. The feat is not often accomplished. But this woman was of an uncommon sluttishness. I had never seen a dirtier face or untidier hair, or a more shapeless and ungirt figure.

"In the name of goodness, Pat," said I, "how did any man ever come to marry a woman like that?"

"You can never tell what makes a man marry a woman," answered Mr. Murphy. "The weemin can't tell, themselves. If they could there wouldn't be mankind in the world left single. But, even as it is, they know that much that many a time I wonder how men escape the way they do. I'll tell you a wee story that come under my own notice years ago."

When I was a young fellow Miss Armytage of the Hall was a settled ould maid, past all expectation, an' near past hope; an' like many another ould maid, she had got odd in her ways. Not sour, mind ye, or carnaptious—just odd. An' some very queer notions she took intil her head from time to time. But with all her oddity she was a good landlord, an' that at a time when there weren't many good landlords; an' she still liked to go in an' out among her tenantry, an' pass a kindly word, ay, an' do more, too, when it was needed. An' though she never had less nor four good carriage-horses eatin' their heads off in her stable, an' kept a coachman, an' a groom forbye, she always went round her tenants on foot. Wet or dry, it was the same to her. She had no regard for the weather. I've met her myself on a winter's day when the frost would be splittin' the stones, an' her steppin' out like a two-year-old, with a pair of woollen stockings pulled over her boots to keep her from slippin'. But though it was well meant of her to put aside her pride an' walk into your house like an ordinary body, there was many a farmer's wife caught in her dishables that would a sight rather the ould lady had driv up in the carriage-an'-pair, an' give her a bit of warnin'.

For Miss Armytage was a great one for people respectin'

themselves accordin' to their station, an' was very severe on dirt. In particular she hated the look of a dirty child. Many a small farmer's family rubbed more soap on themselves in the time it took Miss Armytage to walk from the county-road up to their front door than they'd used in the six months before that; an' many a poor wee mite couldn't crack a smile when she gave it a penny, for the way its nostrils was still stingin'.

But she had one great fad before everything else, an' troth, a kindly one, too. As soon as they were at all fit to do it, all the girls in the Hall school be't to learn needlework, an' fancy needlework at that. An' every child that was born on the estate, an' every grown girl on it that got married, had an outfit, made by the school-children, that would have done My Lady. Miss Armytage paid for all. Them was the two times—when she was a wife an' when she was a mother—that clothes gave a woman most pleasure, Miss Armytage used to say; an' why shouldn't the poor have it as well as the rich?

The same notion of the old lady's done no harm. If it didn't send the population up it didn't keep it down, anyway. Right or wrong, more than one girl got the name of makin' an extra push to get married just on account of the good clothes; an' though the men wouldn't believe that was the reason, the weemin-folk wasn't just so sure about it.

Now there was a fine-lookin' lassie called Liza Cotter used to live with her father in one of the cottages on Miss Armytage's home farm. Her mother had been lady's-maid at the Hall one time, an' made a very poor market for herself, marryin' a labourer; an' Miss Armytage fell out with her about it. But when the poor bein' was lyin' on her early death-bed Miss Armytage went to see her, an' made up the quarrel, an' promised to look after her only child, Liza. She kept her word, too, an' always seen that the child was well-clothed an' well-schooled, an' paid the father a deal better wages than he was worth; for he was an easy-goin' slovenly crather.

A sonsy lump Liza was, with a big wide laugh that would

have near let you see her dinner; an' full of good-nature. As soon as she was got up to a courtin' age Miss Armytage's one wish was to get her married. It was her notion that if marryin' had brought the mother down it might lift the daughter up again. By hook or by crook she meant to hunt up a good match; an' the least was in her mind was a rich farmer for Liza.

At one time she thought she was goin' to get her wish without any bother. When the girl was about eighteen a strong father's son, Hugh Black by name, took a great fancy to her, an' begun to hang about the father's cottage a good deal. Now the divil a thing, in my opinion, was in the young fellow's mind but just to take a bit of a hand out of Liza; an', in any case, if he'd mentioned marryin' her his own folk would have ate him. But when Miss Armytage got hold of the affair, as she very soon did, she jumped at the idea that Black meant business, an' used to go round an' coach Liza on how to behave herself if she meant to catch him.

There was poor results of her teachin'.

In the first place the girl was of too on-comin' a disposition altogether; an' seein', as she thought, a chance of becomin' mistress of a good farm, an', besides, havin' a good deal more than a fancy for the young fellow himself, she clean threw herself at Hugh Black's head. He had only to whistle, an' she would have followed him about like a wee dog. An' I may tell you that sort of behaviour isn't goin' to do a girl much good with a man, even in the country.

All the same Liza was real good-lookin', an' very takin' in her ways. There is no tellin' how she might have done if she'd kept herself at all clean an' trig. But that was what she couldn't do. She was her father's child; an' the slovenly drop was in her.

Miss Armytage was terrible cut about it; for she knew that in the case of a well-brought-up boy like Hugh Black it was clean death to Liza's chances. She used to lecture Liza up an' down about keepin' herself tidy, an' at times would fly into a rage an' scold her wicked; but she might as well have saved her breath. Half a dozen times she washed her hands of the girl altogether; then she would take fresh mind of her word to the mother, an' go back for another try; an' it was all no use. But at last, just when she had determined to give up Liza for good, a new plan came into her head.

She was a great ould match-maker in her way, an' at the time she took up Liza Cotter's love affairs she had another marryin' job on. This was no less than her favourite niece, Miss Rosie, that used to live with her every now an' then until they would fall out. Miss Rosie's father was as poor as Lazarus, an' Miss Armytage was all for her marryin' a neighbourin' landlord that had a great notion of her an' was stinkin' with money, but as old as Methuselem's parrot. The old lady handled the affair well. The pair was engaged to be married; the weddin'-day was well in sight; an' the school-childer had made ready such an outfit of shifts an' underclothes for Miss Rosie as, accordin' to my wife Molly, had never been seen before for lace an' frills. Molly should know, too. Her an' every womankind on the estate was invited to the Hall to see the things, an' had their tea forbye. Somethin' special they must have been; for when Molly brought back Miss Service of the Post Office to talk them all over afterwards, Miss Service wouldn't open her mouth till I was put out of the room.

Now whether it was in the belief that the way the niece was goin' to be dolled-up would set a good example I can't tell you; but, anyway, Miss Armytage thought she saw a chance of reformin' Liza Cotter's ways at last; an' what does she do but fetch her up to the Hall to train her as lady's maid for Miss Rosie.

It wasn't a success, at the first, anyway; an' how it would have turned out in the end nobody ever got a chance of seein'; for about a week before the weddin' here doesn't the niece run off with her own cousin that is in the horse-sojers. All the men-kind in the country said, "Well done," an' all the weemin did the same, but wondered how she'd had the heart to run away from so many good clothes. But Miss Armytage was neither to hold nor to bind, an' abused everybody like a pickpocket.

The weight of her anger fell on Liza. She hadn't been over-well satisfied with Liza as it was; but now she suspected her of havin' a hand in the elopement, an' terrible scenes took place between the two of them. One of the upper-housemaids at the Hall told Molly that Miss Armytage locked up Liza in an empty pantry for two hours, an' stood over her scoldin' her an' questionin' her, an' that the roars an' belyaurs of Liza was desperate, but that she couldn't be got to confess. In the end she convinced Miss Armytage that she was innocent of everything but dirt; an' we heard that Miss Armytage had took pity on her an' promised her one last chance. But it seemed this report was wrong, or else Miss Armytage had flew into another tantrum; for the next day Molly met Liza walkin' home to her father's with hardly an eye in her head from cryin'; an' an hour or so afterwards the groom driv past in a spring cart with all her belongin's in a trunk.

"This is the end of Liza as far as soap an' water is concerned," sez Molly to me that evenin' as we sat at the fire talkin' it all over. "The next time her ears is washed'll be when she's laid-out." An' I agreed with her.

But we were both wrong. For an extraordinary thing happened. From the day Liza went back home from the Hall she was another girl in the way she kept herself. She'd always had good clothes for her station in life—Miss Armytage seen to that—but there's a deal in the way a girl's clothes is put on her, an' you'd have thought Liza's had been blew at her in the Big Wind. Her stockin's was always concertina'd down her legs, an' seldom without a hole in one heel anyway. If her petticoat wasn't hangin' half an inch below her skirt, a piece of braid off it was sure to be, an' if she had one button out of three fastened at the back of her blouse she was doin' well. Half-time a wisp of her hair would be hangin' loose. An' though she may have washed her face every day it wasn't more than once a week that she minded there was a neck below it.

Well, I met her up the road a few weeks after the change took her, an', troth, at the first I didn't know her. She was as neat an' trim as if she was just out of a bandbox, her clothes well-brushed an' well put on, every hair in its place, an' her shoes shinin' that you could have seen your face in them. I turned to look after her when she was gone by—an' that was more than I'd have done a fortnight before—an' then I made off to tell Molly.

But Molly wouldn't believe me at all.

"Ye may say what you like, Pat," she would answer me; "but it wasn't Liza."

"Very well," sez I at the last, "she had a basket in her hand, an' likely was only goin' the length of Jervis's shop. Come down the road with me an' see for yourself."

So off we went an' lay at the back of a ditch an' keeked through the hedge as Liza was comin' back; an' the wife had to give in that it *was* Liza. But she was clean bewildered in her mind, an' went about for the next week or so in a kind of a daze, tryin' to guess how the change had come about.

It wasn't only on herself that Liza wrought the change. She fell-to on the house after a while, an' scrubbed an' polished till you could have shaved yourself in the tins on the wall, an' ate your dinner off the flags on the kitchen-floor. When she had that done she started on the outside with a whitewash brush an' a pot of paint; an' very soon the father's wee cottage would have put many a farmer's house to shame.

But it was in her way of conductin' herself that the biggest change of all come on Liza. From bein' a cacklin' big tom-boy of a hussy, that you'd have heard half a mile before you come in sight of her, she turned to be as quiet an' demure as a house-cat. Instead of stoppin' on the road to collogue with every young fellow she met, an' standin' a guzzle from anythin' in breeches under seventy, she begun to keep herself to herself altogether; an' when she'd meet a young hobble-dehoy of a fellow that a month before she'd have put out her tongue at, now she would give him a distant wee half-smile an' a slow bend of the neck that would fetch the cap off his head in spite of him.

It wasn't long, I need hardly tell you, till other people

besides Molly begun to take notice of all this. An', like Molly, one an' all the weemin-folk fair moidhered themselves tryin' to guess the cause of it. But though they talked, an' compared notes, an' young ones consulted ould ones, an' ould ones consulted young ones, the divil a step nearer findin' out any of them got. Some thought well of the change, an' said they were glad to see the girl beginnin' to have a bit of respect for herself an' her mother before her, an' others set it all down to conceit an' impudence; but whatever folks said they all begun to think more of Liza an' pay more attention to her than they'd ever done in her life before. As for the men, not only did the courtin' kind run wild after her, but the marryin' sort started to hang their hats up, too; an' she could have married up to fifty acres of land half a dozen times inside three months.

None of the followers did any good. Liza had still Hugh Black in her mind, an' gave all the rest of them the go-by. But she altered her ways with Hugh Black, too. He was still welcome when he came to the house. Whenever Liza would go to a meetin' or a swarry Hugh still got leavin' her home. But any courtin' that was done it was Hugh did it, now, an' not Liza. An' while Hugh used to be in the habit of givin' her a towslin' every time he got within reach of her, he owned up to me, himself, that now he was afeard to put his hand inside her arm. It goes without sayin' that all this made him keener to give her a hug than he'd ever been when he could have had one when he liked. But he soon began to see that short of marryin' her it wasn't goin' to be done. Besides that, he was beginnin' to take another kind of notion of her altogether, an' to hate the thought of anybody else gettin' her.

Even Hugh's family was beginnin' to come round a good deal in their way of lookin' at Liza. The mother was a tidy neat woman in her habits, an' had took great notice of how the girl had been keepin' both herself an' the house since the change come on her, an' had give in that Liza would make a good wife for somebody in her own station. As for the father he was a dry cautious ould stick; but I got hold of him one night when he had a couple of bottles of stout in him an' was more like a human bein'; an' he allowed that the girl was a nice girl for her position in life, an' by-ordinary handsome, an' that if a young fellow wanted to be such a fool as to marry a girl without a penny in her pocket or an acre to her name, Liza was as good an excuse as he was ever likely to get.

All this doesn't sound very much, but it was a big deal to anybody that knew the Blacks; an' Molly an' I made up our minds that Miss Armytage was goin' to get her will about Liza, just when she'd given up carin' whether she did or not.

But pride is pride. Liza was only a labourer's daughter; an' though Hugh's mother and Father weren't bitter about her the way they used to be, still they were bound to remember that, an' to mind Hugh of it, too, an', of course, to dangle So-an'-so's fortune before him now an' then, as well.

Hugh hung fire. I begun to wonder would Liza miss him after all. As for Molly, she near fidgeted herself sick about it. She wanted to interfere; an' yet she was afraid to interfere. At last she could stand it no longer.

"Pat," sez she to me, "I'm goin' up to see Miss Armytage. Maybe she has forgiven Liza by now. Her heart was set on this match at one time. If she'll only give Liza the very name of a fortune—and she could do more an' never miss it—it'll come off now; an' surely she'll do that for old times' sake."

When Molly came back I didn't know what to make of her. All she would do was to sit on a chair an' laugh, an' laugh, till I could have choked her.

"What on earth is the matter with you, woman dear?" sez I, in the end. For I was half-vexed at the antics of her.

"Oh, Pat," sez she, wipin' her eyes, "I know the secret, I know the secret."

"What secret?" sez I.

"About Liza," sez she, beginnin' to laugh again. "About the change in Liza."

"What was it?" sez I, all agog. "Tell me."

"I can't," sez Molly. "I can't. I promised Miss Armytage not to tell."

"You can tell *me*," sez I.

"I can't," sez she. "Not even you. I promised Miss Armytage, faithful I promised her.—Don't tempt me, Pat—ah, don't tempt me!" sez she, as I went over to her. "Sure I'm burstin' to tell you; but I passed my word."

"Well, will Miss Armytage do anythin'?" sez I. "You can tell me that, anyway."

"She won't," sez Molly. "She won't lift a finger, though I tried her up an' down for an hour. The niece cured her of interferin', she says, an' she's just goin' to leave Liza to her Creator.—Maybe, she's right," sez Molly, gettin' up off the chair. "Time'll tell. But I wish I hadn't gone near her. For after what she's told me I won't be able to lie in my bed till I see how it all turns out."

Partly to please Molly, an' partly because she had me nearly as much worked up as she was herself, I threw myself in Hugh's road as often as I could, to see how things was goin'. For a few days he slackened off even more than he had been doin'. Then I heard the mother had a big Miss Jennings stayin' with them that was supposed to come into a lot of money when her ould uncle would die; an' one afternoon I met Hugh drivin' Miss Jennings in the trap.

"All's up," sez I to myself. I didn't tell Molly; for I knew she'd be cut about it.

But when Miss Jennings went away Hugh begun to drop up to Liza's house near as often as before; an' sometimes I'd come on them out walkin' together. Then for nearly a week Hugh wouldn't be seen on the road; an' then all at once he'd be as regular as ever. I begun to get exasperated with it all; an' as for Molly, I solemnly believe she lost half a stone weight.

"You'll go into consumption, Molly," sez I to her at the last. "I'll have to do somethin'."

So I took my courage in my hands an' asked Hugh straight did he mean to marry the girl. I found him in a worse swither than myself. He was dyin' about Liza, he gave in to that; but her station in life was again' her; an' he was afraid of what his people would say. For he told me the thought of Miss Jennings's money had stiffened them a good deal again' a girl with no fortune; an', 'deed, I could see that Hugh was a bit shook at the thought of it himself.

He just needed the push of a finger to decide him one way or another; an' I seen him gettin' it. It was as big a surprise to me as it was to Hugh.

I was standin' on the roadside one March evenin', listenin', as usual, to his troubles, when who should come by but Liza herself. She gave us a wee nod an' a smile, an' passed on, lookin' a fair picture.

"Good-bye, Hugh," sez I.

"I'm not goin'," sez he, shakin' his head.

An' as Liza turned up the side-road to her father's cottage there come a swirl of wind round the corner. She clapped her hands to her skirts just a thought too late. The clothes riz to her knees; an' man, the flutterin' of ribbons an' lace would have taken the sight from your eyes.

"Holy Moses!" sez I, lookin' at Hugh.

"Good-bye, Pat," sez he, in an off-hand kind of a way. "I think I'll go after all."

The next day it was all over the country that Hugh Black was goin' to marry Liza Cotter.

I said nothin' to Molly till the news came in; an' then I told her all that had happened the day before. She danced round the kitchen clappin' her hands, an' laughin' like a mad thing.

"Oh, Pat, Pat," she sez, "it was funny before, but this is the best of all. *Now* you know what became of Miss Rosie's weddin' clothes!"

"Lord bless us," sez I, the light breakin' in on me, "was *that* it?"

"That was it," sez Molly. "Isn't Miss Armytage the wonderful old woman?"

I sat down an' laughed near as much as Molly herself; an' the whole countryside laughed on an' off for months after. But many a time I thought what a pity it was that poor old

Miss Armytage should know all she did about men an' weemin, an' yet have to go to her grave wantin' in the end.

"Tell me, though, Pat," said I; "what about Liza herself? Did she remain neat in her habits after she was married?"

A hint of wistfulness tempered the humour of Mr. Murphy's answering smile.

"Ach, couldn't you have left well alone," said he, "an' let me still mind Liza as she came down the road that spring day.—Time and life is too many for the whole of us, Mr. Doyle. Thon was her we seen throwin' out the suds."

Death and a Ploughman

I

THREE persons about Hollybrook farm enjoyed the unquestioning confidence and loyalty of little Bob Menzies—his uncle, the housekeeper, Mrs. Ross, and Henry Leonard, the head ploughman.

His uncle he loved. No feeling of duty or reverence clouded that pure affection. The simplicity of Mr. Menzies had not been impaired by contact with the world. In heart he was still a child. That his generosity was grotesquely streaked with parsimony Bob would not have discerned for himself, but perceived, as he grew older, through the eyes of Mrs. Ross.

Mrs. Ross was the widow of an unfortunate love match. From the humiliating dependence of unpaid drudge in her mother-in-law's household she had been rescued by Hugh Menzies' compassion; and her occasional sharpness of tongue masked real gratitude and affection towards her benefactor. Bob liked Mrs. Ross, and knew her kind and even tender towards himself; but he shrank from her tarter moments, and saw her shrewder but coarser fibred than his uncle.

Towards Henry Leonard Bob's attitude was one of admiration and pride. Henry was the perfect ploughman, even though he knew it. Under his autocratic rule Mr. Menzies' farm was a model. Nowhere else in the neighbourhood were there so well-kept horses, or such shining harness, or so brightly-painted carts and implements. Mr Menzies' crops were first in and first out, his cows gave more milk than any other farmer's cows, his bullocks topped the price for fat cattle, his stacks were models of symmetrical building.

Mr. Menzies accepted these benefits thankfully and with humility; and, though he did not know it, this was the necessary condition of their continuance. Henry was an artist, with all the vanity of an artist. All he craved was recognition and a free hand. No desire for a farm of his own troubled his perfect creation of beauty as he conceived beauty. It was enough for him that the farm was a picture and a model to the countryside. That the ownership and the profit were another's influenced him not at all.

He was not diffident, and never ceased to trumpet his own genius. Mr. Menzies and Bob took him at his own valuation. To them his boasting was a mere statement of obvious truth. Bob, in particular, was an almost worshipping disciple. In his eyes Henry was perfection.

To Mrs. Ross Henry's conceit was intolerable. Her affection for her employer and his nephew made her all the more resentful of Henry's domineering ways; and though she perceived his value and so managed to restrain her desire to "put him in his place," she was always on the watch for an occasion of criticism. It was through Mrs. Ross that disillusion about Henry came to Bob.

One gift of the good farmer Mr. Menzies had been dowered with. He was an instinctive judge of cattle and sheep. In this sole respect Henry Leonard recognized a greater than himself. He never openly acknowledged his master's superiority; but by a tacit arrangement Mr. Menzies accompanied Henry when buying was to be done. It was, however, only in an advisory capacity. Henry's vanity was, on such occasions, soothed by the knowledge that judgment in cattle was only one factor in good buying, and that without his presence Mr. Menzies would inevitably be diddled in the price.

The selling of stock was left in Henry's hands altogether. On a selling errand he travelled to fair or market by himself. His return of prices went unquestioned. Any necessary purchases, such as seed, harness, or implements he paid for out of the cash in his hands; for it was one of Mr. Menzies' idiosyncrasies to run no accounts.

This privilege of Henry's had long been a cause of suspicion and annoyance to Mrs. Ross. In a quiet way she began after a time to keep a check on Henry's outlayings. No discovery to his detriment had rewarded her. With the same unwillingness as she admitted his efficiency she acknowledged to herself that the expenditure was kept astonishingly low. There remained one field of enquiry into Henry's probity, and there Mrs. Ross was by herself helpless. Did he make an honest return of his sales? On the subject of the prices at which he sold, Henry's abstention from boasting amounted almost to reticence; and here Mrs. Ross's suspicions found foothold.

She determined to make use of Bob. There was no one else on whom she could depend; and she had a secondary reason for employing him. Her jealous affection had always been chafed by Bob's hero-worship of the pet ploughman, and she rather welcomed the hope of removing Henry from his pedestal.

About sales in the open market Bob could not help her; but cattle were often sold to dealers who called at the farm. If there was peculation going on it would be at such a private sale rather than in the publicity of a market. To Mrs. Ross's satisfaction an opportunity of testing her theory arose soon after she had formed it.

Bob was no less pleased than herself at the arrival of a well-known cattle-buyer. Cruelty and kindness are conceptions that depend on environment and upbringing. Bob, who had sobbed himself sick when his canary died because he forgot to renew its drinking-water, armed himself with an ash-sapling and looked eagerly forward to the opportunity of belabouring some helpless bullocks. He was hastening to the farmyard when Mrs. Ross stayed him.

"Master Bob," she said in an off-hand way, "I wish you'd just hang about when Henry's selling them cattle an' tell me what price he gets.—Don't let him know what you're after," she cautioned; and saw her mistake as the boy stared at her.

"I've a notion he doesn't get the prices he bums about to me," she put in hurriedly. "You know what a blast he is."

Bob's loyalty instantly rose indignant.

"I'm sure he gets what he says," he protested. "Uncle thinks Henry's far better at selling than he is himself.—But I'll tell you, an' then you'll see!"

No bribe would have bought the lad to spy on his worshipped ploughman; but now he was filled with desire to justify him. When the bullocks had been rounded up Bob took his stand at Henry's side awaiting the battle of wits that he knew would follow. To his disgust Henry directed him to keep an eye on the cattle, and moved off with the dealer before the latter had got beyond the customary "What are you asking for them?"

The pair walked slowly up the yard. Bob could see quite clearly by the casual way the dealer was slapping his leggings with his stick and Henry's calm shakings of the head that they were not come to grips yet. All at once the dealer tucked his stick under his arm, seized Henry's right hand and brought his own down on it with a resounding smack. Battle was joined! The two stopped and faced each other. The low stackyard wall ran alongside them a few feet away. Bob looked at the dealer's dog, and saw him equal to his trust. Bolting into the stable he climbed to the hay-loft above, and from the window dropped into the stack-yard. Between the stacks he could see the bargainers in earnest dispute. Instantly he became a scout, and began to stalk the enemies of his tribe in swift but cautious progression from vast tree to tree of the North American forest. A traitor was plotting against the Great Chief, and his villainy must be exposed.

Bob reached the wall just in time to hear the close of the bargain.

"This is my last word," he heard the sharp staccato voice of the dealer; "fourteen pounds all round."

"It's no use." Bob divined Henry's slow calm shake of the head. "If you want the cattle you'll have to buy them. Fourteen-pound-fifteen, or nothing.—I'll tell you what I'll do; and this is *my* last word. I'll give you back five shillin's a head. Fourteen-pound-ten."

Again there was silence. Bob fretted with impatience. Why was Henry so grasping? He was making a mistake this time; Bob knew he was.

"Aw, well," said the dealer, "there's no use talkin' any more. Good evenin', Henry."

Bob heard the dealer's footsteps turn away. Henry had missed the sale. All Bob's confidence in his hero wilted before the shattering certainty. But wait. That was MacDermott's voice.

"Give me your hand, Henry." There was another loud smack. "You're a regular Jewman. Here; I'll split the differs—fourteen-five; take it or leave it."

"Very good," came Henry's reply. "You can mark them at that." And Bob knew from the voice that Henry was satisfied.

"What a wonder Henry was," the thought beat in Bob's brain as he raced back to his cattle, "what a wonder? How cool and certain of himself. Five shillings a head on eight bullocks was two pounds. He, Bob, would have been a faintheart and thrown away two pounds. How could he have doubted Henry's judgment even for a moment!" As they stood side by side to watch the cattle driven away the boy's upward gaze at the ploughman was reverential.

"These dealin' men thinks they're purty smart, Master Bob," said Henry as MacDermott passed out of sight; "but they'll want to get up a sight earlier in the mornin' before they can best *me*. That's not a bad day's work. Eight fourteens is a hundred and twelve."

"Did you say *fourteen*, Henry?" asked Bob faintly.

"Fourteen," answered Henry with firmness. "I hammered him up from twelve-pound-ten. Away and tell your uncle, Master Bob, if he's about.—An', Bob," he called quietly, in an afterthought, "give that woman Ross inside no information. She's too nosey, altogether."

A sudden darkness fell on the landscape as Bob made his way out of the yard. He turned from the dwelling-house instinctively and sought the fields. Slowly the dreadful fact came home to him. A traitor was indeed plotting against the Great Chief; but it was Henry Leonard. Henry Leonard had cheated his uncle out of two pounds.

Now Bob was familiar with the customary deceptions of farming life. He knew that bulk did not always tally with sample where oats and wheat were concerned. Certain devices whereby fat cattle and milch cows were displayed to more than quite honest advantage were well known to him, and he was not unread in the infinite book of horse-dealing. He felt he could not decline on such deceptions himself; yet he knew that righteous men, that even his Uncle Hugh, practised them with conscience unwrung. But Henry's fault was heinous by any code, flat breach of trust and robbery. The blow was stunning. Coherent thought was for a little beyond Bob. One dominant feeling pressed on his understanding: how was he to continue association with Henry in future? He, not Henry, would be overwhelmed with shame.

In the thickening dusk he saw his uncle pass through an adjoining field on his way to count the cattle. Was it not his duty to tell him of Henry's wrong-doing? He knew it was; and in the same instant saw that the thing was impossible. Let honour and duty lie as they might, Bob *could* not betray Henry.

But what about Mrs. Ross! *She* would question him, closely; for she disliked Henry, and sought his downfall. He must lie, he must tell her the price had been fourteen pounds a head. But could he lie without being detected? He knew his own weakness in dissimulation. Already he felt his telltale face burn as he uttered the falsehood, his eyes fall under Mrs. Ross's keen gaze. He must wait till just before the lamps were lit, and tell his lie in the dark.

But it was dusk already. He had better bestir himself. As he drew near the kitchen door he decided to begin "Oh, Mrs. Ross." And just then Mrs. Ross came round the corner of the house.

"Is that you, Master Bob?" she asked sharply. "Hm; I suppose you went off stravaguin' with MacDermott. Tell me," she said, lowering her voice, "Henry was in a quarter of an hour ago, an' told your uncle he got fourteen pound a head for the eight bullocks. Was that right?"

Fate had made Bob's way easy for him, after all! He had only to answer "yes," and the deed was done.

To his horror, Bob found he could not achieve the monosyllable. Something, he knew not what, rose up within him and forbade him to tell a lie.

Yet he must not allow Henry to be utterly confounded.

"Mrs. Ross," he stammered, "if I tell you, will you promise not to say anything to my uncle or to anybody else?"

In her excitement at the almost certain confirmation of her suspicions, Mrs. Ross would have promised anything.

"All right," she whispered eagerly. "I won't split. What did he really get? Tell me, quick."

Bob had a swift revulsion of feeling. The irrevocable words had not yet been spoken. Could he lie, even at the eleventh hour? A dozen points of view presented themselves to his whirling brain. But the matter had passed beyond his volition. Somebody that was not quite Bob Menzies, somebody that Bob Menzies felt by no means sure was doing the right thing replied sadly:

"Henry wasn't telling the truth. He got fourteen pounds-five.—Oh, Mrs. Ross," the boy cried, seizing her apron, "don't tell; please, you won't tell. And, please, please, never let Henry know you knew."

But in her exaltation Mrs. Ross did not heed him.

"I told you," she cried exultingly, smacking her thigh, "*I* told you, *I* told you," she chanted, beating rhythmically with both hands as she moved toward the kitchen door. "That's your Henry Leonard for you; that's the great Henry that your uncle falls down before, an' blows up, an' encourages till he thinks the farm belongs to him an' not to Hugh Menzies at all. An' if the like of me dared to say a wee word of caution or commonsense I got my head in my hand.—Come in, son, an' get your tea. Your uncle's away over to Sandy Ferguson's. I suppose he's sittin' at the fireside this minit boastin' about the great ploughman he has got. It would make a cat laugh, so it would.—I could have told you, Master Bob, when you were laudin' an' praisin' Henry to the skies, poor innocent child——"

Mrs. Ross's psalm of triumph lasted nearly through Bob's tea; and in the end she became aware of the boy's dejection, and was quick-witted enough to divine the pain she was inflicting, and kindly enough to wish to assuage it.

Bob mustn't take the thing too seriously. All servants were alike; an' Henry was no worse than the rest of them, if he hadn't been allowed too much play-room by them that was too soft an' innocent to be his master as they should be. He had his good points, too, the creature. If he wasn't altogether honest he had put many a pound in Mr. Menzies' pocket; an' he was a great worker, an' kept the farm a picture. An', anyhow, he knew the ways of the place, an' couldn't well be done without now. If he went God knew into whose hands they might fall. It was safer to let well alone. You can't have everything in this world. She would hold her tongue between her teeth, an' just see that a closer eye was kept on Henry in the future.

These scraps of proverbial philosophy and Mrs. Ross's re-affirmation of her promise of silence comforted Bob a little. He saw the commonsense of Mrs. Ross's conclusions. Prudence as well as partiality stood advocate for Henry. But as he sat by the fire his heart was heavy. Dimly he felt how grievous was his calamity. Even his relations with his uncle would be altered by the secret that yawned between them. He would not wait for Mr. Menzies's return, but would go to bed. He shrank from the prospect of their usual confab. His uncle might talk of Henry, as he often did. Bob felt he could not bear that yet, and wishing a subdued "Good night" to Mrs. Ross crept sorrowfully away.

II

But Bob's relations with Henry did not change so much as in his first disillusionment he had expected. His feeling had been sorrow, not anger. He was grieved that the bright being he had looked up to should be so completely dimmed. Indignation against Henry's wrong-doing had never much hold on his mind, and quickly faded. Presently even something of the old hero-worship began to return to the boy. A particularly brilliant piece of horse-dealing accomplished by Henry about this time compelled Bob's admiration though it slightly scandalized his quickened sense of right and wrong. The transaction was something of a triumph for Henry in the neighbourhood. Bob felt that his uncle and himself shared in the glory, and perceived that a certain bluntness of conscience in a servant-man was not without advantage.

Yet Henry did not regain his old place in Bob's heart. He could never trust Henry again as he had once trusted him. But his feeling went deeper than that. Unknown to himself there had come about a little abatement of his trust in human nature. A certain reserve crept into his manner and speech. His boyish enthusiasm became tinged with wariness. He would never again be stunned and bewildered by the revelation of human frailty.

Henry was too much preoccupied with his own importance to be sensitive or observant; but in time he perceived the alteration in Bob's manner and was hurt by it. The incense of Bob's adoration had been sweet in his nostrils, and its diminution had seriously lessened his pleasure in his own accomplishment. That Bob should be aware of any flaw in his conduct it was not in Henry's nature to suspect. But after he had made many attempts to resume their old relations of admired and admirer, he was driven to seek some explanation of the change. The solution that occurred to him was a disagreeable one. It was that Bob had lost interest in farming, and was in danger of falling in with Mr. Menzies' plans that he should give up "that miserable existence," as

Mr. Menzies put it, and go to Belfast to be made a gentleman.

The thought was misery to Henry. He was a younger man than his master by fifteen years, and greatly more vigorous. Reasonably he might expect to be able for fifteen years' service with Bob after Mr. Menzies's death. Now, he saw that fifteen years a desert of humiliation and exile. To decline into subordination in his old age was bad enough; but to be forced to quit his beloved farm of Hollybrook was infinitely more dreadful.

The farm to Henry was a living thing, that responded to kindness, and could suffer by ill-treatment. When he looked on a rich field of grain he saw more than the plenteous yield. His mind travelled back to the pleasant lea field, patiently nursed from the exhaustion of bearing by years of pasturage. In his thoughts he ploughed it again; steadily the team paced; deep and strong the plough shore through the firm turf; the furrow rippled past. Then, next year, the sweet cleansing green-crop, plentifully but wisely manured; and, now, behold the grateful field returning thanks in a bumper harvest, and exalting the glory of Henry Leonard and Hollybrook Farm.

Where was there such another farm, such kindly soil, such sweet lush pasturage? There was good land here and there in the County Down, Henry admitted that. But nowhere else was there a farm like Hollybrook, with just the perfect number of fields, and of the proper acreage; with enough water, but no marsh land, or at least none worth talking of; with a perfect aspect, and just sufficient shelter for cattle? Yet, lacking one man's knowledge and skill this beautiful entity might in a few seasons be destroyed piecemeal. Henry would not have trusted his present master with it for even one season. Too well he remembered the dreadful spring when he lay in hospital with a broken leg, and Hugh Menzies, "the footerin' old dunderhead," as Henry in his bitterness had called him, laid down the Common in grass, out of flax. That was five years ago, and the Common, an annual shame and reproach ever since, was not clean from weeds yet. If in a few brief weeks such damage could be wrought, what heart-wringing possibilities should the farm fall permanently into the hands of some bungler!

That he must sometimes die Henry knew (life and death are ever before the countryman's eyes; in the pursuit of his calling he kills and makes alive) but Henry was little troubled by the necessity. When he thought of death at all he saw the long procession winding through the well-tilled fields; and his spirit, passing among the mourners, swelled as he listened to their praise of the great ploughman that was gone. If it were decreed that he must sometime be driven forth, and spend his last days in exile from that beloved earth, then never more would he look upon it. He would end his life in a far country, and be buried where his dead eyes could not be troubled by the spectacle of Hollybrook Farm fallen from its glorious estate into weeds and poverty.

Henry's departure was nearerhand than he knew. It befel on a fine spring morning when Hollybrook was looking its loveliest. The last of the oats with which the haggard had been so full was being borne into the barn to be threshed. High on a stack Henry paused from time to time in his task of pitching down the sheaves to gaze over the farm almost every field of which was visible from his standpoint. The sight was one to rejoice the heart. It had been a notable spring for the farmer, dry and windy, with occasional showery days and bursts of warm sunshine. Never had the work been better forward. The fields for crop had been ploughed and harrowed, and were ready for sowing. Brown and rich they lay here and there among the grass and the new hay that already showed a tender green pleasantly harmonizing with the deeper tones of the sturdy winter wheat. The red coats of the grazing cattle glowed warmly against the contrasting colour of their pasturage. Lambs frisked on every hillock, and in the glittering sunshine showed dazzling white until one looked at the heavenly fleece that floated above them in the infinite blue.

But this morning Henry's heart did not rejoice. A shadow of melancholy had fallen on him. Only a little while before he had invited Bob up to see the view; but Bob had shaken his head without answering, and the boy's lack of interest had added to the disquiet of Henry's mind. Looking over the bountiful world of which he was partly the creator, Henry was smitten with the transitoriness of life and human effort, and casting his eyes down to Jackie Robertson, the yard-boy, who stood with pitchfork uplifted to catch the sheaves:

"Isn't it an extraordinary thing, Jackie," he said, "that here I am, strong and well, standing on this stack, and yet one false step might send me into eternity."

"Aw, well," returned the yard-boy unconcernedly, winking at one of the women working beside him, "what hell odds?"

The roar of laughter that followed would at any other time have left Henry unscathed. To-day, depressed and disheartened as he was, it struck him like a blow. Incredibly he saw himself not the object of admiration and reverence that he had thought, but a butt and a derision. In a sudden impulse of recklessness he made a stride to the very edge of the stack.

"Ay," he echoed bitterly, "what hell odds!"

Only a second or two had elapsed since Henry first spoke, but in that time Bob Menzies, too, had experienced a shock of feeling. Suddenly Henry's old wrong-doing had appeared to him in a new relation. Unwarned, unrepenting, Henry tottered that instant on the verge of an eternity of agony.

"Henry," the boy shrieked—his voice was high with desperation—"Go back. Go back!"

The ploughman turned to the voice—one of the women remembered afterwards the quick gladness of his smile—and the next moment he was lying, a huddled mass, on the ground.

Bob pushed swiftly through the whimpering women and knelt by the fallen man's side. He had not screamed, nor wept. Horror, deep and dreadful, possessed his whole being.

"Henry," he cried insistently, kneeling beside the twisted figure. "Oh, Henry, speak to me."

"Easy, Master Bob," said William Temple, the old yard-man, laying a quiet hand on the boy's shoulder. "Get up, son, till we straighten him out. Peter's away for the doctor. Don't fret, now. Henry'll be all right."

Quickly and gently they composed Henry's limbs, and placed a sheaf under his head. As Bob knelt by his side again the ploughman's eyes opened and he looked up at the boy for some moments without speaking. Then he smiled quietly.

"Master Bob," he said, "I'll never plough Hollybrook Farm again."

"Blethers, Henry," interposed the yardman gruffly. "You will these thirty years. Lie there quietly till the doctor comes, an' you'll be all right.—Tell me," he asked, moving one of Henry's legs a little, "does that hurt you?"

"No," answered Henry. "I don't feel anything."

Bob caught the look that passed from face to face. The unbelievable thing knocked at his brain; but he fought it back.

The yardman looked questioningly round his fellows, then bent over the ploughman again.

"Henry," he said awkwardly, "you'll be all right, you know; but it—it might be no harm if you had a word or two with the Reverend Mr. Henderson."

Instantly the cloud of horror that was slowly enveloping Bob was shot with light and hope. "Yes, oh yes; that was it! A clergyman: Why had he been so stupid, so blind?—Yes, quick, quick!" He bent over Henry, the words thronging to his tongue, then drew back. He must not expose Henry in his dying hour, before his fellows.—But hell—*hell!*—No; he couldn't do it. Later, by themselves, if Mr. Henderson were not in time.—But Henry had not answered.

"Do you hear me, Henry?" asked the yardman softly. "Would you like to see the Reverend Henderson—just in case," he added shamefacedly.

Henry looked at him, then glanced aside vaguely. His thoughts seemed far away.

"Ay," he whispered at last. "He's a well-meaning oul' creature. Let him come if he likes." He paused. When he spoke again his eyes were clearer and his voice had gained strength.

"William," he said, "I've held a purty straight furr. I don't think they can do me much harm."

His eyes closed slowly. The kindly old yardman motioned to one of the labourers to lead Bob away.

All that afternoon Bob moved through the chorus of praise and sorrow, a tormented, despairing spirit. Distress for the calamity of Henry the ploughman and for his own loss was eclipsed by the thought of the soul damned for ever. Damned, perhaps, through the fault of Bob Menzies, through Bob Menzies' cowardice. He was a partner in the crime. Why had he not done his duty and denounced Henry at once to his uncle?—Ah, he could not have done that!—His old friend. It would have been too mean. A thousand benefits rushed on his memory. Yet though the sinner might have been thrust out of Hollybrook he might thereby have been brought to repentance. The poor soul of Henry Leonard might yet look up with lamentable eyes and silently reproach him from amid the flames of his torment.

Old William Temple, who alone had marked the intensity of Bob's feelings, and had watched over him from a distance, found the child grovelling on a heap of stable straw in an agony of tears. After a little thought William went for Mrs. Ross, and left the two alone together. The housekeeper raised Bob up and held him in her arms.

"Bob, dear," she chided, "don't take on like that; don't now. It's wrong. Poor Henry's gone, an' got a sudden call; but sure we'll have to go sometime. An' if Henry wasn't a regular attender he was a well-livin', decent-spoken man all his days, an' done his work faithfully an' honest; an' that's a religion in itself. There's them walkin' about this countryside holdin' their heads high that has more call to be afraid of their Maker nor Henry Leonard."

Bob looked up in her face, bewildered, incredulous.

"But, Mrs. Ross," he sobbed, "the cattle, the cattle he sold MacDermott.—Oh, why did you make me spy!"

Sudden misgiving flashed in Mrs. Ross's eyes. The boy saw it, and buried his face on her breast in a wilder paroxysm of grief.

"Oh, Mrs. Ross," he cried, "will Henry go to hell after all he's done for my uncle and me?"

"Hush," returned Mrs. Ross in horror. "Is it a few shillings like that again a lifetime of honest labour? If that was the way of things I doubt there'd be little chance for any of us.—Bob," she said suddenly, "come down to the sleepin'-house an' look at him. Do now," she insisted, as Bob struggled in her arms. "It'll drive some notions out of your head. I'll be with you, an' you can go any minit you want.—Come, Bob," she pressed him. "You'll stop thinkin' as you're doin'. An' you needn't be afraid of Henry, son; you above all."

He yielded. White-faced and shrinking he stood with Mrs. Ross in the doorway and looked on the dead ploughman.

Henry lay there, calm and aloof, beyond praise but surely beyond blame also; perhaps to be judged, but then to be judged by something infinitely wise, infinitely remote from human assessment of good or wickedness.

"Bob," said Mrs. Ross softly—but she was speaking half to herself—"an' there's people thinks the Almighty is as wee an' petty as themselves.—Come, now, son."

As they walked down the yard hand in hand the beginnings of peace had begun to steal on Bob.

That night, sitting at the kitchen fire together, Bob Menzies and his Uncle Hugh were long silent. Mrs. Ross was even more active and noisy in the scullery than usual; for at her own suggestion she was to preside later at the wake in the sleeping-house.

"That decent-hearted oul' gawm"—Bob had been quite aware she meant his uncle—"would give a lot of them thirsty blackguards as much drink as they could throw in them. Poor Henry was a sober discreet bein'; an' I won't have any capers an' nonsense at the wakin' of him."

Mrs. Ross had quitted the house a considerable time before Hugh Menzies spoke.

"Bob," he said at last, "there's a wee thing I want to tell you; an' I didn't want to say it before Mrs. Ross, because though she's a kindly good-natured woman, in her heart she never liked the man that's gone.—You might have noticed that the horses, an' the harness, an' the ploughs an' carts about this place were by-ordinary well-kept——"

"I was always proud of our horses, uncle," interposed Bob, and felt himself defending Henry.

"I got a good deal of pleasure out of them myself," said Mr. Menzies. He paused a moment.—"Bob, I don't know whether you ever noticed it, but I'm wee an' miserable about layin'-out. I would never have had the heart to spend the money on them things. Poor Henry that's dead used to humbug me about the price he got for cattle, an' spend the balance on paint an' harness-cream an' saddlers' bills an' things like that."

Bob sat up in his chair. His heart was beating wildly.

"I've knowed about it this many a long year," went on Mr. Menzies, "but I never let on to Henry, because though I was too mean to spend the money myself I seen that it had a right to be spent. Keepin' off altogether the credit that come my own way, the Almighty never created a ploughman like Henry to have him marred by a rusty plough an' dirty horses. An' with Henry spendin' the money, an' not me, I didn't feel that the waste was altogether at my door.—But what I wanted to say to you, Bob, was this. It's better to be straightforward an' have things out. I should have told Henry he was spendin' my money, an' let him do it aboveboard. I do not like the thought of the poor bein' lyin' till the Day of Judgment thinkin' all the time he has done wrong."

But Bob could no longer contain.

"Oh, uncle," he wailed in a passion of regret and anguish, "why didn't you tell him when he was alive? Oh, say in your prayers to-night that you forgive him; and then he won't be punished!"

Hugh Menzies stared at Bob in simple wonder.

"Bob," he said, "you're looking at things all wrong.—No, no; I'm not uneasy about the Judgment. I'll speak for Henry when the time comes an' we're both called. But here, Bob, is what is in my mind. Supposin' just to prevent any mistakes in the meantime I went on spendin' the same amount, or thereabouts, as Henry has been spendin', wouldn't that put things beyond all manner of doubt? An' if Henry got to know, wherever he is, he would understand, as well."

Bob's heart was suddenly wrung with sorrow and remorse.

"Uncle," he sobbed. "Uncle. I knew, too. Only the last time; but I knew and didn't tell you."

"Well, well, well," said Mr. Menzies, gravely nodding his head. "So you knew.—I'm glad you didn't tell, Bob. He was your kind friend.—But you'll do this for him an' me, if you please: You see, there's a miserable drop in me still; an' I might try to pare down the money I should lay-out on harness an' so on, an' not, maybe, cut the dash that Henry would like. I want you to keep me up to the mark. An' if at any time you see me backslidin' in that way will you just yoke the mare, an' the two of us will drive quietly over the length of Drumnaturk an' have a look at Henry's grave. That will bring me back to my duty, if anything will. For to be plain with you, Bob, I don't think we'll ever see a ploughman like Henry Leonard round these parts again."

But Bob, as he wept that night for the friend who had been given back to him but whom he would see no more, hoped that oblivion of earthly things would fall on Henry Leonard after he had learned of his master's forgiveness. For he knew in his heart that never again would the horses be so well-kept on Hollybrook Farm.

•

A Wag of a Tail

IF the moon would have stayed at the full for say a fortnight when Mr. Anthony the solicitor's apples was ripenin' in his new orchard, there's no doubt he'd have had a powerful gatherin'.

But the course of the moon ran along as usual. Everybody in the town was fully aware that Mr. Anthony had such a crop of quantity an' quality as had never been seen in Ballygullion before; for he told them that himself some hundreds of times; an' the first real dark night after the eatin'-apples yellowed the whole children of the population sunk their religious an' political differences an' descended on the orchard like wasps on a wall of plums.

Mr. Anthony sent his office-boy out on errand for me the next mornin' askin' me to come to see him at once, an' when I got there he was in a very bad temper.

"I'll get a dog, Pat," sez he, after purifyin' his system of bad language for about ten minits. "I can't use a gun on the little divils, but, blast me, I'll get a dog."

"Dogs were never very lucky with you, Mr. Anthony," sez I.

"What the deuce do you mean?" sez he, flarin' up. "I was never very lucky with dogs, if that's what you're drivin' at. If I've been cursed all my life with a collection of brainless rabbits with dogs' coats on them, am I to be blamed if I smartened them up now an' again with a pickle or two of shot?—Anyway, what I want this time is not a sportin' dog but a big quiet soft-mouthed animal, all wool an' bark, that wouldn't hurt a blind kitten. I'll train him to walk round the orchard all night—you know very well I can train anything with four legs an' a tail on it—an' whatever livin' he sees or hears he'll just bark at it till I come.—What do you think of that for an idea?" sez he, fixin' me very triumphant with his eyeglass.

"I think you'll need to buy the poor brute a few glycerine jujubes before you put him on sentry-go," sez I. "But if you want a quiet fool of a dog I may tell you Big Billy Lenahan of the Hills tried to sell me one yesterday that he said was the very thing for a family man like myself."

"Could I depend on him bein' quiet?" sez Mr. Anthony, a bit dubious. "I wouldn't put much confidence in the same Lenahan."

"Billy told me the childer might pull the tail out of him an' he'd never look round," sez I; "an' Billy would never let an old friend like me down, I'm sure."

"Ay, but would he let *me* down?" sez Mr. Anthony. "I got him fined again lately for poachin'."

"I'll tell you what I'll do, Mr. Anthony," sez I. "I'll go up to Billy this afternoon an' pick a dog for you myself, an' bring him down to you if I'm satisfied.—Now, not a word!" sez I. "I'd do more than that for you anytime."

An', troth, I did more for him this time, too, before all was finished.

When I told Billy I wanted the dog for Mr. Anthony, he turned over near as much bad language in five minits as Mr. Anthony himself. But in the end he gave in to me.

"Seein' it's to oblige you, Pat," sez he, "I'll let him have a dog to suit his turn; not the one I offered you, for he's sold, but a quiet biddable beast that wouldn't snap within two inches of a midge. All the same it's a sin to expose a kindly good animal to certain death from that handless little pettifogger."

He opened the stable door, an' out came a sturdy lump of an Irish terrier.

"That's a tough-lookin' customer, Billy," sez I, "to be the lamb you say he is."

"Lamb?" sez Billy. "Why, man, a lamb would chase him for his life.—Tommy," he calls to a ragged wee fellow that was hangin' about the upper end of the yard, "are you in your bare feet?"

"No, Mr. Lenahan," answers the boy, "I have my boots on."

"Come down, then, an' kick this dog for me," sez Billy.

The wee fellow walked down the yard all smiles, an' hit the dog a welt with the side of his foot. I laid hold of my stick, to save the child's life; but the dog just turned round an' licked the little rascal's hand, an' wagged every inch of him behind his fore-legs.

"Isn't that a Christian animal now," sez Billy. "Would you like me to take a kick at him myself?"

If I'd thought there'd have been any chance of the dog liftin' about three-quarters of a pound out of the calf of Billy's leg I'd have said "Yes"; but I took pity on the poor brute.

"Don't trouble, Billy," sez I. "If he didn't worry you on sight, he's too good for this world, as it is."

But, lo an' behold you, when I brought the dog down to Mr. Anthony, an' told him my story, he wasn't half-pleased.

"Not that I'd be ungrateful, Pat," sez he; "but blast it, I wanted a dog, not a jelly-fish. Never mind, though," sez he, brightenin' up; "you've seen the hand I've made of a dog before now, haven't you?"

I've buried what bits I could find of two or three of Mr. Anthony's dogs in my time; but tellin' the truth is no way to be popular.

"You're a wonder with anythin' from a flea to an elephant, Mr. Anthony," sez I.

"Well, watch me this time," sez he; "for I'm goin' to astonish you. I've been readin' a book on modern dog-trainin', an', damme, it's more interestin' than case-law.—Did you ever hear of such a thing as a conditioned reflex?" sez he.

"I never did," sez I; an' I was tellin' the whole truth this time.

"Well, it's like this," sez Mr. Anthony: "if you ring a bell ten or twelve times, an' give a dog a piece of meat after each ring, in the end his mouth will water at the sound of a bell.—Now presently I'm goin' to take this dog out, an' every time I meet a child I'm goin' to give the animal a sharp tap with my toe. An' what'll be the result?" sez he, screwin' in the eyeglass, an' lookin' at me very serious. "In half an hour's time he'll hate the very look of a child, an' every time he sees one he'll gowl like the trumpet of a merry-go-round."

"If old Cruelty to Animals catches you at it," sez I, "you'll gowl yourself to the tune of forty shillin's an' costs. But I see your notion."

"An' what do you think of it?" sez he.

"There's a man in Portnagree Asylum thinks his belly is made of glass," sez I, "an' he's sensible compared to you."

"Have you half an hour to spare?" sez Mr. Anthony, layin' hold of his hat.

"I have not," sez I; "but if you'll give me one half-hour

to spend on my own business, I'll come back an' waste another on you."

When I came back he was waitin' for me.

"Off we go, now," sez he; "an' damme, I'll show you somethin'.—Come along, sir," sez he to the dog; an' up the street goes the three of us.

The first lump of a lad we saw, Mr. Anthony waited till he was just abreast of us, an' stirred up the dog pretty brisk with his toe. The dog looked round at Mr. Anthony in an enquirin' sort of way, wagged his tail, a trifle half-hearted, as much as to say, "I don't quite get you," an' walked on.

Then all at once, as I looked at that big tough-lookin' brute behavin' like a hen, an' minded all I could mind about Big Billy Lenahan for twenty years, it come into my head that there was a catch somewhere. The next minit I knew what it was.

Comin' fresh out of Mr. Anthony's we were naturally in the best part of the town, with all dwellin'-houses in the street, an' not a soul to be seen. An', as we walked along, down the front steps of Mrs. Sides's house comes her wee spaniel dog an' waddles over very supercilious to have a sniff with Mr. Anthony's terrier. About three seconds did the whole thing, includin' the growl. The terrier spent another second or two shakin' the body, but it was time wasted.

Mr. Anthony's brains doesn't often move straight, but they move quick. The next thing I remember was watchin' the eyeglass bouncin' off his shoulder-blades as I followed him full-belt up the vennel into Market Street.

But he was still Mr. Anthony.

"Did you see that sideways dive of mine?" he gasps to me, as we came to a stop in the street. "Damme, I've known a blackbird do worse over a hedge."

"Oh, the poor wee dog," sez I.

"Blast the poor wee dog," sez Mr. Anthony. "I collect the whole rents of the Sides' family, that's what I'm thinkin' about.—Home as quick as we can go. Reach me my eyeglass from behind me, an' do you look out for the dog, too. If he as much as wags the end hairs of his tail at me it'll cost me a hundred a year."

"He won't know us," sez I. "Go by him with your nose in the air.—You didn't give him anythin' to eat, I suppose?"

"Anythin' to eat, is it?" sez Mr. Anthony. "I gave him half a pound of steak that was meant for my own dinner. It was part of the system," sez he, catchin' the look I gave him. "No matter who else he fell out with he had to be friends with me."

"We'd better climb over roofs on our way home, then," sez I. "However he was fed where he was stole from, he ate light enough at that Judas, Lenahan's; an' the very memory of half a pound of steak'll make him your friend till eternity."

An' sure enough, when we got by roundabouts back to Mr. Anthony's house the dog was standin' in front of the hall-door with the body of the wee spaniel in his mouth.

He just dropped it in time to dodge the runnin' kick Mr. Anthony made at him; an' by the time Mr. Anthony had done hoppin' round with his toe in his hand the old house-keeper was glowerin' out to see what young villain had threw a brick at the door. The dog wagged "Thank-you" at her as polite as a human-bein', picked up the spaniel an' walked into the house as composed as if he was one of the bearers at its funeral.

The divil a word said the housekeeper, but threw a look at Mr. Anthony, that was peerin' up the road in his short-sighed way, then beckoned me over with a quick little jerk of her hand.

"Where did he shoot it?" sez she under her breath.

But I hadn't time to answer.

"Shut the door quick, Mrs. Jackson," sez Mr. Anthony, all in a splutter.—"Stand beside me, Pat, an' deny every-thin'. Here's the sergeant comin' up the road."

The sergeant walked straight over to us.

"I suppose you know of the tragic occurrence, sir?" sez he.

"Dear, dear," sez Mr. Anthony, all surprised. "What is it? Anybody killed?"

"Worse than that," sez the sergeant. "Mrs. Sides's spaniel dog has been assassinated by a baste of an Irish terrier. An' hearin' you had been observed to have an Irish terrier in your immediate vicinity as you walked down the street some twenty minits ago I took the liberty of comin' up to interrogate you."

"There may have been an Irish terrier followin' me, for all I know," sez Mr. Anthony, "an' he may have chewed the spout off the town-pump for all I care; but he had nothin' to do with me. It's two years since I had an Irish terrier."

"I mind that fellow," sez the sergeant. "You killed him in the bog beyond Drumcree."

"He had the mange," put in Mr. Anthony, very hasty.

"Whatever he had you cured him of it, anyway," sez the sergeant. "If that was your last terrier you're dismissed without a stain on your character. An' it's just as well for you," sez he with a very weighty nod of his head.

"Is she very angry?" sez Mr. Anthony.

"Hellish," sez the sergeant. "I've seen less fuss made of an only child. She came down her own steps, roarin' like a female bull, an' offered me a twenty pound reward if I discovered the depredator.—Do you think, now," sez the sergeant, "if I went through the descriptions of the licensed dogs of this district I'd be likely to get a clue?"

"It's a great notion," sez Mr. Anthony. "Don't waste a minit. Damme, sergeant, if I had your brains I'd die on the Woolsack.—Did you mark that," sez he to me, pullin' out his latchkey. "Did you see how I set him off on a wrong scent just with a hint?—Come in, Pat," sez he, in great twist with himself, "come in an' celebrate my escape.—Here! here!" goin' to the door, an' whistlin'. He lifted a couple of biscuits from the sideboard an' threw them to the terrier.

"To Jericho with these yappin' little abortions," sez he. "No wonder he extinguished the little pismire.—Confound me but I like this dog."

But when I called back in a couple of days' time to hear if all was still well he was singin' a different tune. He opened to me himself, an' as I looked down the hall I seen that the stained-glass fanlight over the door into the garden was all chattered-up.

"Had you a wee storm all to yourself, Mr. Anthony?" sez I.

"Oh, that's nothin'," sez he, hurryin' me into the dinin'-room; "just a triflin' accident as I was makin' ready to shoot the dog."

"But I thought you had taken a fancy to him?" sez I, starin'.

An' then Mr. Anthony cast loose.

"A fancy to him!" sez he, when he came back to Christian expressions again. "Is it take a fancy to that Jack-the-Ripper?—Look there," sez he, slappin' up one of the windows with a wallop that cracked the bottom pane clean across. "Look at that bed."

I looked; an' there was a big square flower-bed with the whole flowers gone, an' it all heaped-up an' out of shape.

"If you buried the dog there," sez I, "he must have swelled."

"If I buried the divil!" splutters Mr. Anthony. "I buried three dogs there these last two days. That beast killed them all, an', blast him, fetched them back here as well.—An' that's not the worst of it," he goes on groanin'. "It's all my best clients in the neighbourhood that have been sufferin'.—Curse the brute, you'd think he read the daily paper, an' went straight out an' killed a dog of somebody he saw I was actin' for."

"So you shot him?" sez I.

"That's the most exasperatin' part of the whole business," sez he, beginnin' to stamp up an' down. "The housekeeper wouldn't let me.—It's the dog himself. He's got round her," sez he, shuttin' the dinin'-room door. "Pat," sez he, "if I wasn't in the twentieth century, an' a solicitor at that, I'd say he was a witch, the way he humbugged an' bamboozled her. Right from the start he behaved like a gentleman, biddable an' clean an' good-natured. It's a miracle he didn't get cramp in his tail he was that grateful for any bite of food she threw him; an' one day she gave him the drumstick of a chicken he wagged five custard-cups off a tray.—But it was through the kitten he got really at her. She had a wee yellow kitten that was just the apple of her eye——"

"Did you say *had*, Mr. Anthony?" I puts in.

"I did," sez Mr. Anthony, a trifle short. "Do you think I passed my law examinations without learnin' grammar?—Well," he goes on, "the brute made up to that kitten as if he loved it, carried it round by the scruff of the neck as careful as if it was made of china, an', damme, even drank milk out of the same saucer.—I'll give in he got the lion's share of the milk, but I don't believe that was why he did it. —You'll laugh at me, Pat, but I declare to you there's times when I believe there's a soft drop in that dog after all. I've been readin' that psychology book of mine again, an', confound me, if there was any way of suggestin' to him that it was a bad thing to kill toy dogs I believe he could be cured of it.—However, in the end he put himself out of court altogether."

"I can guess it," sez I. "He ate the kitten."

"What the divil are you harpin' on the kitten for?" sez Mr. Anthony, very peevish. "That wasn't it at all.—When he brought home Major Henderson's Peke he dropped him in the stock-pot; an' after that the housekeeper swore if I didn't shoot him she'd slaughter him herself with the cleaver. To escape notice I thought I'd do the job inside the house, so I lined up the dog at the end of the passage with two bags of coal behind him to catch any stray shot, an' tied a handkerchief over his eyes.—Damme," sez Mr. Anthony, warmin' up, "it was just like the execution of Marshal Ney.

"The divil of it was that the brute wouldn't act up to the spirit of the thing, but still kept pullin' off the handkerchief with his paws. So I got the housekeeper to throw him a bone; an' as she stepped behind me with her hands to her ears, here doesn't she open her eyes for a second, an' if the dog wasn't waggin' his tail to say 'Thank-you'!

" 'Aw, the poor brute,' sez she, an' glammed at my arm. Up went the muzzle of the gun, an' out went the fanlight. The dog made for the kitchen. I took a snapshot at him with the second barrel, an' had him as good as killed, when confound me if the little fool of a kitten didn't come prancin' out of the kitchen with its tail up, an' get in the way of the charge.—What are you snortin' at, you big booby?" sez he. "Haven't you seen me many a time shootin' a rabbit between one hole in a warren an' another?"

"Twenty times, Mr. Anthony," sez I, wipin' my eyes; "but this is funnier.—Has she give notice?" sez I, noddin' my head towards the kitchen.

"No, confound the old hag," sez Mr. Anthony, very savage. "She hasn't even that much respect for me.—She had the d——d impudence to tell me that if I'd aimed at the kitten I'd have killed the dog.—But no matter. He'll be dead very soon now."

"Dead?" sez I. "I'll never believe it till I see his corpse."

"I poisoned a slice of bread an' butter with strychnine, an' left it in the orchard," sez he, "an' turned the dog out there just before you came.—Oh, my heavens!" he cries, lookin' out of the window, an' clapped his hand to his head. "Mrs. Jackson!" he yells, tearin' the door open. Up the stairs he dashes, an' down them in two lepps with a wee bottle in his hand. "Come on, Pat," he shouts, as he made for the garden door; "come on, quick or we're too late!"

"What is it?" sez I, as I run. "What *is* it, Mr. Anthony?"

"Hippo-wine," he calls back, raisin' the hand with the bottle. "It's all I could think of. Oh, come on, Pat, come on."

"He's for savin' the dog's life after all!" flashes through my mind.

An' as he opened the orchard gate here were a couple of young lads under a tree, an' the wee one of the two had an apple in one hand an' was just takin' a bite out of a slice of bread he had in the other.

The screech Mr. Anthony let out of him wouldn't have disgraced an express-train.

"Stop, boy," he shouts. "Drop it! Don't move!—Oh, why didn't I kill that dirty brute with a hatchet!" sez he, lamentin' as he ran.

Now, as I need hardly tell you, stoppin' was the last thing in the children's mind. They didn't as much as squeal, but just took to their heels an' were out of sight among the trees before you could clap your hands.

"Run, Pat, run," gasps Mr. Anthony. "Keep them goin'. The wee fellow has a bite in his mouth, an' another swallow might hang me!"

But on account of the trees I couldn't pass Mr. Anthony; an' he was makin' no speed himself; for I suppose he must have pulled about a quarter of a stone of apples with his eye-glass before the string broke.

"There they are," he gasps, as he broke through the hedge after the pair, "makin' for the labourers' cottages. We'll be up on the young fellow before he reaches them. If you're ahead just prise his mouth open, an' I'll have the stuff in him before he knows he's poisoned."

"Wherever he's poisoned," I pants after him, "it's not in the legs. He'll beat us to the cottages yet. An' if he drinks water after the strychnine he'll just split open."

Mr. Anthony let somethin' out of him between a groan an' a squeal, spurted fifteen or twenty yards ahead of me, an' kept his lead all the way up the hill. Even with that the fellow beat him to the cottages, an' disappeared round the first one. Mr. Anthony let another whillaloo out of him an' spurted again. When I turned the corner here he had the young lad by the nose an' was jerkin' the contents of the bottle into him between yells. The last mouthful near choked the wee fellow, an' he was half up the steps of the next house before he got back his breath; but he made up for it, for the howl he let out of him as he entered the door was enough to loosen all the slates in the roof.

By this time there was a head out of every door an' window in the whole row, an' the next minit down the steps comes a big red-faced grenadier of a woman an' her with a yard-brush in her hand. She made one rush at Mr. Anthony, an' started to flail at him with the brush as if she was threshin' corn, all the time keepin' up a string of abuse as well as her breath would let her.

"I'll teach ye—ye dirty little pup—my harmless wee fellow—assaultin' an' poisonin' an innocent boy——"

While this was goin' on, between the effects of the run, an' tryin' to dodge the brush, Mr. Anthony could only get stray words out, on his part. He began polite enough in spite of his flurry.

"Madam—Madam—pardon me——" Here he made a glam at his hat to lift it, but the yard-brush saved him the bother. "Let me explain—a minute——"

But with that the woman changed her tactics, an' gave him the point, as the sodgers would say. The bristles took him somethin' wicked in the face; an' when he got them down his nose an' out of his mouth he let one yell of fury, pulled hard on the brush an' then pushed from him. The big woman sat down on the sidewalk an' stopped talkin' as if her head had fell off. She wouldn't have had much chance anyway.

"Confound an' blast you for an ignorant faggot," sez Mr. Anthony, dancin' round her fair stutterin' with the rage, "I didn't poison your brat. He's just after poisonin' himself with strychnine laid in my orchard—where he was stealin' apples, if you want to know——"

By this time the big red-faced woman was on her hands an' knees gettin' up, an' the breath comin' into her again. She riz up about two feet above Mr. Anthony, an' just gul-dhered at him.

"Stealin' apples?" she roars. "My good well-behaved boy, that's only this minit gone down my steps after eatin' his dinner——"

She got no further. A little pale woman on the edge of the crowd let a screech out of her, an' begun clappin' her hands an' callin' out.

"It's my son, it's my wee son. That dirty big loafer of Paddy Finnegan's tempted the poor angel down to the orchard, an' now he's lyin' dead an' buried in his own parlour under the sofa. Ah-h!" She let a yell about ten sizes too big for her, an' up the steps of the next house like an india-rubber ball.

"My G—d" sez Mr. Anthony. "I've dosed the wrong child!" He pulled the bottle out of his pocket, held it to the light, an' up the steps after the wee woman, an' me after him.

The little pale woman was down on her knees beside the sofa, an' had hold of the child's leg, that was stickin' out from underneath. The tears was runnin' down her nose.

"Come out, darlin', quick," she speaks under the sofa.—"Somebody run for the doctor," she calls over her shoulder.—"Let go the leg of the sofa, ye little wasp," sez she, gettin' angry all at once, "or I'll pull the foot off ye!"

Out comes the lad with a jerk, an' as the mother lifted him to his feet I seen he had a wee fragment of bread still in his hand. I jumped to snap it from him, but Mr. Anthony grabbed it first.

"What this?" sez he, with the eyes gogglin' in his head. "There was no jam on *my* bread."

"That's none of your bread," sez the wee woman. "It's off my own good currant loaf, an' this wee heart-scald has jam on it, forbye.—Gimme my switch," sez she, leppin' round the room like a tiger, "an' if I don't warm his hide for the fright he's give us all this day!"

I pulled Mr. Anthony by the tail of his coat, an' we shoved our way through the people that was crowdin' in, an' took to our heels for home.

"That's a sensible little woman, the small body," sez Mr. Anthony, when we'd got our breath a bit. "Did you mark how easily I persuaded her that her boy was in the wrong, an' deserved all he got? But that big pig-faced feather-bed with the yard-brush is a danger. She's venomous, that one. If some unscrupulous lawyer gets hold of her she may run me into a lot of money yet.—Come on," sez he, very savage, pushin' all of himself but one of the side-pockets of his coat through the hole in the orchard hedge; "my luck must turn sometime. Maybe that old bitch of a housekeeper has poisoned herself."

But not even the dog had done that. As we walked along the main path who should come to meet us but himself with the piece of bread very gingerly in his mouth. He laid it down at Mr. Anthony's feet an' looked up in his face as much as to say, "Now, there's a nice wee tit-bit I've been keepin' for you."

"Ah, the poor fellow!" sez I. "You couldn't find it in your heart to be angry with him after that, now could you?"

But Mr. Anthony was long past bein' got round that way.

"Could I not?" sez he, glowerin' at the dog. "I know you," sez he, "you two-faced assassin. You want to see me kickin' on the ground in convulsions, an' you trottin' round me waggin' your tail with your tongue in your cheek. Drop it!" sez he, as the dog took up the piece of bread in his mouth again. "I'll give you an easier death than that; but there's not room for both you an' me in the legal profession in this town.—I'll tell you what, Pat. Come up with me to-night to the waterworks an' we'll drop him quietly in with a stone round his neck."

"Lord bless us, Mr. Anthony," sez I, "do you want the town to get typhoid an' us penal-servitude?"

"Oh, curse him," sez Mr. Anthony in a rage. "I'd be happier with typhoid.—Wait," sez he: "couldn't we throw him in the overflow pool?"

"I suppose we could," sez I, "so long as he doesn't come up later."

"Leave that to me, Pat," sez Mr. Anthony, all himself again. "I'll lay my mind to the job this afternoon with a ready-reckoner, an' calculate to a grain the exact weight of a stone that'll sink the beast nice an' quietly, an' keep him down; an' about nine o'clock to-night he'll pass out of this wicked world without as much as a ripple."

When I got round to Mr. Anthony's at a quarter to nine he fetched me out to the yard on my tip-toes. In the glimmer from the kitchen window I could make out a big square basket with a lid an' a handle.

"That's the dog," sez he. "We can carry him time about."

"Is he paralysed in the legs?" sez I, "or is he just too upsettin' to walk?"

"Are you paralysed in your brains?" sez Mr. Anthony. "Wasn't he near traced to my house already?"

"Oh, come on, then," sez I. "If this job went by common sense it's him would be drowndin' us.—What's that?" sez I, jumpin', as there come a crack from the basket.

"Nothin'," sez Mr. Anthony. "Only the bones of a chicken I gave the dog to keep him quiet."

"Quiet!" sez I. "You'd think he was sendin' off fireworks. The half of the town'll be at our heels before we're there."

But we got to the waterworks unbeknownst, so far as I could make out, an' when we climbed over the palin's, if Mr. Anthony didn't pull a flash-lamp out of his pocket!

"Put that out!" I snaps at him. "Do you *want* us to be catched?"

But Mr. Anthony, as usual, was as obstinate as a he-ass.

"In my readin' of the great Napoleon's campaigns," sez he, "one thing I learned was to make sure of my ground.—This is the town reservoir on our left. Do you see that swirl there? That's the outlet pipe. If we dropped the dog into that the first place he'd stop would be at the polis barrack."

"It's the first place we'll stop, too," sez I, "if you don't switch out that light. Feel round an' get a stone. The overflow pond is on your front. Don't forget that we're keepin' it for the dog."

Away goes Mr. Anthony wanderin' an' gropin' on his hands and knees for a stone; an' the next minit I felt a touch on my arm.

"All right, Pat," sez Billy Lenahan's voice, in a half-whisper. "Come back into your skin again. It's only me. Is this the dog you've got?" sez he, liftin' the basket. "I heard him crackin' nuts as you went past me at the fair-green."

"You can have him back, you big sharper," sez I, "if you'll tell me where he learned his bad habits."

"There's no great mystery about that," sez Billy. "An' I'm safer without him, thank you. Colonel Fitzgerald fell out with his wife about her wee dogs, an' trained this fellow to kill them; an' then he fell in with her again an' gave me a couple of quid to put him out of the road. Since then, as you know, Mr. Anthony paid me a pound for him; an' now you're puttin' him out of the way for nothin'. I'll go off an' look for another dog," sez he; "I done so well out of this one." An' away he slips into the darkness.

"Are you there, Pat?" calls Mr. Anthony's voice in a minit or two.—"*Hell!*" sez he, as there came a crash, "what did you move the basket for?—Will that do?" sez he, showin' me a stone with the flashlight.

"It'll do well," sez I. "Lend me a glimmer till I tie it on him."

"Give me him, now," sez Mr. Anthony, when I'd done. "I bear the brute no ill-will, but damme, if there's any justice in this world I'm entitled to the drownin' of him."

He picked up the dog, hit himself a most lamentable dunt on his knees with the stone, an' started to hop round on one foot.

"For heaven's sake look out," sez I. "If you drop him in the reservoir we're destroyed."

"It's all right," sez Mr. Anthony, an' I knowed by his voice he was keepin' in some terrible observations. "I was just takin' my bearin's."

He hirpled on for a yard or two, an' then he stopped.

"Pat," sez he. "I left my calculations at home; but this stone is far too light. It should be seven pounds and a half, an' it's not that."

"It'll do," sez I, fair dancin' with impatience. "You've been signallin' for the polis all night, an' they'll be here any minit.—Drown yourself or drown the dog; but for heaven's sake do it quick!"

"I can do better," sez Mr. Anthony; an' I knowed by the tone of his voice I needn't contradict him. "The slope of the reservoir is paved with big stones. Take him by the scruff, an' do you show me a light with this thing till I find a loose one. The brute has tormented me for three days; I'll likely be in the Courts over him; an' now, blast him, he's broken my knee-cap. If he's goin' to the bottom, damme, he's stayin' at the bottom."

"Go slow, then, Mr. Anthony," I calls, as soft as I could. "You're in your own light.—Oh, my father!" sez I, as there came a most lamentable splash, "he's in!"

The dog gave a wriggle under my hand at the noise, an' twitched his neck out of my fingers. I caught a glimpse of him tearin' for the reservoir with the stone trundlin' behind him, an' the next minit he was in after Mr. Anthony.

By the time I got to the edge, Mr. Anthony was out, an' crawlin' up the slope on his hands an' knees. As soon as I seen he wasn't too bad I left him on the grass to curse himself dry, an' showed a light on the reservoir for a minit. But there was no sign of the dog.

"Oh, Mr. Anthony," sez I—an' I declare to you I was half-cryin'—"the poor brute jumped in to save you, an' now he's drowned."

"I don't care he was in hell," sez Mr. Anthony. "I expect he was tryin' to knock my brains out with the stone. An' now he'll be up again in three or four days floatin' round the town reservoir an' barkin' for the police.—Come on out of this, d——n you, before I get my death!"

I never saw Mr. Anthony so wicked in my life before. All the way back he never said a word, an' when we got to his house he didn't even ask me for a drink, but slammed the door in my face.

As I turned the corner of his house there came a wee cautious whistle; an' when I crossed the road it was Billy Lenahan.

"Well, I'll be hanged," sez I, lookin' down at his feet.

"Oh, it's him, all right," sez Billy, leanin' down to pat the brute. "The stone came off him an' he swam out just beside me. You might have heard me callin' him quietly by name."

"But I thought you didn't want him," sez I.

"Ach, you could never tell," sez Billy. "A dog's a dog. Some of these nights one of Mrs. Fitzgerald's wee atomies may bite the Colonel's feet in bed again, an' I'll make money on this fellow for the third time."

"Well, I'm not sorry, anyway," sez I.—"Shake a paw,"

sez I to the dog. "You're in bad company, an' I doubt you'll come to a poor end; but, dammit, I wish you well."

He put out his paw to me, hearty enough; an' as far as I could judge by the creature's tail we parted without any ill-will on his side, either.

A Short Cut

Wee John Timoney lived on a small farm about a quarter of a mile up the road from my house. A bit of stony poor land it was; an' like many a man who lives on a small bit of bad land John was hard-workin', an' savin', an' honest. He took a sup, it's true, but only on Fair days; an' he was known by everybody, except the polis, to make a drop of poteen; but with whiskey the price it is, an' John's lonely wee farm just made for the trade, nobody could blame him for that.

So I was a good deal put about when word come over one Fair night by Robert Lynas's yard-boy that a bus had run down John an' the donkey-cart, an' that John was anointed, an' not expected to last beyond mornin'.

I put on my hat at once, an' away up the road to find out was the news true; an' I wasn't right sat down in the kitchen among one or two of John's neighbours when Mrs. Timoney put her head out of the bedroom door an' beckoned me. An' when I went up the room here was the supposed dyin' man sittin' up in bed as merry as a cricket. One of his eyes was black, an' there was a longish cut across his cheek, but, for all that, he was in the best of heart.

"You're not killed, anyway, John," sez I to him.

"Killed!" sez he. "I'm worth half a dozen dead men yet. When I think of the narrow escape I had I'm a thankful bein'."

"It's on his knees he ought to be," sez the wife. "He had somebody's prayers this night."

"But what happened?" sez I.

"It was all that wee donkey of mine," sez John. "One of the Company's buses come round Denver's corner without sayin' a word, an' when it seen us it let a guldher out of it would have deafened you. The donkey couldn't very well put his fingers in his ears, so he stuck his head into the hedge; an' the bus took us in the tail-board. If I had come down on the county road instead of in the sheugh, bedambut, Pat, I would have been hurt.—Give my my breeches, Annie," sez he. "I'll fetch a quart of duty unpaid down to the kitchen. If the neighbours are missin' a wake they'll get a thanks-givin', anyway."

"Now isn't he the wonderful ould fella," sez the wife, "to have come through what he did an' be as well as he is—Who's that?" she calls out, very sharp, as there comes a rappin' on the bedroom door.

"Open, Annie," sez a man's voice. "It's your brother Joe."

She unbarred the door, an' in squeezes Joe Merrick, that owned the pub about three miles down the road.

"What's this I hear about John?" sez he. "Is he much cut about?"

"He's little the worse," sez Mrs. Timoney. "There'll hardly be a mark on him."

I could see Joe's face droppin'.

"Tck, tck," sez he, "that's bad, that's very bad. We'll have to do somethin' about that.—But where is he?" sez he, lookin' at the empty bed.

"He's gone into the wee room to get a drop of what you know, for the neighbours," sez she.

"Are yez mad, the pair of yez?" sez Joe, starin' at her.—"Put down that bottle, an' get back into bed again quick," sez he very snappy to John Timoney, as he came out of the wee room.

"But why?" sez John. "I was just goin'——"

"Off with your breeches an' get in," barks Joe at him. "Do you not know what has happened to you, man? Do you not know that if this is managed right you'll never need to take hold of the handles of a plough again, an' your wife here'll be goin' about like my lady, with a fur coat on her back, an' earrings in her ears. A big bus company, an' an accident like this! —Why your fortune is made."

"But how do you make that out?" sez Mrs. Timoney. "Sure John's not bad."

"He *will* be bad," sez Merrick. "He's in his bed, now, an' he'll not be out of it these two months, with bruises an' pains. An' it'll be six months or a year after he gets up before he'll be able to do a hand's turn.—Leave it to me, now," sez he to John. "I'll have you sick enough before I'm done with you."

"But—but, Joe," stutters old Timoney, his eyes as big as saucers, "I doubt all this wouldn't be over honest."

Little Mrs. Timoney half-opened her lips, an' then closed them again without sayin' anythin'; but I could see that she was beginnin' to turn things over in her mind.

"*Honest?*" snaps Merrick at John. "Dammit," sez he, "are you tryin' to make me out a rogue? Aren't you badly bruised about the body? I can tell that by the way you move in the bed. Isn't your sight injured; an' haven't you a cut across your face half an inch deep?"

"There's no doubt, John," puts in Mrs. Timoney, "it's a very ugly-lookin' gash."

"D——n all it is," sez John, "but the scrab of a brier. Three or four days'll heal it."

"But suppose it festers?" sez Joe. "An' if it was on my face an' I got it in a bus accident I would see that it *did* fester."

John sat up in his bed with a jump.

"Now, listen to me, Joe," sez he, "an' do you listen to me, too, Annie—for you're lettin' this brother of yours carry you off your feet—apart altogether from the fair play of the thing, there'll be no tricks of that nature worked about my face, understand that. I've heard of artificial arms, an' even legs; but I never heard of an artificial head yet, except on a tombstone."

"Well, answer me this," sez the brother-in-law, in a kind of a patient way; "if the bus company offers you money will you refuse it?"

"Aw, begob," sez John, "if you put it that way I'm not above takin' a few quid off them.—Here," sez he to the brother-in-law, "I'll put myself in your charge. Tell me what you want me to do, and if it's in any decency at all, I'll do it."

"That's the way to talk," sez Joe Merrick, rubbin' his hands.—"Come on then, Annie; tear up an old sheet, an' bandage him till there's nothin' free but his mouth.—Show me that cut a minit.—Tck, tck," sez he, "that'll be like a baby's back in a couple of weeks. You wouldn't let me coax it just what you'd know, John?" sez he. "A couple of real dirty spiders' webs on that all night would catch more ten-pound notes nor they ever caught flies."

"D——n the spider will ever spin a thread near the same cut!" sez John, very hearty; "not if I should end my days in the Union.—Go on, Annie; but if I'm to be bandaged, bandage me clean.—Here," he cries out; "you can't cover my eyes! How'll I do when I get out of bed?"

"If I hear of you bein' out of your bed before a month," sez Joe, "I'll be hanged for you. Keep the blinds down when the doctor comes; an' if he wants to pull them up yell out that the light's blindin' you.—Who *is* your doctor?"

"Nobody," sez Mrs. Timoney. "There hasn't been a doctor in the house these fifteen years."

"Good," sez the brother, well pleased. "Then I'll leave word at Dr. Dickson's as I go home. He's well past his work now, though he doesn't know it, an' as blind as a badger.—Have you done, Annie? Bedambut he looks well. Away down to the kitchen now, Pat," sez he, "an' get them one or two callers out of the house on their tip-toes. Come round in the mornin' about ten o'clock to see is John still alive. I'll be here to meet the doctor an' the solicitor."

"What's that?" sez John startin' up again in the bed. "What's that about a solicitor?—Now listen to me, Joe," he sez, "one thing I want to make clear to you. There was a law-suit in our family once, an' it near put my poor father —God rest him, an' send he's in heaven in spite of all he was egged on to swear—out on the road-side. There's to be no law."

"That's all right," sez Joe. "I'm no fonder of lawyers than you are yourself. We'll have to get legal advice for fear of puttin' our foot in things; but I'll answer for it that there won't be any law."

I wasn't long sat down by John's bedside the next mornin' when Joe an' Dr. Dickson arrived. Nothin' could have been more satisfactory from Joe's point of view. The old doctor was a good deal failed, an' desperate cross, an' would agree to nothin' at all that Joe said or hinted at. That was enough for Joe. He pooh-poohed all John's wee bits of injuries; an' the doctor made them out twice as bad as they were. When Joe swore that John wasn't hurt nowhere but on the head the doctor found as many black bruises on John's body as would have kept him from turnin' in the bed for six months, though, troth, a cake of soap would have done more for most of them than the doctor was aware of.

"He's claiming on the bus company, of course," sez Dr. Dickson, pullin' out a notebook.—"Very good; I'll now make a note of his injuries. Pull up that blind further."

He whipped a little ivory ruler out of his pocket, an' first of all stuck it in John's eye, an' then measured the cut on his face.

"Four-an'-a-half inches long," sez he to himself—though an inch-an'-a-half of it was the shadow of his own nose—an' went on writin' down in the book.

"What about your eyes?" sez he. "Is your sight affected?"

"He can't stand the light on them," sez Mrs. Timoney very hasty, before John had time to speak.

"They're runnin' water terrible this minit, doctor," sez Joe.

An' so they were, too; for the dart John got in the left eye with the wee ivory ruler must have given him fair agony.

"Eyes very sensitive to light," sez ould Dickson, writin' away.—"Now, Timoney," sez he, "you'll not leave your bed for at least a month. The bus company will send out a doctor of their own; but I'll be present when he comes; an' do you leave all the talkin' to me. Meantime I'll come out every day——"

"I doubt that'd cost a deal of money," puts in Mrs. Timoney, lookin' all scared.

"Half-a-guinea a visit," sez the doctor, "an' car-hire."

"Oh my Father," groans out poor John, "this is hellish."

"Don't worry yourself," sez ould Dickson. "The bus company will pay, not you. If I didn't make bus companies an' the like pay through the nose I couldn't afford to attend small farmers for half-a-crown a visit, remember."

"There you are, now," sez Joe Merrick, when the doctor was gone. "You heard that. An' if a man like Doctor Dickson makes the bus company pay through the nose, why shouldn't you?"

"It's a great relief to my feelin's, sure enough," sez John. "What time did you say the solicitor was comin' out?"

"Any time, now," sez Joe. "I'm gettin' Mr. Anthony for you."

"He's a bit vain an' light-headed, they tell me," sez John. "He wouldn't be for pushin' me into law just to get himself better knowed? What do you think, Pat?"

"He's not such a fool as you'd imagine from the way he goes on," sez I. "You'll be all right in his hands, I'll answer for that."

But when Mr. Anthony did come, an' begun to let himself rip, I wasn't just so sure about him.

"I'll get you a thousand pounds for this, John," sez he.

Even Joe Merrick gave a gasp.

"A thousand!" sez he.

"A thousand," sez Mr. Anthony. "Any pettifogger could get him five or six hundred; but I'll get him a thousand. Why, damme," sez he, "I got a man fifteen-hundred last year against a railway company for fallin' out of a carriage door on to the line, an' him that drunk at the time that he had taken off his boots, an' thought he was walkin' into his own bedroom.—I'll give in," sez Mr. Anthony, "that he was a great witness."

"But—but, Mr. Anthony," sez poor ould John, goggle-eyed, "a thousand would break the bus company altogether."

Mr. Anthony darted a look through his eye-glass at John;

an' I could see he wasn't long makin' up his mind what sort of a witness John would be.

"Blethers, John," he sez. "Accidents like yours are the makin' of bus companies. There's nobody would travel in a bus nowadays if they didn't see by the papers that they're near sure to be run over if they walk. Anyway," sez he, "it's the insurance company'll have to pay. Show me that cut, now.—Ah, very satisfactory," he sez; "as nice a little bit of disfigurement as one could wish to see. Oh, blast it, if you were only twenty-five an' single, what a poem of a brief I could prepare for a barrister on that cut. Even as it is there's a good few hundreds for you in it, that is if the case is settled before it's too much healed."

I seen a look passin' between Joe an' the sister.

"Will the insurance company not pay up soon?" sez Joe.

"Soon!" sez Mr. Anthony. "What would they do that for? Every day this case hangs on, John'll be gettin' better, an' his face'll be gettin' smoother. Why, damme," sez he, "if they had a solicitor of my class actin' for them the case wouldn't be right started before this time next year. As it is they'll be in no hurry. In about three months' time their doctor'll come to see you, John. Burns of Liscree does all their work in this county. I know him well—a big breezy noisy man—they chose him on that account. He'll come blusterin' in like a March gale, an' hit you a slap on the back'll make you near swallow your false teeth, an' ask has he been sent here in mistake, you're lookin' so well. Before he's been talkin' to you five minutes you'll feel you want to buy the bus driver a box of cigars, an' write the insurance company a cheque for fifty pounds for curing you of your rheumatism. He's good," sez Mr. Anthony, "damme, he's good. With a little promptin' from me he near got Sam Twining up out of bed for his own funeral this time last year.—But pay no attention to him, John. If the other side get old Dickson properly riled he'll swear Burns into hell an' out again.

"An' now," sez Mr. Anthony, fetchin' out a notebook

about three times the size of the doctor's one, "we'll jot down some details of the claim.—First of all, the doctor. He'll make—let me see—say fifty visits. What's he chargin' a visit?"

"Half-a-guinea, sir," sez Mrs. Timoney. "I suppose it's not too much, for an insurance company."

"Blethers," sez Mr. Anthony. "Does the old ass not remember that he's a professional man?—One guinea a visit," sez he, writin' in the book, "say seventy-five pounds."

"But, Mr. Anthony, sir," sez poor John, "will a bill like that not make these insurance men angry at the very start?"

"Wait till they see mine," sez Mr. Anthony; "an', damme, the doctor's bill'll make them burst out laughin'. Wait till you hear a barrister on your sufferin', an' blast me, but you'll be ashamed of yourself that you didn't die the night you were hit."

"Mr. Anthony, sir," sez John, rising up on his elbow, an' speakin' very determined. "There's one thing must be settled between us. There must be no law. *You* can tell whatever lies you like; I take it that's your job, but I'm an honest small farmer, an', on the lines you're layin' down, into a witness-box my conscience will not let me go.—No," sez he, "I'll settle all right if the case can be settled; an' you can open your mouth as wide as you like, because I see these insurance fellows is nothin' but cheats; but *no law*."

Mr. Anthony took the eyeglass out of his eye an' began to polish it with his silk handkerchief, an' by the vicious way he rubbed I could see that he was vexed.

"Mr. Timoney," sez he, "let me tell you that you're not givin' me much assistance in this case. I'll go further, an' say that you're actually hamperin' me.—Listen to me, now; an' do you all listen to me.—I'm instructed to settle this case, an' I'll settle it. The insurance company will meet us half-way. In the first place, they're liable. An insurance company against a poor man with a donkey-an'-cart is always liable. Fitzsimons down the street from me is their solicitor; an' he'll tell them that, stupid as he is.

"In the next place, they'll hear that I'm in charge of the case, an' the minit that comes out the managin' director's hand will go to his cheque-book—that is," sez he, lookin' round us all very weighty, "*if they think you are goin' to law.* —But do you hear me, now; if the insurance company hears or believes or guesses that you won't go to law, you're a done man.—Here's my last word," sez he, screwin' the eyeglass into his eye as if he was closin' a tin of petrol, "either you'll let me give out that you're as quarrelsome as a jilted weasel an' as big a liar as Beelzebub sellin' a horse, or, confound me, I'll leave you to any half-educated numskull that'll take up a case I've washed my hands of."

When Mr. Anthony was gone, after gettin' his own way about everythin', there wasn't a word spoke for a long while. John was still upon his elbow, an' though I wouldn't altogether like to say that he was lookin' like Beelzezub, I would hardly just have liked to trust him with a copy of the New Testament an' a friendly barrister.

But neither John nor the missis were goin' to touch the insurance company's money as easy as they thought. For divil a word came from the company, good or bad; an' no doctor came to see John.

After all the warnin's Mr. Anthony had given us I wasn't surprised about the delay; but the old couple, an' especially Mrs. Timoney, were greatly put about, an' at last she came over to see me one mornin', looking very worried.

"Pat," sez she, burstin' into tears, "if things goes on any longer the way they're doin' poor John'll never touch a penny piece in spite of all he's come through."

"How's that, Mrs. Timoney?" sez I, astonished. "What's gone astray?"

"It's his face," sez she. "I managed it well enough for a while, with the hint I had from Joe——"

"You didn't put the spiders' webs on it!" sez I.

"I was afeard to," sez she. "If a spider had got into the wound God knows where it might have come out. No, I just worked with dirty cloths, an' did well enough; but seein' how time was slippin' by I thought one mornin' I'd drop a little dust from one of the rafters into the wound; an' the second day after that John had convulsions in the night an' bit a piece out of a cup."

"Lord save us!" sez I. "Is he bad still?"

"It's worse nor that," sez she, beginnin' to cry again. "His face is closed up, an' he's healin' like a child.—Oh, now, aren't them insurance people just behavin' divilish on a poor old man an' woman like us!"

"I'll go in to Mr. Anthony in the mornin'," sez I.

"Mr. Anthony," sez I, when I went into his private room, "John Timoney's wife says his face is near healed, an' there's no time to lose."

But Mr. Anthony remained cool.

"It's just what I would have expected from John Timoney's face," sez he. "I've never had a client that gave me as little support as the same John Timoney. But I won't act yet should his face move round to the small of his back.—Listen," sez he. "Doctor Burns goes on his holidays for the month of August; an' do you think it's an old, wise, experienced fellow like himself he'll get for a locum. Don't you know very well that a good-lookin' girl's chum always has a face on her would stop a clock? What Burns'll leave behind him in August will be some brat of a boy, either cocksure enough to poison his father or too scared to prescribe anything stronger than Glauber salts, if it was for double pneumonia. On the first day of the same month of August I'll threaten the insurance company with a writ; an' if that superannuated old bear, Dickson, doesn't growl down any medical man under ten years' experience that's sent out to examine John Timoney, damme, I'll eat the Law Directory between two slices of bread an' butter.—An' I'll see that Mrs. Timoney's brother is there, as well," sez he. "A most intelligent fellow that, an' might be helpful."

"He'll be helpful, sure enough, if he gets a chance," sez I to myself. "He'd cut John's throat if he thought the widow would get another two hundred."

A week afterwards there came a message for me that I was wanted in John Timoney's. An' when I went, here was

Joe Merrick sittin' in the kitchen with a very flushed face, an' him laughin' to himself every minit or two.

"I've done it, Pat," sez he, jumpin' up an' slappin' me on the back with another great guffaw; "bedambut I've done it!"

"What have you done?" sez I. "Some rascality, I'm sure."

"The insurance doctor has been here," sez he, "a young gawm of a fellow, an' as raw as a mountainy servant-girl. Dr. Dickson was late; an' as I sat lookin' at the young fellow the idea come into my head.

" 'Have you ever tasted poteen?' sez I to him. An' he never had.

" 'You must sample it,' " sez I.

"Before he had two mouthfuls down, his tongue was beginnin' to loosen. He held out his mug for a second dose, an' by the time he had that in him he was bletherin'. One look at John did him; but he believes every word I said; an' as he went off he shook me by the hand an' told me he would recommend John for four figures, if it was only for the liquor he made."

"Was he tight?" sez I.

"Tight?" laughs Joe. "With two mugs of John's brew in him? Why it's enough to muddle an addin' machine."

"You had very little to do, to expose the poor young fellow before Dickson," sez I. For I was a good deal disgusted.

"He was gone before Dickson came," sez Merrick. "An' that was as lucky a stroke as any; for the old man took himself off in a towerin' rage, an' swears he'll learn the insurance company to send other doctors out behind his back!—But come on up an' see the sick man.—John," sez he, "I've been tellin' Pat the fortune you're goin' to get now that the insurance doctor has been with you."

But John wasn't in near as good heart as his brother-in-law was in; an' even Mrs. Timoney was lookin' very sober.

"Tell Pat what you did," sez John to the brother-in-law. —"Tell him, now; for I'm not easy in my mind about it, at all."

Joe looked at me a bit foolish, an' begun to laugh again.

"Well," he sez, "for your life don't say a word; but I looked at John's face before the young doctor was let up to the room, an' the cut looked very dry an' healed; so I just nicked my finger with John's razor an' ran it along the scar. —An' a d——d expensive-lookin' wound I made," sez Joe, all pleased with himself. "The young fellow just glanced at it, an' sez 'Erysipelas,' an' covers it up."

"Pat," sez poor old John, very anxious; "you don't think there could be anythin' like that wrong with me?"

"If you don't get gangrene from this ruffian Joe's blood," sez I, "all you're in danger of is about six months' hard for fraud."

"There now," sez John to the wife, near cryin'. "I told you!—Write to Mr. Anthony this minit, Joe, an' tell him to settle the case at once, an' put me out of my misery. For I'm uneasy in my mind about this day's doin's."

It wasn't long till he was uneasier. Three days later Joe Merrick drove into my yard, an' the curses of him would have fired an axle.

"We're ruined, Pat," sez he, "ruined an' destroyed by that little spitfire, Mr. Anthony. The minit he got my letter up went his tail among the stars, an' he started to engage King's Counsel as if he was pickin' a football team. He has two trysted already, an' there'll not be horse-hair enough in Ireland to fit out the drove of them he'll have round him before he's done. Come on up to the cottage quick, or John'll lose his senses altogether."

An', troth, poor John wasn't very far from it. There he was sittin' up in bed, moanin' an' lamentin' as if he was at his own wake. It was no use tryin' to reason with him. He would listen to nothin'.

"I see it all," he'd say over an' over again. "It was law he meant the whole time.—Pat," sez he, catchin' me by the hand, "what'll I do? It's hell or the poor-house for me, now; for if I don't perjure myself in the witness-box the house'll be sold over my head. Go to him, Pat; go to Mr. Anthony if you don't want to see me hangin' from a tree!"

"Mrs. Timoney," sez I, gettin' her down to the kitchen

by herself, "go in to Mr. Anthony in the mornin' an' tell him to settle for anythin' he can get, or you'll have a lunatic on your hands."

"I'll go," sez she, all flustered an' upset. "It's a terrible pity John's so timid; but I will.—Should I—should I tell him about Joe's wee bit of cleverness?" sez she, hesitatin'.

"It'll put Mr. Anthony in a fix if she does," sez I to myself.—"Better not," sez I to her.

But I went in early next mornin' to Mr. Anthony, just to see should I tell him myself.

"Mr. Anthony," sez I, sittin' down in his private room, "I thought you promised you wouldn't go to law in this case of John Timoney's?"

"I'm not goin' to law," sez he, lyin' back very easy in his chair.

"Well, then," sez I, "barrin' to frighten the very life an' sowl out of wee John, what do you want two Counsellors for?"

"Pat," sez Mr. Anthony, stickin' his glass in his eye an' fixin' me with it very superior, "you have heard me comparin' myself to the great Napoleon?"

"Several times, sir," sez I.

"Very well," sez he, "Napoleon won victories with his big battalions, but I've bettered him, for I've brought up my big battalions an' won a victory without a shot bein' fired. The minit Fitzsimons heard the news he came down here an' settled for six-hundred-an'-fifty pounds.—There's only one condition. He's to see John Timoney before the agreement is signed."

"I don't like that, Mr. Anthony," I blurted out.

"I would rather not, myself," sez Mr. Anthony. "That wound of John's isn't so satisfactory as it was, I'm sure. But if their doctor's report wasn't damagin' they wouldn't be talkin' of a settlement. An' Fitzsimons can't go into the witness-box. I'll let him see John if he wants to."

"I'd better tell him about Joe," sez I to myself. An' I did. Mr. Anthony listened to me without sayin' a word; an' then he swore very bitter for about five minits by the clock.

"This is what comes of the common ignorant layman havin' to do with what's a matter for lawyers an' gentlemen," sez he. "Oh, my father, if I had only wooden dummies for clients the cases I'd win would fill a library.—What time ought Mrs. Timoney to be here?" sez he, gettin' business-like all at once. "Half an hour?—Don't come back till then. This campaign will take some plannin'."

When I went back Mrs. Timoney was just leavin' Mr. Anthony's room. I could see by her face she had been cryin', an' made up my mind to find Mr. Anthony in a very bad temper. But he must have calmed down.

"Don't speak to me for a little," sez he. "I want to think."

He sat there I suppose ten minits, windin' an' unwindin' the string of his eyeglass on his forefinger; an' then all at once he tossed the glass in the air an' caught it.

"Away an' finish your business," sez he, "an' come back in an hour. Mr. Fitzsimons an' I will be goin' out to John Timoney's then, an' you may as well come, too."

"You're wrong, Mr. Anthony, sir," sez I. "You should settle here, for what you can get. There's somethin' queer about Fitzsimons goin' out to John's. As sure as death he has a card up his sleeve."

"Pat," sez Mr. Anthony, jumpin' up an' slappin' himself on the chest, "Napoleon got a settlement at Elba, an' could have lived comfortable enough on it till the end of his days. But did he? Not a bit of him. He tossed head or harp at Waterloo, an' damme, if he'd had me at his elbow to advise him he'd have headed the ha'penny.—Listen, now," sez he; "keep quiet till Fitzsimons an' me are in the room with John Timoney. Hold your tongue so far—an' then, if you don't hold your breath my name's not Anthony!"

Not one word did I say till we were in John's kitchen at any rate; an' then only to bid the time of day to Mrs. Timoney. Mr. Anthony shook hands with her, too, very easy an' affable. Fitzsimons was a deal dryer an' cautiouser, an' didn't even commit himself to sayin' it was a fine day. The more I looked at him the more it come into my mind that he was wound up for somethin', an' only bidin' his time. I tried to catch Mr. Anthony's eye an' give him a warnin' to look out for trouble; but Mr. Anthony was skippin' about all careless an' gay, an' I don't suppose would have took a warnin' if I'd give it to him.

"I presume I can bring Mr. Fitzsimons up to see John?" sez he to Mrs. Timoney. "Just as a matter of form, before the settlement's signed."

"Certainly, sir," sez Mrs. Timoney, leadin' the way.

John was lyin' back in the bed, with about twice as much bandagin' over his face as I'd ever seen before. When Mr. Anthony spoke to him he answered very feeble an' low; an', whether it was Joe's doin' or not, I could see John was beginnin' to learn the business.

"He's very weak after the shock an' his long illness," sez Mr. Anthony, turnin' to Fitzsimons.

"I can tell that, "answers Fitzsimons. "Of course our doctor reported as much." An' his tone was cordial enough, for the dry old stick he was.

"Dammit," sez I to myself, "this is a cake-walk after all."

"Need I take the bandages off?" sez Mr. Anthony very airy. But I thought he looked a trifle away as he said it.

"Oh well—just as a matter of form," sez Fitzsimons.

Mr. Anthony turned his head towards Mrs. Timoney; an' as he bent down over John I seen her slip to the window an' pull down the blind a couple of inches more.

"Steady, now, John," sez Mr. Anthony; "I'll not hurt you.—The wound has never closed, Fitzsimons," sez he, "an' it's very painful still.—A glance will show you."

An' as Mr. Anthony lifted the bandages, Fitzsimons skipped to the window, an' up with the blind. I looked at John's face; an' there right along the wound was a red streak of wet blood, an' some over his cheek as well.

"I never would ha' believed it of Mr. Anthony!" sez I to myself.

But as Mr. Anthony went to put the bandages back, Fitzsimons grabbed his arm.

"Just as our doctor reported," sez Fitzsimons, beamin' very dry an' frosty all round; "a clear fake.—Clever young fellow, that locum, Anthony," sez he; "but one of the toughest medicals ever went through Unity. The poteen was just buttermilk to him.—Allow me."

Too late I seen what he was after, but didn't step forward in time. He plucked the handkerchief from his pocket an' drew it sharply down John's wound.

I can hear the screech that John let out of him, yet!

The next minit he was sittin' up in the bed yelpin' like a docked puppy, an' the blood patterin' down the whole front of his night-shirt.

"Oh, my heavens an' earth!" sez Fitzsimons, glarin' at him, with his face like a sheet. Then all at once he took a wickeder glare at Mr. Anthony, an' stalked out to the motor-car without another word.

We were half-roads to Ballygullion before he spoke.

"You've trapped me, Anthony," sez he. "You can't deny it. I was fool enough to believe that drunken young ass of a doctor; an' now I've made matters ten times worse. But it was a dirty low-down trick to give him poteen, an' I'm surprised that you would be concerned in such a transaction."

"It serves you an' the company jolly well right," sez Mr. Anthony—"tryin' to cheat an old man with your delay. I had neither art nor part in the poteen business, though, an' to convince you I'll still settle for the sum we agreed on, six hundred an' fifty pounds.—But, Fitzsimons," sez he, "unless you want to be laughed out of the country we'd better say nothin' about your assault on a poor old sufferer. Pay an' let the matter drop. An' the next time you're dealin' with decent people don't be too ready to listen to cock-an'-bull stories, that's all."

"Did you notice how I closed Fitzsimons's mouth an' ears about the case?" sez Mr. Anthony, when we had the car to ourselves. "He'll eat the head off anybody that even mentions it from this time on.—An' yet it's a pity, too," sez he. "If we dare only face the Courts after Fitz's blunder to-day, blast me but we'd get a million."

"Mr. Anthony," sez I, "what did Joe Merrick cut John's face open with?"

"Cut?" sez Mr. Anthony, lookin' at me all injured innocence. "*Cut!* Do you think for one moment that I'd lend myself to any such piece of rascality!—The old fool got up out of bed for a drink in the middle of last night an' nearly knocked his brains out on the edge of the kitchen door, that's all.

"Pat," sez he presently, gazin' at me very solemn, "when you consider the low trickery of the insurance company wouldn't you almost say the thing had happened providentially?"

I looked at him for a minute or two, an' he never turned a hair.

"There's just one thing I'll say, Mr. Anthony," sez I, openin' the door, "an' that is that I'm goin' to get out an' walk. For if Providence should take it into its head to interfere with you again in connection with this affair I'd just as soon not be in the car."

Turkey and Ham

WHEN wee Mr. Anthony the solicitor was courtin' Mr. Livingston's daughter, Miss Betty, he had only the one trouble. It wasn't his girl; she was a quiet simple affectionate slip of a grey-eyed girl, an' thought the sun riz an' set on him. The bother was, Mr. Anthony was so pleased about it that he begun to put on fat. He told me his trouble, one day we were out shootin' over the Bermingham estate, that Miss Betty's father was agent for; an' I only laughed at him.

"What odds does it make," says I, "if your young lady takes no notice?"

That comforted him for a while; but the followin' week a thunderbolt fell on him.

"George," sez Miss Betty to him one evenin', very timid, "I'm thinkin' of tryin' to slim. It would never do for the two of us to get fat," sez she. "People would look after us as we went down the street."

Mr. Anthony jumped as if he had touched an electric wire.

"That settles it," sez he. "I needed that jog. Not that I'm greedy, dear; but I'm a great judge of food and wine, and it seemed a pity not to exercise my talent. Now, my mind is made up. As from the end of to-night's dinner—I'll have to eat that, since it's cooked—I go on a diet till I've lost a stone and a half. I will not have you slimming, Betty. Curse it," says he, "I don't care if you grow as round as a dumpling. I love you. But we mustn't become ridiculous. Listen to me, darling," he says, warmin' up; "from to-night I go on to Dr. Thompson's diet. It's a corker, mind you. It slimmed old Mrs. McGimpsey till she rattled in her coffin; and it may kill me, too; but my word is my oath. Damme, if it wasn't boiled chicken and bacon I'd give to-night's dinner to the dog."

"Don't overdo it, George," sez Miss Betty, a trifle frightened. "You might injure your health. And you forget that to-morrow's Christmas Day, and you're dining with us."

"I was doing more than that," sez Mr. Anthony. "I was dining in the middle of the day as well, just to spite my old housekeeper. She has my Christmas dinner bought, a turkey and a ham, and sausages and chestnuts and heaven knows what; and I got a present of two bottles of champagne from Mr. Bermingham—the Widow Clicquot, 1921—that would make a tombstone angel play jazz tunes."

"But George, darling," says Miss Betty, "were you going to eat and drink all that? And I was sympathizing about your figure!"

"Confound it, no," says Mr. Anthony. "I never get anything but a morsel, a couple of slices of breast, and maybe a wing and a sausage or two; and then off goes the rest to her relations. She has a sister married to the gamekeeper of the Bermingham estate, and another to the keeper of the back lodge-gate, and you'd think she was married to them herself. They get about two-thirds of all the food I pay for; and now they're going to get the whole of my Christmas dinner."

"But it's a shame," says Miss Betty, "an imposition!"

Mr. Anthony stopped on the road.

" 'Gad," says he, "I never thought of that. It *is* an imposition. I've been weak, Betty," sez he, "and that's not like me. I can't eat my Christmas dinner—grape-fruit and toast, the doctor's diet says—and I can't drink my Christmas champagne; but, begad, if I fast the housekeeper's relatives may fast, too. Pat Murphy's coming round this evening after dinner to fix up some shooting for St. Stephen's Day. I'll give my dinner to him. Not a word!" says he. "I want to show you that you're getting a man that loves you better than his meals. It's a point of honour with me, now. Damme," sez he, "I'll stick to the diet should I go up the aisle with you, and the people looking through me as if I was a rainbow."

But when Mr. Anthony offered me the dinner that evening it was far too late.

"I just daren't take it, Mr. Anthony," says I. "We have a turkey of my wife Mollie's rearin' that she cried over when she was killin' it, as if it was a child; an' the least I can do is to attend the funeral. An' as for champagne, I wouldn't have the wee bubbles out of my system before the New Year. Eat an' drink the whole lot yourself," says I. "Miss Betty'll never know."

"I wouldn't do that," says Mr. Anthony. "Is it deceive poor Betty even before I'm married to her? Never!" says he. "I'm a man of principle. Beyond what the doctor's diet permits—not a crumb," says he, "not the pop of a cork. I suppose the housekeeper's clan will have to get the dinner after all."

"Give it to some decent poor family," says I. "It'll be a friendly turn. An' if a solicitor's soul *can* be saved it may do somethin' in that direction as well."

"Tell me the name of a family," says he, "and if the champagne goes to heads unaccustomed to anythin' but porter, damme, I'll defend them myself."

"The O'Greens of Creel's Row are decent people that would be glad of an extra bit an' sup on a day like that," says I; "but, sure, if you sent your Christmas dinner to a Nationalist family there'd be a revolution."

"This is where brains and experience come in," says Mr. Anthony, all pleased with himself. "There's an Orange family called Williamson on the far side of the Row. We'll split the dinner between the two families, an' I'll throw in a drop of whiskey, each, to warm their stomachs after the champagne."

"If you do that," says I, "your soul an' body are safe for the Christmas holidays, anyway. But if your whiskey is so plenty could you not spare me a drop, now?"

"I can," says he, "and will."

He took down a bottle an' filled out about half a glass.

"Isn't it an extraordinary thing, Pat," says he, twirlin' the glass in his hand, "the way people let drink get a hold of them. Now here I am," says he, takin' a sip, "that have given up this stuff maybe for ever, and I don't care a fig. There's nothin' to give up," says he, takin' another sup. "I've lost the taste for it already. Bless my soul!" he says emptyin' down the last drop, "I've dirtied your glass. Wait till I get another."

"All the same, Mr. Anthony," says I, "you'll find it a long Christmas day."

"It can't be helped," says he, lookin' a bit glum. "Principle is principle. But, do you know, Pat; I think it would be a kindly act if you and I dropped round to the houses of these two poor fellows to-morrow. They'd like to see the giver of the feast; and it might console me under the diet if I saw other people doing themselves harm instead of me."

"I'm with you," says I, "if you'll make it early. We're not eatin' our dinner till four. The brother-in-law and his wife are comin' down on the afternoon train from Belfast."

"Good," says Mr. Anthony. "What time do these unfortunate people dine?"

"They don't dine at all," says I. "As soon as the grub is cooked they eat it."

"Very well," says Mr. Anthony. "I'll not be up myself;

but I'll tell the housekeeper to send the stuff about ten. And three hours will cook a ham."

"It doesn't take near as long to cook drink," says I.

"We'll have to take our chance of that," says Mr. Anthony. "I can put a flask in my pocket. Let us say half-past twelve at Johnson's corner. Oh, just a minute," says he. He tossed up a shilling. "The turkey goes to the O'Greens, and the ham to the Williamsons. We'll call on the Williamsons first, to accustom me to the smell of food. If I encounter the turkey first I might be tempted to taste the stuffing. Don't be surprised if you find me thinner in the morning, Pat. There'll be nothing in me but half a grape-fruit and some kind of sawdust toast. Curse that doctor fellow," says he, forgettin' himself a little. "And to think that he'll be eating bacon and eggs."

The next day about a quarter to one o'clock Mr. Anthony an' I walked up the path to Robert Williamson's cottage. About six feet away from the door Mr. Anthony stopped me.

"Do you smell it, Pat?" says he.

"What?" says I, after a hard sniff.

"The ham," says he. "Pure Limerick. I would know it a mile away. They're a queer lot in the South of Ireland, but damme, they can make ham. Lovely," says he, takin' a sniff himself. "I feel well paid already for my little bit of self-sacrifice. Don't let me stay too long. That smell is making me ravenous."

When we went into the Williamson's kitchen there was nobody there but Mrs. Williamson, an' the two children. The fire was barely in, an' there wasn't even a saucepan on it. Mrs. Williamson was blowin' the bellows; an' she looked up all surprised. Mr. Anthony stammered a little.

"I was just taking a Christmas morning walk with my friend Pat Murphy," says he; "and we thought we'd call and wish you a Happy Christmas."

"Thank you, sir," says Mrs. Williamson, well pleased, "you were always very kind. Shake hands with the gentleman," says she to the children, "and say 'Thank you'."

It's very hard to have a child sayin' "Thank you" for nothin'. Mr. Anthony put his hand in his pocket an' fetched out some silver. I looked, an' the divil a thing smaller was among it than two-shillin' bits. He gave the children one apiece; but you could see by his face he was addin' it to the cost of the ham.

Mrs. Williamson thanked him herself with the tears in her eyes.

"The boss got half a day's work this mornin' at double pay," says she, "an' he'll not be back till half-past two, so I haven't a bite cooked in the house that I could offer you."

Mr. Anthony's face fell, an' he gave a very straightforward sniff. Mrs. Williamson took the hint.

"You've said it, sir," sez she. "It's a bit on the elderly side, sure enough; but maybe you would take a morsel."

She went to the cupboard an' fetched out a piece of very broadminded-lookin' cheese; though the green was beginning' to get the better of the Orange.

"Try a piece of that an' a sup of whiskey, sir," says she, "you an' Pat Murphy; just for the credit of the house."

Mr. Anthony turned his back on the cheese, an' filled himself out a stiffish glass. It pulled him together a good deal, for he faced round manful again.

"Thank you, mem," says he; "but I'm on a diet, and cheese is specially forbidden. But you're right to eat that piece at half-past two; for I doubt it will be past its best by three o'clock.—Now don't be drinking all the woman's whiskey, Pat," says he to me, that was barely takin' a poor man's drink. "I thought we were neither to eat nor wet our lips till we got home."

But I lingered a minute to speak to Mrs. Williamson.

"You should have thanked him for the dinner," says I. "He's not well pleased."

"What dinner?" says she, gapin' at me.

"It was half his dinner was sent you this mornin'," says I. "He's on a diet, an' didn't want the good food wasted. A whole Limerick ham, an' whiskey an' champagne wine. Did you not open the parcel yet?"

"If there was a parcel sent me it must have gone astray," says she; "for as true as I'm here I never got a crumb."

"That's queer," says I. "The housekeeper was to send it —half to you an' half to the O'Greens."

Mrs. Williamson looked very hard at me, an' the colour riz in her face.

"Oh, 'fare ye well, Killeavey'," says she. "That's all we'll ever hear of it. The ould faggot," says she. "Not that I would give offence to anybody of your persuasion, Mr. Murphy; but I expect she has gone an' sent the whole jing-bang to the O'Greens because they're her own sort. Run away, dear!" she says to the little boy that was hangin' round her. "Not a word, mind you, to Mr. Anthony. I'll say nothin' to my man. He'd want to stand on his rights; an' there's no use havin' a row between neighbours on this of all days in the year. But it's not very Christmas behaviour of her, I'll say that. An' I haven't tasted a bit of Limerick ham since I was at service in the Berminghams! Never mind, Mr. Murphy. It's not your fault. But there'll no blessin' follow it."

I suppose the whiskey did all the better work on Mr. Anthony on account of him bein' near empty; but when I caught up on him it was beginning to lift his heart a little.

"Now not one syllable out of you," says he, "about the teaspoonful of whiskey I had. If that cheese wasn't an excuse for at least half a pint I'll go back and eat the stuff. Isn't it a pity we went into the house at all? If I hadn't this cold in my head I'd have smelt it at the gate. Are we near the O'Greens?"

"It's somewhere about this part of the Row," says I. "Take a sniff an' try if you can smell a turkey."

"There's Mrs. O'Green just gone into the door," says he, very hasty. "Come on. I don't want the neighbours to think I'm serving a writ. You haven't four sixpences for a two-shilling piece Pat, have you? No? Curse it," says he, "I must have put in my pocket the money I had for the Bermingham servants instead of what I got for the poor. How many young O'Greens are there?"

"Seven," says I, "an' three dead."

"Thank heavens," says Mr. Anthony. "I mean for the three dead. My goodness," says he, fishing among his change, "this is going to cost me fifteen-and-sixpence. Can they all walk?" lokin' at me with a bit of hope in his eye.

"There's two of them can't, Mr. Anthony," says I; "but I doubt they could hold on tight enough to a couple of two-shillin' bits if they were put in their hand."

"D——n them," sez he, good-natured enough. "But I'll give the Berminghams' butler sixpence, and have my revenge."

Mr. and Mrs. O'Green an' the seven children were all in the wee kitchen; an' the five that could walk fell on Mr. Anthony an' near tore him to bits.

"An' very kind of you, sir," shouts Mrs. O'Green through the noise. "You were always gentry, Mr. Anthony, an' had somethin' in the heel of your hand for the poor man; an' God bless you an' the purty girl you're goin' to marry, an' may you raise as hearty an' healthy a flock as my own an' as many of them, though I doubt the mistress is a bit light in the make for it."

Mr. Anthony had been holdin' on to his money so far; but this was too much for him. He hauled out the silver, an' in his splutter began at the half-crown end, an' cost himself an extra sixpence. There was great enthusiasm; an' Mr. Anthony's Sunday breeches aged six months in about three minutes.

"We're just goin' to have our Christmas dinner," roars Mrs. O'Green. "You'll have a bite with us. Hold on till I try the pot."

"Good gracious," says Mr. Anthony in my ear, "I hope they haven't put in the champagne, too."

She laid a big dish on the table. The boilin' pot cleared a way through the crowd for itself, an' out tumbled a stew of rabbits an' bacon an' vegetables that would have tempted a sick millionaire, let alone a man on a diet.

"It's hardly done yet, but take that in your fingers, sir," says she, handin' him the leg of a rabbit, "an' just pick it as you stand there. Now, take it! It won't talk to you— barrin' you prosecute my man for shootin' it accidentally in Mr. Bermingham's demesne, an' a gentleman like you won't do that. Fetch the whiskey, Michael," she shouts at her husband. "I'll hold the twins. There's plenty more where that bottle came from," says she slippin' the twins' two two-shillin' bits into her husband's hand with a wink; "but porter'll be better for you."

Mr. Anthony leaned over to me as he was standin' with a glass in one hand an' the leg of a rabbit in the other.

"Take this bone out of my mouth," he mumbles. "I've near swallowed it twice; an' it would be sure to go down with the whiskey. I can't refuse to eat with these poor people," says he. "The Irish are very proud, and it would be taken as a deadly insult. And, curse it, I'm entitled to somethin' for my sixteen bob. By the way, did you see any sign of the turkey, or has it got lost in the stew?"

I shook my head as if I didn't hear him, for, troth, I'd been wonderin' about the turkey myself. An' when we were goin' out of the house, after me an' Mr. Anthony had drunk another couple of sups of whiskey an' Mr. Anthony had bought two reserved tickets for a concert in aid of the new chapel, I drew Mrs. O'Green behind the open cupboard door.

"What became of the turkey?" says I.

"What turkey?" says she. "My man shot no turkey, or if he did it was an accident."

"Mr. Anthony is on a diet," says I in her ear; "but had his Christmas dinner bought, an' sent you an' your family half of it, a turkey an' dear knows what besides. The housekeeper was to bring or send it, an' Mr. Anthony came round hopin' for a wing or a leg, so that he could eat an' still keep his conscience clear."

Mrs. O'Green took a look at me, an' then a half-scared look over her shoulder at her husband.

"Come outside," says she.—"It's that ould bitch of a housekeeper," says she. "Oh, well I know where our turkey is gone. It's decoratin' the insides of her an' her two sticks of sisters that hasn't chick or child between them, an' me with five hungry children an' two I'm feedin' myself an' wouldn't have a bite in the house this day if my hard-workin' man hadn't shot three rabbits an' a water-hen yesterday evening' an' him skulkin' behind hedge an' ditch to keep out of sight of the gamekeeper that's leatherin' into our turkey this minit—an' I wish he had shot *him*, too. But, for the love of mercy, Pat Murphy, say nothin' to nobody; for Michael has a wee sup of drink on him, this bein' Christmas mornin'—that was why I gave him the twins to hold, to keep him at peace—an' if he hears this news there'll be the siege of Athlone! Away with you," says she; "for he has his eye on me, an' for all he's a good faithful husband he's wicked in drink, an' might do somebody a mischief if he found out. God send I'll be able to keep it from him an' save his soul from sin this holy day, an' me with a couple of mouthfuls of whiskey in me, too, an' long-tongued with it, that the like never crossed my lips since the two blessed twins were christened Aloysius an' Timothy by Father O'Leary in this very house an' them dyin' but lived since, an' we had half a pint of whiskey that isn't paid for yet, an' I hope that ould extortioner down the street won't keep Mr. Anthony's two shillin'-bits again' it an' not let us have the porter."

Mr. Anthony was a temperate man, generally, more used to eatin' than drinkin'; an' when I caught up with him I found him two or three notes higher in the tune than when we left Williamson's, an' a little inclined to hiccough, though he handled it in a very gentlemanly way.

"There's a native courtesy about the Irish people, Pat," says he, "a fine old standard of princely hospitality—*hmph!* I beg your pardon," says he.—"Look at that poor creature with one miserable rabbit in a pot along with very bad company, and, damme, she was handing round legs of it as if it was a centipede. She wanted me to take whiskey, too. I wish I had. There's something sticking in my gizzard about half-way down, blast me but I think it's a claw. She should have cut the claws off, shouldn't she, Pat? No system about the

Irish, all happy-go-lucky. Now I'm a me-methodicalman," says he, takin' it in a rush. "It runs in my mind"—he stopped in the middle of the road an' began to grope in his pockets—"that I've lost somethin'.—What do you think, Pat?"

"What do you think you've lost?" says I.

He looked at me a bit wanderin' an' peevish.

"I don't *think* I've lost," says he. "I know.—Wait till I think what it was. I have it," says he. "What became of the turkey? An' if it comes to that——" he looked at me all surprised, "what became of the Limerick ham?"

An' then the divil entered into me.

"Mr. Anthony," says I, "should we not call round by the gamekeeper's house? Your old housekeeper is sure to be there, an' she would take it as a great compliment."

"So she would," says Mr. Anthony, stoppin' in the middle of the road again, an' forgettin' all about the turkey an' the ham for the time. "A very proper thing, too. Lord of the Manor visits old retainer—what? Lead on, Macduff. Wait a minute," says he, wrinklin' up his forehead as if he was still tryin' to remember somethin', "do I look like a man that was on a strict diet?"

"You look like a man that will be on a quare strict diet to-morrow," sez I.

An', sure enough, the whiskey was gettin' more of a hold of him every second.

"I don't mind about to-morrow," says he, devil-may-care all at once, "so long as I'm all right to-day. And I don't care for any keeper—gate-keeper, gamekeeper, or house-keeper. If she opens her mouth to say the word 'diet'—if I even see it in her eye—I'll give her a month's notice without the option of a fine. Come along!

"Wait a minute," says he again; an' this time he looked worrieder than ever. "If we should meet Betty! *That* would be awkward, Pat. I couldn't give *her* a month's notice, could I?" He wagged his head very solemn as if there was nothing to be said for the opposite side. "And she could give *me* notice on the spot. Hold on," says he. "What day is this?

Christmas Day. And she'll have had her lunch. She couldn't come out full of lunch on Christmas Day and sack poor Anthony that has nothing inside him at all—at any rate nothing that's doing him any good. No, no. Posterous.—I mean," says he, pickin' his steps through the syllables very carefully, "*Pre*-pos-terous.

"Now, listen to me, Pat," says he when we got under way once more, "we must do this in style. The old castle—the gamekeeper's house is the old castle. The wicked Baron—that's the housekeeper; and very wicked she was this day when she found I'd given away the family's dinner. The gallant knight—quite clearly that's G. Anthony, Esq., solicitor-at-law except on Christmas Day. And the beautiful damsel is Betty."

"But she isn't here," says I.

"I know that," says he, shakin' his head very mournful. "It's just as well."

"An' where does Pat Murphy come in?" says I, humourin' him.

"You don't come in at all," says he, "if you have any sense. For, there's going to be bloody wars. Do you think," says he, lookin' at me as if he was an owl that had sat up playin' cards till night-time, "that I didn't spot what that old deceiver had done with my Christmas gifts? Well, I did *not* spot it. I'm a man that makes so few blunders that I can acknowledge when I do make one. The whole way along there was something appearing and disappearing in my mind. I thought for a while it was my eyeglass. It was fluttering about me like a butterfly; but I caught it at last. And then all at once I saw that old harridan of a housekeeper carrying away my good dinner to her friends and leaving the poor and hungry with nothing to cover their nakedness but some d——d bad whiskey. Halt!" says he, pulling up on his toes. "We're at the gate. Form fours! Do you see that?" says he, pullin' a wee tin-trumpet out of his pocket. "The youngest walking O'Green child gave me that—and I'm still two and fourpence down over the transaction. When I blow three blasts on that—over the top!"

He blew three blasts on the wee trumpet—the first two were misfires—an' away up the path with me a good distance behind him—for the whiskey was beginnin' to die in me, an' I was feelin' a trifle ashamed of the whole transaction. When I got into the eatin'-room he was standin' at the head of the table holdin' a champagne bottle by the neck. The gamekeeper an' his wife, the lodge-keeper an' *his* wife, an' the housekeeper were all seated round such a spread as you never saw, bar in a picture—a turkey, a ham, plum puddin', cakes, sweets, bottles, an' glasses. They were just goin' to begin. There was a big salmon trout in front of the gamekeeper, an' he had dealt it all round the party an' given himself the ace.

Mr. Anthony was lookin' down on them with what would have been a frown if his features could have kept their places in the class.

"It *is* my dinner," says he, catchin' a hiccough just as it was tryin' to escape. "'S *all* my dinner. That's my trout you're eating. You might think that's boiled trout; but it's not. It's poached trout. And I got a present of it because I proved to the satisfaction of a magistrate that it wasn't poached trout. *So, where are you?*" says Mr. Anthony so loud all of a sudden that the gamekeeper raised his knife an' fork to protect himself.

You never saw five people as willin' to be in another place as the party round that table. But the gamekeeper gathered himself together.

"You're wrong, sir," says he, very soothin', a thing that didn't help his case at all. "I got this fish from Big Billy Lenahan of the Hills."

"So did I," says Mr. Anthony; an' the gamekeeper didn't know the answer.

"The fish was a present to me," says he at last. "That it may choke me if it wasn't," says he, gettin' desperate.

"Very good," says Mr. Anthony with great satisfaction. "*Let* it choke you. Stand up and swallow a mouthful; and if the fish doesn't choke you I'll make it apologize."

The gamekeeper looked at his wife most pitiful, but she

had nothin' to say; an' Mr. Anthony seemed very determined. So the gamekeeper stood on his feet with the plate of fish in one hand, balanced about a couple of ounces on the blade of his knife, an' made a shot at his mouth. He half caught the piece of fish, saw it was slippin', took a sudden suck; an' between that an' six pairs of eyes watchin' him, two of them in hope, sure enough he choked. An' the right name of it was chokin'. He was a short-necked, red-faced man when he started, but before you could count three he was purple, an' the eyes were comin' out of his head. I think it was his bad conscience more than the fish; but one or other looked like bein' the death of him. The three weemin let a combined family yell an' gathered round him cryin' an' lamentin'; the brother-in-law got him under the arms; an' between pullin' an' haulin' they had him out of the room an' into the kitchen in a twinklin', an' the door shut. I didn't know till the next day whether he lived or died.

For Mr. Anthony wasn't a bit put about, but laid down the bottle of champagne an' took up a whiskey-bottle.

"Seeing I'm on a diet, Pat," says he, "and have to deny myself, and you don't like champagne, we'd better begin the wake with whiskey."

He poured out two tough ones; an' he had finished first.

"Now, Pat," says he, "do you take the turkey an' I'll take the ham."

But I was beginnin' to feel the weather a bit myself, now; an' somehow it didn't seem right that I should have the honour of carryin' the turkey.

"No, no, sir," says I. "I take the ham."

We didn't get it settled; for, just as I spoke, a big boulder of a stone came flying through the window an' carried about a quarter of the plates an' glasses to their long home.

Mr. Anthony seized the champagne-bottle again, an' dived under the table-cloth.

"Take cover," says he. "He isn't dead yet."

I got behind a chair, waitin' for the second bomb. An' as Mr. Anthony poked his head out from the folds of the table-cloth, holdin' the champagne-bottle at the "Present," in rushes Michael O'Green with his two eldest boys on his heels, an' him wild-lookin'. He didn't even hear the pop as Mr. Anthony fired.

"Yez stole me Christmas dinner," says he, "but yez'll never eat it."

An' with that he lays hands on the turkey.

"Grab all you can, lads," says he. "What's not ours we'll make ours."

But even in the state he was in by this time Mr. Anthony was still the legal man.

"Justice and fair-play," says he, risin' to his feet, with his thumb in the champagne-bottle, an' it thinkin' it was tryin' to put out a fire. "Take what you like; but leave the ham."

It was like a ghost risin' before Michael. He let half a prayer, half an apology, out of him, lifted the turkey, called off the family with what plunder they'd laid hands on, an' away down the road, gallopin'.

But nothin' could shake Mr. Anthony by this time.

"You were quite right, Pat," says he as solemn as if he was on the Bench; "you do take the ham. I'll carry the champagne, if I can get it to my head without being drowned. Fetch one of those bottles of whiskey as well, or the battle of the Boyne will be fought over again in Creel's Row this day."

He wasn't far out. Robert Williamson was a quiet determined man that liked to get to the bottom of things, an' insisted on what was his due. When he came home his wee son told him enough about the dinner he had missed for him to get the whole story out of his wife. He put on his hat.

"Leave the dinner till I come back," says he. "I'll either have that ham with me or Michael O'Green by the hair of his head."

When he got to O'Green's the family was just takin' their places in triumph for such a feed, between rabbit stew an' the turkey, as would go down in the family history for generations to come. Robert wasted no words.

"I see you have your turkey," says he to Michael. "An'

that old bigot of a housekeeper let you have our ham as well. If I don't get it in two minits, I'll kick the stuffin' out of you an' the turkey both."

Any other time, Michael would have asked nothin' better than to let him try. But he had been greatly soothed by his victory about the turkey.

"Mr. Anthony kept the ham, Robert," says he. "As true as death I haven't got it."

"Then I'll have the turkey," says Williamson, quite simple an' straightforward; lays hold of it by the legs, an' lifts it from the dish.

"Will you, by my sowl?" roars Michael, flamin' all at once, an' lays hold of the turkey by the neck; an' in a minute the two of them was pullin' tug-of-war all over the kitchen floor, with the family yellin' to raise the thatch. There was already a fair knot of Creel's Row people gathered since word had gone round about Michael O'Green arrivin' with a whole cooked turkey in his hand; so Mr. Anthony an' I got through unbeknownst, an' into the kitchen just in time for Robert Williamson to miss Michael with the turkey an' hit Mr. Anthony in the face. It was the first time I saw Mr. Anthony real vexed the whole day. He brushed the loose bits of the turkey off his face, snatched the ham from me, an' liftin' it with his two hands felled Robert like a sheep. Then he came to himself again.

"There's your ham, Robert," says he in his ear, as Robert stood up half-dazed. "I'm sorry it slipped out of my hand. But I'm on a diet; and a trifle weak with the hunger."

The sergeant of police had got wind of the turkey, an' came in with two constables just in time to prevent a European war; for Michael an' his family weren't too well pleased with the condition the turkey was in by this time, an' wanted to lay claim to the ham. But the trouble was settled, for the time bein', with the help of the bottle in my pocket. The sergeant sent Williamson an' the ham home under escort, an' volunteered to drive Mr. Anthony an' me back in his own wee car; an' when we got there Mr. Anthony got round him to fetch word to Mr. Livingston's that

Mr. Anthony had been slightly injured while heroically separatin' two men engaged in a party fight, an' wouldn't be able to go for dinner.

As my head began to clear I could see that he was wrong. "You'll have Miss Betty back here as sure as eggs are eggs," says I; "an' where'll you be, then, with the state you're in?"

Mr. Anthony loked at me, an' would have turned pale but for the gravy of the turkey that was crusted on his face.

"Curse it," says he; "isn't it hellish the way a fine brain like mine is blunted by even the smell of drink. Come up to the bathroom with me, quick, and do you pour water on my head. I'd miss myself with Niagara Falls."

I thawed the gravy off him with hot water, an' had got him into purty fair order with cold, when sure enough we heard wheels; an' the next minute Miss Betty was in the hall.

"He's puttin' on his dressin'-gown, Miss Betty," says I, runnin' out with a towel in my hand, "an' will speak to you over the banisters. Don't let her within ten steps of the stairs of you," says I to Mr. Anthony before he went out; "for between wet an' dry that you've put into you this day your breath'll be like a pole-cat."

So Mr. Anthony perjured himself from the top of the stairs, an' made it all sound like sober truth, though it was neither; an' Miss Betty's eyes near lit up the stair-rods she was so proud of him for reddin' the party row when the police couldn't do it.

"You'll be able to come to dinner," says she, coaxin'.

"I think I will, after all," says Mr. Anthony, never heedin' the kick I gave him. "But, mind you, Betty, not even my injuries are to be an excuse for breaking the diet. I'm a man of my word should it snow turkeys."

"Oh, *George*," says Miss Betty, "how obstinate you are —and how dear. I think I'll have to run up and kiss you."

Mr. Anthony cursed under his breath, an' took a very frightened skelly at me.

"Just a minute, darling," says he, lettin' on to wrap the

dressin'-gown tighter round him. "Has Stubbs the chemist anything?" he whispers to me.

"He has capsules," says I, "would make violets of a bad egg; but they take a while to work."

"Betty, dear," says Mr. Anthony—"it sounds very unromantic, I know—the truth is my lips are a good deal bruised. But Pat Murphy is getting me something from the chemist; and I think, darling"—his voice would have lubricated a stripped bearing—"I think they'll be healed by dinner-time."

The Hennesseys

THE Hennesseys lived a little too far away to be called neighbours, but I knew all about them. The whole countryside knew, an' pitied them; an' when anybody speaks kindly about you it's no great sign that you're doing well.

No one expected them to do well, from the day the pair got married, second cousins, with a history on both sides of weak chests and early death. Hugh's family were even more again' the match than Cissie's; for Hugh's father had a deal the more land of the two; but neither family wanted the match, an' speyed evil for it. But the young couple were in love, deep an' true they were in love; an' they thought true love must be a shield again' harm.

For a long time it seemed to be so, though even in their good luck there were things to make a body pause an' be afraid. Hugh's father died in a ripe old age, but he left no one but Hugh behind him out of a family of seven. Cissie's mother died, under fifty; an' Cissie was the last of her little flock of five. But, with the two farms, Hugh an' Cissie were well-off, an' could eat better an' take things easier than them that went before.

An' so they did, in the beginning. Then their family began to come along, thick; an' the pair grew anxious an' a little bit greedy for their children, an' began to buy land.

They would have done better to build a good slated house first; for there was nothing on either of the farms they had inherited except thatch an' mud walls. But they wanted their whole family to be as well off some time as their father an' mother had been; an' so nine children herded together for years in a kitchen with a mud floor that was seldom dry, an' slept in two rooms with not a single window that would open.

They say book-learning hardens the heart. Maybe so. People were loving to their own an' kindly to their neighbours in those days, more than they are now; but I think if they'd had a little more education a good deal of misery would have been saved.

Still, the Hennesseys grew up till the older ones of them were young men and women; a little too bright in the complexion, maybe, but strong an' healthy to all appearance. The eldest girl was nearly finished for a National school-teacher, an' the eldest boy had got a job in Belfast. It wasn't worth while building a new house now. There would soon be more room as the children made their way in the world. Hugh added another lean-to to the house they were living in, for the benefit of the bigger girls, an' bought fifteen acres of land from the executors of the Widow Reilly. But the crows were coming home to roost.

The first to go was Mary, the school-teacher—simple enough. A wetting at a school treat, a bad throat made little of because the girl was courting an' didn't want to lie-up, an' Mary was in the graveyard. The boy in Belfast found city life didn't agree with him, an' came home to work on the farm; not for very long.

The new house was begun then; but a country mason is hard to hurry. Only five children moved in along with Hugh an' his wife, a changed Hugh, an' a changed Cissie, worn an' anxious an' weighed down. Hugh, that straight big handsome man, had grown into a stoop, an' the skin was stretched tight on his cheek-bones; an' Cissie's cheery smile was gone. She was a still, faded ghost of a being, now, with a hand always out to draw one of the children to her.

In seven more years' time the family was brought down to two; an' then Hugh gave up, an' died himself, leaving his wife with two sons, a young man of twenty-three called Samuel, an' George, a school-boy of thirteen.

The family was well-off now, an' for a long time had lived comfortably, an' lifted their heads a bit, an' were driven about by their yard-man in a very nice turn-out of a trap, with a hackney horse that wasn't allowed to plough; an' mixed a good deal with a better class than they used to know. People were still sorry for them, but not as sorry as when they were struggling to bring up a large family. One an' another would shake their heads an' say it was a pity that in the end there'd be nobody to inherit all that land; an' everybody had a comfortable feeling that though the Hennesseys had got on in the world there was no reason to envy them. Still, in spite of all the history that people had seen passing before them, Samuel could have found a hundred girls willing to close their eyes to what they all knew in their hearts would happen. But Samuel was a quiet, book-reading, thinking young fellow, wise an' sober beyond his years, an' seemed to keep from all intimacy with girls, as if he never meant to have anything to do with them; an' was more like a young priest than like an ordinary man.

All these things that I have told you passed before my eyes, too; but, as I have said, at a little distance. An' though, like everybody else, I had talked about "those poor Hennesseys" an' been curious about them, an' had pitied them as far as a human bein' can pity anyone but his own an' himself, it wasn't till the Great War had reached the rationing stage that I came into close contact with any of the family.

Although I always patronized Michael Cassidy's public-house when I was out with a few friends enjoying myself, the family provisions an' any little sup of drink we kept at home was always bought at Henry Doonan's spirit-grocery. Henry had been very thick with me when we were both young men kicking football. The friendship had never dropped; an' when shortage an' rationing of some few things begun, Henry was very helpful an' friendly in the way of giving our household a little advantage in the matter of butter an' sugar an' the like, an' a drop of whiskey when it was required.

But one evening after dusk when my wife had sent our youngest son along to Doonan's for the usual weekly supply, the boy came back with the butter short, an' just our bare ration of sugar, an' a message that Mr. Doonan would be obliged if I called with him that evening or early the following morning.

Henry Doonan was a pushing man, keen on business, an' matter of fact; but simple in many ways, an' kind to the heart's core. When I went to him next morning I found him all flustered. He wiped his forehead when he saw me, though it was the month of October.

"My heavens," says he, "I thought you weren't coming."

"What's wrong, Henry?" I asked. "What has upset you?"

"Come in an' sit down," says he, beckoning me into his office—"I have a letter from Samuel Hennessey, an' the like of it you never read. He's going the way of the rest," says Henry; "I suppose you know that."

"I did not," says I; "though I'm not surprised."

"Well, he's going," says Henry. "He's taken to his bed now, an' will never get up again. An' do you know what he wants? He wants me to do him a favour an' supply him with whiskey an' extra groceries for his own wake an' funeral."

I stared at Henry. I could feel myself turning white.

"Aye, you may look at me," says Henry, wiping his forehead again; "but it's true. I'm going there this forenoon to let him know what I can spare.—You'll come with me, Pat," says Henry, a kind of imploring. "I've given you a day in harvest before now. Go there by myself I cannot do. I didn't sleep a wink all night thinking about it."

It wasn't a job I'd have picked for myself; but Henry had been kind; and I saw he was more upset than even I would be. So I said I would go.

Samuel was sitting propped up in the bed. He was as thin as a rake, an' gone waxy in the face. The eyes were burning in his head, but he was quite composed.

"I brought Mr. Murphy with me," says Henry, fumbling with his hat. "He was in the shop, an' thought he'd like to come an' ask how you were."

Samuel looked at me an' wrinkled his face about the cheekbones an' mouth; but it wasn't a smile.

"Thank you, Mr. Murphy," he said. He nodded his head a little.—"You see how I am.—Will you be able to oblige us in that little matter?" he says, turning to Henry.

Henry shuffled his feet.

"With—with pleasure, Mr. Hennessey," says he, an' then turned as red as fire. Something like a laugh winked in Samuel's eyes, an' went out.

"You're obliging us very much, Mr. Doonan," says he. "You see, there was a shortage at my brother Joseph's funeral, an' for the credit of the family we wouldn't like that to happen again.—Knock on that door an' call my mother, please, till we see about quantities."

I opened my mouth to speak, but couldn't.

"Oh, Mr. Samuel——" says Henry, an' stopped.

"It's all right," says Samuel quietly. "We've got over that, years ago. She's waiting."

Mrs. Hennessey came in like a mouse, an' stood at the foot of the bed. When I was able to look at her I saw she was quite calm on the surface, but was holding herself in.

"Mother," says Samuel—he spoke in a matter-of-fact ordinary voice—"Mr. Doonan can oblige us." The mother bowed her head but didn't look at Henry.—"You can tell him about the groceries. An' I think we'd better have a gallon of whiskey if he can spare it. That was what we had for Robert's funeral."

"I can't remember, dear," said his mother after a minit. She spoke in a half-whisper.

"Yes," says Samuel, thinking, "that was it.—What about making out a list of all you think you'll need, an' then we'll see what Mr. Doonan can manage? I would like things to be done no worse than usual."

The mother turned without a word, an' went out.

"Strange," says Samuel, half to himself, when she had

shut the door—"strange that they should all have to go, one after another—an' now me. An' yet it isn't strange. It had to be, once we were born. But if my father an' mother had known as much as I do, lying here, they'd never have married; an' then we would never have been born."

He paused to gather his breath. Henry an' I said nothing. What was there to be said?

"All that is left for the Hennesseys now," went on Samuel, "is to depart quietly, an' leave a good name behind them in the country. I'd like us to do that. Not that it matters. But I'd like it."

He lay back for a while, an' closed his eyes. Then he sat up again as if a thought had struck him.

"Tell me, Mr. Murphy," he said, "how long do you think the War will last?"

"Some say another year, Mr. Hennessey," I answered. "Not less, anyway."

"Mr. Doonan," says Samuel, "if butter was salted down in a jar, would it keep for a year or better, do you think?"

"I think so," answered Henry.

"Sugar will keep, I know," goes on Samuel—"an' whiskey. You won't need to put any salt in *that*," says he, smiling a faint wee smile. "If we ask you for double quantities of butter an' sugar an' whiskey could you—as a great favour—let us have them?"

Henry thought for a minit or two.

"You'll get them, Mr. Samuel," says he.

Mrs. Hennessey came in, an' he speaking, with a piece of paper in her hand.

"Mother," says Samuel, so brisk an' sharp that I wheeled round, "Mr. Doonan holds a good stock at present. There may be more scarcity an' more rationing. I'm ordering a double stock of sugar an' butter an' whiskey."

The mother looked at him a long while without speaking. Her fingers closed on the rail of the bed.

"Yes, my son," she said at last.

Henry an' I went into the next room with Mrs. Hennessey. We said no good-byes.

The youngest boy was there, playing with the cat an' laughing. I mind that well. The mother lifted a pencil off the table an' began to alter the paper. She seemed quite composed, but I noticed there was a shake in her hand.

"Let me do that, Mother," says the boy, jumping up.

"No," says the mother very quick. "No, no, NO!" she cried out. She threw her two arms round the son an' crushed him to her. Her tears ran down the two faces.

The boy slowly drew back in his mother's arms, an' stroked her hair an' comforted her as her own man might have done.

"What is it, Ma dear?" he said. "What is it, that you're worried an' crying more? Is Sam not so well to-day?"

But I looked in the child's face; an' I doubt people had been talking.

Cupboard Love

MAT HARRISON was the leading auctioneer in Ballygullion when I was still a youngish man—big, blustering, red-faced, an' greedy for business.

People said the wife had been pushed into marrying him because of the money he'd made; but she was a cut above him, an' knew it.

The third member of the family was Doreen, a tallish fair-haired girl, that took after her mother, an' was as scared of her father as if he was the school-teacher.

What would have been the fourth member of the family, if he could have managed it, was young Denis Seeds, Mat's assistant an' clerk. He was come of nothing at all; but in time Mat came to depend on him a good deal; an' took out a second licence so that Denis might do deputy now an' then when business was throng. As for weemin folk, they just lay down at Denis's feet. Mrs. Harrison kept him at arm's length; but he could wheedle two eggs for his breakfast out of her any morning he liked.

Denis and Doreen had grand opportunities for courting. Any auctioneer's premises is a through-other place; but Mat's was by-ordinary. He was that greedy that he would take on to sell things couldn't even have been given away. "Send it in an I'll see," was one of the names they had for him in the country. The back half of the big auction-hall was just a forest of ould wardrobes, an' dressers, an' hat-stands, an' clock-cases, an' rubbish.

Not too far back in all this was a lamentable big mahogany double wardrobe that had come out of the Hastings's dower-house when the second Mrs. Hastings died, an' would have made a house itself; an' after some very unfortunate courting among delf an' fire-irons an' so on, the pair happened one day to peep into the big wardrobe. Denis opened the door a little thought wider, an' looked at Doreen; Doreen drew back an' shook her head—an' then went in; an' the two of them stayed till there was little but third-hand air left.

Denis was very downy about the affair. With pushing an' shoving an' coaxing, he made a couple of separate ways to the wardrobe, an' either of them twisty enough to baffle a ferret. The young couple never went along the same pad together. All at once, when they'd manœuvred into position like sailing boats at a regatta, their eyes would meet an' telegraph; a couple of ould plates would be tramped into smithereens; an' the pair of them were in the moon.

But one morning Mat Harrison came down to breakfast in a very bad temper. Just as the razor was turnin' the angle of his chin, he'd seen in the looking-glass Denis an' Doreen disappearing into the wardrobe.

Now, unbeknownst, as he thought, even to his wife, Mat had Doreen as good as sold to a farmer about three miles out of the town, a big good-natured ruffian with a countryside of land an' plenty of money; an' the sight of Denis and Doreen courting was a terrible sell to Mat.

But he told nobody about spotting them. His wife had her own plans for Doreen, as Mat well knew. A fly-blown specimen she had picked, one Bobby Hastings, a do-less crather that had been a younger son of the Hastings family, before he got middle-aged, had an allowance from an old aunt, an' was hail-fellow with anybody that would stand him a drink.

He knew good drink from bad; an' it wasn't auction whiskey Mrs. Harrison set before him; so he used to drop in occasionally when Mat wasn't about, an' play high-faluting compliments to Doreen. The child took no heed, till her mother explained that Bobby was trying to court her, an' scared Doreen so much that after having hysterics in the wardrobe with Denis in the afternoon, she slipped off to the Reverend Mr. Forsyth after dark, an' nearly washed away the Rectory, crying on his neck.

The reverend gentleman was a kindly sporting old boy, but a bit inclined to run at things. He flew into a terrible pucker, swore it would be clean barbarous to marry a young thing like Doreen to either of the two was laid out for her, an' went down next day an' raised such a rumpus with Mr. an' Mrs. Mat that the pair of them said they'd go over to the Presbyterians.

Two days later Mat had bills out over town and country for "a general sale of furniture, including a magnificent mahogany wardrobe." There was more in this than stopping the courting—he could have done *that* by turning the key in the wardrobe door—it was a warning to Denis an' Doreen, all they ever got. But it was enough, especially for Doreen. She didn't change words with Denis the whole week before the sale, went about like a mouse, an' never lifted her eyes higher than her father's boots.

On the morning of the sale she broke down, an' slipped into the auction-hall for a farewell look at the wardrobe where it was sitting ready for the sale. It won't surprise you that Denis was saying good-bye to it, as well.

"For the last time," he whispers to Doreen. The next minit they were inside—an', the minit after, Mat turned the key on the pair of them.

All that was in his mind was to give them a fright they wouldn't forget, an' then let them out before anybody seen them. But on the instant there came a call from the house that he was wanted for a second; an' the second ran to ten minutes. By the time he got back, the auction-hall was beginning to fill with people; an' the only thing to do was to go on with the auction, an' let the couple out in the evening.

What would happen in the meantime Mat couldn't think. Apart from the courting altogether, he'd muddled himself up in his job. He had the sale of a big farm out at Mulrenn in the afternoon; an' meant to let Denis finish the furniture sale while he was away; an' now he was clean balked. He did the worst thing he could do, an' let black rage take possession of him all at once.

"Fetch the wardrobe forward," he roars. "I'll begin with that."

But if Mat outside the wardrobe was in a pucker, the couple inside it were in a bigger pucker still. They suspected who had turned the key on them, but weren't quite sure; an' that kept Doreen from going out of her mind altogether. As it was, she was in a poor enough state, an' clung round Denis in a way she'd never done before; because she was a timid bashful creature; an' for a while Denis didn't care if they were locked up for life.

But the sound of Mat's voice put that notion out of his head.

"Wedge your knees again' the front, quick, Doreen!" he whispers. "I'll hold you tight." An' I've no doubt he did.

"Four of you go to it," shouts Mat's voice. "There's a lot of rubbish inside that I'll clear out later."

"It *was* your father locked us in," says Denis in Doreen's ear. An' if Doreen wanted to cry, the backward dive of the wardrobe put every notion out of her head but getting hold of Denis again.

"How much am I offered for this beautiful piece of furniture, big enough to rear a family in?" sez Mat.

"He has said it, Doreen," sez Denis. "We'll get wheels an' a chimley on it, an' live rent free together on love."

It was the first word of anything so serious as marrying that Denis had uttered yet; and Doreen just hid her face under his left ear, leaving her own one handy for anythin' more he might say.

"How much for it?" sez Mat outside.

"How much for Doreen?" whispers Denis in her ear.

"One pound," sez somebody outside.

"One hug," sez Denis, an' paid it.

"Thirty shillings," comes another voice.

"A hug an' a half," sez Denis; an' the half was as big again as the hug.

The bidding stopped at four pound fifteen.

"Am I selling for four pounds fifteen?" asks Mat.

"Will you marry me for love?" whispers Denis.

Doreen said nothing. There was no distance between her an' Denis, but she made it less.

"Going—Going——" sez Mat. He made the usual pause. Denis turned Doreen's mouth under his own.

"Gone!" sez the two men at the one time; an' if Mat didn't hear Denis, Denis heard Mat still less.

"I wonder who has bought us," sez Doreen, when the pair had come back into the world again.

"I wonder how we'll get out," sez Denis.

"Is there any hurry?" whispers Doreen.

"There won't be," sez Denis. "We'll have to stay here till the sale's over, an' the people gone. Then I'll knock on Jimmy Doran"—that was the yard man—"an' any small key will let us out.—Doreen," sez he, very earnest, "do you depend on me? For if we're to get each other we'll have to skip this night."

Doreen said nothing again, but in some way that was quite satisfactory. The two lay quiet, an' then all at once Doreen gave a jump.

"Denis," sez she. "We're sold. Might we not be taken away?"

"Come back," sez Denis, gatherin' her into his arms again. "This sale can't be finished to-day. The boss must go to Mulrenn. He'll be making an announcement presently—Listen!"

"Put in the horse, you stupid booby," comes Mat's voice.

"I'm late as it is. This furniture sale is adjourned till eleven o'clock to-morrow," he barks out, "an' nothing can be taken out of the yard in the meantime.—I said 'nothing, nothing, *nothing*,'" he roars, "an' if you don't like that cancel your bid, an' cancel yourself, an' go out of the yard backwards for fear your face should make somebody's horse run away——"

"That was big Mrs. McEntee he was talkin' to," sez Denis. "She always rubs him wrong.—Doreen," sez he. "Once we're out of this we'd better not stay long in the one place; for the boss is not going to be in good twist when he comes back from Mulrenn.—An' with bad air, not to speak of hunger an' thirst, I don't think we'll be in very good twist ourselves, then, for facing him."

They stayed quiet for another while; an' all at once they heard a voice near the door of the wardrobe.

"If the boss comes back in as bad a temper as he went away," sez Jimmy Doran to somebody, "he'll want to murder me for letting you take this wardrobe out of the yard before it's paid for. But, when he hears who you were bidding for, he'll know his money is safe.—Back your lorry up close, an' I'll get the men to put it on."

"Oh, Denis, Denis," sez Doreen, clutching him. "They're taking us away; an' what'll we do at all!"

"Hold hard," sez Denis, letting on to be a deal cooler than he was, "an' brace yourself with your knees the way I told you before. I daren't call out. The yard's half full of people yet; an' you'd be scandalized to eternity."

"All together," comes Jimmy's voice outside. "Closer a bit with that lorry—*Now!*"

Back tilts the wardrobe as before; there was a trampling of feet an' a heave, an' then a bang that near loosened the teeth in the two heads.

"Away with you, now," sez Jimmy to the lorry man. "I clean forgot about what's inside; but whatever there is you can bring it back when you come in to settle."

The lorry owner climbed up, shook the reins, an' off he went with Denis an' Doreen an' the wardrobe.

"Oh, Denis," sobs Doreen. "If we only knew where we were going."

An' though Denis showed no sign, he'd have given a good deal to know, himself.

But if the lorry took away a load of trouble it left near as much behind it. Of course Doreen's mother had missed her long before, an' when Denis wasn't to be found either she put two an' two together at once. At first her whole feeling was anger at her daughter throwing herself away on what she deemed little better than a servant; but presently far more anxious thoughts came into her head. Denis had got Doreen away; an' mightn't she have to be glad if he *did* marry her?

All at once Mrs. Mat run up the stairs half sobbing, put on her bonnet an' cloak, an' away to the Rectory.

The Reverend Mr. Forsyth was quite light an' airy about the business, an' gave her no comfort at all.

"What did you expect, my dear lady?" he said. "What did you expect? A healthy, good-looking young woman and a healthy, good-looking young man, thrown together a great deal, owing to the preoccupation of the young lady's parents with—shall we say?—providing a marriage portion for her. —Ah!" sez he, throwin' up his eyes, "in my romantic youth I used to think innocent love the best marriage portion.— Then, look at the alternatives before the girl: *your* choice for her, my dear lady—and your husband's! Which of the two would *you* have liked to marry?"

He looked a trifle sideways at Mrs. Harrison, an' she started to cry.

"We were both wrong," sez she; "both Mat an' me, but sure all will be well yet. Denis is a good boy."

"Quite, quite," sez the Rector, still off-hand. "But good boys can be bad boys sometimes, where foolish girls are concerned. However, I'll see what I can do," sez he, taking pity on her. "You'll consent to their marriage of course?"

"I'll consent to anything, sir," sez she. "An' I'll stand up to that man of mine, too, if he should eat me.—I'd rather see her married to Denis than to that big tub of guts *he's* picked for her," sez she, in a sudden fury.

"My dear lady," sez the Rector, beaming on her, "if you continue in your present Christian frame of mind I think we'll have little difficulty in circumventing Mr. Harrison.—Come to my study, and give me particulars about when and where the—shall we say the happy couple?—were last seen."

The words weren't out of his mouth till there came a clatter of galloping hoofs an' rattling wheels up the avenue. Down lepps Mat Harrison, through the open hall door, an' into the room.

"The wardrobe," he gasps out, "the wardrobe. Did Murphy bring it straight here?"

"Bring what here, my dear Harrison?" sez the Rector.

"The wardrobe Pat Murphy bought for you," sez Mat, "an' a nice d——d trick it was, gettin' an outsider to bid for you—all because you an' I had a bit of a row."

"Oh, the *wardrobe*," sez the Rector, glidin' over the remarks about me bidding for him. "Yes, it came an hour ago."

"Oh, my heavens," groans Mat. "Where is it? Quick! Quick!"

"Mr. Harrison," sez the Rector, very dignified, "if you don't wish me to have the wardrobe you can take it back. A far more serious thing has happened. Your daughter Doreen——"

"I know," shouts Mat. "Come on. I locked them in the wardrobe four hours ago, an' never thought what might happen till now."

The Rector threw up his hands.

"In the wardrobe. Four hours ago. Oh, my dear sir!"

But Mrs. Harrison pushed him aside, an' lepped at her man like a wild-cat.

"You devil," sez she. She caught him by the lapels of his coat; an' that wee woman fairly shook the big bullock of a man. "You've killed my only child sooner than not get your own ignorant bullying way."

"Hush, hush," sez the Rector, pulling her off. "Give me the key, Harrison, an' come on."

"I'm coming, too," cried out Mrs. Harrison, "to look on my dead child. Oh Doreen, Doreen!"

The Rector shook his head at Harrison as much as to say she couldn't be kept back, an' rushed out through the kitchen into the yard.

"Put on your jacket an' hat," he called to the housemaid.

The big wardrobe was lying on its back on some straw in the yard. Mat took hold of one end, an' tried to lift it.

"They're there still," he said, an' the voice choked in his throat.

The Rector rapped on the door, then put his ear down an' listened, holding up one hand for silence.

"There's no sound," sez he, very quiet. "Run for the doctor, Lizzie," sez he to the maid. "Tell him it's urgent—desperately urgent."

He stood up, an' put the key in the wardrobe lock.

"Before I open the door," sez he—"if this poor young couple aren't past recovery will you give them their way?"

But the pig-headedness was in Mat still.

"Wait till we get them out, an' then we'll see," he sez.

"Yes," sez the wife, drying her tears very fierce all at once; "wait till we get them out!"

Mr. Forsyth turned the key an' pulled the door open. An' the big wardrobe was chock-full of old books of all shapes an' sizes! There wasn't room for a brick, let alone for Denis an' Doreen.

The Rector turned an' looked at Mat. But Mat's mouth was too wide open for him to speak. Mrs. Harrison stopped crying, an' looked at her husband as if she had swelled to his size an' him shrunk to hers.

"You big blundering ass!" sez she. "You couldn't even make a good job of your dirty work. The pair of them never went into the wardrobe at all. They've slipped round the back an' away together; an' now we'll *have* to let Denis marry her."

"I think so, my dear people," sez the Rector, stroking his chin. "Yes, I really think so——"

Mrs. Harrison looked at him, took another poisonous look at Mat, an' then nodded, glum enough.

Mat didn't look at her. He was gazing at the wardrobe.

"Find them if you can," sez he to the Rector, "an' then marry them. I'll pay for all."

The housemaid came running out of the kitchen and stood panting.

"The doctor's at the door, sir," sez she.

"Tell him to go up to my study," sez the Rector; "and bring Mr. and Mrs. Harrison up, too. And, Lizzie," he whispers, "put a bottle of sherry—the *good* sherry—in the decanter. We're going to drink a toast."

When they were all inside, he came round the corner of the stable an' called to me:

"*Pat—Pat Murphy!* Ah, there you are. Where did you tell Denis and Doreen to hide while ye were putting the books in the wardrobe?"

"They're in the hayloft, sir," sez I. "An' if you don't want *them* badly, they can do nicely without *you*."

"Tell them to come up to my study at once," sez he, "an' get their wedding-day fixed.—And, Pat, when you're removing the books, would you mind keeping an eye out for my second best hat? I missed it off my head somewhere about *Barnes on the Minor Prophets*."

Pity

STRANGE figures, likeable, terrifying, absurd, or sad, visit me now and then from my boyhood at my uncle's farm. The other night there came stealing into my mind the piteous and grotesque wraith of the Dummy Morrison.

She was completely deaf; and, save for an unintelligible, half-animal note when goaded to rage by thoughtless small boys of whom I remember with shame that I was one, was also dumb.

But she came of decent people who had fallen in the

world; and when her father, and then her mother, died, in a distress the more poignant for her own helpless existence, enough money was raised to provide her with a foster-mother, and afterwards to send her to an Institution where she learned to read and write, and gained enough skill in dressmaking to earn a slender living from house to house in our part of the country.

I remember her as small and pitifully thin, sallow of complexion, with dark hair of which the side locks hung in ringlets; and noticeably dark eyes that looked out on the world with a mixture of pain and anger. Her teeth were yellow, and broken with much biting of thread. Their colour may have been due to the vast oceans of tea that the Dummy drank. In the course of her profession she arrived at irregular hours, and was given irregular meals of which one constituent was always tea. It was better to give her tea before she began to work. She would work without it; but crossly and badly. I have heard my aunt say that the Dummy's stitches were always longer when she had no tea.

In consequence of all this tea-bibbing she suffered greatly from indigestion, and used to consume huge quantities of baking-soda, which she did not mix with water, but licked off the palm of her hand. Suddenly, as she sat working in the small parlour to which at our house she was relegated, she would utter her inarticulate cry, run to the kitchen, thrust her fingers into the tin of baking-soda, and then return to her task, licking her fingers as she went. A tom-boy of a maid of ours hid the baking-soda once, but only once; for the Dummy charged her with a sewing-needle, and obtained an unconditional surrender. I can hear the squeals of Margaret yet.

The Dummy was very much annoyed if anyone interfered with the materials of her craft. Before beginning work she laid all her requirements round about her in order. To substitute the scissors for the needle-case was enough to call down her wrath. I have received a tap of her thimble on the head for no more. It was her customary retaliation. She had become very skilful in inflicting it; and could bring the tears to a small boy's eyes with a single tap.

But it was hardly necessary for me to offend. Girl children she liked, and loved to adorn. But boys she detested; and did not willingly work on the clothing of a male child after he had passed from cotton to cloth. She had good reason to dislike boys. They plagued her sadly. When they found it was waste of time "calling her names" they used to throw small stones to draw her notice, and then thrust out their tongues in derision; or pluck her dress from behind, and sometimes snatch her hand-bag and provoke her to fury by proffering it and drawing it back again.

Nevertheless, she was somewhat susceptible to the presence of a man, and when there was one in the room kept continually patting her hair, and adjusting her ringlets, and tugging at her dress. If any man she met on the road was polite enough to raise his hat she always bowed with grave formality. But women, even her own customers, she ignored, unless they stopped to shake hands with her.

Late one Christmas Eve, when the spirit of festivity was already in the air, Dick Murray, our second ploughman, being dared thereto by my uncle, kissed the Dummy under the mistletoe. She remained quite still in his arms, but seemed very much flustered, and dropped her scissors and thimble. She was always very gracious to Dick afterwards; though now and then she would shake her finger at him and moan, but not in her angry note. It was the general opinion in our house that night that she was secretly pleased with Dick, and that he ought to kiss her again; but he had been chaffed so much about his act of cheek or chivalry that he could not be brought to repeat it. And, besides, our maid Margaret, who was currently supposed to have a notion of Dick, strangely took offence at his kissing the Dummy, and didn't allow him to kiss herself again till Christmas Day.

But this slip at mistletoe-time was the only lapse into feminine weakness on the part of the Dummy that I ever knew of. She was in general abnormally modest in her demeanour; and when, by some blunder, she omitted a trifling but indispensable modification of my cousin Robert's first breeches she was so much abashed that she would never enter his mother's house afterwards.

The thing is hardly credible, but there was at one time on foot a project to arrange a marriage of the Dummy to some poor fellow who suffered the same affliction as herself; but she received the proposal, when its nature was made clear to her, with such an extremity of horror that it was shamefacedly abandoned.

She was given to the wearing of rings and brooches and other fal-lals, all of them gaudy, and that not because they were of necessity cheap. Though she was a tolerable dressmaker her taste in colours was garish. A certain elderly young woman in our neighbourhood who after many years of angling for a man was flattered by something in the nature of a bite, was seduced into the belief that one of the Dummy's imaginings might possibly take a year or two off her, and had a new hat trimmed by the Dummy, in scarlet and orange. The hesitating admirer tried to give his doubtful fancy a lift home from church the following Sunday; but his horse took so much notice of the hat that not only had poor Miss McKim to foot it home, but the subsequent ridicule extinguished her first and last chance of a man for ever.

Probably it was the needs of her profession that caused the Dummy to become a human pincushion. Nothing in the form of a pin or a needle escaped her eye, or failed to be impounded and thrust into some part of her clothing. In addition, she always carefully stored away any scraps or snippets of linen or cotton or bright-coloured silk. No one knew what she did with them; but after she died a cupboard-full of rag dolls was found, all gaudily dressed and with complete and elaborate underclothing.

It is with awareness that I have painted the Dummy Morrison as a figure of comedy; for she was looked on as a "character," and except for an occasional and conventional word of pity her name always produced a smile, or a mildly absurd anecdote. But though the knowledge took a long time to come home to me in its full significance, I learned that there was another side to her life.

As I was coming home late one night from a Magic Lantern show, escorted by one of our farm-servants, I passed the little cottage where the Dummy dwelt solitary. There was a light in her sitting-room window, but for the first time in my knowledge she had forgotten to draw down the blind. The thing was notable and astonishing. We did not consciously agree to spy on her, the man and I, but without speech we found ourselves looking in on the Dummy as she sat at tea.

She was not alone. On the chair opposite to her at the little round table there sat a large doll. Her doll's cup and saucer were on the table, and before the Dummy poured out her own tea she went through the pretence of pouring out tea for the doll. She paid no more attention to the doll, then, but finished her own meal. After she had washed the tea-things she pushed back the table and sat down before the fire, looking into it. I cannot tell why my companion and I did not go away then; but we did not go, but continued to look on in silence. Presently the tears began to fall from the Dummy's eyes. They shone in the lamp-light, and ran down her cheeks, and splashed on the front of her dress. She did not wipe them, but sat very still, looking into the fire.

No one, certainly not a boy of eleven, could plumb the depths of that poor alien being's anguish and despair. I am afraid I should have known dislike and dread of the Dummy Morrison again; perhaps I should again have tormented her, and provoked her to helpless wrath. I cannot tell. A few weeks after I had looked with uncomprehending eyes on her suffering she was found dead, sitting before her grey hearth. Complete loneliness had fallen on her spirit at the last. There was only one cup and saucer on the table, and the second chair was empty.

Why is it so much harder to be pitiful to the living than to the dead?

Yellow-man and Oranges

MY cousin William was a teetotaller, and would not allow whiskey in his house even for the stomach's sake. Yet I have heard him declare that he would rather take his chance with a drunkard than with a gambler, any day, and in time came to agree with him. In my early years, certainly as far as my twelfth, this great truth was hidden from me. I was sportily inclined, given to reckless wagering with buttons and marbles, and had once or twice gone the length of withdrawing a halfpenny from my pocket, and, for a giddy second or two, tottering on the verge of the pitch-and-toss that our farm labourers played every dinner hour.

Only the incidents of the story I am going to tell prevented me from becoming a frightful illustration of my cousin's axiom.

It must have been about my ninth year that I became material, relinquished an eternal for a temporal recompense of my good behaviour, and fixed the limits of my reward on being permitted to go to B—— races.

My disposition towards gambling had nothing to do with this backsliding. Quite literally, my god was my belly. I had been to several fairs, hung with empty longing round the stalls of country dainties, and listened to the siren voices of the owners: "Here you are for the yellow-man, the cakes, the cheese and the oranges!" The other eatables explain themselves, but yellow-man has, I believe, passed into limbo, and become legendary. It was a sweetish substance, yellow in colour, and about the consistency of sandstone; and the large, thick, round bannocks of it were paved with knobs of clear candied sugar of great attractiveness. The cheese was none of your fancy brands; not Cheddar, or Cheshire, or Gruyère, or Camembert, or Stilton—just "cheese," a damp, flabby, pinkish substance that, I can see quite clearly now, could only have been digested by a stone-crusher; though in those days I tossed it to my stomach with nonchalance.

For long I had regarded these fair-day stalls as the last

word in the lighter gastronomy; then one day a small and depraved classmate "mitched" from school, went off to B—— races, and brought back tidings of an incredible world, where, he averred, the stalls were as big as a circus-tent, the lemonade fizzy beyond earthly gassiness, and the yellow-man crystals from Aladdin's cave. It was from this day that I put aside all worthiness of ambition, and declined on B—— races.

But although I knew that men and women, and even children did go to B—— races, I did not really believe it possible that I should ever be there in the flesh of a small boy. My aunt, for excellent reasons, reversed the order of my cousin William, and placed the drunkard in a lower and hotter hell than the gambler; nevertheless the gambler's position on her thermometer was far above comfort. She was fond of horses, and had, as a young girl, ridden hardily to hounds; but I do not think that in her mind racing was connected with horses as she knew them. To her a race-meeting was a place where men lost fortunes, and women's hearts were broken; and a racehorse was a serpent-like familiar of the Evil One. It was only by taking scandalous advantages of my aunt's integrity that I reached B—— racecourse with her consent.

Among the fowl from which my aunt enjoyed the personal income denied her by my uncle, her heart had chosen a small, brown hen of indeterminate breed, but extraordinary laying powers. The hen's fecundity had been her first recommendation to my aunt, whose rewarding attention and care had awakened cordial response. I think it might be said that in time they came to love each other. I can still hear my aunt's greeting to her idolised "Chuckey," and see the bright sideways glance of the little fowl as she made deep-throated inquiry after my aunt's health and welfare. I came to have a certain affection for the wise little bird myself; and during the dreadful days when nesting overcame friendship, and "Chuckey" was lost, my feet were the most unwearying in search of her. My aunt marked my devotion, and in one of the small gushes of enthusiasm that not even a lifetime of disappointment had been able to suppress, vowed that if I found the hen I should have whatever I asked. But I do not believe she ever thought of my wishing to go to B—— races.

Still, she was a woman of her word. Once I had brought myself to dare the thunderbolt, my boon was secure. But after the first hour of delirium, care began to mingle with my joy. The races were nearly three months away. How much could I amass, in that time, toward the day of glory?

I remember clambering to my nest on top of the straw at the end of the cart-shed, and coming to grips with the problem. To placate the gods, I pointed out firmly to myself that half-a-crown was the very most I could hope to gather, and that even this sum was preposterously high. But my desires were now exorbitant. Eating and drinking still occupied my foremost thoughts; but in the background were confused imaginings of reported delights: side-shows, strong men and bearded ladies, conjurers and tight-rope walkers. In a little pigeon-hole in my mind, peeped into only now and then, there glittered the bright image of an incredible five shillings.

Since those far-off days I have learned—to my grief—something of the larger borrowing; bonds and coupons, debentures and preferences, redemptions and—alas—repudiations; yet I have never thrilled to any of these transactions as I did to the progress of the great B—— race fund.

It was my misfortune that the aberration of the brown hen occurred a few weeks within the New Year. A little earlier, and I might have tightened my belt and opened the fund with a shilling or maybe eigheeen-pence. As it was, the rich yieldings of the kindly Christian festival had dwindled miserably to fourpence. To begin the foundation of a fortune with such a sum, and so shortly after Christmas, was the very insanity of optimism. Purses are light and hearts hard in that meagre season. If Dick Whittington had heard Bow Bells in the early weeks of a New Year, they would have bidden him follow his nose till he reached home. Even though my cousin William's occasional halfpenny had risen to a penny at the first of February, and I had got a windfall of sixpence from Barney Connor the cattle-dealer for timely help with an obstreperous herd, the extremity of parsimony had raised me to no more than one-and-fivepence by the first of March. Then a gleam of fortune shone my way. "For "being a good boy" and praying—I fear ineffectually—for my uncle on market-night without pressure, I received a threepennypiece from my aunt. But the devil was not neglecting his business. It was from below that the blinding radiance of chance overwhelmed me.

The B—— races were due in mid March. A week into the month, when I had resigned myself to half-a-crown, and was even prepared to be grudgingly content with two-and-threepence, my Uncle Alec—my wicked uncle, about whose doings folk lowered their voices when I appeared—suddenly took to himself wings, suddenly, though in stages. One wing sprouted on him the evening he carried me off to D—— Hunt and the subsequent supper, where I over-ate myself (it was in these words my conduct was reported to my aunt), "worse than a stray beagle"; the second burst from his shoulders when he made over to me his hand of cards at Nap while he hurried off to reason with his hunter, which was, it seemed, kicking a loose-box into matches. He would pay my losing declarations, he said; but anything I won I might keep. To this day the other players are unaware of the miracle, but, though their gross eyes could not perceive it, the small boy sitting among them held in his imperfectly clean fist not five cards but a gloriously bewildering jumble of yellow-man, cakes, cheese, oranges, lemonade, fat ladies, jews-harps, acrobats—but why be diffuse?—held the quintessential delights of B—— races. For, though he was a little boy, and in most things innocent, and in all things honest as he understood honesty, yet he was clear-headed enough to discern the shining principle that the way to make money for himself was not to be too chary of losing money for his uncle.

The general who heroically risks his men's lives is seldom cheated of victory. The details of my fight are a blur in my memory now, though I can recall a double Nap during the playing of which my heart nearly choked me; but I know that when my Uncle Alec came back to his place he had lost seven or eight shillings, and was either too much relieved or too good a sportsman to draw from me the fact that, in what had been a little boy's empty pocket, three shillings and nine-pence of profit now pulsed through his system an almost infinite voltage of joy. I should dearly have loved to drive home that night with my Uncle Alec; but the risk was too great. If he had lost money on the whole evening (and my Uncle Alec was too reckless to have much chance of winning) I did not see how I could in decency avoid offering up my three-and-ninepence. It was clearly a case where ignorance was bliss. I feigned sleepiness betimes; and went home honourably but dully in the doctor's brougham.

And so, on a gusty forenoon of March, I set out for B—— races in the care of Dick Murray, our second ploughman, with five shillings and fivepence in my pocket. B—— racecourse was three miles away, but the whole distance was keyed up to the emotion of the last hundred yards to a circus-tent where the band is already playing. Our little party walked thrilling, though not all to the anticipation of the same delight. A hundred yards out of view of my uncle's house we had become three. About that time Dick Murray was at the height of his customary love-affair with our latest maid. Even then I knew the handsome scallywag as a successful lover. I knew, too, that Maggie (the third Maggie of his affections in my knowledge) loved Dick. She had told me so; and told me, with a breathless joy, that he was taking her to the races. I had even witnessed her preparations; for in Maggie's eyes I was too young to be accounted masculine; but I was old enough to be horrified by the appalling condition of her underwear (she was a dreadful slattern) and as we walked to the races I beheld a very different Maggie from the gaudy siren that kindled Dick's ardent glances. I was half inclined to warn Dick that Maggie was not quite what she seemed; but felt that this particular matter lay entirely in the feminine world, and was no concern of a man's. Besides, I was anxious that Dick should love Maggie very much this day of B—— races, knowing that in such a situation three would not be company.

Things fell out as I hoped. I traversed the fields between the road and the racecourse, tugging at Dick's arm like a kite at a string, thereby making a similar tugging of the willing Maggie's hand incumbent on Dick. But when we had threaded the crowd, and drew up before the first stall, quiet fell on me, and a little awe. The great, the miraculous hoped-for but never believed-in day appeared to have come! I awakened from my trance. Dick was bending down to me, a little shamefaced. Could I look after myself, and meet him here when the last race was over? and would I be sure not to let-on to my aunt or uncle? Gladly, enthusiastically I consented and promised; and in a trice had vanished among the stalls lest Dick should change his mind.

Once out of view I slowed down, and walked amazedly, solemn as if in a cathedral. Even then I was not quite convinced that my dream had become reality. Gradually I descended from the spiritual into the carnal world, and disengaging in my pocket a shilling from my other wealth, I returned to the stall I had quitted. The proprietress held up her most beguiling dainties. But I kept my hand in my pocket. This was not a day to squander light-heartedly. I must be sparing of my very moments. Not yet was the hour of yellow-man and all the other delights of the palate. A little abstinence first, a nice choice, before the orgy began that I promised myself should begin, and should be an orgy.

I spit upon the doctrine of guardian angels. The most happy-go-lucky of the tribe would have caught at my hand and plucked me past the little rosy-faced man with the three thimbles.

These instruments of destruction were laid out on the end of an upright orange box. As I looked, the little man began to weave the thimbles in and out with smooth dexterity, and I was for the first time aware of the pea. To this day I cannot tell whether it was vegetable or mineral, grown by man or minted by the devil; I only know that I shall never forget it. Aimlessly, innocently it gambolled among the weaving thimbles, that seemed to love it; for when it offered to wander they controlled it tenderly into their mazy circle again. Suddenly the weaving of the thimbles ceased. The pea had vanished. Obviously it was beneath one of the thimbles. The little rosy-faced man chirruped pleasantly, enticingly. There was money to be made. He would pay even-money for the finding of the pea. If we did not speculate we could not accumulate, he said.

Alas, I did not observe the flaw in the little man's logic. A quick-witted guardian angel might still have redeemed himself by whispering in my ear that even if one did speculate, one hadn't a dog's chance of accumulating. There are, I reiterate, no guardian angels. I was smitten with the desire of accumulating at the expense of the rosy-faced man. He was willing that I should do so. As I pushed among the gathering little crowd, he called out cheerfully to let the young sportsman through. I took my stand beside the orange box, and with a wisdom beyond my years, as I remember pluming myself, I decided to reconnoitre carefully before venturing my money.

But the period of probation was short. No one was betting. The little rosy-faced man moved the thimbles swiftly about the board, covered the pea, uncovered it. Half a dozen times I betted with myself which thimble it was under, and I always won. I began to be a little abashed by the foolishness of the rosy-faced man. He was clearly a misfit in his profession. It would be a shame to take his money. Yet in my heart I felt that something ought to be done before he became aware of his incompetence. I took a shilling in my hand, drew a deep breath—and found to my disgust that I was too shy to bet. A jaunty-looking bystander nudged me.

"The middle one, sir, don't you think?" he whispered. "I'm going to have two bob on this."

"No," I breathed earnestly, "the right-hand one."

"The middle one," insisted the obstinate fellow. He cast down a florin, and lifted the middle thimble. There was nothing under it.

"Right you were, sir," he whispered to me, as the rosy-faced man picked up the coin.

But I was hurriedly fumbling for a second shilling. I lifted the right-hand thimble.

"Some wins and some loses," remarked the rosy-faced man without emotion, pocketing my two shillings. "If you don't speculate you can't accumulate." But I heard him as from a great way off; for my attention was occupied by a portion of orange box on which there was no pea, and which was surrounded by waving darkness.

"Both of us fools," murmured my new friend. "Don't bet again till we both choose the same thimble."

There was hope and common sense in this. My courage somewhat returned to me. I felt in my pocket again. A shilling? no; we couldn't fail this time. I would recover my loss and then flee. I felt I had not the resolution to persist on this nerve-racking road to fortune. I took out two shillings. My friend and I scanned the board narrowly, consulted with our eyes, differed—agreed. The middle one this time? We nodded to each other. I cannot describe the crashing dismay that struck my brain when the thimble was lifted. That other people could suffer disaster I knew already; but this had happened to *me*!

I looked in sick misery at the dapper man, my friend. He clapped his finger to his lips. His face was alive with mischief. He looked round the ring of faces, then jerked his thumb at the rosy-faced little man, who had turned his back on the board, apparently to beckon to a passer-by. Swiftly the dapper man snatched up a thimble in each hand. There was no pea under either. He looked meaningly at me as he threw down half-a-crown. Not myself, certainly; not even the devil, for he couldn't have had time; pure mechanical obedience to a stronger will took out my last shilling. The rosy-faced little man turned round, laid his hands on the thimbles, barely stirred them. I lifted the third thimble—and remember nothing but groping uncertainly through a misty forest of faces and shapes till I recovered from my passion of hysterical weeping, and found myself lying under a hedge some hundred yards away from the unthinking crowd. I have grown old now, and can never know such misery again.

It would be more convincing, I am aware, if I wound up by saying that there and then I renounced gambling, and never "turned a card" or betted on a horse during a long life. And indeed the memory of the thimble-rigger, and the dismay and anguish he brought on me, came back to me later when I was better able to profit by them. Thereafter I avoided such cony-catching fellows, to my great profit, doubtless. But in simple truth I must confess that I did not immediately avoid evil, and returned disconsolately to the course, and there encountered my Uncle Alec. He questioned me about my tear-stained face. I told him my sad story, not unhopefully; but, with a glimpse of that streak of hardness that sometimes appeared in him he did not tip me as I expected, but gave me sevenpence to make up my cash to a shilling, and told me to fight my luck and back a certain horse, whose name, I remember, was "My Lud." And "My Lud" must have charged the gods of chance favourably on my behalf, for he came in first, at two to one; and in my exaltation I I must have found special grace in the matter of gastric juice, and did not die on the way home, though my internal economy by that time can have been no more fit for human contemplation than that of our maid Maggie.

De Mortuis

I WAS standing in Ballygullion churchyard, said Mr. Patrick Murphy, looking down into Richard Roney's grave, when Ralph Christy pushed in quietly beside me.

"Poor fellow," says he, "he was early cut off. An' it seems all the sadder on a fine day like this."

It was a true word. The time of year was the end of April, a bright crystal day, with a clear blue sky that seemed as if it stretched to eternity. There was a small rise in the ground just beyond the grave, an' on it a sapling fire-tree, tall an' straight, an' as beautiful as a young girl an' her not knowing you were looking at her; an' there came into my head, that it was a sore thing to die while life was still sweet.

I walked back into the town with Ralph, both of us looking as if we were of much the same mind, an' saying little. But he was no wet blanket, Ralph. Even if he had prospered, an' put by a deal of what he had made, there was still a spark in him. As we came abreast of Michael Cassidy's pub he took me by the elbow.

"This is terrible dismal crack we've been having, Pat," says he. "Come into Michael's till we drown melancholy. There'll be one or two neighbours here on the same errand."

An' so there were: Hamilton, the opposition grocer to Ralph, an' Brice the vet, an' Ferguson the draper, an' a few more. The solemn faces were beginning to smile, an' now an' then a laugh would break through. At times somebody would remember himself an' say: "Poor Dick," but it would be a kind of an afterthought.

Ralph Christy was greatly cheered up, over an' above the effect of the two half-ones each we had drunk.

"This is the way things ought to be, Pat," says he. "Dick Roney would have enjoyed himself if he'd been with us."

An' then Ralph came out with an unexpected thing—for him.

"Why should he be missing the fun that, look at the matter how you like, he's the cause of, Pat," says he suddenly, "wouldn't it be a great thing to come to your own funeral?"

"You wouldn't raise much of a laugh," says I, taking a skelly at the street door as I spoke.

"Lord bless me," says he, very hasty, "I didn't mean *that*. I mean to hold your funeral before you died, while you could still enjoy the crack as well as anybody else.—As true as death I'll do it!" he says, hitting the counter a thump. "An' we'll hold it here in Michael Cassidy's."

"If you do," says I, a trifle dry, "you'll have to pay for all the drinks would have been consumed if they had got rid of you. An' you may swear there'd be a by-ordinary gathering of mourners."

"Oh, I'm not going to ask the whole town an' district,"

says he.—"Still, there would have to be a brave few. An' we wouldn't want stray customers coming in. I'll tell you what," says he, "we'll hold it in Michael's bar-parlour here. It can be made private if necessary."

He went over an' pulled along the sliding panel that cut off the bar-parlour window from the bar itself.

"There you are," says he in my ear. "The bar-parlour's quite private now. There's another advantage, too, that I'll let you know about later."

"You don't mean to tell me that you're in earnest about this notion?" says I. For I thought he'd been just codding me.

"But I am," says he. "Why not? Will you not come?" he asks, quizzing me.

"I wouldn't miss it for a pound-note," says I. "It's the only time in my life that I ever heard of anything new going to happen in Ballygullion."

"That's a bargain, then," says Ralph. "You're the first mourner invited. But what about the others?" says he, plucking at his lip. "Come down to my wee snuggery behind the shop. There's too much noise here."

"The point to be decided," says I, after we'd got out paper an' pencil, "is what kind of a party is it to be. Is it just to be a quiet wee drinking-party of your friends, to show that they're glad to have you among them still, an' to wish you long life?"

Ralph thought for a while before he spoke.

"No," he answered me; "that's not what is in my head. I want there to be more of the funeral atmosphere than that. I want them to behave as if they were done with me for good; as if my shop was closed an' my seat on the Town Commissioners vacant. I'd like them to talk about me as if I were lying in the burial-ground above, an' someone brought my name up."

"Well," says I, "there's only two ways for you to manage that. The one is for you to *be* lying in the burial-ground; an' the other is to fill all the mourners that full that they'll tell you what they think about you, straight out. But I doubt it would be something more good-natured than the truth."

"Pat," says he, "this was only a frolic of a notion when it came into my head at first. All I thought of was a pleasant hour among my friends, while I was still with them. But as I looked through Michael's service-window it came into my head that a body could be standing there listening, an' nobody in the bar-parlour know."

"It came into my head, too," says I. "An' I'm going to speak quare an' well about my friends while I'm in there, from now on."

"Yes, but," says Ralph, "suppose it was *I* that was standing there? Suppose I came into Michael's after they had all arrived, and stood a while at the service-window without them knowing? Wouldn't I hear the truth then?"

"You might hear more than you bargained for," says I.

"I'll take my chance of that," says Ralph. "At any rate I'd know where I stand in the town. An' I don't think there'd be anything said about me that I wouldn't like to listen to."

An' then all at once I saw how things were with Ralph Christy. He was a shrewd business man, an' not rash with his money, but kindly an' charitable, an' never hard on anyone honestly trying to pay his way. In Town Council work he was clear-headed an' public-spirited. No jobbery for Ralph, nor for anybody else if he could prevent it. If he had any fault at all it was that he was too retiring an' cautious, never letting his right hand know what his left hand was doing, as the saying goes; an' not seeming to care tuppence about what anybody thought of him.

An' here, all the time, as I saw now in a flash, was a man wanting to be well thought of by his fellow-citizens, an' hoping for a little sympathy an' praise. All his life he had refused praise an' flattery, an' would let no man make a wonder of him because he had done his duty. But now he was growing old, an' lonely. He felt that his own time was drawing near, an' thought he'd like to know what baggage he had to bring with him into the next world.

A body didn't need to be very wise to see that with human nature being what it was, there was more than a chance Ralph was riding for a bad fall. I was about to warn him of that, an' then I closed my mouth. Ralph Christy was an obstinate man, an' not likely to listen to me. But there was another thing, an' no credit to me; but I'll be as honest as Ralph himself, an' own up to it. My own nature is human, too; an' I doubt I wasn't unwilling that he should get a skelp or two in among the praise. If that was so, God forgive me.

But none of these thoughts came to my tongue or showed in my face; an' the two of us got at the choosing of the mourners. It was no easy task, as you may guess. Where you pleased one you were bound to offend twenty. In the end Ralph decided to ask only what friends and associates of his were at Richard Roney's funeral, as being regular funeral attenders who could take a sup of drink in a neighbourly way. He picked up eight an' myself. Among them were two or three acid enough gentlemen; an' I made up my mind that on the big day, whether Ralph listened outside beforehand or not, nobody but myself would get saying very much till he came into the bar-parlour.

An' I wasn't there myself, after all. Ralph knew that if word of the party got out there'd be a deal of talk in the town, so all the guests were sworn to keep it a dead secret. But my wife Molly saw there was something on my mind, an' gave me no peace day or night. An' when she got the story of the mock funeral out of me she nearly went into hysterics. It was flying in the face of Providence, she said. All the guests would die within a year. The devil would run away bodily with Ralph Christy; an' Michael Cassidy's pub would be consumed with fire an' brimstone.

Molly was young an' slim in those days; an', though it nearly broke my heart, I didn't go. I've been sorry all my life since.

All the invited guests turned up on the appointed afternoon. All in good time, too. For there was a flavour of something new an' out of the way about the party; an' the very pleasant additional feeling that drinks were bound to be free.

There was a bit of a hitch about that. As I would have expected if I had been there, Ralph didn't appear in the bar-parlour at the appointed hour. But, what I would *not* have expected, he didn't appear in Michael Cassidy's premises at all. Twice the party sent out to the bar to make enquiry, but there was no word of Ralph. An' what was worse, no drink was forthcoming.

At last Harrison, the hardware man, could stand it no longer.

"We're wasting time," says he. "Drinks are on the corpse at *this* funeral. Whiskey, boys?" There was no answer. He rang the bell. "Eight glasses of your liqueur whiskey, Michael. An' we'll not insult it with soda-water. Just a jug from the pump."

Then Michael made a mistake.

"You're paying for this yourself, of course, Mr. Harrison?" says he.

"Of course I'm doing nothing of the sort," answers Harrison, very sharp. "Ralph Christy is paying for all. Didn't he ask us here?"

Michael tried to recover himself.

"It's all right, gentlemen," says he. "I'm not thinking about the money, you know that. An' to show I'm not, I'll let this drink be on the house if Mr. Christy doesn't offer to pay."

But he had done harm.

"You'd wonder," says Harrison, when the drinks had been brought, "that Christy, if he couldn't be here in time, wouldn't have taken steps to prevent us being affronted by that big jelly-fish."

"It's not like Ralph," says old George, the army pensioner. "He's always willing enough to pay his turn."

"He pays his turn all right," says Harrison, "whenever he has a drink or two safe inside him. But I never saw him start a round in my life. You might lean over a bar with him for five minutes before he'd open his mouth."

"He's giving us all something to mourn for," squeaks Bates, the spirit-grocer. "Maybe that's his idea."

One word led to another, everyone vying for who could get in his little stab.

Even old Ferguson, the draper, a kindly old fellow, had his criticism.

"This was a stupid idea of Christy's," says he. "A decent, friendly man, but not much brains."

"He has brains of a kind," says Dorrian, the builder; "but it's in a pettifogging, shopkeeping way. No breadth of mind for politics or local government. But I supppose he's the big noise in the grocery business in this town. I beg your pardon, Mr. Hamilton," says he, as Ferguson made a face at him. "Of course I forgot about you."

"No offence," says Hamilton. "Christy an' I fill our own places in this town. But there's two things I will say about him. The man has no notion of dressing a window, an' he can't buy bacon."

An' away the whole of them went in a chorus to the same tune.

Now all this time Michael Cassidy had the slide of his service-window a little crack open, an' him listening to every word. It came into his head that if he had to leave it to attend to a customer Ralph Christy might come in an' hear how he was being scandalized. So he calls to Liza Reid, his sister's child that kept house for him.

"Away down to Ralph Christy's shop," says he, "an' tell him his friends are here. I don't know what's keeping him."

"I know," says she. "The railway-porter has been run down by a lorry at the foot of the street. I'll hold you Mr. Christy is looking on, or giving a hand."

"Well, say to him he's a-waiting-for in the bar-parlour, an' to hurry up. Put your head in an' tell this grumbling pack you're going." An' then a strange notion came into Michael's head. He gave a bark of a laugh. "Hold on," says he; "I'll do it myself."

He opened the door of the bar-parlour, an' walked in very slowly.

"Gentlemen," says he, holding up his hand. They all stopped talking when they saw his serious face.

"I have had bad news," says Michael. "There's been a lorry-accident near the station. Somebody's killed, an' Miss

Reid hears it's Ralph Christy. I've sent her down to find out the truth. Stay where you are. I'll come back."

There was dead silence in the bar-parlour, one looking at another. Then they began to talk, very quiet.

"An unlucky notion, this mock funeral," says Ferguson, the draper. "An' has come home to roost. Poor fellow. Oh, poor fellow. There weren't many like him."

"Ay," says Brice, the vet. "The people'll recognize now what he did for them on the Town Council. They'll stop yapping about the Assembly Hall, an' see it for what it is, an ornament an' a blessing to the town."

"Yes," says Dorrian, the builder. "It'll be his monument, an' the monument he deserved. He held me tight to my contract; but I respected him for it; an' did him a great job."

One after another sang his requiem; an' all to a changed tune. Hamilton, the grocer, sat silent.

"Gentlemen," says he at last, "I would like to say a word. Ralph Christy an' me have been in opposition for years; an' I'll tell you this: He was a hard man to be up against. I'm not saying that to his discredit. There were no underhand tricks in him. He had brains, an' minded his business. The honest truth is: I'm sorry anything should have happened to him; but I'm d——d glad he's out of my road; for I'll have some chance now."

"Fair enough, Hamilton," says Mr. Ferguson. "It's the best thing has been said about him yet. But listen, friends," he says, "haven't we all forgotten that maybe Ralph isn't dead at all?"

"An' he isn't, either," said Michael, coming in of the door. "What'll you drink, boys? He'll grudge you nothing. He's been standing at the service-window these last five or six minutes; an' seeing that you had changed your tune about him I let him listen. Now, don't be angry with me! If you could have watched his face you would have been glad. I declare to you he was like a wee child that has been given a penny for saying his task well."

But they never got their drink from Ralph Christy. It was he that had been knocked down by the lorry—an' died about a quarter-of-an-hour afterwards.

The Burying of Maryanne Corbally

THE story of the burying of Maryanne Corbally was told me in a Donegal village forty-five years ago by my old friend, Dr. D——. Like many other doctors, he was given to dwelling on death. He had seen with what simplicity humble folk die and leave their sweet possessions, and had told me of many such wayfarers. Most clearly, out of all his tales, there comes back to me this deathbed of an old woman:

I had been attending her for some time, said Dr. D——, but then the old heart began to give up, and I saw she wasn't going to do. So I told her; that she might put her bits of affairs in order. She owned her little house, and some sticks of furniture; and it was thought she had a pound or two of cash stowed away. Father X—— went to see her, and talked about her making a will. But he wouldn't make the will.

"Let the doctor do it," he said.

However, I was too cute for that; for well I was aware the rows it might get me into. But I knew she must be feeling bad, and I went to see her again. She was all alone. I examined her heart, and she was no better.

"The ould clock is in a bad way," she said. "Don't be scared to tell me, doctor. Will Maryanne Corbally be here long?"

"I'm afraid will it be more than two or three days," I answered her.

"Will I last till morning?" she asked me.

"How can any of us tell whether we'll last till morning?" I said.

"Send for the priest, then," said she. "And do you come back; for I want to talk to you."

I went back, and sat down by the bed.

"My hour is come," she said, "and I don't want to stay. I've had my good times when I was a young one; better than people knows. I was a gallus young heifer when I was a girl."

"Were you, Maryanne?" I said. "How was it you never married?"

"No, I never married," she said. "And I'll tell you why. I was very thick with a fellow of this town, an engineer on a boat he was. I was out with him a lot after one of his voyages, and my mother not knowing; and one night he began to talk of marrying me. He asked me to meet him the following night. And the following night I went up to the loft to dress myself; and I put on my muslin dress with a gauze scarf, and my white hat trimmed in black, with black velvet strings tied under my chin. And as I was dressing my mother calls up to me:

" 'What are you doing, Maryanne?' says she.

" 'Och, I'm just giving my face a rub,' said I.

" 'Come down this minute,' says she, 'and get yourself off to confession. And I'll be at the altar to-morrow, and will know if you were there.'

"What could I do? I was afraid of my mother, and deadly scared would she know of my goings-on with the sailor. However, I said to myself, 'Maybe there won't be many there and I'll get a quick run-through.'

"And when I went into the chapel wasn't all the ould voteens in the town there; and I had to wait, and me fidgeting like a racehorse. And when my turn came the priest had been delayed with the ould wan before me telling him her history; and he was down on me, and scolded me, and gave me the seven penitenial psalms to say——"

"Oho, Maryanne," said I, "I know what a girl gets the seven penitential psalms for."

"Never mind about what it was," said she. "It wasn't that. The priest made a mistake. I went on up the road hurrying, and presently I met Lizzie Hourahan. And I threw open my jacket to let her see how well I was looking."

" 'You needn't have bothered,' said she; 'he won't speak to you.' "

"He came round the corner.

" 'I had to go to confession,' I said. 'My mother made me.'

" 'Go back to your mother,' he said.

"I went home, and he went to sea; and I never saw him again. He was drowned in the Baltic; and from that day to this I never had the heart to take a whirl with a young fellow again. What about it, now! But I had my good times like the rest of them when I was young. A gallus heifer I was.

"But what I want to say to you is this: You are my friend. I don't want to be stuck in the ground as if I was a bundle of ould rags. The Corballys were decent people; and I'd like to think I was being buried like decent people. First of all will you see that I'm laid-out as I should be? I've a few pounds saved; and I didn't know where to put them that they'd be safe; and I bethought me of an ould quilted petticoat I have, and cut open the quilting and put a sovereign here and there. It's under me. Get it out."

So I went and brought in a trustworthy neighbour; and we cut the petticoat open. It was no very pleasant task, as you may guess. There were twenty-five sovereigns.

"Now," she said; "that money is to bury me. And whatever ready money is left goes to Father X—— for masses."

I thought she might have given a pound or two to myself; for I got no fee from her; but what matter?

"You should leave your house and furniture to your niece Aloysia," said I. "She hasn't very much."

"Divil a bit of me cares for that," she said. "I've had plenty of trouble with her."

But her bark was worse than her bite; and in the end I persuaded her, and wrote it down.

"Now don't make little of me when you're burying me," she said. "And, first of all, see that my face is well washed. For there hasn't been water on it since I lay down, six weeks ago; and I would like to have my face clean and me looking my best. And could I have candles in my three brass candlesticks?"

"I have three candles," said I, "that I got from a patient, and they came from the nuns of Belmahon, and them all covered over with holy paintings. I'll put them in the candlesticks with my own hands."

"That would be grand," she said. "Could I have two or three flowers in a cup?"

"They'll be in no cup," said I, "but in two cut-glass vases, and out of my own garden."

"You're very kind," she said. "And the neighbours will be out of their minds."

"And now there's more I want you to promise me: Don't let me be left in that cowld chapel, and me all by my lone. Let there be two nights' waking of me, and the people that comes to wake me treated decent. For I want the burying of Maryanne Corbally to be remembered in this town.

"And about the coffin: Nothing but solid oak, plain and respectable. It will last longer, and the very man that makes the coffin will think more of me. And let it be covered with good broadcloth. None of your black rep for *me*. And let there be three crosses in white Llama on each side, and one on each end, and a big cross on the breast of the coffin. And a brass plate; but don't let my age be put on it. I don't want every old woman in the town to be reading it and saying: 'Is that all she was?' For, this long while, I have given out I was ten years less than I was; but some people I told I was more. I used to wonder why people didn't want their age to be on their coffin; but I know now.

"And I want to be laid beside my father and mother along the hedge at the top of the hill. It will be hard to find, for I wasn't able to go there this long time. But see that it *is* found, and see that I'm buried deep. I don't want to be stuck in as if was into a rat-hole.—You'll do this for me, doctor?"

"I will, and more," I said.

"I would like it," she said. "I would like the burying of Maryanne Corbally to be talked about in this town long after I was gone."

"It will be," said I. "There hasn't been such a funeral in this town for twenty years as you'll have.

"I'll get Grace Derrison in to sit with you to-night," I said as I rose to go.

"Ah, what bother?" she answered me. "Amn't I used to being by myself." But I got Grace.

Early in the morning there came a knocking at the door. I put out my head.

"She's gone," says Grace Derrison; "and I was lonely and fearsome."

"I'll get up," said I. "Go for Patty Barrett while I dress myself."

"I will not," says she affronted. "What can she do for her that I can't do?"

"I'll go myself," said I; for I knew Patty would make a job of it.

Now Patty was old and inclined to be fractious; and at first she was disposed to get on her high horse.

"What would I rise out of my bed to go and wash an ould dead woman for?" said she.

"Is it your old friend Maryanne Corbally," said I, "that took you by the hand to school?"

"She did nothing of the sort," said Patty. "I'm five good years older than she is."

"Well, she's dead now," said I, "and her face dirty. You'd hate the neighbours to see her.—Come now," said I, wheedling her; "you'll maybe need a lick yourself, some day. And you'll be well rewarded," said I; "for I'm pay-master."

She got up and came with me, though she grumbled at me for being so particular.

"Sure isn't she only an ould dead corp, now," she said.

But she made a good job, as I knew she would. We tied Maryanne about the middle—that's where they're inclined to give—and I combed her hair, and she began to look well.

"What'll be done about the sheets?" said Patty.

"I'll go home for a pair," said I. And I did, and brought back the best pair of linen sheets in the house.—I never found that out till afterwards; and wasn't I the fool didn't send for them, later.—And I brought the candles.

"What do you need, now?" I asked Patty. For I heard her muttering to herself.

"A valence for the bed would set her off all to pieces," she said.

So I went for a single sheet. Another of my linen ones gone! But it made a complete job of the old woman.

The next day I saw about the rest. And since the bother had been left on my shoulders, I was determined I'd be no niggard.

I went to Peter Renahan.

"First of all," I said, "the coffin is to be of solid oak, and covered with black broadcloth.—That's all wrong, of course," said I, "but she wanted it, and let it be done."—Then I told him about the crosses and the coffin-plate. "The coffin itself," I said, "is to be lined with white satin. And it's not to be stuffed with hay, but with cotton-wool; and the pillow satin; and the covering good stamped paper lace."

"In the name of heavens who do you want this for?" says Peter. "Is it for Queen Victoria?"

"It's for Maryanne Corbally," I said; "and we're not going to affront her."

Then I gave directions about the funeral.

"And treat the men well," I told Peter.

"Ten shillings?" says Peter.

"A pound," I said. I had qualms of conscience, later on, that I was doing the priest out of money; but it was too late, then.

The wake was a great success; the house full for two nights, and people out in the street. At the funeral hay was thrown on the coffin before the grave was filled in, a thing never done before in the town. A few old women grumbled at this, and thought the corpse was being pampered. But in general there was great admiration of the burying; and if Maryanne could have been standing at the graveyard gate as the mourners came away, I think she would have been satisfied.

Predestination

I HAVE had a great many interesting experiences during the course of my business, said my friend the auctioneer. Yet the one that rises most clearly in my mind is of no auctioneering importance at all. A good many years have gone by since it happened; but I was then already past middle age, though not quite come to the time when I would admit that.

It was in September, well on to the end of the month, but balmy, calm weather; the skies as still as sea sand, not a move in the trees, and the upland meadows just glistening with sunshine and gossamer webs. All that was over, for the day. I had done a long afternoon's and evening's work, and was tired, but well satisfied with the job and with myself. In the afternoon I had let Sam Soame's big farm in con-acre, and then, in the evening, to oblige my life-time's crony, Richard Wead, I had let his little outfarm, on the same terms. It was too far from his homestead for him to labour it him-self; but he was a romantic old fellow, and wouldn't part with it altogether, because it had belonged to an uncle of his own name that one time had a great reputation for fiddle playing, and was still remembered.

When I saw Richard's auction was going to keep me late I sent my horse and trap on to his home farm, seeing there was neither hay nor oats where we were; and, when all was over, and the promissory notes signed and the balance of the auction whiskey drunk, Richard and I set out for his house, to eat our own supper. It was falling dusk by this time, so Richard brought a lantern and a candle with him, to use when we came to the short-cut of lanes and pads near the end of our journey.

There was no scarcity of crack as we went along, even if it was a trifle one-sided. Both of us had drunk a fair sup of the auction whiskey, Richard more than me, or maybe I had more experience of it, and the stronger head. The whiskey was coarse stuff, meant for country throats, and very stimulating to talk, especially in the form of bids. Anyway, it had loosened Richard's tongue. He kept talking to me all the time, but more as if he was talking aloud to himself, and arguing things out. A word now and then from me was enough to keep him going. And his subject was the usual one with him when he was in company with what he knew to be a friend: womenfolk in general.

He was about fifty-five at this time, and his wife a year or two older. He had married her for the twenty-five acres of land that rounded off his home farm, and had got more with her than that. She was a steady careful woman, a gatherer, and not only a great housekeeper but a good nurse when Richard needed one, as he did now and then. He liked an odd sup of drink and was fond of anything in the nature of an outing, say a wedding or a burying, or the like, and sang a good song at a Harvest-Home or a swarry without having to be coaxed. The wife was a fine cook, kept her house in apple-pie order, and made it a kind of child to herself, seeing she had no children of her own.

It was a disappointment to Richard that there had been no family, and he was inclined to blame it on his wife. He told me once he thought she was too serious-minded to have children. Still, the two got on well enough together. She was attached to him in a faithful, steady-going way, but she looked on him as not being quite grown-up and having a lot of outlandish notions in his head; and for the most part let him talk away without listening to him. When he got tired of talking to the clock on the kitchen mantelpiece he would go out to some neighbour's house where he would be listened to with more attention, though seemingly without any damage to his high opinion of his wife. It was just that he was good crack, and knew he was, and liked to have it acknowledged now and then. And, as far as I could gather, his wife was always glad enough to see the tails of his coat, so that she could get on with her dusting and mending and polishing. I needn't tell you that whenever he did talk to her it wasn't about women.

But he talked to me about them from time to time; to

me, especially, because he deemed I had a more than usual knowledge of them, as well I might, having been heart-scalded with them at furniture sales for half a lifetime. It wasn't that side of women he was interested in, however, at the time I'm telling you about. Like many another man of his years he saw love slipping away from him for good, and leaving an uncomfortable feeling behind that maybe he hadn't taken enough advantage of it while it was still within his grasp. And, like some men of that class, he was inclined to treat himself now and then to a wee sniff of the scent of the roses that was shortly going to leave him for ever. This night I'm telling you of, the sunshine and the good weather and the sup of auction whiskey all combined to turn his thoughts to his favourite subject. As we padded steadily along the darkening road he delivered himself of a lot of what I would call wisdom that has missed the boat.

As usual, it was about women in general, but no names mentioned, and I let it go in of one ear and out at the other; for he wearied me about them, whiles. Presently he came to a pause. Even in the dark I could see him looking at me sideways a couple of times, as if he wanted to say something, but was held back. Then he found his tongue.

"Marriage is all right, Sandy," he said to me, suddenly, but not unexpectedly. I knew right well he had been meditating something on the matter for a long time.

"Marriage is all right," he went on, not waiting for me to answer him; "but it mustn't be allowed to dry up. You mustn't treat it like a branch of a beech-tree that you tear off and carry home and put in a vase on the top of a dresser or against a wall. The fresh green will go, but when that is faded there's a lovelier thing comes in its place, all reds and crimsons and yellows and golds. Yet after a while they fade, too, and the branch grows dry and dusty, and in the end you get tired of it, and throw it on the dunghill.—It's a sapling, marriage should be, that you water and dig round, and clear of weeds, and keep limber and growing."

"You're a nice old sapling for anybody to dig round,"

said I, jeering at him. "The only digging that'll ever be done round you will leave you neither one nor the other."

"Hold on, now," said he, "but I might sprout again in a bit of fresh ground."

"Oh, the divil a twig," I said. "You should be ashamed of yourself, you old rascal, letting such notions come into your head at your time of life."

"Why should I?" he asked, a little tart. "Even a bullock will look over a fence at a bit of new grass."

"It doesn't get him much further," said I.

"He mayn't want to go any futher," he answered me; "but even if it only raises a longing in his heart isn't it better than being dead?"

"It ends in him lepping over," said I, "and then coming back with a stick at his rump, and his tail between his legs. And looking's as bad as lepping over, if we're to believe all we're told. You must have been looking at something purty sappy, yourself, lately, by the way you're talking. Where did you come on her and what age is she?"

"She's the new barmaid at Shennickan's bar in B——," he answered me, "and she's about twenty-four or five."

"It's a bit old," said I. "Eighteen's more the mark for a patriarch like you. I've often wondered what age Methuselah wanted them."

"Oh, mock away, Sandy," he replied, not a bit put out. "But, say what you like, the kiss of a girl of eighteen is sweet."

"Sweeter than the kiss of a man of sixty," said I.

"I'm not sixty," said he, getting warm again, "or near it."

"Not in your notions," said I, getting drier in my tone. "But there's a difference between dream and reality."

"Never mind," said he, all huffed. "Anyway, she's going to have tea in Belfast with me, one of these afternoons. She told me she would rather listen to me than to half the young fellows that are going about nowadays."

"You'd better sell a bullock," said I; "for you'll shortly be needing ready money."

"Now, don't mistake me," he said, drawing in his horns a

bit. "I'm not going to need money, because I'm not going to spend money. Whatever I have in the way of money and property is my wife's as well as mine, and I'm not entitled to spend it on anybody else. I know that. I'm after no harm and I'm going to do no harm. I'm an elder of the church; and you forget the harm my bad example could do, forbye the scandal that might arise. All I intend is to let the sun shine on me while I'm still able to feel it warm on my back. There's no more in my mind than that. It's just as if I was only out of the nest again, and feeling my wings."

"You'll not feel them very long," I said to him. "When you give them a singe or two at that barmaid's curly hair you'll come down to the ground again purty sudden, and it won't be the weight of your pockets that'll fetch you.—Here; lengthen your step a bit. It's high time you were home. We can talk these matters over at the supper table," I puts in, a bit wicked.

"Lord forbid!" he burst out. "I might leave the country."

"There you are," said I. "And you were doing no harm, by your own way of it. Come home, anyway. I won't split on you.—Where are you going?" I called out to him as he turned left at the fork of the roads. "The right hand is shorter. We can cut across the fields presently."

"Come this way, Sandy," he said. "I love the wee bit with the overhanging trees. Wait till I light the lantern. I'll shine it on them as we pass under. The horse-chestnut leaves will be a shade turned; and I need some wee glint of beauty and heartening after the way you've been tramping on me."

"D——n the bit will I!" I said. For I was getting scunnered with his blethers. "It's the road to the County Asylum you should be on."

"We'll toss a halfpenny for it," he said, shifting the lantern to his other hand. "Head or harp?"

"Harp," I said.

"It's head," said he. "Come and look."

I wasn't sorry. When we stepped out again it was lovely, sure enough, to see the rays of the lantern wheeling and searching among the dark green trees, with here and there a branch of yellow or red striking back.

"It's a wonderful thing, too," I said to myself, "but without this old dreamer's fool notions I would never have thought of looking at all this.—That and the whiskey, of course," I put in, to hide my own foolishness from myself.

And as we walked along, each thinking his own thoughts and a bit lifted above himself, here from a little scroggy bank on the left-hand side there rose a young fresh voice of a girl. She was half singing, half soothing an old northern air: "I know my love by his way of walking;" but as we stood there, with Richard's free hand on my arm, holding me back, the voice rose up clear and sweet, and then fell away in a lament: "But if my love laves me, what will I do?"

The voice stopped, and the pair of us tip-toed along the grassy edge of the road to where it was coming from, Richard with the lantern half-covered by his coat. When we came fornent the place, he flashed the light on it. And, here, in a wee grassy clearing among the elm and sycamore saplings on a ditch-side, was sitting a girl of nineteen or twenty, and beside her, lying in a kind of little creel you could carry on your arm, a baby of about three months old, sleeping sound. There were two or three scarlet poppies and purple teasel on the top of the ditch-side, and a scatter of yellow stinking-weeds on the face of it; and in the light of the candle the whole thing seemed like a picture on a magic-lantern screen. The girl looked up at us, laughing, and not a bit put out. I could tell by her that she had seen the light of our lantern coming down the road towards her, and was waiting for us.

She was a bold-looking piece, afraid of nothing on earth, I would say, if only it had breeches on it. Her eyes were dark, and well-deep, and dared you to come on. Her hair was purple-black in the light of the lantern, with heavy black eyebrows; her lips half open on strong white teeth, and pouted, and nature's own paint not dry on them yet. The sort of a girl that at my time of life cut you along the flanks, and then reined you back into a jog-trot with your spine sagged and your head drooping.

As I stood there turning her over on my tongue, half smiling, and half sorry for myself, Richard spoke to her, sharper than I would have expected, the old farmer rising in him first of all.

"What are you doing there, my girl?" he demanded.

"Just thinking of going to bed," she answered him. "If you swing your lantern to the right you'll see the haystack."

"You haven't matches about you?" he questioned her, still sharply. "You aren't going to light a fire?"

"I have no matches, and I'm not going to light a fire," she answered. "I'll be warm enough without one," said she, looking straight at him. "Don't you think I will?"

He didn't answer for a moment.

"I don't believe the child will take cold," said he; and by the tone of his voice I knew the farmer was softening in him.

"Where do you come from?" he asked her.

She looked hard at him again. The top of the lantern was spouting light through the air-holes, and I could see he was filling his eyes with her.

"From the Garden of Eden," said she; "an' I've lost Adam by the way."

"You've a tongue in your head," said he.

"I'm fully furnished as a girl from head to foot," she answered him, putting a bit to it with her eyes.

"Is the child yours?" he went on. All the time I said nothing, but just kept thinking to myself how much better a hand I could have made of the business, if I'd wanted to.

"You should give me a paper to fill up," she said, very easy and pleasant. "Yes, he's mine."

"Where's his father?" Richard asked.

"Dear knows," she said, as if it didn't cost her much thought.

"Who *is* his father?" he went on.

"Dear knows that, too," she answered, with no more appearance of care on her.

"Are you not ashamed of yourself," demanded Richard;

and I could feel he was looking for the support of the elder of the kirk.

"Divil a bit," she answered. "The world must go on. The child'll be good to me some day, and maybe his father wouldn't have been. And he's earning more than his keep for me, meantime."

Richard stood there a minute, silent, but shuffling on his feet.

"Are you hungry?" he asked suddenly, as if it had just occurred to him.

She leaned over lazily and half opened a wee schoolboy's satchel. It was pang full of meat and bread bursting out of paper, and pieces of cake, and broken buns. I saw two packets of cigarettes—and a box of matches.

"I've even a drop of whiskey," she said, with a kind of a knowing air; and showed a wee naggin' bottle. "All the requirements," she said, and looked hard at Richard.—"Shine the light on yourself and the dummy," she told him, "till I make my pick between you."

He turned the lantern on me. The light of a lantern isn't strong, and I never blinked, but tried to look as beautiful as I could, with a skelly in her direction that hinted there was more in me than appeared on the surface.

"You could speak if you wanted to, dummy," said she. "But you could hold your tongue, too, couldn't you?"

I didn't answer her; for I knew she wasn't speaking to me.

"Now, turn the lantern on yourself," she said to Richard.

"I will not," Richard answered her, and there was a warming of jauntiness in his voice. "I'm a better man in the dark."

"Hello!" said I to myself, and began to take more notice.

"Are you a bachelor?" the girl asked Richard. It was unexpected, and Richard stammered.

"I—I am," he said. I could twig his head as he half turned it to look warning at me.

"I could give you a night's lodging," she said; and as she looked at Richard her eyes were shining brighter and richer and fuller of promise than the lantern.

"Come on home, Richard," I said all at once, catching him by the arm.—Good night, young woman," I called out, as I pulled him with me. "Good luck and good sport to yourself and your wee child, all the rest of your lives."

I meant it, too; and a whole lot more that I couldn't put into words.

When Richard and I had gone down the road a few steps I took the lantern from his hand and flashed it back on her. She had turned on her side and was groping for her supper in the wee satchel, and paying no attention to us at all. The battle was over and she had lost; but she would live to fight another day.

We walked along, side by side, without saying a word, both no doubt thinking of the same thing. At last Richard delivered himself.

"That's a grand little heifer," he said. "There's bird-lime on that one, right enough."

"More than on the curly-headed barmaid?" I put in.

"Ach, hold your tongue!" said Richard; and I knew he was going to save money on the barmaid.

"It's a pity of her, too," he went on; "tramping the roads with her child. I'll hold you some fellow has put is across her and won't marry her."

"She doesn't seem to mind very much," I said.

"That's the worst of it," he answered. "She'll come to a poor end. The men will light on her like flies."

The pair of us walked a bit further, and again nothing said. All at once Richard checked his foot.

"We ought to have given her some trifle," he burst out. "I'll go back and give her a shilling, and say some few words of warning to the creature. I hate to think of what may happen to her. Sit down on the ditch-side there till I come back.—No, I don't want the lantern."

I listened to his feet striding off in the dark, and noticed that they seemed to be gradually moving quicker. But I didn't let it bother me. That's the best of seeing as much of human nature as you do in my trade. In the end you just take people as they come.

I sat there a good while, smiling to myself, and listening for Richard's feet coming back, and then I lit my pipe and watched the smoke turning blue and seeping away into the darkness. I finished that pipe, and half another fill of it, and wondered what excuse I'd make to Richard's wife for keeping the supper late. Then I heard Richard's feet coming down the road. He didn't speed up this time as he came to the end of his journey.

"Come on," he said, very gruff, laying hold of the lantern.

We took the road once more, nothing said for a long time.

At last Richard spoke.

"Better not tell when we get home about me going back," he said. "My wife might grudge the money."

"She'd be sure to," said I.

"Maybe better not mention the girl at all," said Richard. "A man's wife is jealous even at the mention of another woman."

"Better say nothing," I agreed.

I meant to speak in my ordinary tone; but for the life of me I couldn't keep a little dryness out of my voice; and it frayed him.

"Is a man to blame for a thing that's not really his own fault?" he let out of him suddenly and with a good deal of heat.

"I don't see how he could be," I said.

"It all depended on that halfpenny," he said; "on whether it turned head or harp. Isn't that so?"

"It would seem to be," I answered, very impartial.

"I had nothing to do with that, had I?" he asked.

"Nothing at all," I answered; "no more than if I'd tossed it myself."

"There you are!" he said; and he sounded easier. "I was turning all over in my mind as I came along, and that's the conclusion I came to. But isn't it shocking to think the whole thing was in the power of a bloody halfpenny that was spun in the air before the beginning of the world. I have been weighed in the balance and found a little wanting, before now; for, after all, I'm only human flesh and blood.

But to-night the weight of a halfpenny has caused my scale to kick the beam."

"If you'd been the weight of a penny yourself that wouldn't have happened," I said, and could have cut my tongue out the moment after.

"Oh, why wasn't I?" he uttered in a kind of a wail. "Why wasn't I? And now, if I live to look down on my wife's dead face I'll never know peace of mind again."

The Longest Way Round

THERE are some weemin, said Mr. Patrick Murphy, an' the longer they live with their husbands the less they think of them. They see all their man's wee failings; he can't get up in the mornings; he likes a bottle of stout with a friend; or he doesn't make as much money as the man next door. An' she forgets that, for all these wee deficiencies, he has been keeping her an' her children in food an' clothes an' house-room for more than half his life; an' that nobody else ever offered to do that for her. Timothy O'Reel's wife was that sort, an' Timothy was the kind of wee man—a bit feckless, but willing an anxious—that puts up with it. The time I'm speaking about was more than a generation ago. Timothy was an agent for farming implements; an' seeing that in those days the driving power of most agricultural machines was a man's arms an' the small of his back, Timothy found it easier to keep his wife's tongue in grist than her teeth.

Just at the beginning of autumn a stroke of luck fell his way. The new threshing-machines were coming in, with a traction-engine instead of horses to draw an' drive them; an' did more work, an' riz more dust, an' sold more bottled-stout than would have served half a countryside the old-fashioned way. A big farmer in our neighbourhood, Joe McIlhenna, took a notion to launch out into one of these contrivances, an', knowing Timothy for the decent, struggling wee body he was, had pity on the crather, an' put the buying of the thresher through him, to give him the commission. Timothy had to go up to Dublin to see about it, a long day's journey there an' back; an' the job riz more noise in the O'Reel household than the thresher itself would have done if it had begun operations in the parlour.

Mrs. O'Reel was near out of her mind with excitement. She seen a new dress for herself, an' new boots for the children, an' curtains for the front room, an' a silk petticoat for herself that would twist every woman's face in the congregation round to her backbone every time it swiss-switched up the aisle.

An' of course she got to work an' near driv Timothy out of his mind. She told him he was a useless loafer, an' that Mr. McIlhenna had given him the job only out of charity, an' that he'd make a bauchle of it an' lose the address of the firm in Dublin, or fall out of the train on his way back; till, if the threshing-machine *had* been in the parlour, the first thing it would have dealt with would have been a stoutish red-headed little targe of a woman called O'Reel.

The big morning came. The wife was sleeping in the attic, where the morning sun would be sure to waken her, if she slept a wink at all. The dog had got no supper, so that he'd be wake-rife. The children had been promised welts on them as thick as a man's thumb if they didn't call their father an hour before it was necessary. The cat had been put out because she'd yowl to be let in, an' the alarm clock had been wound up that tight that it cost eighteenpence, later on, to make it loosen its tongue again. All was set for raising a useless dunderhead of a man that nobody but Providence knew why his wife had married him.

An' Timothy woke of his own accord. He didn't know why or how. He was half asleep as he moved through the house. But he woke nobody. The fairies were with him that morning. The fire lighted, the kettle boiled, the tea was strong enough for the spoon to stand up in it, a thing that hadn't happened Timothy since his first child was born. He caught the train. He closed his eyes, an' here he was just coming into Dublin, after a few hours' sleep. All day, things went with him like magic. He selected the thresher, after finding fault with two or three. He threw his weight about as if he was Julius Caesar. He'd never felt like that before. He came to the conclusion that it must have been the strong tea, an' had some more of it; out of a pewter tankard, strange enough. He made up his mind to do a lot of other things he'd never done before, to be a man instead of a mouse. If he'd only known sooner how easy it was! But he knew now, an' it wasn't too late.

He noticed that he was in a first-class carriage, going back. But it didn't matter. He could pay the excess fare. And he mustn't fall asleep. But he dozed. When he awoke he was out of the train and walking through the village of Cymbally, the station before his own. It was a lucky accident. Suddenly he remembered—who was it had told him?—that his old flame, Mrs. J——, now a widow, had come to live there. He'd drop in to see her an' talk of old times. His wife would be vexed. But he'd be doing nothing wrong. If she didn't like it she could lump it.

Mrs. J—— liked it. She cried out with astonishment an' pleasure when she saw him. The two sat down before the fire, a torching fire for October. She brought him food, such food as his wife had never cooked. She brought him tea, blacker an' stronger and sweeter than the tea he had made himself in the morning. She fairly beamed on him. It was like old times, she said, when he used to come courting her. If she had married him she wouldn't be a widow now. And all at once Timothy saw that this was true. He wanted to explain, to say that the mistake could be righted. It was his wife who was dead, not Mrs. J——'s husband. But Mrs. J—— would keep talking. It had always been a weakness of hers. He rapped on the table for silence. And all at once a thundering sounded on the door. His wife rushed in, his children, the barking dog.

"You stupid fool," his wife screamed. "I knew it. You've slept in, an' you'll miss the train!"

Timothy never forgot that morning as long as he lived,

that half-hour of being pushed about, an' having his collar buttoned while somebody was lacing his boots, an' drinking tepid water with tea-leaves floating on it, an' being scolded an' abused an' jeered at by his wife an' family. He caught the train, an' he did his business, or let it be done for him. And he caught the evening train from Dublin. But all the time he felt angry an' miserable an' ashamed. He saw himself despised an' made little of—ay, by his own toddling infant. He had had bad luck when he married. The thought of his old sweetheart came back to his mind. He blew on the red coals of his anger, an' courage riz in him. He'd get off at Cymbally station, an' see if the widow was anything like his dream of her. If she was glad to see him, if she gave even half a hint that she was sorry she hadn't married him, it would lift his heart an' his pride in himself.

The evening was falling dark; but he counted the stations carefully from the junction. His heart beat as he drew near Cymbally. He jumped out, an' stood bewildered a moment or two. The train moved on. His brain cleared. It wasn't Cymbally. It was his own station. He was at home.

"Hello, Mr. O'Reel," said the stationmaster, "what's a bother to you?"

"Doesn't this train stop at Cymbally station?" Timothy asked.

"An' what put that notion in your head?" said the stationmaster. "Don't you know the place is clean derelict an' abandoned now the salt-mine is closed?—But aren't you better where you are?"

Timothy stood looking at him for a moment or two in a dubious kind of way. Then, all at once, he pulled himself together.

"Yes," he said over his shoulder, as he stepped out, briskly and determinedly; "it's the shortest way home."

Cautious Cupid

WHEN, in my wanderings round the less frequented roads of my native county of X——, I come on a country churchyard, it is my practice to stop my car and explore. Some folk will think this a melancholy and even morbid habit, but I do not find it so. There is the consoling thought that in spite of the inevitability of death (in which, indeed, nobody really believes, so far as he himself is concerned) one is still a survivor. And there is interest and even amusement to be found in the inscriptions on the tombstones. Sorrow does not always bestow dignity, especially when it has a pen in its hand; and still less often when it it reading with tear-blinded eyes a newspaper's album of mortuary doggerel. But a monument to the dead will sometimes puzzle without awakening our shamefaced sense of absurdity. I came on such a one in the derelict churchyard of Drumdirly many years ago when I was more certain that I was immortal than I am nowadays. It was a largish four-sided cenotaph. Each face of the square portion before it began to taper off contained an inscription. On the East face, looking towards the cemetery path, the lettering ran: "The Family Burying-ground of John Penny," on the South: "Here lies the body of Julia, dearly-loved and deeply regretted wife of the said John Penny. She was lovely and pleasant in her life;" on the North: "Here lies the body of John Penny." Then came the circumstance that made the monument remarkable. On the West face, and not to be seen from the path, the inscription read, "Here lies Anthony Stenton, husband of Julia Arbel." The date of death was given in each instance. I saw that Anthony Stenton had been the first to die, and John Penny the last. But who was Anthony Stenton, and why did his body share this grave? How did he, too, happen to have married a "Julia?" Was it the same Julia; and if this were so, why was not the fact stated?

Being curious about the matter, I put these questions to my friend, Sandy Morrison, the auctioneer, knowing that his humorous eye and all-retaining memory had gathered a vast store of Co. X—— character and incident, and that his ironic but unembittered tongue could best deal with it. He told me this story:

The village of Drumdirly has disappeared. It was never very big, nor the parish it stood in very throng with people, but on account of an old yarn connected with the churchyard it was a great place for weddings. It seems that in days gone by the youngest son of the then lord of the soil ran away with a shopkeeper's daughter from Belfast, and got to the wee church in time to be married before the young fellow's father, Sir Joseph B——, that was chasing the pair, took up with them. He met them on the steps as they came out of the church, and the bride, who didn't know Sir Joseph, seeing her husband coming up to meet them looking thirty years older than he'd been that morning, twigged her chance, just launched herself at him, kissed him on the mouth and called him Father. He pushed her off, had a good look at her, and then kissed her just as hearty, and decided on the spot that he could put up with her, shop or no shop. After that the little church had the name of being lucky to be married in.

The John Penny whose name you saw on the tombstone was under-gardener to Sir Joseph's great-grandson, another Sir Joseph. He was a simple faithful creature, the sort that would have carried a snail half-a-mile to eat somebody-else's plants sooner than put his foot on it. Sir Joseph had a kind of smiling fancy for him, left him a small pension in his will, and got him the promise of being appointed the next sexton of Drumdirly church, the then man being far-through. It was me put the sexton notion in Sir Joseph's head, because I had a fancy for John Penny myself, he was so comic in his mixture of simplicity and odd wisdom; and John found out what I had done for him, and ever afterwards would open his heart to me like a pod of peas.

At the time of John's actual appointment as sexton he wasn't above thirty-five years of age, and good-looking in a moon-faced kind of way; and when Sir Joseph died, which he did shortly afterwards, John, what with his sexton's salary, and his pension, and the little gratifications the happy bridegrooms gave him that came to be married at the church, was looked upon as a great catch by all the young women in the neighbourhood, and some not just so young. Simple and all as John was, he wasn't so simple as not to know that for himself. It went to his head at first. He ran ram-stam at every girl of his own class, or better, that he came across; but, like a wild sheep-dog in a fieldful of young sheep, he wasn't able to make up his mind which of them he was after. If he'd kept on that way it wouldn't have mattered. Some lassie was sure, in the end, to take him by the ear and lead him up to the chancel steps. He used to come to me in my office here in B—— and keep me off my work picking between this girl and that for him, and, God forgive me, moidering him more than ever. But when a couple or three years had gone by, and he was able to come to no decision, I began to notice him cooling off.

"What's wrong with you, John?" says I to him, one day. "Are you going to roam lonely about a double-bed, like a bull in a field, for the whole rest of your life? You're over forty, mind you. A deal of sweet apples have ripened since you got your pension and your good job; and you've never put out your hand. If you don't watch, you'll be left with a crab or a windfall at the last. How many young, sappy girls have you seen these last few years go down the church steps to a pair of warm blankets, and you've never made a move, yourself. What's holding you?"

He looked at me with a long serious look, like a calf over a hedge.

"That's what's holding me," says he, "I see too many of them. But that isn't all. If they went away in their white clothes, and their faces shining" (the poorer class of girls used soap in those days, interjected Sandy) "and I never saw or heard of them again, it would be all right. By this time my eldest boy would have been tugging at the church bell-rope. But I *do* hear of them, and see them. They come back to other people's weddings, to gape at other poor fools caught in the net. And, man, there's the sore change has come on them nearly all. They don't know I'm doing it; but I mark them down. I see a lump of a young woman pushing forward in the wee crowd. Her face has got only a lick and a promise, and her hair looks as if it had been done with a rake. She has a dirty-looking brat by the hand, but she's that eager gaping at the little deceiver and her poor dupe coming out of the porch, and into double-daylight if he only knew, that she can't spare time to wipe its nose. And, says I to myself, 'that's Rose Anne Dibler, that was married here four years ago, and that I had a notion of once when I was gardening with Sir Joseph, and was so like a flower herself that I was afraid to put out my hand to pluck her. But look at her now! And her name might be Penny, and that snottery child be mine'."

"They don't all grow dirty and throughother, John," says I to him. "There's still some fine sonsy young married women come into my office that I like the look of far better than my wife knows."

"Ay, there you are," says John, with his solemn bullock's face looking seriouser than ever. "If your own wife was still what she used to be, or what you thought she was when you married her, you wouldn't be gaping at other women."

"Oh, come now," says I, "you may have a good juicy apple in your hand, but it doesn't keep you from taking an odd skelly at the basket."

He looked at me very serious and weighty.

"There may be a speck on the one in your hand," says he, "but you swallow it, and don't find out till it sickens you. There's all kinds of flaws in women as well as in apples. Every year I take part in the execution of mankind at the altar, I see more. When they've got a man as far as the church they know he can't run away, and they begin to lose caution and let themselves be seen in their true colours. Even their women comrades begin to tell the truth about them. Up till that time they never let on all they know about their friend the bride. After all, she's one of the great clanjamfry of women; and, damage one and you damage all. But now that she's safe they let her have the cutting edge of their tongues. When I'm dandering in and out among the crowd at a wedding the women take less notice of me than usual, they're so busy gaping and criticizing; and, man, I pick up as many wee biographies as, if they were spread abroad, would leave this part of the world childless."

"How do you keep mind of them all, John?" I asked, drawing him on.

"I couldn't keep mind of them all," says he. "I tried it at the beginning when my attention was first awakened to the difference in women between the seed and the sapling; and I couldn't do it.—Might I sit down a minute, Mr. Morrison; for I want to go into this matter thoroughly, so as to clear my own mind as well as to give you information that may be of value to you, even in your own calling. For marriage is just an auction-sale of furniture. We men are the bidders. We don't half examine the lot we're bidding for. We're never allowed close enough to do it, and we don't see the chipped corners, and the crooked legs, and the lick of paint or varnish that hides so much, and the cracks filled up with putty. When a lot is put forward you may have a sort of idle fancy for it, and you throw in a bid or two half out of good-nature. Then somebody begins to bid against you. You say to yourself, there must be more in this lot than I thought; and before you know where you are you can't do without it. I've seen some tasty enough bits of furniture coming down the steps of that wee church I have charge of, on a man's arm, that must have showed a very different appearance before they were long brought home. The first thing, Mr. Morrison, I would say to a man who was thinking of attending one of your auction-sales would be: 'Examine carefully the lot you fancy, and then put it to yourself if you haven't seen as showy stuff as that crack and chip before it had well dinted the carpet'."

"The first thing," says I, "that I'd do to you if I saw you entering my auction-yard would be to put the dog on you."

"You would not," says he; "you're too honest and too

good a friend. You warned me off two or three very flighty bits of stuff in my early days at the church that, but for you, might have taken me in. Now, I'm nearly what you might call a professional. I see them at the church, and I come to my own conclusions about them, making a big discount for the fact that, for that one day, they're in the shop window, with the tears darned, and the wee wrinkles ironed out. Then they're brought back to me by nearly every wedding, like it might be for an inspection, and I enter up the change in my book, good or bad as the case may be."

"So you keep a book?" says I.

"I told you my memory wouldn't hold them all," says he. "You see, it's not just a case of remembering different women's names and general appearance. Each one has her own little curlikews, of fun and figure and character, that time works on, and the kind of life she leads. You'll take note of a lassie coming down the steps good-tempered looking enough; and at some wedding a couple of years or so later, if you stand close to her, the corners of her lips will have drooped, and the wee up-and-down wrinkles will have creased between her eyes, and her mouth pouted out; and then you know she has grown a temper and you're well rid of her. Or, as I told you, she may have got slovenly. You'll see that first in the childer, and then it spreads to herself. As for gossiping, bad cooking, and a dirty house, those you'll gather as you pass in and out among the lookers-on at the wedding, especially if they're kept waiting. That annoys women; and then they don't know how to fill in the time; and if there's any woman acquaintance they feel like knifing, then's when they'll do it."

"What fault are you most afraid of being caught with, John?" I asks, just to keep him warm on his subject.

"Fat," says he. "Fat is the great enemy of womankind. It's the curse of the good as well as of the bad. In troth I think the good-tempered, good-natured women are the most addicted to it. It's a sore mar to them as far as men are concerned. A woman may be as kind as a milch cow and as beautiful as Venus the evening star; but if she has a belly on her like a poisoned pup how the hell can a man love her? The only good thing to be said about fat is, you can see it coming on, if you have any gumption at all. Look for it under the chin," says he, gazing at me very solemn. "There's where the first sign of it appears; so far, that is, as my opportunities have extended. I've taken notice of a wee ripple of fat on the wedding-day that by that time next year was a fold as thick as your first finger. In another year that one is thickening about the hips; and then her bread is baked! You may respect her, and you may like her, but, as far as romantic notions are concerned, it's: 'Good-bye summer and flowers.' But, as I've said, the language of fat is easy to learn. I can see two stone ahead in any bride's life as clear as if it was on her bones already."

Now, all the time this sermon had been going on I had been half-listening to it, and half absent-mindedly totting up my accounts. In the end I laid down my cash-book that I might listen better, and my head began to shire.

"Tell me," says I, "all these women that you've been putting on the dissecting table were getting married. What good or what protection was it to you to have that information about them? It's the young single ones you ought to have been thinking about."

"It's them I have been thinking about," says he, "all the time since I first got a blinding flash of daylight on the whole matter, and was saved from a life of torment and misery. But I was only an amature at the start. I had to learn the profession, beginning in ignorance and learning from my own mistakes till I had passed from doubt to certainty. And how could I do that without seeing actual results? It was Liza Jane Bren that first opened my eyes and enlightened my understanding. I mind her a bride coming out of the porch, smiling and sonsy, with cheeks as pink as a rose-petal, and her eyes just melting in her head with love. My teeth fair watered for her. I could have had her, mind you, if I'd showed any push; and my heart ached to think that she might have been handed to me like a Christmas Box and me to have only to cut the string and take off the wrappings. She married a bit of money, and I suppose it was the better eating that did it; but six months after—for a woman chum of hers told me, even if I couldn't have guessed it for myself—she wasn't able to get her wedding-dress on her to go to a dance—No," he says, catching the look in my eye; "it wasn't that. The first child wasn't born till a year later. I wish you saw her now, when she has four!

"She was the eye-opener," he went on after a minute or two. "And they've never shut since. At the beginning, as I told you, I marked the brides down and followed their career for a few years, anywhere I came on them, but mostly at weddings. And I learned the signs I told you of, year by year: fat, and ill-temper, and witless gabble, and towsled hair, and greasy skin, and dirty children. I noted them in the book I started, with columns for all those things, and others I can't remember at the moment. The first column was for what I thought they would turn out, and the last—that one I filled in a good deal later—was for what they did turn out. And it was the differs between the two that has kept me single till now, and looks like keeping me that way till I'm carried to the grave. For I got real skill in the matter, and made rules, and in the end I could apply them to a single girl as if they were prophecy. I can mark the danger-signals a long way off, now, and shunt into a siding. When I see a girl and hear her history I don't even need to follow her up. As our late rector was so fond of saying, there are concomitant circumstances. Take fat, for example. Well; beware of a girl with a fat mother. She may be as thin as a sunbeam when you see her first; but she'll thicken in the end. And it's the same with a gabbler, especially if she's of the foolish giggling kind. I dread them even more than the other. Think of having the church bell in your ears all day, and, worse still, part of the night."

"Maybe you're a bit too sensitive about bells," says I, "having so much of them already."

"Maybe I am," says he. "But when I stop pulling the rope they quit."

"John," says I, "you've taken a wrong road. If you keep on looking for perfection in a wife you'll never come down the aisle in your own church till you do it in a wooden box. Most of us have to be content with less. My wife has no great impediment in her speech, as you're no doubt aware; but she and I get on bravely, all the same."

"Ah, well," says he, quite serious and matter-of-fact, "it's hard to talk down an auctioneer."

"You needn't be afraid to marry a talker," says I, when I'd done laughing, "if you always keep a bucket of water like that at your hand."

But he was thinking too busy to see what I meant.

"Mr. Morrison," says he, "do you really think I'm taking this business of choosing a wife too serious-minded?"

"I'll tell you what I think," says I. "I think you'll turn up your nose at one woman and another till they're all scunnered at you; and in the end you'll have to be content with some old runt that's marrying you for your savings."

"I wouldn't like that," says he, thinking again. "I would not. A man can manage wonderful well while he's active and tolerably young. But he needs a kindly woman by his side when he's going downhill."

I had heard of other uses for a woman than that; but I said nothing. It would only have been thrown away on him. But I gave him a little prod.

"Do you not think," says I, "that it might be your duty to give her a hand up the climbing side of the hill before she started on her real job of being your housekeeper and nurse?"

He sat there another while without speaking; and I could see there was something he was anxious to say, if he could only make up his mind that I was to be trusted.

"Come on!" says I, at the last. "Get it off your chest. You know I'm your friend, and you know by this time, surely, that I can hold my tongue. What more do you want?"

He took one more look at me, and then drew a deep breath and let it out again. I knew he had swallowed me as father-confessor.

"Mr. Morrison," he says, "I'm slow to trust anybody, even

a man; but there comes a time when a body can't depend on himself alone, when he must look out through somebody else's eyes because he has got a speck of dust—and maybe a handful of it—in his own. That time has come to me; and you are the only man-kind that I would place dependence in. I have weighed you in the balance this long while, though you may not know it; and, barring when you were led away by some bit of light-mindedness, I never found you wanting." He rose up and shut the door of my office very quietly. "Listen," he says, when he had sat down again, "I think I have found one at least—Julia Arbel."

"I think I know her," says I. And I did. "What evidence have you collected about the girl?"

"I'm going to put it before you," he answered, "and see whether you can help me to make up my mind once and for all."

"Can you not make it up for yourself?" I asked him. Then I looked at his right hand playing the harmonium on the table, and I knew he couldn't.

"Have you her in the book?" says I.

"I have," says he, "this year and more. And her mother and sister as well, for a guide to me."

"And how does the girl herself come out of it?"

"*Well*," says he, nodding his head to drive it home. He paused a minute. "Except for one thing."

"And what is that?" I asked, as he hesitated.

"She's young," says he.

He looked down, and cupped his right knee in the palm of his hand, then shook his head very disconsolate.

"What age?" I asked.

"About twenty-one—or two," he says.

"You're double that, or near it?" I put to him.

"I am," says he, beating on his knee. "But I'm told," says he, cheering up, "that a steady man like me lasts longer than one that has spent his early days running after the women."

"You're satisfied with her, then, every way but the age?" I asked him.

"I'm pretty well satisfied about that, too," says he. "At

my time of life you begin to need a shake of pepper in the milk. But there's a little uneasiness at the back of my mind, still. It would be a terrible thing, Mr. Morrison, if she turned light-headed and began to carry-on with the boys. Think of showing the people to their seats and all the time knowing that the early-comers were nodding their heads and smiling at one another behind my back, and her maybe keeking sideways out of her hymn-book to see her jo.—I don't believe it!" says he, suddenly, hitting his knee this time with his closed fist. "Point by point I have compared her with the book, and she has never made a miss."

"Her mother's as thin as a red-herring, too," says I, "and her near fifty.—Though I like them a trifle plumper, myself."

"The mother's on the skinny side, I give in," says he. "But the father's well-covered; and that should even Julia out. Her sister Rose is thickening up a shade about the middle. But then she's had twins; and, please God, that's not going to happen to us."

"You're going to face, then?" says I.

"I think it. I do think it," says he, fidgeting on his chair. "Look here," he says, pulling a sheet of paper out of his pocket. "I've checked her off on all these points for a year and more.—Fat I have dealt with," he mutters, running his finger along the paper. "Listen now, Mr. Morrison, while I sum up: She's clean in her person, and neat in her dress without too much show. I've been looking for a hole in the heel of her stocking these three months, and never spotted one. She's kind to her father and mother, and biddable to both. Her mother pushes her to the front more than the girl wants, but that's done for her own good. She's punctual at church, and no doubt everywhere else. I've had three hearty meals in the house lately and kept the mother in talk all the time they were being prepared; so the daughter must be a good cook. She has a kindly, merry word for everybody; but she lets her mother do most of the talking. And if the mother lights on any of her neighbours too hard the girl has always something to say in their defence. 'She's not two-faced,' the mother said to me. 'Anything that's in her comes out.' And she was very sympathetic about her father's rheumatism, and rubbed his knee with liniment while I was there. I took particular notice of that," says he; "for there's times I get a kind of a catch of pain in my right shoulder as I pull at the bell-rope, and it has come into my head latterly that it might be rheumatism."

"She'll not marry you just to keep her hand in at the rubbing," says I. "I would sing dumb about the rheumatism.—Tell me," says I, "how much money have you put-by?"

He looked at the door and the window, and then wrote down the figure on the back of his piece of paper and handed it to me.

"Tell that to the father," says I, "and he'll fetch her down to you by the scruff of the neck."

He shook his head slowly, looking at me very sober and earnest.

"No," says he, "I won't do that. What happiness could I expect with a girl I had bought? I never thought much of Jacob's dealings in connection with Leah and Rachel. I'll be married for love or not at all. And I think she likes me," says he. "She smiles at me, both coming and going, at Morning and Evening service; and if I'm not on the spot when she's leaving the porch she hangs back till I show myself. She talks to me and questions me about my duties, and knows near as much as I do about them. Only the other day she told me she believed she could conduct a whole wedding-service by herself, and got very red in the face as she said it. I thought that very encouraging. And on the Thursday night, when there's only a handful of a congregation, and her father and mother never there, she slips round to the bell-house and watches me pulling the rope, and sometimes puts a hand over mine and helps me to pull."

"That'll help you to make up your mind, too," says I.

"It warms me like ground ginger," says he. "The words have been on my tongue to ask her, more than once; and I believe she would say 'yes.'—If I could only be sure she wasn't flighty."

"Have you ever seen any sign of it?" says I.

"There's a fellow has been coming after her to the Thursday night services," says he; "for I'm sure he's not coming out of piety. Anthony Stenton, older than herself, but still young; and he has the name of being a bit of a playboy with the girls."

"Do you ever see the pair of them carrying-on?" says I.

"I do not," says he. "When I come out of the bell-house he's often talking to her. But I've never seen him nearer her than, say, three or four feet. And not a flush on her face, or a hair awry. Just a modest young girl talking to a young man, and keeping him in his place."

"Then what do you want?" says I. "You can't expect her to live in a band-box.—Away up to her father's this evening, and ask her. Short of putting her through a sieve you can't test her any more. And I'll take a clash at the bell, myself, the day you get her."

He thought a while.

"I'm going to give her one more test," says he. "Your words have put it in my head. If she passes that I'll stand by her to all eternity. I may be slow to ring, but I'm bell-metal to my note."

He wouldn't tell me what the test was, though I tried him up and down. All I could get out of him was that it would be made the following Thursday.

On the Friday evening he came into my office as I was making up my books after a sale. I couldn't tell by him was he pleased or disgusted.

"Well," says I, "do I order in two glasses of whiskey from across the street?"

"No," says he, "neither whiskey nor wine.—She was a cracked bell, after all."

He stood there, saying nothing. The water gathered in his eyes, and he rubbed it away with the back of his hand.

"Don't laugh at me," he says. "She was a bonny creature, and had crept up my sleeve more than I knew.—You're aware," he says, "that on Thursday nights I ring the bell for a quarter of an hour before the service. She was there as usual, a bit before I started to ring; and, man, she was looking like one of the angels in the end window of the church. We had a daffing word or two before I struck the first clap on the bell. When I took hold of the rope she leaned against me and put both her warm soft hands over mine. As she turned away she kissed her fingers to me for the first time. My heart smote me for the thing I was going to do; but I couldn't bring myself to go back on it. I pulled the bell for five minutes, and then my neighbour Tompkins's young son, as I had arranged, came into the bell-house and took over from me without breaking the time or altering the note. I had him trained to do that for times that the rector was likely to want me. There was no sign of Julia when I went out of the bell-house. I slipped in among the bushes, and had planned, if all was well, to tell her I could thole no longer, but had given up the bell to come and ask her would she marry me. And there, as I turned the big yew bush, she was standing in young Anthony Stenton's arms, on her toes, with her arms round his neck, and giving him wee laughing kisses very dainty and careful, so that—I knew it d——d well," he moaned—"her hair wouldn't be tossed for me to take notice."

"What did you say or do?" I asked him.

"Nothing," says he. "They never even saw me. I just went away and sat down on a tombstone and crossed her out of the book, in my mind. I don't know what the lassie thought when she came back and saw young Tompkins pulling the bell-rope. Anyway, she didn't face into the church afterwards. I suppose she'll be kneeling at the chancel steps beside Anthony Stenton one of these days.

"Well, well," he goes on, pulling himself together, "after the first gunk I wasn't so much taken down as you might expect. For all she seemed so good and steady, there was a wee glint in her eye that I'd always doubted. That's why I put the last test to her. And wasn't it well I did?"

"I don't know about that," says I—and I meant it. "I'll hold you she'll be as much gunked as you are. I believe the father and mother must have been recommending her to marry you; and from what you tell me I think she wasn't unwilling to do it, and was only taking a last fling of her heels before she was langled. There's honest blood in her, forbye a bit of fun."

John straightened himself up, and looked at me very pitiful. His mouth half-opened; and I knew it was to say he'd give her another chance. Then his shoulders slumped down again. He shook his head, slow and disconsolate.

"No," says he, "I daren't risk it. She's a bonny creature, and kindly, I do believe. But I'd never be sure of her, short of keeping her tied to the bell-rope."

II

For a long while after this disaster of his I saw little of John. It was plain that he was sheering out of my way any time he was in the town; so I left him to lick his sores, the best thing you can do for a man or dog. Anthony Stenton married Julia a year or so after, very much against her father and mother's will. They thought they had her safely planted with John Penny; and Stenton was far from being so well-off or so dependable. The pair settled down on Stenton's small farm, a good few miles distant from Drumdirly, with a different market-town. Presently they went out of my mind, and, I presume, out of John's, too. But he was a methodical kind of man, as a gardener must be—I often thought women must be a sore trial to one, after the regular ways of plants. —It can't have been very long till he was making notes again; for I was at the wedding of a client of mine's daughter in Drumdirly church something less than a year later, and I saw John taking some great skellies at the bride and the bridesmaids and the female relations.

"You're for the book, my poor girl," says I to myself as I saw her thin acid-looking mother coming down the aisle at her heels looking as if the bridegroom was a full twenty acres short of what she had expected for her daughter. And there's something to be said for John Penny's system. The man that married the same daughter got an ill-tempered bitch in the end.

But, whether the examples that came before him were poor or whether he was still suffering from the setback he had got, years went by and John wasn't seriously tempted again. Then he got a couple of further disappointments, both of them with young girls. Like most men after a certain time of life he began to prefer them younger. The wife has noticed the same thing about myself, I may tell you; but it hasn't taken any years off *her*.

The first of these disasters was Rosie Stiles, a bright, lively lass, but not so on-coming with the men as to scare John, and as good a child to her father and mother as could be. And though she had plenty to say for herself she was no gossip. That left her pretty clear on John's book but for one thing, her figure and the future of it. John was by this stage more tolerant of a little plumpness; but he still abhorred fat. Here Rosie was beyond question. Her mother was betwixt and between, and her father the same; but Rosie was as thin as a yard of pump-water, and could—and did—eat like a beagle without even putting on an extra ounce. Maybe she was abusing her food fortune. All I know is that just as John was well on the hook, and ready to be landed, here doesn't Rosie's appetite start to fatten her. It wasn't that she began slowly to thicken up and lose her greyhound lines. She just suddenly began to blow out like a football. It was a sore bewilderment to her, and a sore disappointment. By this time John's reputation for having money had been raised so high with talk that, though he was showing signs of age, all but the romantic ones would have lepped at him. Word of John's book had got about, too; and Rosie had more than an inkling that she stood high in it. But all was no use. John had a question-mark against her the first Sunday she loosened her stays, and in two months' time she was ruled out of the book altogether.

However, she hadn't got as far under John's skin as Julia, and he soon forgot her. Time went on again, and another girl began to get high-marks. This was Susan Rice, young, lively, by-ordinary good-looking, and with a very floostering tongue in her head. She set her cap at John; for though she was 'fond of the boys,' as our expression goes, she had made up her mind to get on in the world by hook or by crook; and John was a good mark. Before long she had worked herself high-up in near every column of John's biography of her. It was in my mind to warn John that she wasn't just all she seemed; for she had flattered me into giving her a "short knock" for a second-hand piano she was bidding for, and then laughed at me behind my back. But it wasn't necessary. She cut her own throat with John in a very simple way; and I was there when she did it. He had followed her and her two sisters and her young brother up the street on our market-day. The four went into Jamey's sweetie-shop opposite my premises, and John ran in to ask me to take a good look at her and give him my opinion. When the four came out of the shop they divided up the sweets they had bought, and stood there eating them, and laughing and joking together. I looked at John's fancy and forgave her the piano. There was no doubt she was a taking piece. She finished her sweets first, then looked round the other three as they were eating. The young brother, a little chap of about six or seven, had held off his, to lengthen the pleasure, and had still most of them. He stretched out his hand with the sweets in it to John's girl, showing her how much he had left. She didn't seem to take notice. But all at once she swooped on him, grabbed half the sweets and more, crammed them into her mouth, and ran off laughing as loud as her bulged cheeks would let her. I looked at John to see how he'd take it. He was gaping after her with *his* mouth half-open, clean flabbergasted.

"How will you enter that in the book, John?" I asked him quietly.

He had pulled himself together a little; but he couldn't hide the slap in the eye he had got.

"First place for being two-faced, greedy, and selfish," says he at last. "Oh, man, Mr. Morrison," says he, "haven't I had the merciful escape from the hard-hearted devil!" And he turned away without saying another word.

"That'll about do him," says I to myself as I watched

him going along the street, an elderly man by his walk and his stooped shoulders. "He'll go down to the grave a bachelor now; and the Protestant Orphans will get his money."

But though the years went on mounting against him and me, John never gave up his hankerings after romance. He still came in from time to time to see me, and have a crack, and turn out his queer character to me. And though he wasted a power of my time I encouraged him. He was childish, but he wasn't ordinary in his notions; and, besides that, I liked the old fellow. You encounter so many cute lads in an auctioneer's business that it's a pleasant change to meet somebody, now and then, with a simple heart. They pay for their simplicity, but they sometimes get good money for their money.

All these years John continued to keep his book. But it was now more of a hobby with him than a means of guiding him to a wife. In the end it began to operate on him the other way altogether. He got to know that much about the deceitfulness and the unexpectedness and the changeableness of women, both in body and nature, that, forbye his advancing years, the chances of his taking one to himself had nearly become nil. He could have married more than one, mind you. A man known to have money can get some sort of a woman so long as he has enough breath in him to blow out a candle. But by this time John was scared of them all. He'd been so long looking out for the red signal that he had lost nearly all power of seeing the green.

I thought at the last that he had given up all notion of meeting the perfect woman and was going to be content with making up one for himself out of the broken bits he had collected. He didn't talk about them nearly so much; and, though he sometimes checked up on a married one in his book, he seemed to have made an end of entries. And this worked a change in him. He became more contented, and more charitable to women with his tongue. There were honest and two-faced of them, he said, and good and bad; and he hadn't been clear-eyed enough to see the honest and the good. He surprised me at times by pointing out some young married woman who had turned out better than he'd expected.

"There's young Mrs. Robb of Cooledan," he said to me one day, "and she had a noticeable double chin on her the time she was married, though she was well short of twenty-five. I can tell you what I thought of her future," says he, as usual pulling a piece of paper out of his pocket; "for I have had reason lately for making an extract or two from the book. Here she is as she came down the church steps: 'Twenty-four years and twenty-one days old'—You'll understand," he broke off to say, "that there's no chance of a young woman of our own congregation deceiving me about her age; I see the water go on them all—'bright blue eyes and looks you straight in the face. Hair fair, plentiful, and well-brushed on all occasions as well as on her wedding-day. Teeth good, though she eats too many sweets for a girl with a mother of that weight and build. Shoulders straight, and holds herself upright. Fine in the waist, but a good deal bulged above the stays. Ankles trim and feet small. Thickening about the hips. About five feet four inches in height, and, I would guess, not more than eight-and-a-half stone weight. Character'—well, we needn't go into that. But here is a special note about her: 'I would say she will weigh well over ten stone before she is thirty.'

"I was wrong about her," says he, putting the paper in his pocket. "She took her weight in McGran's shop last Tuesday, while I was there, on one of those new-fangled contrivances that does it for a penny. I keeked over her shoulder, by the way I was looking at the price ticket on a ham. She'll be thirty-two next July; and I declare to you she weighed only eight stone three."

"There you are!" says I. "If you'd had a little more charity and common-sense the last twenty years you might have had as many wives as the Sultan of Turkey."

"I might have had *one*," says he, turning away very down and disconsolate. "I might have had *one*."

"Ha," says I to myself, looking after him. "I wonder who he's regretting."

I was too busy to think more of it at the time; and I saw nothing of him for weeks and weeks after. But happening to be in his part of the country, making a valuation, I drove round that way on my road home. I found him in the house. The wee sitting-room was as clean as a new pin, the curtains fresh, the furniture polished, and the ornaments bright and shining. There was even flowers on the mantelpiece. And I knew that he kept no servant.

"John," says I, looking round me, "why do you ever bother yourself about women? Give up searching for a wife. No woman that ever lived could do better for you than this."

But I had said the wrong thing. He held up his hand to stop me.

"Don't believe that. Not for one second," says he, and stuck fast. I looked closer at him; and he was better dressed than usual, very trig and smart-looking, a bit too much so for his years. A notion began to dawn in me.

"You surely couldn't have found the perfect woman at last?" I asked him. And still I didn't believe it would be that.

"I have," says he, very sober and quiet; not at all what I would have expected, seeing he had such big news to tell me.

"You *haven't!*" says I, near in a shout.—"Clear on the book?"

"Clear on the book," says he. "Too good for the book."

"Will she marry you?" I asked.

"No," he says, still very quiet; "she's married already. It's Julia Stenton, that I let slip out of my fingers when I might have had her, years ago. I was in the townland of Tollylum a couple of months since, the first time I'd been in that direction since I lost her; for I couldn't bear to see her again and her married to that waster. But I met a pleasant-looking woman on the road, that I liked the look of. She didn't know me and I didn't know her till she was gone by. Then all at once it flashed into my head who it was. She was as slim in the figure as that Thursday evening she first laid her two warm soft hands on mine, in what I thought was a Judas trick. Her hair was still plenty, and though there was grey among it you would hardly have taken notice of the differs between that and the fair hairs. Her eyes were still bright, but steadier than they used to be; and though the face was lined it was a kindlier, patienter face than the one that used to smile on me, and, as I thought, on everybody else. Maybe her waist *was* what you'd know thicker; but it went all the better with her years.—Lord bless her! she's far over forty; and she seemed as light on her feet as ever.—Och, och," says he, and stopped again.

"So that's why you've given up talking to me about women the last two months," says I. "You've been checking up on her in the book."

"Now, how do you know *that*?" he asked me, all surprised. He hadn't much acquaintance with the auctioneering trade.

"Did she come out of it well?" I asked him.

"Well enough to break my heart," he answered me. "I do not know how I came to make such a miss.—No," he goes on after a minute or two's consideration. "I do know. She has got it hard. Life has changed her. Life has sprouted the good seed that was in her and has choked the tares. It's a melancholy thing to say, Mr. Morrison; it's a very melancholy thing for me to have to say, but I believe she has grown better grain on the stony ground. I would have pampered her, given way to her whims, and made a doll of her instead of a woman."

It was an odd saying to come from John, sure enough, but I wasn't surprised. With all his simplicity he never stopped trying to hoke out the truth.

"What sort of a man did the other fellow turn into?" I asked him. "Not very dependable or easy to do with, I would gather."

"Neither of those things," says John. "If I had kept a book of men as well as a book of women he would have cut a poor figure, from his neighbours' account of him.—I begin to wish," says he, breaking off, "that I'd done that. I would have been fairer to the women, then.—I have inquired about him and her up and down in a quiet way, not with a pencil in my hand and a book in my mind; for I see now that it's an inhuman way of dealing with your fellow-creatures; but just listening to what folk said and chewing it and turning it over in my thoughts. Here's what it all comes to, as far as I can make out: He's neither good nor bad. I would call it just a poor middling. He's selfish to the core. He always was. He's harsh and unreasonable with her from time to time. That, most women can put up with from their men. They have to, if their men are farmers, especially in a climate like this that would try the temper of an angel; and he's none. But he's oncoming and taking with other women all the time; and that's not so easy for a woman to thole. I don't know how far he lets her down with other women, and I don't think she knows herself, or wants to know. He's lazy, and leaves the driving of the servants to her; only, the servants work for her without driving. He takes a sup of drink pretty often, and is hard to put up with when he's doing it. But when he isn't drinking, and has cleaned himself up, he's a handsome figure of a man still, though red and bloated about the nose and face, particularly after a spree. When he's on with the wife he flatters her, and makes much of her, and will spend money dressing her up, and make her take an excursion with him here and there even if the farm work should suffer. In short, he acts the playboy, and doesn't care very much what she does or has to put up with so long as she lets him do that. She takes the good with the bad, but both smiling; and if, as seems not unlikely, she's sometimes sorry she married him, she gives no sign of it to the world. Now and then he curses her because there have been no children, and swears that it's not his fault and she's a cold-blooded bitch. She takes that with the rest and shows no sign; and there has never been hint or word against her own good name."

Before John had done I could see Julia and the husband before me plain and life-size. I saw that all of his observing and note-taking hadn't been thrown away, even if he'd got little good of it himself; and I felt sorry to think what an auctioneer's clerk had been wasted in him. He wound up by telling me that Julia's husband was in bad health; and bogged in debt; and that the general opinion was that if he lived much longer they'd be evicted out of their farm.

I got no more out of him that day. It was only by degrees and over weeks and weeks that he disclosed to me all the patient, cautious inquiries he had made about his old sweetheart and her man, and her life with him; and how he had built her up as time and marriage had changed and remade her. I'm no way sentimental—I wouldn't need to be—and I didn't believe John's Julia was anything like the saint he made her out. But when I did come in contact with her, later, I had to admit that in putting her in his Book of Judgment as A1 he wasn't very far astray.

The strange thing was that he kept harking back to his notion that she was the better for not marrying him. It wasn't like John. With all his inquiring about other people he had come to have a considerable opinion of himself as far as women were concerned. But he returned to it again and again when he came to see me, and that was pretty often, once more. Then all at once I twigged what was in his mind. All was for the best. Julia had been shaped and improved by life and marriage, for his benefit. She was the finished article, now; and he, with all his thinking and experience, was the one man able to recognize that, and to profit by it, and to give her the treatment she deserved. Providentially, her first man was going to be taken away now that his work was completed, and his place left for John.

I wouldn't just go the length of saying that he was knowingly waiting and hoping for the husband's death, though I've a notion that was the honest truth of the matter. Always, before he left me, he'd drop a word or two on the subject. "I hear he's not so well," or, "I'm told his cough is growing on him," or, "They say he looks like a walking skeleton;" and without asking or any name being spoken I knew who John meant. He had made a kind of business connection in the neighbourhood by taking to buying flowers and plants for the church graveyard and his own little grounds from a market-gardener in Julia's direction. In that way he kept himself up to date in the news about her and her man. The news wasn't good. Beyond all doubt the husband was dying of consumption. He had worked for it, by drinking and neglecting himself, and sometimes of a market day lying out a whole evening in the cold and wet at the back of a ditch till his wife found him. She had many a job like that with him, but did them all uncomplaining; and got doing them, as the like of her will. If she'd just let him lie out a whole night sometime, and get a good drooking, she would have had less hunting for him in the future, or John would have had a chance of her sooner.

Then the money end of things got worse. I made quiet inquiry myself, at John's instigation. The husband was in a bad financial way. He was behind with his rent, and he was behind with his rates, and he was in as much debt as she would let him be. At times they were in want of ordinary groceries for the home.

When I told John about this—for I knew he would hear it sooner or later—he fairly cried out. It mustn't be, he said; it must *not* be. Not while he was a well-off man with nobody to come after him. He would gladly put his hand in his pocket if I would only show him how to help her without hurting her feelings.

"How much have you now?" I asked him. He told me, and I was surprised, though I knew he had been growing more penurious as he got older. I considered for a long while before I advised him. In general the worst thing you can do for anybody is to give them money, because in the first place it's easy-come, and in the second place instead of being grateful they think it mean of you not to give more than you did. But I decided to let John help his old flame. He had plenty; and though he liked me I was never going to get any of it myself. She had done him a good turn by maybe keeping him from getting married to some targe of a woman that would have squandered it, and made him miserable as well. And there was a chance that he might have an opportunity side by side at a hearth with her yet.

"Listen, John," says I, "if you take my advice you'll lend nobody money. If you do you're only heart-scalded waiting and hoping for them to pay you back; and they're hiding behind the trees and round corners for fear you'd see them and take mind of the debt. Even if they mean to pay you back—and not many do—you're little better off. If you wish them 'Good-morning' too hearty, they say to themselves, 'he's trying to keep in with me;' if you make it too dry, they say to themselves, 'what's he in such a hurry for; does he think I mean to do him?'

"There's another thing you ought to take account of," says I: "it's a dangerous business having intercourse with a woman—even financial intercourse—behind her husband's back, especially when he's in bad health. If you want to be kind to Julia for laying her two warm hands on yours once, *give* her the money. I'll pass it on to her as coming from a relative that wants his or her name kept dark. I'll take her receipt, so that all will be business-like, and no hanky-panky. She'll know who it came from, you may swear; but you had better deny it, for the present. It'll keep her husband longer alive, mind you; and she'll not be sorry, though that may surprise you. But it's a good woman's fault. I can hold my tongue, you know I can. And I'm glad to do Julia a turn. I mind her a dashing girl, with a laugh like joy-bells, and I gather from you that she hasn't changed for the worse." I didn't tell him that I had kissed her, myself, more than once, when she was a slip of a thing; no harm meant and no harm done.

He fetched me money next day, how much, is between him and me. (Once, twice, three times he did it, and then it wasn't needed any more.)

So I called on Julia, making the excuse of inquiring about her husband. He was in bed and too ill to see me. I sat down in the parlour and began to talk about old times. She had kept her shape and looks wonderful for a woman well over forty; but she only smiled, now, when I mind the time she would have laughed. I worked the talk round to the position of her husband and herself, and drew her on to tell me more than she had intended at first. Then I said to her very diplomatic that I had an offer of help for them from a far-out friend of hers who didn't want his name known. She looked at me, with a wee smile on her lips at first, then she began to laugh; and then she took out her handkerchief and wiped her eyes.

"Ooch," she says, beginning to smile again, "the decent, kindly old hen, that I had half a notion of marrying one time, and changed my mind."

I remembered what John had told me; but I didn't say a word. All women are alike about some things.

"How do you know it was him?" I asked her.

"Ach, Mr. Morrison," says she, "sure the whole country-side here knows about him. He's been snooking round ever since my poor Anthony took bad, making inquiries about me and taking an inventory. I even heard you were at the back of it.—Are you putting me up for auction, or is it to be private treaty?" she asks me with a touch of mischief.—"But isn't it just like him! I wonder am I as little changed."

"How would it have done if you'd married him, that time?" says I.

"It wouldn't have done at all," says she, shaking her head with a wee laugh. "There was a bit of a spark in me then—more than there is in me now, I doubt," says she, her face turning serious. "He would have jennied after me, and weighed every bite went into my mouth, and noted me down in his book, till a woman of any spirit at all would have kicked over the traces. Anthony let me alone, and kept me wondering what he was going to do.—He put me through it, all right," says she, with a bit of a sigh; "but it was maybe better for me than getting my own way."

"It's not so long ago," says I, "since John told me nearly the same thing. He said you were a finer woman this day through him not getting you. He's not such an old hen as you think."

"Did he say that?" she asked me, all interested. "It was plucky of him; for he fancies he's no miss.—Is he thinking of me still?" says she, with another wee smile.

"He never thought of anybody else," says I. There's no

use cheapening what you're trying to sell. And, besides, I knew it would please her.

She wasn't displeased, I could see. But she was staunch.

"Ach, well," says she, "there's no use talking about it, now. And this is no sort of crack for me, with my man lying sick and fighting for his life. He has his faults, Mr. Morrison, I know that. But we had good times together, him and me; and I'll never forget him or put another man in his place."

I left it at that. For I knew when to let well alone.

"You'll take this bit of money that's offered you?" I asked her. "From your old relative!" I put in, before she could open her mouth.—"Now, it's from an old relative. I'm a business man, and those are my business instructions. You say your husband is lying sick; and the countryside knows he's near broke. You have no right to refuse it."

"No!" says she, standing up and stamping her foot. "I may have had my little disappointments; but I'm not come down to charity."

She was torn two ways, I could see.

"It's not charity," says I; "it's love and affection." I let that sink in for a minute, for I saw the struggle growing in her mind.—"Take it, now," says I. "For the giver's own sake take it. You say your marriage did you good. Well, to give this will do *him* good. Even to think of it has done him good. He told me on no account to let you even guess it was he was offering the money. But he's only human. He knows right well you'll find out sometime, and he'll want you to. But what's in his mind is to show you that he bears you no ill-will for what happened in the past."

I took a good look at her, and could see that she was hesitating. I knew the time was come.

"I'll tell you more," says I. "The decent man came over here in the first instance to inquire for your husband when he heard he was ill. He was told about you by one and another; and he has a bigger notion of you than ever. But he knows it's no use, and never will be, if you were free this day twelvemonth."

"It *is* no use," she says. I could see the spirit rising in her. "If I was free to-morrow, and he was the last man on earth, I wouldn't marry him. And here is why, among other things. I told you I wouldn't have him years ago. It wasn't the truth. He never asked me. He forgot that I was an ordinary, healthy girl and that there was red blood in me, and that he wasn't the only man on earth, taking his time before he'd crook his finger. He played a mean trick on me, and when he had caught me out he went off and left me in the lurch, though he knew well I'd have married him if he'd asked me."

"Tell me about it," says I, letting on I didn't know. So she told me word for word, the story I'd heard from John already. They were both simple at heart, and both truth-tellers.

"I'd never have thought he had it in him," says I.

"I didn't think he had it in him," says she, sitting down, and the anger dying in her. "If he'd come to me next day when the rage was off me, and I'd begun to laugh, I do believe I would still have taken him. But he missed his chance, and I got a better man."

"You're beginning to laugh, now," says I.

"I am beginning to laugh," says she, "though I haven't much to laugh about this minute. And I forgive him, on account of what he's doing now.—After all, it's a kind of a pat on the back for me, isn't it?"

Her eyes were still shining with tears.

"Julia," says I, "take this money, and whatever more is offered that you have need of in your present trouble. You'll be doing a kinder action than you know."

"But my husband?" says she. "I will not make little of him for anybody—not even for himself."

"No one will ever know, I tell you. John's a bit of an old hen, if you like; but he's an honest hen, and as true as the sun. And, if the worst comes to the worst, a lie or two is no great difficulty to an auctioneer. I can swear a hole in a wall if it's really necessary. And you won't need to marry John over it. I'll poison my own wife and take you myself."

She looked at me with a bit of the old sparkle in her eyes. "You're wearing well, Sandy," says she.

I put the notes in her hand, and went off on the laugh. I didn't want her to commit herself to anything definite about not marrying John. For I knew that if she did she would feel she had to keep her word, even if she didn't want to.

On my way home, I went round by John's, and warned him.

"Keep away," says I. "If you wish to give her any more money, send it by me. At the moment she'll be thinking better and better of the man that's going to die; and she's a soft-hearted loyal creature anytime. If she got a notion in her head of you just sitting waiting for his death, that you might lepp at her, you wouldn't have an earthly chance."

"It's what I would expect of her," says John, "and what I would like. She was a good loyal wife to him, and she'll be a good loyal wife to me if I get her. I don't deserve to get her," says he, "after the sore mess I made. I thought I knew all about women; but she has taught me something I didn't know. I'll burn the book," says he, "as soon as the breath is out of her man's body."

"I would burn it now if I was you," says I. "Then you can tell her there was never anybody in it that mattered but herself."

"I'll do that," says he. "I should never have had the rest of those women in it.—There's another thing has been bothering me," says he. "I suppose he'll be buried in Drumdirly here?"

"I would think it," says I.

"I'd give her the money to take him to Castledoor where he comes from," says he. "It's twenty miles away, but I wouldn't grudge the expense. She'd be more mine then when we came to lie down at the last."

"You haven't got her yet, remember that," says I. "But she was married to him in Drumdirly church, and to Drumdirly she'll bring him, you may swear."

"I've been thinking that, too," he says. "It's hard on me,

that'll be resting there as well. I'd like to have had her all to myself. But I suppose I'll have to put up with it.—Tell me," says he, "would it hurt her feelings or maybe choke her off me if I tolled the bell when he was being buried?"

"So long as you didn't break into a wedding peal," says I. But he never smiled.

"She might like me to ring the knell," says he. "She might think I was showing a delicate respect to the dead."

"If I were you I'd give the job to Tompkins's son," says I.

He looked at me very dubious, and I could see that he was unwilling to give up his notion. Then he nodded his head.

"You're right," says he. "I'll do that. I'm only human, after all; and every pull I took at the rope I'd be throwing a sod on him and tramping it down hard. The thought might come into her mind."

"You can let the young fellow ring the joy-bells at your wedding," says I, "for a treat."

He did ring them. For she married John, as anybody would have known who knows women at all. And she earned him, and all the peace and rest and easy circumstances she got with him. She nursed her first husband as no paid woman *could* have nursed him, and she looked after the farm just as before, and kept trouble and anxiety from his dying bed. He did her one good turn, that she was too kindly-natured to know; he was so thankless that he must have eased John's way for him, later, forbye making a saint of her to John. And a saint she was. She gave her life for her bad bargain; for she sucked in the poison of the consumption that took her off before her time.

John and she were happy together. He fussed after her too much, but now she was ready to be fussed after. He would have spoiled or scunnered any other woman, or herself earlier. But she had earned the right to be spoiled. It did her no harm. She laughed at him, before his face, and a little behind his back; but she would let nobody else do it, except perhaps me, that knew all.

As for John, he nearly kneeled down before her, partly because of herself and partly because of the injustice he had done her long ago. In the end she became nearly as fond of him as she was of the first man. And she was just as good and kind and unselfish to John. No matter how he vexed her—and his old-maidish ways would have angered a real saint—she never threw up to him the trick he had played her about the bell-ringing. It was the one fear of John's life that she would.

When the sickness was on her, and she knew beyond doubt what it was, she tried to persuade him to let her go to a Sanatorium. But he wouldn't even listen. No, he said. He wasn't afraid. It wasn't smitting with people of his age. Anyway, she had been willing to risk her life for the first man, and he would do no less for her. She called me in to try and persuade him, but it was no use. She lay back on the pillow at last, and gave in.

"I don't know why everybody's so good to me, Sandy," she says. "For I can't be much use, to have had two such men and not to have raised a family for them."

She smiled on John as she said it; and, though you'll think it a queer comparison, no dog ever bestowed on a human being a look of such love and longing and gratitude as I saw in John's eyes.

She was buried beside her first husband in Drumdirly churchyard. It was her wish, and she made me promise to tell John, though I'd rather have lost the sale of a two-hundred-acre farm than do the job.

"I'm going to see him," says she. "The good in him will still be there, and the bad will surely be forgiven, when I could forgive it without a thought. I'll keep the second marriage to myself till John comes. There's no marrying or giving in marriage in the grave; and the three of us will be friends together—I hope," says she. There came the smallest wee bit of lightening in her face as she spoke; very near a smile. She was a woman of a great heart.

God forgive me—for I couldn't think she was dying—I was going to ask her which of the two she would choose if she had to make a pick. But, when I looked at her, all at once death was in her face; and I called out on John and ran away.

Head or Harp

I WAS passing Sandy Morrison the auctioneer's premises one day when he was seeing a friend or client off; and he gazed after the man so long and with such apparently mingled feelings that I too looked hard at the fellow as he went past me. He was to all appearance a middle-aged farmer, a sober-looking, well set-up man, dressed more carefully than is usual with his class. From the finicky way he picked his steps so as to keep his shoes free of mud, I took him to be a precise person, probably a bachelor.

"A cautious bird that, Sandy?" said I.

"You never can tell," answered Sandy. "I've known him play pitch an' toss when he was a younger man."

"Not for much money?" I said.

"For more than you'd think," returned Sandy, raising one hand for silence, and continuing to follow the man closely with his eyes. Then he relaxed.

"A year or two ago," he said, "I told you a story about a halfpenny. I'm only killing time at the moment. Come into my office, an' I'll tell you a story about a penny."

. . . . .

It began with a courting match between two people that got on better with each other than with anybody else, but just wanted the jag of love to drive them together for good—or bad. At the time I'm going to talk about, the man held some thirty-five acres of a farm a mile or so out of this town; rich land, but not enough of it; for he was a pushing, greedy farmer, an' hadn't sufficient elbow-room. The girl had a good job up the street here at McGompsey's the builders, an' would inherit sixty or seventy acres away down in the south when an uncle of hers died. She was certain to get this; for the reversion of it was left to her in her grandfather's will. The uncle, though he was a bachelor, wouldn't have her there while he was alive. He liked her well enough, an' there had never been a cross word between the two of them; but he thought she was too fond of her own way.

James Linchahan—that's him that's gone down the road there—an' she, an' I, were all of an age. We bumped up against one another a good deal at the wee parties there used to be in those days when we were able to make our own amusement; singing-parties, an' dancing-parties, an' even sitting round a hearthside, telling stories an' asking riddles, an' the like. In the end we three became good friends. But I was always the odd man out. When either of them wanted to talk about anything that they wished the other not to know about, they came to me; an' I used to give them what I thought was good advice, though even in those days I wasn't conceited enough to think there was much chance of them taking it.

But the pair were drawing nearer to each other; there was no doubt of that. Our little society of three was beginning to split up into two an' one, even at parties. People took notice of it in the end. When there was a bit of a carpet-hop, no young man of any discretion would ask Sarah to be his partner until James Linchahan had had his chance at her. An' when there would be a regular, invited dance at some biggish farmer's house in the countryside, an' Tommy Dickson's two old shandrydans of carriages were called into use, James and Sarah would now an' then fill one of them by themselves, going or coming, or maybe both ways.

It had come to the time when folk were beginning to ask each other, "What's holding them back?" But I knew what it was, though I kept my mouth shut. Being the cautious couple they were, an' both very independent-minded, they had sat down to think out, and in cold blood, what—say as you like—is far better done in hot. Both came to me in the end; or maybe, in troth, I picked it out of them, for I've a bit of a gift in that direction.

"If I ask her, an' she takes me," said James, in his dubious way, "I might have to go off to her farm in the south when her uncle dies, an' live there with her all the time."

"You couldn't very well carry on the marrying business by telegraph," says I, "unless there's been some improvement brought in, meanwhile."

"An' I'd have no independent life of my own at all," says he, paying no attention to me. "I'd be clean under her thumb."

"Oh, well, maybe she'd be poking you in the ribs with it," says I. But I was wasting my breath.

"Do you want the girl, or do you not?" says I at last. For I was getting tired of his shugglety-shooing backwards an' forwards.

"It's a toss-up with me," says he; "that's the truth. I want her—an' I want nobody."

"Well, *toss up*," says I. "I've seen you toss up about near as important things before now. An' didn't you toss the winner of the Grand National last year an' make fifteen pounds?"

It was curious; but it was true. Behind all his caution an' his Presbyterian upbringing, James, when he was clean beat about making up his mind, had a sneaking notion of a gamble, an' thought he was lucky in one. I've seen him decide whether a day was going to rain or to dry up because three crows flew over the barn roof instead of two.

But this time he shook his head.

"No," he said. "Marriage is a shocking serious thing. I must commit it of my own free will an' inclination, or not at all."

"Listen, then," says I. "There's a dance being held at McCrum's of Liskeel, over the engagement of his youngest daughter to Sam Toner. The whole three of us will be asked. Fetch Sarah there an' back in one of Dickson's old buses—I'll make my own arrangements—an' if, between food an' drink (for it's not a teetotal house) an' dancing—an' Sarah herself, you don't throw your arm round her on the way home an' pop the question, then give her up for good, an' she'll be well rid of a skim-milk-blooded sheep."

He sat up on the chair an' smacked his knee.

"Bedambut," says he, "I will—if I don't change my mind, that is."

McCrum's dance came an' went; an' all had shaped well at it, so far as I could see. At the beginning of the night

James had gone bald-headed for Sarah. If any other man seemed to want her, James as good as shoved him out of his way. Three times out of four he danced with her. Everybody in the room thought the affair was as good as settled, even myself; an' I went out to the grounds with a good-looking slip of a girl from that part of the country an' caught James's disease without James's caution.

When I got back to the dancing-room my first look was for James an' Sarah. They didn't seem just as keen on each other as before. I thought once or twice I could see James checking his step as he made towards her when the piano started, as if it had come into his head that things were moving faster than he was just ready for. An' once I saw Sarah certainly turn away an' hide behind somebody else when she saw James making in her direction. But I took no notice of this bit of manœuvring.

"After all," I said to myself, "a couple of courting sparrows'll do the same in a bush. Wait till the pair of them are going home in the carriage together."

I did wait; an' the next day at dinner-time in comes James to me. He was in very poor heart.

"Well?" I asked him; though I could see for myself.

"No luck," says he. "The divil's in all weemin."

"Tell me about it," says I. "Just as it happened."

"All seemed to go right at the start," said he. "When the dancing was over she came out of the dressing-room to meet me as we had arranged, an' I could see that though she had her out-of-door coat on her she had dolled herself up a bit, an' fixed her hair. She put her hand on my arm as we went to the covered car, a thing she had never done before, an' it gave me a kind of queer feeling *I'd* never got before, either, as she maybe intended.

"An' then I made a mistake. I may tell you I always found a girl handier lying in my left arm than in my right. When I saw the way the horse was facing I made to get into the carriage first; an' I could feel by the way Sarah stiffened up that she didn't like it. She's a very nice girl in many ways, an' can milk a cow an' make butter as if she never had a pen in her hand; but she's a bit inclined to think that nobody in the world can do anything right but herself. Her an' I had had several wee tussles over me wanting to be boss, as she put it.

"However, the thing blew over once the car started. Bit by bit the stiffness went out of her backbone. The calf of her leg pressed just what you'd know again mine, an' began to feel warmer an' warmer. Slowly I slipped my arm round her, an' closer she came. An' then all at once her body turned to indian-rubber, an' she laid her head on my shoulder an' nuzzled into my neck.

"It was what I had been hoping for; but all the same it came on me with a kind of shock. Like lightning the thought flashed through me: '*Now* you've dont it, my lad. This is the end of you're carrying-on round the countryside.' I couldn't stop myself, but drew away just what you'd know. An', d——n it all, she stuck a pin in me!

"I gave a start an' a yelp, an' pulled from her.

" 'What is it?' she says, all taken aback, by the way. 'What's wrong?'

" 'It was a pin,' says I, sucking in my breath with the pain. 'Oh-h; it was a corker-pin.'

" 'I'm sorry, Jim,' says she, an' you'd have thought she meant it. 'It must have been the one in my outside coat collar.'

"She fissled at her neck, an' then drew nearer me again; but I hadn't come to myself yet, an' I fought for time.

" 'Maybe we were sitting too close,' says I, an' could have bitten the tongue off myself. But the harm was done, if it *was* harm. D——n the finger she would let me lay on her at all, after that. What do you think about it, Sandy? An' what do you think *she* thinks about it?"

"Yes," said I, "*that's* what matters. I'll tell you something, an' let you make up your own mind. She was in with me this morning already."

He paused for a moment, looking at me between anxious an' cautious.

"Did she say anything about last night?" he asked me.

"She told me all about it," said I; "or as much as a nice girl could tell with decency. I think the pin was an accident, James."

"Did she say anything about *me*?" asked James.

"She did," said I. " 'What a fool he was'," she said.

"What a fool *I* was, or what a fool *she* was?" he asked me.

"What a fool *you* were," I answered. "Think it over; an' not too long."

An' the next morning he came in to tell me that Sarah's uncle was dead, an' she going away down the country by the evening train. I could see that he was near out of his mind with trying to make up his mind.

"What'll I do, at all at all?" he asked me.

"What'll you *do*?" I asked him, vexed with the fool. "Go away down to her uncle's place with her, a lonely girl now, with her heart soft. Ask her in the train, before the young fellows get wind of her down there; for now that the farm is hers, every farming man, young or old, single or widower, in the district will be asking her as she comes back from the funeral, or, in troth, maybe at the graveside."

"I suppose I wouldn't have a day or two to think?" says he in desperation. For he knew I was right.

"If you go on shilly-shallying like that you'll just be in time to miss the train," says I.

But he looked as if the train would have time to arrive at the uncle's wake, an' him not in it.

"She'd want me to sell my own farm here, an' live with her," says he; "an' I'd never get calling my soul my own. Should I bother about her at all?"

I put my hand in my pocket an' pulled out a penny.

"Here," I said, "if you leave the deciding to yourself you'll put it off till she's nursing some plucky fellow's grand-children. Do what I'm going to tell you. Away down to the wee hiding-place among the trees by the river, where we used to play pitch an' toss when we were all boys together—you were always lucky there, or thought you were—an' toss head or harp whether you'll propose to her or not. Now go on," I said, as he stood looking at me, open-mouthed.

"An' if things turn out badly you can always blame it on Providence."

He thought a minute or two more, an' then put out his hand an' took my penny.

"I was always lucky down there, sure enough," he said. "D'ye mind the fifteen pounds? Bedambut, I'll do it!"

Off he went, half a dozen steps an' a consider; an' I turned to do a bit of work, but couldn't for wondering how his gamble would turn out. In ten minutes or a quarter of an hour he came back.

"Well?" I asked him.

He hesitated a trifle before he answered me.

"Nothing settled yet," says he. "The penny fell on its edge an' ran in among some big stones."

"Did you not go to look for it?" said I.

"I did not," said he. "There's no time, if I'm going to travel in the train along with her. I'll maybe miss her as it is; an' I'm not too sure that I wouldn't just as soon do that."

He stood thinking for a minute or two, saying nothing more, an' waiting for a prod from me, as I very well knew. Then he gave me up in despair.

"Listen, Sandy," says he. "I'll go off in the train with her this evening, an' commit myself to nothing, but just keep the door on the jar without shutting myself in or out. When I'm gone do you look for the penny; an', if you find it, telegraph me in the morning : Head or Harp. As the penny has fallen, so will I stand or fall. Will you do that for me?"

"I will," says I; "but if she ever hears about it she'll pour boiling water on you. Away with you!"

Now I was a busy man even then, an' had neither time nor inclination to go looking for pennies, especially as it was drawing on to dusk an' I might have to finish the search with a lantern an' be found out an' become the laughing-stock of the whole town. Being human, I very soon persuaded myself that, anyway, I would be doing wrong to place a decent man's happiness on the turn of a coin, an' that the proper thing to do would be to make up my mind, after due consideration, what would be better for the happiness of the pair of them.

I trotted James an' Sarah up an' down before me like horses at a fair. They kept step with each other; an' at that moment I was inclined to think well, myself, of double harness.

Next morning I walked across to the post office an' wired to James the one word: "Head." The next news of him I heard was that he was troth-plighted to Sarah. Nothing at all had been said between James an' me in the meantime about the penny. I was beginning to feel a bit ashamed of my share in the transaction; an' I think he was waiting for me to speak. There was only the one thing for me to do now.

As we walked to the church together on the morning of the wedding day, I told him I had gone an' looked for the penny, an' had found it between two stones; an' it was a head beyond doubt.

The news gave him great heartening, I could see; an' the proof is that, later on, when he was living with his wife on her farm, an' she was pressing him to sell his own farm which he had stuck to in spite of her, he came to consult me.

"I suppose I should sell, Sandy?" he asked me, hesitating as usual, an' still more anxious about his independence than I quite liked. "I'll be in her hands with a vengeance then, mind you."

"Sell," I said. "A man's happiness is in his wife's hands, anyway. If she's not actually with him she can always get at him."

He looked down at the ground, wetting his lips one with the other.

"You stick to it that the penny was head?" says he.

The worst of telling a lie is that it rears a whole family.

"It was head," I answered him.

"I'll sell," says he. An' he kept his word.

Now, how his marriage turned out I never knew. Sometimes I was afraid it hadn't been a success; for after he'd sold his own little farm he never came back to the town here to see me, nor sent me a scrape all those years. My conscience used to trouble me more than an auctioneer's conscience is supposed to do. An' when he was here to-day, as you saw, about a wee bit of property that had been left him, I asked him plump an' plain if his marriage had turned out well. He fenced with me, as I might have known he would.

"How could it have turned out badly," he said at the last, "if the penny was a head?"

Then all at once I cleared my conscience, an' told him I'd never seen the penny at all, had never even searched for it.

He took it better than I expected; just looked at me hard for a minit, wagged his head up an' down, as much as to say: "What better could I expect?" an' turned an' walked off to the station. "So I'll never know, now," said Sandy; "but what odds?"

I could see that he wasn't altogether satisfied; an' I had become interested in the question now, myself.

"You don't think he would have gone to look for the penny on his way to the train?" I asked Sandy.

"After all this time?" said Sandy. "Not him!"

But I had aroused Sandy's curiosity.

"I'll tell you what we'll do," he said. "The gambling-ground got damp an' unpleasant as the years went on. Nobody ever goes near it. James's train be gone shortly. We'll go an' look, then, ourselves. The penny might be there yet."

An', foolish an' all as it sounds, go we did.

We walked up an' down the deserted plot, kicking away the weeds and peering between the stones. Suddenly Sandy gripped my arm and pointed with his other hand to the impression of a man's boot in the soft ground. It was fresh, beyond doubt.

"James's big feet for a pound!" he said.

"If he has found the penny, won't he have taken it with him?" said I.

"Sure to," Sandy answered, vexedly.

But he still continued to scan the ground in a half-hearted way. All at once he stooped, then stood up and beckoned to me, his face alive with half-incredulous mirth. I hastened over. There, in the shadow of a moss-covered stone, lay, not a penny, but two halfpence, pocket-clean. One of them was head, the other harp. Sandy picked the two up and looked at them soberly as they lay in his palm. Then the wisdom of half a lifetime of auctioneering and matrimony spoke by his mouth:

"The divil moan him," he said. "What better did you or I do?"

The Picture

MY story goes back said my friend Sandy Morrison, the auctioneer, to the time when weemin, old an' young, covered themselves from head to heel; an' some, even young ones of them, wore flannel petticoats in the winter. But that time was near over; an' the first hints of this day of ours was beginning to dawn, when the more you take off a girl going to a party the more you're dressing her up.

Roger Harber an' his brother Harry started the new system in our town. Both had served their time to fancy drapery in Belfast, because both thought little of farming. When their father, a widower, died, the farm was sold, an' the price divided between the brothers. Being brought up near Bally-gullion, they made up their minds to start a drapery business in the town, on up-to-date lines. Up-to-date it was; an' a year or two ahead of the times, to satisfy Harry, who was a bit sportier than Roger. I'll admit there was plain respectable clothes somewhere at the back of the shop premises; but the bulk of the stock was made up of shiftings of the high and low-water mark, an' wee mimity decorations that caught your eye so strong that you forgot for a minit to look at the figure they were hung-on. Clean "gardening of Eden," my wife called it; an' went to a good deal of trouble to see that I didn't play the divil there, now an' again, with some of her young female friends.

But Roger didn't go quite so far as Harry in his up-to-date notions of shopping. His wife threatened to leave him if he did. The brothers fell-out with each other over the affair, an' couldn't be reconciled; an' in the end, dropping the partnership they had begun with, they started two separate shops; Roger's fancy enough; but Harry's, for those days, fairly outrageous.

The division of the brothers split the town, or the weemin section of it, anyway. Young weemin an' girls clustered round Harry's windows—when their elders weren't about. Middle-aged weemin walked past, but turned on their heels for a skelly; an' sometimes half walked-past, an' then whipped into the shop like a hunted rabbit into its hole. But the two shops were one too many, or near that. An' the competition between them was ferocious. It was hard to be quite sure which was doing the better. There was a lot of mixed buying by old an' young, an' swopping carried-on afterwards. Young weemin were seen buying in Harry's shop what was purty flighty, even for them; an' later-on the old weemin cronies would take note that it was the girls' mothers were wearing the stuffs. An' many a husband didn't know of his wife's new youngness of heart till he saw it glittering down the road on the arm furthest away from him.

Competition between the two shops grew worse an' worse; an' the two young proprietors were driven to all sorts of attempts to get business. But a body like myself, the nature of whose own business brought him into touch with nearly all that was going on in the town, knew that both of the pair were having a tough struggle to make ends meet; though Harry, being a bachelor an' not bad-looking, was getting his nose a bit in front of the brother. An' I needn't tell you that the pair weren't thinking very highly of each other, an' were barely on speaking terms.

Now, in my job as an auctioneer, it behoves a body to know nearly everything that's going on in the neighbourhood; an' a wee bit of harmless gossip, or a funny wee tale, may do a good deal towards putting an auction-crowd in good bidding humour. So anything new or out of the ordinary usually brings me snooking round for information. There came to my ears the fact that a young painter-fellow had got leave to occupy an' old mud-an'-thatch cottage up in the hills, a few miles out of the town, an' was going to stay there a while, painting the countryside. Of course that was into *my* hand—pictures to be sold; an' another little connection with the outside world. So I made an expedition out to him one day; an' we liked each other, an' became friends.

But he wasn't the only pebble on the beach. His temporary cottage was three-roomed. To keep house for him while he painted the district, he had brought with him an elderly woman, with a young daughter say about eighteen; an' if I'd been the painter I'd have let the countryside alone, an' painted nothing but that young lassie for the rest of my life; or this was my first notion of her, anyway. Hair that fairly burned on her head, a figure like a sapling willow-branch, an' an eye that could have been left to do all her talking for her; an', as it was, said a lot of things about her that she'd have maybe done better to keep to herself. Even the very old working-man who carried water to the cottage was lifted out of himself, an' said to me that "a couple of drops of blood from them rosy lips would paint a cart." Chorley, the artist, hadn't painted her yet, I found out later. He was keeping her for the latter end of his meditated show; an' I think had planted her an' the mother up on that desolate hillside because he didn't want any painter in Belfast to get hold of her first.

I was a wee bit more attracted myself than my wife would have liked, an' visited my friend the artist maybe oftener than was necessary. An' then a fancy notion came into my head: Why not, when Chorley the painter was done with her, get Roger Harber to take her into his shop as a counter hand? There wasn't a stitch of clothing or decoration in his whole premises but would look worth twice its present price with her handling them. Even the very fittings of the shop would seem better; for folks wouldn't be looking at them. Weemin-folk, old an' young, would hate the sight of her; but they would come in to look, an' then would buy; an' with a few special male knick-knacks in the line of ties an' breast-pins left lying about, young men would have an excuse to go back an' look at the lassie after they left their own lass home. The girl was a trump card for a smallish country-town like ours. She mightn't be just up to Belfast style in manner an' dress an' decoration; but my private notion was that she'd put Harry out of business within six months. An' I didn't care whether she did or not; for Harry was an impudent pup; an', besides that, Roger was married, an' had a young family to rear.

I told my notion to the artist. How long would he want to keep the girl himself, painting her, I asked him; an' did he think she would take a job in our town when he was done with her?

He took a while to think; an' decided that he'd be done with her in about a fortnight. The countryside he was as good as over-with. All he meant to do now, bar a few finishing-off jobs on scenery and sketches, would take little time. But before he quitted that part of the world he was going to paint a portrait of the girl. She wasn't, maybe, just the raving beauty these simple country folk deemed her; but he was going to paint an oil colour of her that would make her worth looking-at. He had sketched her in bits, an' with all sorts of mediums: water-colour an' chalk, an' crayons, an' lead pencil; but this time he'd tackle her full length in oils, standing upright, an' turning peoples' heads like spinning-tops. He was all het-up about it; an' in troth I paid little heed to him; for he was given that way before he did a piece of work; an' the result didn't always come up to his notion of himself.

Let *me* talk to the girl, he said; and then *he* would talk to her. He might want her again, an' he didn't want the price pushed too high.

There was little or no trouble fixing up the engagement. Be*at*rice, as the mother called her, would be let go to Roger, as a counter-hand, for the fifteen shillings a week the artist had been paying her, if digs could be found for her as well, an' she would promise to write to her mother once a fortnight at the least, an' to be a good girl. I fetched Roger to see the girl—for I knew she would stick in his wife's throat—an' all was as good as settled. Meantime, the artist would clear-off his odd jobs, an' fall-to on the painting of her, as soon as he could get some extra fancy clothes for her from Belfast.

"Wait till you see her when I'm done with her," says he to me, privately. "Wait till I clean her up a bit, an' do her hair—for *I* know how, I may tell you—an' lower an' raise the high-water mark of some of her clothing; an' she'll surprise you. Up till the present I've been letting her exist in her dirt an' her dishables, as they call them hereabouts; for I don't want some other wandering artist like myself to see her; but now I'll let the sun shine on her, an' her shine back. Don't you come near me till I send for you when the job's finished; an', when you do come, you'll open your eyes."

Now, I'm no artist; but in the course of my job as an auctioneer I've put a good many pictures through my hands; an' looking at Be*at*rice when Chorley was finished with her, I was fair bowled-out. If I might put it that way, he had just taken the wrappings off her, an' let the real girl turn from a bud into a flower: hair, eyes, figure, smile, notion of herself—an' the last not least. She had seen herself with another body's eyes for the first time, an' now she was showing what she thought of herself; an' mind you, it wasn't too little.

I nearly ran home to the town to fetch Roger, an', when I told him he'd put his brother Harry out of business in three months, he wasn't maybe as vexed as a brother should have been.

But we got a gunk from the new Be*at*rice. She wasn't going to sell her hen on a rainy day. A couple of good looks at her picture, an' she wouldn't go to Roger short of twenty-five bob a week, an' her keep!

An' Roger wouldn't pay it. He couldn't afford it, in the first place; for he was just holding-on with his toe-nails as things were. An', if he'd been willing to take the risk, his wife wouldn't have let him. I knew his wife, a jealous wee she-cat; an' I knew the second reason was the stronger. For all I an' the artist could say, he wouldn't give-in. The bargain was off; an' the mother an' her girl left a day or two before the artist did, an' went back to their home.

But the news of the picture had leaked out round about the cottage district where the artist had been working; an' who should get word of it but Harry Harber; an' being a bachelor, an' a livelier bird than his brother, he made a special expedition up the hills, to see for himself.

The mother an' her girl were gone the day before; but the picture was there, still unpacked. An' Harry fell for it, clean-work; not only as a healthy young fellow, but as a cute business-man. His own affairs, owing to price-cutting against his brother, were pretty desperate too. Call it rash or call it plucky; but he borrowed money on his shop, with a little assistance from me—for I was a trifle vexed with Roger—an' the next thing was that, propped-up on the top of the glass-case in Harry's shop where all the female fancies of brooches an' rings an' neck-chains were displayed, was the artist's picture of Be*at*rice, framed an' glazed.

An' dammit, she had risen above herself; a man-trap, a looking-glass for a man to see what he wanted, an' for a girl to see how she could learn to give it to him. The artist was no miss, for a not very celebrated provincial painter; but this time he had risen into the Academy line for once in his life.

An' Be*at*rice just conquered the town. Big an' wee, well-to-do an' poor, bowed down before her image as if it was herself—haunted the shop an' bought. Mothers brought in their daughters, an' some few of them their husbands; an' husbands came of themselves; an' young men by the score, an' winked at each other sideways as they went off, the way young men *do* wink about a nifty bit of female flesh. They came in so often on the excuse of wanting cigarettes that in the end Harry took out a tobacco-licence an' did a roaring trade in smokes. The picture was so lifelike a rendering of a living breathing good-looking young woman, that folk mistook it sometimes for life itself. Harry told me that a constable of the police lifted his cap the first time he caught

6

a glimpse of it; an' then was going to lift Harry himself for laughing at him. An' Barney Tillick, coming in, with a sup on him, to buy tobacco, fell in love with it, an' trying to kiss it, pitched forward on the top of the glass case an' smashed that to atoms. In the end Be*at*rice's picture had become one of the citizens of the town; an' Roger an' his wife were nearly out of their minds. Trade was leaving them faster every day. Roger lowered his prices, but it only meant that he was losing more money.

All this time, I had been mad with him for not taking my advice an' hiring Be*at*rice when she'd finished with her artist friend. But at last he came to me in despair. We had a talk. I took pity on him, an' went up to Harry's shop, bought a packet of cigarettes an' had a good look at Be*at*rice's picture. The more I looked at it the better I liked it, an' the less I thought of Roger's chance. "He's done," said I to myself. "He can't conquer that." An' then a thing happened that I thought nothing of at the moment. Walking up the street I ran into Gostering Pete, the chief scandal-monger of the town, an' the second-greatest "soak." I couldn't escape him, or his cute eye an' mind.

"You were in looking at Be*at*rice a while ago, I saw," says he. "Wonderful, isn't she?"

"Wonderful indeed," says I. "You'd think she was a living-being."

"She would make a bit of stir in this town if she came alive," says he.

"She certainly would," I answered him; an' passed on, smiling at the thought.

It wasn't more than a week after when I met the fellow again.

"Sa-Sandy," says he, "do you believe in ghosts?"

His voice sounded all disturbed an' stammery. I stared at him.

"You look as if you'd seen one," said I.

"Am I drunk," says he, "three hours before my usual time? If I'm not, I've seen a ghost.—Listen to me," says he, putting out a hand. "As true as death that picture in Harry

Harber's shop met me in the street two minutes ago, smiled at me an' went past without speaking."

"Drink stays a long while in a man's system," says I. "Were you in Martin Toney's pub as usual, last night?"

"No," says he; "but I'm going there now. Either that or to the lunatic asylum.—I will tell you I'm just after meeting Harry Harber's girl-picture in the street!"

I looked at him closer; an' I could see he was real shaken.

"It's a sore thing, this whiskey," said I to myself.—"Come up to Harry's," I said to him, "an' we'll see is the picture still there."

Off we went, him clinging to my arm, an' shivering.

"Some rascal has slipped out the picture while Harry is at his dinner, an' has set it up against a wall," thinks I. Then another thought came to me. I made old Pete turn past *Roger's* shop door on our way. An' there in the doorway, who was standing but Be*at*rice, in the flesh, smiling at me till she, an' the notion she'd got of her new self, near filled the frame of the door.

It was a new Be*at*rice, I very soon saw. The divil a word she said to me, good or bad, but threw her arms round me an' kissed me like a full brush kissing canvas.

"It's me myself," says she, drawing back a step. "Roger" —none of your "Master" Rogers, mark you—"has engaged me to shout down my picture. "He's paying me two pounds a week; an' I'm worth double that to him already, an' will be more when I get my feet under me. I'll redd out the trade from *Harry's* shop till he'll have to go down on his knees to me to *get* me myself, an' pay me double. Less than three pounds a week I'll not take, anyway. An' if he doesn't give me that, Roger here will—provided his wife doesn't hunt me——" says she, in an afterthought.

The wife didn't; though I'm sure she wanted to. Be*at*rice didn't get the three pounds a week; but she must have got the most of it, an' been worth near double.

I needn't tell you what stir an' diversion the contest riz in the town. For more than a while Be*at*rice an' her picture fought it out in the two spendthrift shops, as folk called them. Spendthrift they were, an' spendthrifts they made; Roger an' Harry buying dear an' selling cheap; dress an' undress; hats that the very crows took fright at, an' shoes that near shaped a girl's feet into semicircles, with the points digging-up the worms. As for ear-rings an' brooches, the younger weemin had as much imitation gold and jewels hanging on them as set some of them jingling like a tinker's cart.

But, riding an' shining above it all, was the contest between Roger an' Harry, an' between Be*at*rice herself, an' the picture of her. Standing alone, the picture might have worn Be*at*rice down or taken her all her time to fight it; but Be*at*rice had a tongue as well; an' every day got cleverer at managing it. Even Mrs. Roger was afraid of it; an' now an' then laughed at it near as hearty as the hated Be*at*rice. Very soon Be*at*rice's sayings were dancing in the same ring with her looks. The 'crack' in the town was that Roger had won, an' that Harry might shut up shop, anytime.

An' Harry began to think that, himself. I could see it in him, an' hear it in his voice when he spoke about the contest to me, as he sometimes did. Even simple kindly Roger was satisfied of that, an' began to crow a trifle; an' his wife openly. Public opinion among the groups had agreed with them, an' folk were beginning to deal more in his shop, an' avoid Harry's more an' more, except to look for sacrifice bargains.

Harry was near wild with distress an' rage; but there was pluck in him.

"I won't give in," he said to me. (For I had begun to turn a trifle more towards his side now that he was getting the worst of things.) "I'll offer her *five* pound a week, should it break me. D——n it," he says, "her company would be worth that to me, forbye her work altogether."

I kept my eyes an' ears open; for I felt something was going to happen. But I misdoubted whether Harry would be able to incur that amount of expense an' keep solvent, even if it *did* tempt Be*at*rice. I heard little or nothing of it all for a wheen of weeks. I'd kept away from Roger's as much as possible; for though I still liked the man, his wife was becoming clean insufferable with triumph as her husband's takings in the shop crept up.

Everything went on as before; Be*at*rice filling all eyes, an' Roger inching-in on Harry's business every day. An' then, one evening, when I could hold out no longer, an' was sitting with Mr. and Mrs. Roger in their parlour (for there'd been nothing to be got out of Harry) a great big square brown-paper-covered parcel was brought in by a messenger-boy, an' with it a closed envelope. I looked hard at the oddity of the size and shape of the parcel, an' all at once I bethought me of what it was; for, as you know already, I'd been accustomed, at one time, to haunt Chorley the painter's cottage in the hills.

"*In the name of goodness!*" said I to myself; an' stopped, as Roger began to pull off the brown paper.

I was right. It was Chorley's picture of Be*at*rice. An', when Roger read out the sheet of writing-paper, here was an invitation to the marriage of her an' Harry! Be*at*rice, it rubbed in, very unnecessarily, would not be coming back to Roger's shop.

There was dead silence as Roger laid the letter down. When he turned to his missus his face was white.

"We're done, Mem," he grinds out. "We can't stand against Be*at*rice herself." He lifted the picture. "I may put my foot through this thing that he has sent us in mockery."

But Mrs. Roger, though she was a jealous wife, was no dunce.

"Do nothing of the sort," says she. "Did you never hear of the old saying: '*Look at me now, an' the day you got me*'? We'll hold her picture, if we can, for five or six years, till we see what has happened to *her*."

The husband looked at his wife, an' his face creased into a smile.

"Bedambut!" says he, an' took up the picture in his arms. "This lassie is going back on a glass-case again!"

. . . . .

"But which of the brothers won in the end?" I asked Sandy, impatiently.

"If you walk up a certain street in this wee town," answered my friend, Mr. Morrison, "you'll come on a respectable-looking draper's shop with the name 'Roger Harber' on the sign-board. There's no other Harber in business in the town, now."

Dangerous Documents

WHEN what we called the Troubled Times came to the South of Ireland, said Mr. Patrick Murphy, people began to sleep very uneasy at night, even in the North, especially if they lived in the country, or on the outside edge of a country town. For when they lay down at night they never knew but they might have to walk straight to the chuchyard when they got up, an' stay there for good. Wee Mr. Anthony, the solicitor, being the peppery wee man he was, got into a terrible pucker about it all, an' at an early stage, as he had a habit of doing, sent for me to advise him, so that if anything went wrong he would have somebody to blame it on.

"I know what's wrong with him," says I to my wife Molly, "as well as if I was inside him. He's afraid the authorities will want to take his gun and ammunition from him, while this fuss is on; an' they might nearly as well take away his life."

"They'd cause very little bloodshed of man or beast by leaving them both with him," says Molly.

"Ay, but somebody might get the gun off him in the night-time, an' shoot *him*, Molly," says I. "I'd better call up at the house, an' see what he's up to."

When I went into his study I found him still in a pucker.

"What the devil," says he, fixing me with his eye-glass as if I was the whole cause of the trouble, "what the devil are we going to do about these rascals who are going round at night, waking up decent law-abiding folk, and searching their houses? And, damme, the Government-men are the worst of the two; for *they* can take their time about the job, and the other fellows are in a hurry."

"You'd better get rid of your gun an' ammunition, Mr. Anthony," says I. "If the *law* isn't after you on account of them, some of the lawless *will* be."

Mr. Anthony wasn't as much put about as I expected.

"They won't take the trouble," says he, very off-hand. "I doubt if you could kill a policeman with Number-Three shot; though I've sometimes wanted to try, when they were giving evidence against my clients. Never mind about the gun and cartridges. It's my private and confidential papers I'm thinking about.—Listen to me, Pat: Why am I everybody's friend in Ballygullion, from the Hastings's of the Hall to the town idiot? Why does everybody smile at me as if I was a fine day, and touch their hats, and tell me where there is a covey of partridges to be found; even, blast them, when there isn't. Why do women, old and young, pull me into dark corners as if I was their sweetheart, and give me ties and scarf-pins till I look like an Autumn Sale? I'll tell you; it's because I know so much about everybody's private affairs—from a hammer-toe to a miscarriage—that, if I let my tongue wag, the whole grown-up inhabitants of the town might light out for Australia."

"You must have a great grip of your tongue, Mr. Anthony," says I. "I never heard of you letting any of the stuff loose."

"Have you, now?" says Mr. Anthony, all pleased. "Now, have you, Pat?—But all the more reason for keeping my lips still locked. Damme, if some of these patriot fellows began to read some of my confidential letters, they'd sit down on a ditch-side an' put off the freeing of Ireland for another hundred years! But come out to the back-garden, and I'll show you where I'm going to hide this inflammable matter. You wouldn't guess it in another *two* hundred years; and even if you were looking at it you wouldn't be able to see it before your very eyes. Don't let the housekeeper take notice of us," says he, lowering his voice as we walked past the kitchen door. "She's as inquisitive as a hungry hen in a stable-yard.—What do you think of *that*?" says he, pulling me up suddenly under the window of his bedroom. An' here, lying face downward on the ground, was a big stone kitchen-sink, say three feet by four. It was made of granite, not less than an inch-an'-a-half thick; an' must have weighed above three hundred-weight.

"The man who could pick that up with his finger an' thumb an' balance it on his nose," says I, "is wasting his time, either as a patriot or a policeman. He'd be worth fifty pound a week on the Halls. But how will you get the papers *in*; an' then how the divil will you come at them when you want them?"

"Aha!" says Mr. Anthony, putting his finger to his nose. "Wait and you'll see something.—Can you eat eggs?" he puts in, unexpected.

"If they've a shell on them like that," says I, looking at the granite sink, "I may as well say I'm not going to try."

"They're not in there, you old fool," says Mr. Anthony. "I'm going to send my housekeeper to the grocer's for them, for our supper. I don't want to let her know too much about this apparatus of mine.—Stay here a minute or two. I have to go up to my room, as well."

An' off he went, leaving me taking a deal more notice of the sink than the sink was taking of me. But I could make little of it, beyond spotting that, in addition to having it lying face down, Mr. Anthony had the outlet-hole, that once led into the drain-pipe, plugged with metal. There was no gossip going to escape that way, anyhow.

When he came down from his room he had a bundle of light strong chain in his arms. He threw it down beside his dog, an' scared the seven senses out of him.

"D——n the brute," says he, very hasty, looking after him as he belted down the garden path; "did he think I was carrying sausages?—Now, pay attention, Pat. My bedroom window is straight-above. Do you stay here. I'll go upstairs again and lower this chain to you. Fit these four hooks to the four corners of the sink. I have a make-weight upstairs, and a pulley on the window-sill. When I release the make-weight up comes the sink a couple of feet from the rubber-square I have under it; an' I can then get out what papers I want. I lower the sink again and remove the mechanism; and no one but a genius could guess the stuff was there, or how to get at it if they did.—Masterly, eh? and harmless. Curse me," says he, "if I had the handling of an explosive bomb I could tame it down to frying bacon."

"You'd better keep your bedrom door locked when you're getting out papers," says I. "If somebody was to put the make-weight up on its perch again, when you're doing the job, you'd lose more than your toe-nails."

"You're one of those folk," says Mr. Anthony, all annoyed, "that can see no good in anything they haven't done themselves.—Look out, now, when I call down to you. I'll raise the sink a couple of feet, and then lower it again." He disappeared into the house. In a couple of minutes I heard him shout, an' then, sure enough, he did what he had said. Up the sink went, an' down it came. I made a hasty glam for the dog, but I was too late. He was under the sink already, I suppose taking shelter from the chain. Not much of his tail can have been nipped, for there was no hair to be seen; but the gowls of him from under the sink would have come out through the walls of one of King Pharaoh's pyramids.

"Up with it again," I shouted. "The dog's under the granite!"

The wee man put his head out of the window, an' his features were tied in a knot.

"To pot with him, and you too," he yells. "I've let the make-weight graze my foot; and my toes are raspberry-jam."

But things weren't just as bad as the dog an' Mr. Anthony thought. All the dog left behind him was a few hairs at the end of his tail; an' Mr. Anthony's toes were only skinned. So, after a deal of coaxing, I agreed to help him with the fetching down of his papers to the sink, a couple of days later.

All the next day, however, I kept thinking of what had happened to the dog; so I sent Mr. Anthony word that I couldn't go, because my mother-in-law was dead. So she was, too; but it was five years before. Mr. Anthony wrote back very furious, that he would do the job without me; an' I might go an' bury myself if I liked; but with no granite over me.

But I knew he'd forgive me if I'd go an' praise the job when it was done. An' a good job it was, I had to give in. The chains held firm. The make-weight worked like a clock. As for the dog, he kept clear of trouble; for the minute the sink rose in the air he took to his heels, with his tail so far between his legs that he near tripped over it.

Mr. Anthony had all the papers ready, made up in labelled packages; each family's trouble by itself. My teeth watered as I looked at the wee bundles; for I knew there was costs an' damages in every one of them, enough to buy a farm.

When I'd buttered him up sufficiently about what he'd done with the papers, he showed me what he'd done with his shooting-materials. The gun he had up the chimney; the cartridges he had packed, very neatly, on the shelves of his bedroom, in brown paper tied with red tape; and each parcel labelled with the name of some imaginary lawsuit, written by his own hands. I will say, they looked very legal and business-like.

"I wouldn't let that old targe of a housekeeper lay a finger on them," says he. "She's that full of curiosity she would hold a hen's egg to the light to see was the yoke web-footed. —Look at them," says Mr. Anthony, capering round the parcels. "Nobody would think there was the death of hundreds of game birds and animals under those pieces of brown paper, now would they?"

I knew too much of Mr. Anthony's shooting to think it, either. But there was no use vexing him, so I held my tongue.

"You can laugh at all sorts of raiders now, sir," said I, as I went off. "An' you're not far astray about the housekeeper. If she gets a guess of what family history is hidden under that stone-sink she'll break into it should she do it with her teeth."

The very next day he beckoned to me from his office-window to come across the street an' speak to him. I couldn't tell, when I went in, what was up with him. He was half-vexed an' half-pleased.

"You were right about the old faggot of a housekeeper," he said. "She's after that sink-full of secrets of mine. I looked out of my bedroom window yesterday, an' confound me if she wasn't lying on her belly beside it, trying to poke a bit of stick up the safety outlet-hole that I hadn't bothered to plug up, it was so small."

"She wouldn't get many of the Ten Commandments out through that, Mr. Anthony," says I.

"No; but she'll have found out that there are papers there," says he, "and she'll know there must be something special, when I'm hiding them so carefully.—I'm delighted about it," says he.

"Delighted!" says I, gaping at him.

"Yes," says he. "It has given me a chance of matching my wits with hers. I'm packing her off to her sister-in-law's to-night, for gossip and fresh butter, and when she comes back she'll be circumvented; and not a sign of that.—No, I won't tell you how. Come out to see me to-morrow night. I wish you to guess in the meantime what I've done. Damme, the thing is so simple that you'll want to kick yourself for not having had the brains to think of it."

When I went out to Mr. Anthony's house the following night he was standing at the gate, waiting.

"Well?" he says, all smiles an' pats on the back for himself. "I declare you're looking quite worried. Are you still puzzling your head about my conundrum?"

"All I'm puzzling my head about," says I, "is whether or not I should sue you for the loss of a night's rest.—What was it you did?"

"I *still* won't tell you," says he, in high feather with himself. "I want to take the conceit out of you a little further. Come and have another look at the Sphinx first."

"The spinks?" says I, staring at him. "What kind of a contrivance is that?"

"It's the same as the sink," says he, "only its spelt differently."—But it was the sink itself he brought me out to, after all.

I walked round an' round it; an' stubbed my big toe kicking a piece of mud off one end that looked as if it might be hiding something new. But the sink still took no more notice of me than if I was a sink myself, an' no great friend of the family. The dog didn't appear at all; an' I wasn't surprised.

Now, during this time, I'd seen or heard no word of the housekeeper, though I'd expected to find her snooking round, trying to spy farlies. But all at once there riz the divil's own row in the kitchen premises; shouting in a woman's voice, an' banging of tin pans; an' something that sounded like a whole tea-set committing suicide. An' along with it all was the barking an' yelping of a dog, time about, as somebody missed him, or didn't. Suddenly out comes Mr. Anthony's dog himself, with the housekeeper at his tail, an' her with a red-hot poker in her hand. All at once I saw that the pair of them were chasing a mouse. Mr. Anthony, standing back gloating over me, didn't spot this at first. When he did he let a screech out of him that turned the mouse in its tracks an' checked the dog on all four feet an' his tail as well. The mouse spotted the wee safety outlet-hole in the sink that Mr. Anthony hadn't thought worth-while stopping-up, an' bolted through it; the housekeeper kicked the dog out of her way an' plunged the red-hot poker into the hole, after the mouse. If Mr. Anthony yelled again he came in second; for the sink just opened up in a flash an' a crack of thunder; an' followed up with as many small shots as if Mr. Anthony was missing a flock of snipe with a hundred-chambered revolver.

Things might have been worse. The house got the bulk of the damage. The breakfast-room window went-in out of the way; an' Mr. Anthony's bedroom window, up-above, came down to see what had happened. Mr. Anthony's eyeglass would have been splintered, he told me afterwards, only that he saw the piece of granite coming, an' side-stepped it. The housekeeper fell on her back, an' that saved her face; an', if she was hit anywhere else, she was too modest to say anything about it. As for the dog, he made up his mind about the sink for good, an' was never seen again. Wherever he took refuge, I'll go bail it wasn't in a stone-quarry.

Mr. Anthony wasn't as much upset as you'd have expected.

"You can't blame me, you know, Pat," said he, "for exchanging my papers and the cartridges. Who the devil would have thought of mice and red-hot pokers? But all is for the best. Word will get about that half the local scandals have been blown broadcast; and every woman will be so scared of provoking every other woman, that, confound me, Ballygullion will be like Spring-cleaned Paradise; till the next generation grows-up, anyway."

Widow's Weeds

LONG ago, said Mr. Patrick Murphy, Mr. Lecorr, the then landlord on a big scale in our parts, thought he could teach his tenants how to farm land. I suppose he deemed he could get more out of them, that way, in those days when a landlord owned all of a tenant except his clothes and his wife. So he picked on three adjoining small holdings on his estate that, taken together, would raise all three things a farmer needs: root-crops, an' corn an' hay, an' grazing for cattle an' sheep; threw the three tenants out on the road, an' made his model farm.

Now, as you know, or ought to know, any man can be a tenant of land, but not every man can be a farmer; an' when Mr. Lecorr had lost as much money on his model farm as he wanted to do, an', besides that, was near his end an' wished to go where the very ploughs are made of gold, he gave back the farm-in-three-bits to the representatives of the folk he'd put out long before. Moreover, an' I suppose hoping to get a bigger size of a farm when he went aloft, he put up three dwelling-houses in lieu of the three he'd knocked down, an', thinking to show himself clever as well as good, he lumped the three new homesteads into what was a kind of wee town of three families.

The three houses were in a triangle. One was on the top of a short brae which ran down to the other two, that were opposite each other on a flat plot. The ground between the two below an' the one on the wee hill was roughish an' bumpy, but fit for people to walk on.

Now, knowing what you know of human nature, you'll expect to hear that every one of the three tenants lived in the hope of pushing out the other two an' making the model farm again, for himself or herself. But it hadn't come off. The two lower houses and farms were in my time held by two separate weemin, one a widow-woman called Leish, the other a Miss Wister, a convinced old-maid, but young enough to have a bit of an itch on the fourth finger of her left hand now an' then, especially in the Spring. The Widow let-on loudly that she was tired of men, an' glad she had no childer to bother her. But any mankind passing the two lower houses of the wee village was taken more notice of from both than he was aware of. Yet the two weemin were good enough friends, an' went in an' out of each other's houses, an' shared the gossip of the countryside between them, as far as they could gather it.

But though they behaved in this extraordinary fashion—for weemin, that is—it wasn't altogether because of their natural kindliness, though both had a fair share of that. The truth is that the house on the wee hillock was for long of no interest to the pair, because it was empty.

The tenant of it had been a widow-man called Nestley, an ould fellow of a political turn of mind, always muttering about Home Rule for Ireland; an' hating landlords like hell. Although he'd been given back his farm, like the others, he'd never forgiven his landlord for throwing him out of it; an' wouldn't begin farming again, but carried on the job he'd taken up as head-groom to ould Jollicks, a gentleman-farmer with plenty of money, an' a good distance away. When Nestley died, some years later, his master kept the son, Frank, on in his place—for he had taken a fancy to him—an' Frank continued to let the wee farm he'd inherited from his father; but never came near it.

When ould Jollicks died, himself, there was great excitement in the three-house village of two weemin. But it was all thrown away. No change was made. Frank's land was still let, an' the hill-house still lay empty. Worse than that, the new tenant of the wee farm had never let himself be seen. Ould Jollick's fancy for Frank had lasted; he'd found him so quiet an' biddable an' respectful, an', moreover, able to hold his tongue. In the end Frank became half a groom, half a body-servant to him; an' when the old man died an' the establishment was broken-up, Frank got a legacy of three hundred pounds. This time he came home to his house an' his wee farm.

But he didn't come home the wee farmer's son he was expected to be. Ould Jollicks had been a bit of a swell in his way, an Honourable an' a J.P.; an' these things counted a deal more in them days than they do now. He was an old bachelor, too; an' though he had plenty of servants he did a lot of things for himself; for he kept late an' far from regular hours, an' wouldn't let the household sit up for him, but would call Francis, his man, to make a bite of supper or the like, especially if it was for more than one; an' Frank, though in the beginning he was a rough enough diamond of a country lout, did his best, an' as the years went by became quite handy about a house. An', more than that, he got dressy in his own way, an' washed every morning, an' kept himself neat an' spruce; an' though he was a big stoutish fellow in his build, would have begun to look nearly as well on horseback as his Master if his horse an' him hadn't had a fall that twisted his thigh an' made him have to sit in the saddle a kind of sideways, forbye giving him a clumsy limp.

Well, ould Jollicks died before his time, partly on account of drink, an' partly on account of weemin. There was nothing for Frank to do but to come home to his wee farm; an' if the three hundred pounds didn't travel with him, at least the word that he had got it did. Neither of the two of them made as much differs in the countryside as you might expect, not even with the two weemin at the foot of the hill. Whether or not it was his long association with his Master an' nobody else, had done it, nobody knowed; but anyway, Frank kept himself to himself. The letting of his wee farm had some months yet to run, an' he had plenty of leisure on his hands; so he hired no help in garden or house, but worked away by his lone, cooking an' cleaning an' washing an' all the rest of it, an' even mending his own clothes. How he got on was guesswork; for he would hardly let an outsider enter his door. But he still kept very trim an' trig in his personal appearance, an' always as clean as a new pin. An', though he was a year or two on the wrong side of forty, many a woman in her forties—by her own way of it—would throw a bright eye on him.

But it was mostly only in gossip, an' in guessing who would marry him, that Frank came under the generality of weemin's tongues. All of them knew in their hearts that, situated as the three were in their backwater of land, either the Widow Leish or Mary Wister would get the langle on him, unless they divided him in two, an' each took half. Mary Wister would have taken the upper half, an' wanted no more, I think, for she was wearing near the boundary line of courting, an' looking for company, mostly, an' more money an' land. The Widow wanted a whole man to herself; an' made no secret of it.

But, if there was no hope about Frank in the neighbourhood, I need hardly tell you there was plenty of curiosity. Even the wives of farmers with fifty or sixty acres of land would make an excuse of some kind or another to drop into one of the two houses in search of gossip. My own wife, Molly, wouldn't go herself; but she was always very willing to listen to anything I could pick up. It was for this reason that having—or making—an errand in that direction, I found myself on an afternoon sitting at the fire in the Widow's kitchen with, not only one of the weemin in the case, but with both. For the two had lived side by side in their lonely houses for upwards of five years, an' even now, instead of being bitter enemies over Frank, an' not on speaking terms, they consorted together like twin sisters. There were people who said it was in order that the one could keep her eye on the other!

Anyway, I found the pair willing to talk on the matter, the widow like a running bubbling stream, but the old maid needing a cautious turn of the tap, as you might say. We hitched our three chairs nearer the fire, myself in the middle, to see fair-play; for we all three of us knowed there was going to be gossip, an' what it was going to be about.

"Have yez never married him yet, Mrs. Leish?" says I, going straight to the point.

"Och, houl' your tongue, Mr. Murphy," says she. "A woman can't marry a man. She has to get him into the frame of mind when *he'll* marry *her*."

"An' can't either of you do that?" says I. "Even if land could marry land what could be a more suitable match? Your farm marches Frank Nestley's; an' when ould Greedy-guts" (for that's what folk used to call the late landlord) "when ould Greedy-guts gave it back to your husband he was fitting your good corn-growing land into Frank's father's good root-growing land, that it should never have been torn away from. On a join of your land an' Frank's a body could grow nearly anything."

But here Mary Wister broke in.

"What's the matter with *my* thirty acres of grass-land that my uncle left me, an' that I have no trouble in letting every year?" says she, very acid. "It's not *tied* to grass, keep mind, an' could raise anything for man or beast."

"Everything but childer," says the Widow, winking at me. "If Frank doesn't marry something sappy, the late Mr. Lecorr's picked farm'll likely never come together again; an' that would be a pity. Listen to me, Mary," says she, with one side of her face a question-mark, an' the other side winking at myself, "if I snaffle him will you sell your farm to him an' me, an' turn the three farms into one again? Unless I've lost the trick of getting round a man, I'd make Frank give you a good price."

But the old maid took a short-cut, though it turned her very red about the gills.

"What was the name of your child by Mr. Leish?" says she to the Widow—"or did you just call it 'Pussy'?"

She didn't wink at me; but she pressed her lips into a straight line an' nodded her head, as much as to say to the Widow: "Take that, since you asked for it."

The Widow side-stepped her, though her eyes looked something between shame an' woman-slaughter.

"It wasn't my fault but my father's that I married thirty acres of land instead of a man," says she; "an' I'm not going to do it again. But, barring his limpiter-leg, him on the hill here is a big sonsy fellow, if he just wasn't so distant an' shy; an' possession of the three-into-one farm might put a bit of spunk into him."

"What age of a man is he?" says I, just to stop them short of war.

"About Mary's age, there," says the Widow, hitting back; "not a day over fifty, an' well preserved; though I'll give in he's a trifle pot-bellied," she puts in, for peace-sake.

"Tell me," says I, losing patience with the war that was still threatening, "which of you has the best chances? Out with it. I'm making a book on the contest, an' I want to lay the right odds."

The Widow sat up in her chair, an' threw out both her hands.

"Neither of the two of us," says she; an' this time meant what she said. "He couldn't keep us more at a distance if he was prodding at each of us with a pitchfork. The truth is, Mr. Murphy, he was spoiled by his late Master, ould Jollicks. The ould fellow could keep no maids in the house owing to his drinking ways and the effect they had on him so far as weemin were concerned. Fresh sets of them kept coming; but in-between-times Frank up the hill here had to do not only bottle-washer but cook. His ould Master, between his bursts, behaved himself like a gentleman; an'

Frank after a while began to copy him, first in his speech, then in his clothes, so far as a poor man could do it; an' then even in his care of the ould fellow's delph an' silver an' furniture. An' since Frank came back to his father's house he has still kept on copying his late boss in every way he can, even to clean-shaving an' polishing his nails. When I go up to call upon him, maybe to borrow something—we mostly go together," says she, with a comical look at Miss Wister—"he'll hardly let us in; an' we have to clean our feet on the ould potato-bag he has for a mat till you'd think we were polishing our boots for a party. An' forbye that——" She paused in her speech an' looked at Mary Wister, that was all frowned-up, an' making signs at her with her hand.

"Will I stop?" the Widow asks her.

Miss Wister nodded her head, an' near girned her features into a knot; an' when that failed half rose to her feet.

"Och, blethers," bursts out the Widow. "I can tell Pat, an' ould married man with a family. Sit down, you; an' don't be so mimity. You can hold the shovel before your face if you think the fire is getting jealous of your complexion."

Miss Wister sat down, but very gingerly; an' every other moment looking at the door to see could she run, if she was pushed to it.

The Widow looked from me to her, an' from her to me: an' then took the bit in her teeth.

"Here's the wholly-all of it, Mr. Murphy," says she. "But tell nobody but your wife, an' her only when you've pulled the blankets over the pair of you. Mary an' I *are* after this man on the hill.—For his own good," says she with a grin. "His bit of land isn't near big enough to keep him in comfort. If he marries one or the other of us two he'll have a farm big enough to keep a family as well as himself."

"Wait now," I puts in. "If Frank marries one of you he'll have only two bits of the landlord's big farm, unless I've forgotten to count."

"He'll have three," says the Widow. "The one of us that misses him'll sell her farm an' quit these parts, she'll be that gunked."

I looked from one to the other, an' both of them were sitting bolt upright, with their eyes crossing. I could see that what the Widow had just said was true.

"What's the betting, then, I ask you again?" says I. "Who'd get most out of being married to him? I'd lay odds on her; for she'd make the most push."

"Both of us," says the Widow. "*I* want to prove that I could have had a family, if I'd been given a fair chance. An' *she*"—here she jerked her thumb at Mary Wister—"wants to show that it wasn't through her own fault but by the stupidity of men-kind that she's been left on the shelf."

The natural colour had been coming back to Miss Wister's face as she listened, an' she could hold-in no longer.

"I don't see why I shouldn't have a family as well as my neighbours," says she. "I can handle childer as well as anybody else in this island. My brother John's three just dote on me when I go there, an' are a sight more biddable to me than they are to their mother."

The Widow looked again at me, an' arched her eyebrows as much as to say: "Lord help the poor innocent creature." But she must have let about ten minutes of ridicule go to sleep on her tongue.

"Well, well," says she. "We may put that aside. Anyway, Frank'll make a good father if he can rise to the occasion. He's as kind to the dog an' cat as if they were Christians; an' the very chickens love him. But he has oddities, an' that's the truth. I've told you, Mr. Murphy," says she, "what a pet his late Master made of Frank, an' how Frank copied the old man in his way of speaking, an' in his dress. Well, all this went further than most people knowed or thought. Even in his eating an' drinking he copied his boss. When the old man came here in his trap to see some particular early-flowering bulbs I had the name of growing, I offered him a cup of tea. He thanked me, but refused. He never took tea, he said; an' indeed he had no great word of it. An', behold you, Frank said *he* never took tea, either. I gave them coffee instead; an' damn the either of them would take sugar in it, though it was bitter enough to throw a knot on a pig's puddings. But, if you can believe me, Frank carried things further nor that.—Now shut up you!" she put in to Mary Wister.—"All the quality, I'm told, takes a cold-water bath in the morning just after getting out of bed. It's the thing to do, for anybody who is anybody. One jugful of hot water in it, an' you belong to the common dirt. The ould Master took his cold bath every morning, pure cold water without even whiskey in it. An', will you believe me, when Frank found out about this, an' how it was the correct thing to do, he began to take one as well. He laid hold of an old metal cylinder that had held tar for some roof, cleaned it out, scraped an' polished it; an' every morning he could get water on the sly—for he was a bit afeared of being laughed at—he lepped-in, up to his neck.

"Now his old Master if he liked you, he liked you. He was flattered an' pleased when he got word of Frank's cleanliness, an' he had the tar-barrel specially cleaned an' painted, an' fixed on a ring of bricks in the lean-to attached to the stable. An' into it every morning Frank got, summer an' winter, cold an' hot; an' there were times, I'm told, when he had to break the ice on the water. An' now, Mr. Murphy, he has got a rain-water barrel set on stones just at his own kitchen-door, an' there's a sough round our neighbourhood that he keeps it full of cold water an' gets into it stark-naked every morning the way he used to do at Hollyberry House."

"He must be a hardy fellow," says I, shivering, myself, at the very thought of it.

The Widow got up, walked to the kitchen door, turned the key in the lock an' put it in her pocket; an' I knowed I was going to hear something worth listening to.

"Sit at peace, now, you," she says to Mary Wister. "You can't get through the window.—Now, Pat," says she to me, "her an' I aren't going to fight over Frank. We're after him on a plan. Each of us will do her best; an' the loser will go to the wedding; an' if there's a family, will sell her farm to the winner. We've begun the campaign already, each in her own way. I'll give you mine first. Frank has been hauchling round the premises trying to start a garden. We can see that, beyond the bushes that hide the house itself. Now I'm a bit of a gardener——"

"More than a bit," puts in Miss Wister. I could tell she was growing easier in her mind.

"More than a bit, if you like," says the Widow. "I will maintain that there's nobody in the countryside, even at the Hall, can show earlier or bigger blooms than I can. But Frank's wee garden must be a wilderness. He gave in that to me, the only time he's been in mine; an' I sent him away with his arms full of roots an' bulbs an' cuttings. Now Mary, here, is no gardener. A single woman very seldom is. Eating an' drinking are her weaknesses, generally. She can put as much into herself as she likes an' still keep purty thin. So Mary's having her own particular slap at him. The day I trapped him I had her over; an' when he went off she hung a basket on his arm with a tin of her own flesh honey in the comb, an' as many cakes an' wee jam tarts as she could put in. So now, Pat, it's 'pull devil, pull baker.' "

"Well, good luck to the winner," says I, half-rising from my chair. "He'll not have room for the two of you up there, anyway."

Miss Wister was on her feet already, looking a trifle shamefaced at the plain talk. The Widow pulled her down again with a pluck at her skirts that nearly pulled them off her.

"Now stay there, you, an' none of your mock modesty. It's in your mind, what I'm going to say; an' you may as well see it on the wall. The truth is that Frank's oddity goes further than I told you, Pat. They say that for the last few years, since he got the cowp off his Master's black stallion, he has never loked at the side of the road a woman was on. The question is, are Mary here an' me wasting our time. Does he want anybody at all, or should anybody else want him? I'll give in he still looks well on a horse's back; but a woman can't keep a horse in the kitchen for him.—What do you think? What would you advise? Out with it. Mary can bend down her head and let on she's tying her boot."

I reached for my hat from in under my chair, an' stood up to go.

"Let me have a day or two to laugh," says I; "an' if the case hasn't settled itself by then I'll come back an' give you my verdict."

But, lo an' behold you, the whole matter was as good as decided within twenty-four hours.

The year was wearing towards autumn by this time, an' the bad weather beginning. That very night there came the father an' mother of a storm, with a waterfall of rain towards morning. As I looked out of the bedroom window there come into my head the thought of Frank Nestley climbing into his barrel, an' I said to myself: "I wonder will he just step out of the house this morning an' stand in the rain. I'll go across this very day an' find out, should Molly leave me." For it ran in my mind that the storm might have whummled some of the bushes guarding the house. An' so it it had; an' here's the whole history for you:

About a quarter past seven on the morning of the storm, but when it had well died down, there came a hellish knocking on Mary Wister's front door, an' with it a loud shouting like the Widow's voice.

"Her house is blew down," says Mary to herself, lepps out of bed, throws a few duds on her, an' opens the door. It was the Widow, sure enough; an' her eyes were goggling with divilment.

"There's two bushes blown down from round Frank's house," she splutters between her giggles. "Put something more on you, Mary. I'll go an' get a wrap. You can see the barrel plain; an' it's just about Frank's rising-time. Come on quick, an' we'll maybe get a keek at him."

Miss Wister gazed at her open-mouthed.

"I'll do nothing of the sort," she snaps. "I was brought up to be a lady, if you weren't."

But the Widow was ready for her.

"Lady be damned," says she. "We're not going near enough to be unladylike. But it'll be quare fun to see thon big hauchle of a man climbing into his barrel like an elephant into a tea-cup. An' if it was nothing else, we'll find out whether or not his twisted leg would interfere much with his nursing childer. Come on, now.—Did you never see a man with nothing on him before?"

"I did not, indeed," snaps Miss Wister. "I never even saw myself in a glass.—*You* look," says she; "an' you can tell me afterwards."

"Wait a minute, then," says the Widow. Off she went to her house, an' when she came back she had a loose wrap round her shoulders. "Come on now," says she, "an' none of your capers. If he looks round we can pretend we're raising blown-down plants."

But, while this was going on, Frank had come out of his back-door. The wee falling hill from his house to the weemin's, though it was steepish, was short. Frank heard the voice, looked down, saw the two weemin, put his foot on the step he had fixed on the barrel, an' made a hasty sprachling lepp-in. Whether the barrel saw the two weemin on the flat ground below an' did it for divilment, I can't tell you; but, anyway, it fell on its side off the stone support an' started down the hill with Frank inside yelling first help an' murder, an' then for the weemin to get away.

But the barrel paid no heed to him. Down the hill it rattled an' blundered, nearly threw Frank out, an' then rocked sideways just in time to keep him in. An' when it reached the bottom of the hill, an' it going no slower, you may swear, it whanged against the beech-tree-stump that Mary Wister kept her bees'-skep on, an' poured out Frank at the weemin's feet.

The Widow let a yell out of her as he riz, an' threw her loose wrap over him. But Miss Wister didn't interfere. The thundercloud of battered humanity roarin' down the hill had been too much for her. She looked back at the Widow, as she fumbled at the latch of her own door.

"Do you stay here," she said to her friend. "I think, after all, I'd rather be neighbourly."

Pilcher's Parable

I'VE told you stories about Pilcher (said Mr. Patrick Murphy) the wee Scotchman that came to Ulster to make peace among us; an' about the ups an' downs he had while he was trying to do it. I'll tell you one more; though whether it was an "up" or a "down" I can't just make up my mind.

He had hopes of us folk in Ballygullion getting the length of agreeing, or, maybe, *dis*agreeing to build a Public Hall where everybody could meet, Catholic or Protestant, Orange or Green. Either of the two sides was to use it, separately, or together if they could agree on any subject that might be discussed without blowing off the roof.

It was Pilcher's job, first of all, to accustom the two parties to the notion that the thing could be done short of a miracle. The way he meant to set about it was to invite twos an' threes of us to his wee house, an' get them to talk about the proposal without him being there.

"I'll not be in the room, Pat," says he. "I'll not even be in the house. I'll give them a good meal, food an' drink; an' that'll soothe them down, an' incline them to peace. After all, the Soul is at the mercy of the body. An' that little servant-girl of mine, though she's a rough diamond, an' no doubt a Papish like yourself, *can* cook a meal would have changed the colour of King William the Third's hair.

"Public-meetings an' crowds," says he, all worked up, "are the seed-beds of rows an' ill-feeling. I'll sow this notion of mine, about a Central Hall, in the minds of twos an' threes, in circumstances when it'll sprout *good* feeling an' common-sense; an' in the end may spread an' blossom over all Ireland!

"I'm making a start this night," says he. "Hugh Geary an' Peter Screene are coming up to the house to have a quiet bit of supper all by themselves, with wee Sally, the maid, to feed an' look after them. I'll eat early, by myself, an' then go off to that auction at Parker's that I'm to meet you at;

an', if you'll come back with me, later, to my place, we can hear how my visitors got on."

"Hugh Geary an' Peter Screene!" says I. "Lord help your wit. A weasel an' a rat would agree better together!"

"Nonsense," says he. "They'll have a full meal in them: one glass each of good whiskey before they go to the table; an' then they'll sit down to peace an' porter. They'll have the foundations of the hall laid before you an' I come back."

"We'll be picking the bits of them two selves off the floor," says I.

"Not on *porter*," says he. "They're going to get nothing else, *then*.—An' listen, Pat," says he—here he looked just what you'd know foolish—"I mean to try out a grand an' fancy new notion that has come into my head. You know my wee collection of delph-an'-china ware. There came a political turn on it after I settled in Ireland. An', when these two half-enemies sit down to-night, there on the table will be sitting, beside Peter Screene, the Irish patriot, a big Orange-an'-Blue jug; an' beside Hugh Geary, the Ulster patriot, a Green-an'-White one.

"The two men will be a trifle surprised at first, an' maybe a little put about; but then, as the meal draws-on, an' they're each drinking good porter from the other side's jug, it'll begin to steal on them that maybe *some* good can come out of evil, after all. It's a kind of a parable I'm putting up to them, Pat," says he, smiling at me as innocent as if he was about twelve years of age; an' dammit, with the simplicity of the crayther, I actually began to wonder if there mightn't be something in what he was saying.

"How would it be," said I to myself, "if an outlandish plan like this, but on a bigger scale, should be the way to bring peace to Ireland?"

"All is set for the meal," says wee Pilcher; "an' Susan has been instructed *where* to sit down *who* at the table. You an' I will go straight back from the auction, an' see, an' find out from their own lips, all that has happened between what I hope will by that time be two fast friends."

The plan was carried out as arranged; an' when Pilcher

an' I arrived back at his house together after the auction we slipped into the hall, an' listened at the dining-room door.

All was quiet, sure enough! Two gentlemen-born couldn't have eaten their dinners with less noise.

"Peace, perfect peace," says Pilcher with a smile on his face, an' his finger at his lips.

"By heavens," says I to myself, "the wee man has done it for once; if he should never do it again."

An' when we opened the door, behold you, the room was empty; the table-cloth was hanging sideways, an' half-sodden with porter; the plates an' dishes all higgelty-piggelty over the table, an' one or two on the floor, some of them in bits; an' among them, very noticeable an' bigoted, great whacks of the two delph jugs of different politics, cured of politics forever!

The decent wee servant-lass ran out to us from the kitchen, wringing her apron with both hands, an' them supper to the elbow.

"Oh, sir, sir," says she—an' you couldn't have told was she laughing or crying—"there's been hell's own delight between the two jugs; as I knowed in my heart there would be. At the start of the meal I began to think I'd been wrong, an' there was going to be peace between the two men. They eyed the jugs a bit sideways at first; but I could feel that they were trying to let-on that there was nothing unusual about them. The two started eating as peaceful as lambs, an' talking about nothing but the weather an' the crops; an' I kept feeding their grinders, so as to keep their thoughts at peace.

"But no ordinary man-being can eat long without drinking, if there's any drink about; an' at last Peter Screene, after just wetting his lips with buttermilk, an' getting no answer from it, laid hold of the Twelfth of July jug beside him, poured himself out a glassful of porter, an' emptied it down.

" 'Hugh,' " says he to Geary the plumber, 'if we don't put a few sups into us before the wee prophet comes back, we'll not have enough in us to keep us friends that long.—Fill-up!'

"'By heavens,' says I to myself, 'the Master has been right, after all!'

"An' it looked that way. Geary filled up good-an'-hearty, an' poured-down, twice; though I noticed that he laid-hold of his Green-an'-White jug as if it was going to burn him. Then Peter filled-up again, to be even with him. All seemed well.

"But presently I heard a voice in the eating-room as if the wind was rising; then I heard a clatter; an' after that, smash upon smash upon smash! I glammed the dish of pudding off the range, an' made for the room, as the boss had warned me to do if I heard the stoor rising. An', lo an' behold you, when I got to the room door, the Nationalist jug met me as if I'd been an Orange-woman, an' scattered itself against the pudding-dish in my hands. An', the next minit, as I pushed on in, I near fell over the remains of the Orange-an'-Blue jug on the hearth-rug. The two men were at each other, hammer-an'-tongs! Geary was fighting the cunninger, just throwing boiled-potatoes at Peter Screene from behind the eight-day clock; but Peter had laid hold of the leg of lamb by the ankle, an', I do believe, would have massacred Hugh, if Hugh hadn't used his own living legs an' skedaddled through the door without looking behind him!"

I could have listened to more of the battle; for the wee lassie told it well, an' as fair as if the one half of her was Orange an' the other half Green. But Pilcher put a stop to her. He was quite cool an' calm, very much to my surprise; an' I could see that he was beginning to come down out of the clouds.

"Clear up this mess as soon as we're gone," says he to the lassie. "In the meantime spread a corner of the dining-table, an' bring a couple of bottles of porter, if there's any left. Mr. Murphy an' I are going to attend another meeting, later in the evening. In the meantime we want to have a talk."

But the wee girl was hanging-back, a wee bit gunked-looking as she eyed the floor.

"What'll yez drink your porter out of, sir?" says she, "now that the two political jugs is gone?"

Wee Pilcher thought a while; then his eyes brightened, an' I knew some fresh fancy had laid hold of him.

"Fetch the *good* jug," says he. "You know the one I mean."

The girl looked at him, mouth open.

"Will you risk it, sir?" says she. She looked at me, between a qualm an' a grin. "Unless Mr. Murphy has *turned*! —If you'll pardon me, sir, that jug isn't ordinary."

"Neither is Mr. Murphy," says wee Pilcher; an' it warmed my heart to be so well-thought of by the simple wee man.

"Now what new notion has come into his head?" says I to myself; for, as he fussed out after the girl, his face was all lit-up an' his eyes were once more shining.

An', when he came back, here he had in his hand, an' carrying it as if it was gold an' jewels, the beautifulest white-china jug you ever seen in your life; purty in shape, an' purtier in colour, with what was left of the evening sun showing through it in rainbows; an' it shaped graceful enough to be growing in a bed of flowers.

"Oh, man," there burst out of me, "what a heavenly thing! Why didn't you bring it down for the two quarrelsome ruffians to see? They'd never have had the wickedness to break *that*, not even on a party row!"

The wee man held the jug up; an' his eyes were blazing through tears.

"Yes, Pat," he says. "I'm seeing things clearly at last. *That's* what we all need," says he, throwing his free hand in the air. "Something above us but not beyond us, to lift us out of the rut of hate an' jealousy we're in, an' give us more imagination about ourselves an' our neighbours, an' what we're all intended for by Providence.

"Come on down the town with me, Pat," he says, all carried away. "We can't eat here and be in time for the wee talk we *must* have, now, in Rogers's carpenter's yard. But we'll have some bread an' cheese in Mrs. Ruttledge's wee tea-shop, after it, an' then come back here an' talk over this new notion that the jug has bestowed on me; an' maybe will bestow on yourself, though you belong to a different *sort*.—

Jenny!" he calls to the maid in the kitchen, "redd-up this mess as well as you can. Pat Murphy and I are away to that meeting I told you of. Don't bother about a meal for us. We'll eat somewhere or other. Go out an' meet that big sweetheart of yours if you can. Or fetch him in here if you like. He can gorge himself on the remains of the battle! By the time that big fellow has done with them there won't be much left.—Come on, Pat," he says. "This new notion of mine will make history; an' beyond these islands.—Look at it!" says he, turning back for another loving gape at the china jug. "It's showing up among that man-made wreckage like the spire of a church."

All the way to the meeting he was singing the same song; an' in the carpenter's yard he fairly *preached* toleration an' good-will for both political sides; till, coming back home with him, when the meeting was over, I felt as if I could play the flute in an Orange Band!

An' as Jenny, the maid, opened the door to us when we got back, lo' an' behold ye! even in the half-dusk we could see that her nose was red an' her face all plastered with tears.

"Oh, sir, sir," she lamented, clapping her hands together, "there's been the very devil to pay! That rascal, Joe Turpenny, that I thought was my wise an' sensible sweetheart, an' used to vex me at times, putting his tongue out even at his own side, arrived here half-drunk from sitting in a pub after quitting-time, blethering about yourself, Mr. Pilcher, an' nearly everybody else. I set him down at the dining-table—a thing I'd never done before—to put food an' wisdom into him; but sorrow-all he would talk about but of the hard-times of the poor working-man; an' the downing of the rich; an' calling yourself, sir, a bloody wee paraside, living on other folks' sweat. He swep his right arm across the table, an' redd-off near half of the glass an' delph that was left on it; an' when that clearance let him see the lovely, lovely jug that your heart is set-on, he hit it a sideways skelp with the big carving knife that just divided it into two halves.—Look at it, sir!" says she, throwing the eating-room door open.

An' there, sure enough, in the middle of the debree, lay the beautiful white-china jug, split in half plumb through the two angels that, joined together by their wings, had made the lovely belly of it.

"He hit it vicious, sir, before I could grab his arm," she moaned. "He'd been talking working-man's politics down at Raftilly's pub, an' came here full of them, an' booze. 'Look at that bloody thing,' says he to me, saving your presence—'what the Quality—mauryah! drinks wine an' brandy out of while the rest of us sucks porter out of a tin mug!' For, in troth, sir," says she, "when I saw the state he was in when he arrived, I ran into the kitchen an' fetched out an ould rusty tin pan; an' he drank out of that till he nearly went home by the dining-room window instead of the hall-door.—You'll never forgive me, sir, I know; but what can a lonely woman do with a half-drunk man but make him drunker!"

I thought well of wee Pilcher. He listened in peace an' patience till the servant-lassie had gone, then picked up the two halves of the white-china jug, an' joined them together in his hands; saying nothing, good or bad, but wagging his head up an' down, as if he'd clean lost hope of all he'd been striving for.

"I wouldn't give up, if I were you, sir," I says, to hearten him. "Could the two halves not be joined together, near as strong as before?"

"Maybe," says wee Pilcher. "Maybe. Though a great many folk have tried to do the like, an' failed. But if they ever *are*, Pat, it will have to be done with a big broad band of rusty metal; and I doubt that'll make a lamentable change in the flavour of the drink."

Postscript

(To Patrick Murphy of Ballygullion)

DEAR Mr. Patrick Murphy, dear to me,
  Nor inexpensive to my gentle readers,
(For years you've cost them many an author's fee;
A faithful band; there have been few seceders).

Why have you travelled so far and lived so long?
Gained many a—what *you* would call a collyum,
Told countless stories, risen into song,
And now stepped forth with yet another volume?
I cannot say. But this I hold for truth,
And not my warmest partisan will doubt me,
Had I not thought of you in days of youth
Not very much would now be heard about me.
Beneath your tattered coat and greasy hat
I hid myself and uttered many a libel,
Mocked friend and foe, and, let me tell you, Pat,
Put forward truths not always from the Bible.
Your dialect has sanctioned phrase on phrase
That standard language would have deemed profanity,
And, many a time, for censorship or praise,
I borrowed the colour of your Christianity.
I used to think the debit on *your* page;
You owe me much, your substance, form, and gesture,
Your pawky country crack, your axiom sage,
Your farm, your wife, your—not expensive—vesture.
But now I see that, as I feigned your life,
And listened for your voice, and sought around me
The cheery humour that assuages strife,
Truth, charity, and understanding found me.
Merchant or farmer was my brother man,
Not Red, brown, black; nor Right nor sinister;
A blind man tapping through the eternal plan,
Yet laughing more than King or Minister.
For your sake, then, I chose the humbler lot,
Shunned chief and princess, leprechaun and fairy,
Stirred up the thorns that crackle round a pot,
And loved the human rather than the airy.
Good-bye, old shade, my playmate and my friend,
I speak your praise in sadness not bravado,
Soon for me too will laughter make an end,
And, like yourself, dear Pat, I'll be a shadow.